SPIRIT

SPIRIT

MAUREEN HARTMAN

SPIRIT is dedicated to my two sons, who influenced me in ways they could never have imagined, and to my husband, whose strength I've relied upon throughout our own journey through grief, and without whom I could never have had the fortitude to complete this story.

CHAPTER ONE

LUCY ENDURED THE LONG LINES AT THE CROWDED FARMERS' MARKET. HER TOTE bag was heavy, her feet hurt, and she was tired—but not too tired for a fat sticky bun. She closed her eyes and inhaled the heavenly scent of cinnamon and sugar as she waited her turn in line and opened her eyes abruptly when she heard a familiar voice.

A shudder radiated throughout her body and her tote fell to the ground, spilling its contents around her feet as a small man in a tattered jean jacket ducked behind the neighboring stand. *It couldn't be him*, she thought. *He's in prison.*

Lucy struggled for breath—disoriented, and dizzy with confusion. She stood motionless as other shoppers bumped and pushed past her to the front of the line. Her shaky legs were about to give way when a firm hand grabbed her by the elbow. She stumbled along, blind and deaf with shock as the concerned grip on her arm pulled her from the crowd to a nearby bench.

"Are you all right?" He spoke calmly. "Hey, are you okay?"

She struggled to understand him through the overriding noise in her head and shut her eyes to the world in a desperate grasp at clarity, reconciling what she'd heard and seen with the improbability. It was just a jacket, after all, it could have been anyone, but the voice…

Lucy thought she'd left the days of that constant presence behind her. His lurking figure waiting behind each corner and the aftershocks which had haunted her thoughts and dreams for the last three years.

"Hey." She felt the grip on her arm again. *"Are you all right?"*

She nodded robotically, while visions from her past flashed in her head. *A Clockwork Orange* slideshow of terror, panic, and pain.

"Should I call someone?"

Lucy tried to pull her arm back, but the grip tightened. *Go away*, she thought, *whoever you are, just leave me alone.* She focused on her breathing the way her therapist had taught her as a dull jumble of sounds and voices from the market dimly reminded her of where she was. A rhythmic *scree-scraw* of the swing set sliced through the air, while the small voice of a child prattled on behind her.

Slow breath in, she reminded herself. *Slow breath out.* She was revived slightly by the strong breeze brushing across her sweat-dampened face.

In due course, Lucy's racing heart eased, and her breathing became more regular. She looked down at her hands, no longer trembling. Her Good Samaritan, patiently sitting beside her, looked closely at her face. He appeared not much older than her—twenty-six or twenty-seven—with unruly black hair; thick eyebrows; and full, beautiful lips.

Lucy looked into his gentle gray eyes and cleared her throat. "I'm sorry." He cocked an eyebrow. "You know," she went on. "*This.*" She indicated her lack of composure with embarrassment, longing to be left alone, but unable to peel her eyes away from his gaze.

A small boy approached and hoisted her tote up onto the bench, then climbed up beside it. He was missing one shoe, and a dirty sock dangled from his toes.

Lucy gazed idly at the child, dressed in a denim shirt and tan corduroys. His healthy head of bouncy black curls and the sweet look of inquiry on his soft face reminded her of one of her younger students.

"I'm fine," she reassured him, trying to stand. His eyes narrowed in doubt as he placed his hand firmly on her shoulder. Lucy pulled away. "I'll *be* fine. Thank you for ..." But he waved it off.

Their bench was beneath the heritage tree planted in the center of Drake Park long ago to mark the center of town. The Old Oak, the locals called it. The "Middle of the World."

A weathered bronze plaque at the base of the tree, proclaimed its official status with an engraved dedication by Franklin P. Drake, for whom the town was named.

Lucy's cheeks flushed. Her tangled nut-brown hair, liberated somehow from its ever-present clip, flowed over her shoulders and lashed about in the rising wind. She thought, self-consciously, that she probably looked like a train wreck.

"I'm Eli. This is my son, Owen. He has a knack for losing his shoes. Don't you, Little Bird?" Owen flashed a dramatic smile, displaying two perfect rows of tiny teeth. Eli straightened the boy's sock and retrieved the missing shoe from beneath the bench.

"Nice to meet you both, but I need to get going." The farmers were packing up their displays and loading their trucks and trailers. *How long have I been sitting here?* Lucy stood unsteadily and looked around for her shopping bag. "Thank you again." She was eager to get home.

Eli finished tying his son's shoe and lifted the boy from the bench as a sudden gust of wind blew his shaggy dark hair into his eyes. He pushed it back and handed Lucy her bag with the now-familiar look of concern. "Owen managed to salvage most of your shopping. I'm afraid the eggs were a total loss." He paused. "Could we at least walk you to your car?"

She took the tote bag from him and slung it over her shoulder. "No, thank you. I'm on foot." *Slow breath in, slow breath out.* "I live nearby." Why had she said that? She chastised herself. "Um, all right then. Thank you again."

Eli reached for her arm once more. This time, the touch was electric. "See you around?"

"Yes." She clutched her tote tighter, and her heart raced as the warmth from his hand radiated into her forearm. Owen hopped off the bench and held out the remainder of his cinnamon roll to Lucy. His big brown eyes nearly melted her heart with their pleading for her to accept the offering. She lifted it from his tiny, sticky hand. It was soft and fresh and thick with frosting. Lucy thanked him with a nod and pulled a gooey length off. The sharp bite of cinnamon struck her palate the instant Lucy stuffed it into her mouth. She swirled the icing around with her tongue and let it trickle down her throat.

Lucy stopped on the other side of the street to adjust the heavy tote when the glint from a crystal hanging in a shop window caught her attention. She admired the spray of color surrounding it. It was a small joy, worthy of her indulgence, so she turned for the door—and careened directly into Eli's shoulder.

"Ouch!" Lucy's hand flew to her nose. The sting made her eyes water, and she sneezed. What was he doing here? she wondered, looking up at him. Eli grinned, then placed a finger to the corner of his mouth as if to say, *you've got something there.*

Lucy discovered a glob of frosting on her lip and wiped it away with an embarrassed laugh. Her reflection in the display window of the Lucky Duck Toy Shop made her cringe—her loose hair whipped madly about in the wind. She pried a strand from her mouth, another from her eyes, gripping what she could in one hand while trying to tuck the rest of the unruly mane behind her ears.

"You sure you're all right?"

"Stop. Really. I'm fine." She was lying, thinking again of the man in the jean jacket. Her heart fluttered, and the pavement seemed to roll beneath her feet like a California fault-line. She turned back to her reflection. "Though I look like a train wreck."

"You look radiant," he said, as their eyes met in the shop window. Lucy smiled, revealing the small gap between her front teeth.

Was he flirting? Lucy still wasn't accustomed to Midwestern friendliness, though she had moved here from California right out of college, three years earlier. The lack of boundaries made her uncomfortable with everyone except her roommate and fellow teacher, Summer.

Owen ogled a Millennium Falcon kite that hung in the window beside a mobile of flashy silver dragonflies and the dazzling crystal that had gotten Lucy's attention—the latter hanging from a silver thread. She looked down at the boy, who was wearing the delight of Christmas morning upon his face.

"That's the one I'm getting," he said, pointing to the kite.

"Excellent choice," she said, holding her hair back with one hand to keep it from flying about in the wind. She smiled down at the boy. "I'm thinking about that crystal. See it there?" Lucy repositioned her heavy bag over her other shoulder.

"C'mon." Owen took his father's hand and pulled him to the door.

Lucy followed father and son into the shop, wondering what had gotten into her. Was it just the crystal or her curiosity about Eli?

A door chime alerted the clerk—a beautiful, brown-skinned woman in her early thirties—who glanced up from what she was doing with a look of recognition.

"How's Owen, eh?" asked the clerk with a sweet smile, twinkling eyes, and a hint of a foreign accent. Her combed-out Afro, playful patchwork skirt, and bright yellow sweater suited her occupation. "I've been waiting for you, birthday boy." Owen rocked on his feet—heel to toe, heel to toe—as the clerk reached under the counter for a package and laid it on the counter.

"Happy Birthday, Owen."

"You didn't have to do this, Mia, but thank you." Eli walked around the counter to the clerk and embraced her. She held onto his hand as he stepped back.

"Oh, Eli, it's nothing."

Lucy watched the scene, shyly analyzing the interaction, trying to put the pieces together: a smile, a touch, a laugh; each indicating a degree of familiarity. Wife? Girlfriend?

She wandered through the shop, past a display of whirligigs and a bin filled high with small stuffed animals, then stood in front of the window and gazed across the street at the large park within the four corners of small-town commerce. A small duck pond lay on the other side, where young cattails swayed in the breeze. Flowerbeds, not yet planted. Crabapples, just beginning to bloom. Benches tucked into boxwood and honeysuckle hedgerows.

The farmers had evacuated, and the square was all but deserted, leaving the giant oak standing guard. From this perspective, the massive tree looked haunting—contorted from years of over-pruning, or dead limbs which had dropped off years ago. It looked like a creature reaching toward her. Again, she recalled the spirit she'd seen earlier. *It wasn't just the jacket.*

The thin layer of clouds had dissipated, blown north of them with the steady wind, leaving a brilliant blue sky in contrast to the dark, gray bark of the gnarled tree. Lucy watched a plastic bag hop and tumble into the street, lifted by a gust over a passing car. A subtle shift in her focus rested on the kite in the window display. *The Millennium Falcon.*

She thought of the small boy with his inquisitive eyes, and looked over her shoulder to find Eli looking directly at her from the counter. With a smile, she placed a finger to the corner of her mouth as if wiping the frosting from her face. He returned her smile and nodded.

Turning away again, Lucy reached for the crystal in the window, and then plucked a boxed dragonfly mobile from a nearby shelf.

She heard the ting-a-ling of the door, and when she turned back around, was surprised to discover that Eli and Owen were gone. They had left without saying goodbye—and she felt a mystifying twinge of regret. Hadn't she been hoping to be left alone? Why then did she care that they had left?

"You know Eli, do you?" asked the clerk, pulling Lucy out of her thoughts.

"No, not really. We just sort of met at the park." Heading to the counter, Lucy fished around in her tote for her wallet and spotted her hair clip. Mia nodded toward the street.

"He's single." The words were practically sung. Lucy turned, following Mia's gaze, and caught sight of Eli and Owen standing on the sidewalk just outside the shop. She quickly tucked her purchases into her bag and tried to appear nonchalant as she combed her fingers hastily through her tangled hair and fastened the clip.

Outside, Eli and Owen were still there. Eli looked up, alerted by the door chime. "We're headed to the high school field to get this beast airborne," he said, holding up the kite—which, now that it was unfolded, was larger than the boy. "You're welcome to join us," he added, in that Midwestern, never-met-a-stranger way.

Lucy tightened her grip on the heavy tote until it felt like it was cutting through her shoulder. She looked at her feet, as if they were holding her back. She thought of her sister, Julia, who was currently traipsing around Europe with her trusty backpack. Julia was the spontaneous one—the one who jumped at every opportunity without a second thought, and seldom said no.

Owen looked up at her with his big brown eyes, and she smiled.

"I'll meet you there. I need to get my shopping put away."

CHAPTER TWO

LUCY ROUNDED THE CORNER TO GOLDEN AVENUE, THINKING ABOUT ELI, HIS SON, and the disarming quality that had convinced her to accept their invitation. By the time she'd reached the Methodist church on the corner of Fox Street, she'd talked herself out of it. As she tramped up the steps to the covered porch of her century-old four-square house, she'd reversed herself again.

Lucy threw open the door and looked into the brilliant blue eyes of Summer, her roommate, who was dressed in an oversized sweater with knee-length leggings. Her long red hair draping across her shoulders.

"I was just headed out to get some ink for the printer," Summer said. "Need anything?"

"No. Nothing." Lucy tried to slip past.

"Whoa—what's the rush?"

Summer and Lucy had lived together for over three years. They were more than roommates. They were business partners in the Chrysanthemum House Home School Project. They were best friends. And they were as close as sisters.

"I ..." Lucy didn't know where to start. "I'll tell you later."

Apparently unsatisfied, Summer followed Lucy into the house, past the dining room table, and into the kitchen. Placing her shopping tote on the floor, Lucy opened the refrigerator and stood, staring into a void, thinking about her strange circumstances as Summer leaned on the door, waiting for an answer.

"I ... met someone."

Lucy reached into the tote and produced a block of craft cheese and a jumble of other items in small paper bags. She set them one by one into the fridge. The carton of eggs had been removed and disposed of, but the bottom of the tote still held bits of shell and a smear of yolk.

"A guy?" Summer knew Lucy's history and how it impacted most of the choices she made in life.

"Yes, and his son." She folded her bag and set it beside the farmhouse-style sink. "I'm meeting them at the high school to fly kites." Summer's jaw dropped, and Lucy laughed. "It's not a date."

"Then what is it?"

"Just flying kites."

"There's more. What are you not telling me?" Summer crossed her arms.

"I'll tell you everything when I get back." Summer shook her head in resignation as Lucy stepped past her and scurried up to her room, where she dragged a brush through her hair and unearthed her own kite from the closet, where it was hidden behind her wool coat and a random collection of scarves that reminded her of winter, snow, and icy streets.

As a California transplant, Lucy did not tolerate Midwest winters well—but that was a small price to pay for anonymity.

SUMMER'S CAR WAS gone when Lucy emerged from the house with her kite in one hand and a fistful of almonds in the other. The bells of St. Michael's tolled the quarter-hour. It wasn't too late to change her mind.

Her neighbor across the street was sitting on the front step of his duplex, apparently deep in thought, until Lucy's screen door snapped shut behind her—and his head shot up as if a gun had been fired. *Sorry. Not sorry.* Lucy and Summer called him GI Joe. It was creepy, the way he skulked around in his ragged camo pants and his MAGA hat. His beard had grown thicker by the day since he'd moved in a month earlier.

She did her best to ignore GI Joe, as she unlocked her vintage Schwinn from the signpost and peddled up Fox Street toward the church. The high school was another two blocks down Golden Avenue, but she already could see Owen's kite high in the sky and felt glad she hadn't missed them.

Lucy coasted past the weather-beaten concession stand and crossed the track, circling the outer rim of the playing field to where Owen was kicking up streams of the little rubber beads embedded in the artificial turf. Eli was trying to hand off the kite to Owen when he noticed her.

"Hey! We thought you forgot about us," he called. Lucy waved and laid her bike on its side. Owen rejected the spool of string and ran to her.

"Lucy, look how high it is!"

"I see that. Way to go, Owen." Lucy pulled her blue-and-white striped kite from its nylon sleeve and snapped it together—one, two, three—as Owen watched. Eli at last handed the Millennium Falcon to his son, who took it and ran back to the center of the field.

Eli gestured toward the old aluminum bleachers on both sides of the field. "This was practically my home in high school," he beamed, pushing his wind-blown hair from his face. Two boys were chasing up and down the steps—from the track up to the announcer's box and back again. "Football, track, soccer, and my favorite, lacrosse. I played them all."

Lucy looked from end to end, and where she imagined Eli saw his glory days and felt the hometown pride of a Mighty Mallard, she noticed the age, wear, and evidence of a school district strapped for cash. She was ashamed to compare this to her high school in Monterey, with its seemingly limitless budget.

The steady wind took Lucy's kite high above the goalposts. The fat reel of string spun in her hands as the blue-and-white stripes soared higher and higher. Eli whooped excitedly.

"So, you grew up here in Drake?" asked Lucy.

"Yep. I never planned to stay, but life happens." Eli glanced at his son, and Lucy understood that it was Owen who had happened. "You're not from here, though," he went on. "I would have remembered you."

"Not from here, no. I moved here from California three years ago."

"You've been here that long?" He turned for a moment, distracted. "Owen! Knock that off, or you'll bust it! Sheesh." Owen was running with his kite dragging and bumping along the turf behind him before it lifted into the air. Eli pushed his hair back again. "Where have you been hiding?"

"I don't get out much."

She could tell he was waiting for her to elaborate—but how does a person expand on nothing? She had no life outside her house, her school, her students.

"Owen!" Owen's kite had taken a sudden nosedive. Lucy rushed to the crash site and handed her kite to Owen while she inspected the damage.

"Well, the crew looks good," she said grinning, "but the ship needs some repairs." Owen squinted at her, unsure of her meaning. "I have a repair kit at my house," she explained. It'll be good as new in no time."

Eli took the kite from her. "I'm glad you joined us. This was fun." He touched her arm briefly with the tips of his fingers. It reminded her of where her day had begun, and the jean jacket was suddenly on her mind again.

"Thank you," she said then, out of the blue, "for …" Where were the words to express her gratitude for the way he had rescued her? For his kindness, patience, and friendship without expectation or judgment?

Eli waved it away.

Owen reeled in the string of his broken kite as Lucy did the same with hers. She watched the reels grow fat in a playful race with a loveable, silly boy.

"You're great with him." Eli grinned, with a nod to Owen, who had quickly finished his task and was skipping away from the football field, the clear winner. Lucy collapsed her kite and returned it to the nylon cover. She wasn't sure how to answer, so she just smiled back and walked over to her bike.

Owen held tight to his father's hand as the three crossed the deserted street to an older model BMW—Eli's car.

"Follow me," Lucy said.

"Are you sure?"

"I said I would fix the kite. I'm a woman of my word." She waited for them to get settled in their car and pushed off from the curb to lead the way to her house.

SUMMER WAS WAITING on the porch swing when Eli pulled slowly up behind Lucy.

Eli followed Lucy up the front steps and held out his hand. "Eli Moon." Summer accepted it as Owen scrambled up, lugging his damaged kite. "This is my son, Owen."

"Eli, this is Summer, my roommate." Summer acknowledged the strangers on her porch with a generous smile, and winked at Lucy.

Lucy invited her guests in for a drink of water—and in Owen's case, a fistful of rice crackers, which soon turned into possession of the whole box.

A warm, natural light enhanced the artistic craftsmanship of the home. Lucy had always appreciated the wood floors, the narrow stained-glass window, and the built-in sideboard in the dining room. There were four bedrooms upstairs, and full baths up and down. The house felt spacious yet cozy. A far cry from the two-bedroom bungalow where she had grown up.

She watched Owen run his finger along the chair rail, which surrounded the dining room and rounded the corner to the foot of the stairs. Then he stepped cautiously through the pocket doors opposite the dining room and stopped short, with his father right on his heels.

Eli looked from a glass door leading to the back garden on one end, to a picture window where he spied Summer on the porch swing on the other. In between sat three large round tables set with colorful bins filled with school supplies.

"You live in a school?" Eli asked. Owen was in awe as he followed his father into the middle of the room and made himself comfortable at the center table.

Lucy stepped past Eli and handed Owen a few sheets of paper. He set down his box of crackers and promptly began drawing pictures with the fat Crayola markers, looking up sporadically at the *Wind in the Willows* posters tacked up around the room. Mr. Toad, Badger, Ratty, and the rest of the gang were keeping company with multiplication tables and an artistic rendition of the alphabet, which included examples in three languages.

"It's the Chrysanthemum House Home School Project," Lucy said. "A mouthful, I know. We just call it the Chrysanthemum House. I opened it three years ago with my landlord's two kids and two others from down the street. Summer joined me soon after that. This year we're at capacity with twelve." Lucy felt proud of the accomplishment, especially when she saw the look of wonder on Eli's face.

Lance Kirsch, her landlord, owned a number of rental homes in Drake and the day Lucy signed the papers on the Chrysanthemum House, he'd told her that her Home School Project was going to take the country by storm.

Eli looked down at Owen, who held up his empty water glass. Lucy took it and walked out of the room, listening to Eli's footfall behind her.

She patted the head of a bronze bust on the cluttered dining room table. "Good afternoon, Your Highness." The bust of a glamorous Victorian woman with hair piled high on her head had been Summer's contribution to the house. Eli laughed and gave the small statue a pat, too. Her Highness ruled the stack of papers she sat upon, as well as the folders, books, and laptop computer that surrounded her.

Eli followed her into the kitchen—a small room with low countertops and high cupboards. Lucy set the empty glass down beside the farmhouse sink and then stretched to prop open the tall double-hung window behind it with the stub of a broken ruler. The stiff breeze pushed and drew on the bright yellow cafe curtains.

"What's a home school project?" Eli asked as she refilled Owen's glass from the tap.

"It's something I dreamed up in college as a student teacher.

Looking at the system from that perspective, it seemed to me the whole thing was pretty screwed up." Lucy filled her own glass. "Thirty kids to one teacher; no one was getting what they needed, and the teacher was at her wits' end trying to keep up. The Home School Project started out as a concept I used for my thesis. When I found this house, it became a reality. I totally lucked out, especially when Summer answered my ad."

"You're a teacher. It makes sense, you know, the way you handle Owen," Eli said. "I'm a social worker."

"Aha. That explains a lot."

"What," Eli smiled at her.

"A fixer. You know. You saw me struggling and had to help." Lucy thought of the pains he'd gone to to get her on her feet that morning. He'd turned her whole day around.

They leaned back against the sink and sipped their water. Lucy could hear Summer in the classroom with Owen, answering his questions.

"Well, I do what I can," he laughed. "It's hard to resist a damsel in distress," he teased.

Damsel? Lucy tilted her head in doubt. Not once in her life had she considered herself as such. Not even in her Disney princess stage. "Hey, we're not in the way, are we?" he asked.

"No, not at all." Lucy opened a drawer and pulled out this and that until she found what she was looking for. It was a metal box with two clips on either side. She flipped it open and showed Eli the contents. It held just about anything one could hope for in a tool kit, in miniature.

"Well, that's adorable." He marveled at the interchangeable bits as Lucy reached deep into the drawer for a bottle of Gorilla Glue and some cloth tape.

"Let's get to work." They joined Summer and Owen in the classroom and spread the damaged kite out on the next table. "Owen, you can be my assistant."

Owen took his job very seriously, holding the bottle of glue as Lucy lined up the broken wing. She glued the cracked plastic rod, and then taped the finger-length rip beside it. She tightened the loops and re-threaded the string. Owen had a hand in all of it.

"So, Owen, your kite was a birthday present." Owen grinned up at Lucy, nodding. "When's your birthday? Not today, is it?"

"Yesterday, May fourth," Owen said, beaming. "Get it? May the fourth?" It took her a moment before she put it together with the Millennium Falcon kite. She slapped her forehead and laughed at herself.

"Of course! Happy Birthday, Owen!"

"I'm six." So like a six-year-old to proudly volunteer his age.

"Hey, Owen, would you like to see the garden out here?" Summer asked as she struggled with the door leading out of the classroom to a small, fenced in yard at the side of the house. The old door swelled with the humidity and it always took a few strong pulls to get it open.

"Sure!" Owen excitedly climbed from his chair and followed summer out to her garden, so full of promise. Two garden boxes, side by side, had been planted recently with green beans, carrots, tomatoes, and kale. The beans were just breaking ground, their white cotyledons reaching up to the sky. Tomato cages surrounded three six-inch-tall starts.

"Early days," Summer said. "But we'll have plenty to share before you know it."

"I don't like tomatoes," Owen said, studying the colorful lables at the end of each row, "but I *love* carrots."

"We need to get going, Little Bird," Eli said. Owen's shoulders slumped with disappointment.

"But the glue needs time to set," said Lucy.

Eli nodded and grinned. "We'll come back for it later."

Lucy followed them out of the small yard through a wooden gate to the sidewalk and watched as Owen clicked himself into his booster seat, while his father lingered outside the car.

She stood on the curb facing Eli, hands in her pockets, struggling to put what she was feeling into words. *Just say SOMETHING. ANYTHING.*

"Dad!" Owen's impatience hurried things along.

"So…"

"So…"

"Dad!"

"Be right there, Owen." Eli rounded the car to the driver's seat.

Lucy waved as they drove away, wondering what the hell had just happened.

CHAPTER THREE

SUMMER STOOD IN THE HALL, PEERING THROUGH THE CRACK IN LUCY'S BED-room door. "Knock-knock," she said, nudging it open. Lucy invited her friend to sit, and Summer made herself comfortable at the end of the bed.

Lucy's red-headed friend had left behind the same opportunities that faced every graduating student when she joined Lucy at the Chrysanthemum House. In Chicago, she also left behind two over-protective parents, and an uncertain future with a bandmate. In some respects, she and Lucy were both runaways.

"He's cute," Summer said. Lucy smiled as she hung the crystal from a small cup hook in the center of the window frame, then closed the blinds.

Eli was cute, Lucy acknowledged. She imagined him as a little boy, with his mischievous grin, his messy hair, and the bounce in his step—quite like his son.

Summer went on. "He was totally into you."

"Stop it," Lucy said, blushing. He'd left with a practical reason to return. Lucy did not want to delude herself into reading more into it. She thought about her reflection in the window earlier, her hair flapping in the wind. *Radiant*? He'd seen her at her worst. A shell-shocked imbecile, unable to walk, speak, or cope with the trauma that had been inflicted years earlier. Just the memory of it was enough to make her nauseous.

"So, what's the story?"

"It's so embarrassing," Lucy began. Summer tilted her head. "I had a moment. I thought I heard … I thought I saw him. Ben Wyatt. Just as my knees started to crumble, Eli caught me."

"What?" Summer grimaced.

"He caught me."

"Not that. Wyatt."

"I know. It couldn't have been him, but it seemed so real."

"It's only been three years."

"Precisely." Lucy thought back to the moment the jury returned with one guilty conviction of the three charges. Sexual assault—not guilty. Attempted homicide—not guilty. Assault with a deadly weapon—guilty. Altogether the max would have been twenty years. But he would only get four of them, and only because there was a witness who saw him flee from her unconscious body.

He'd argued that the stabbing was her own fault—that his back was literally against the wall, and he'd had no intention of hurting her. But he did hurt her, and she had the scar to prove it. Any sexual contact, he'd said, was her imagination—a case of "he said, she said." The smudge of semen left behind tested inconclusive.

Lucy entered Benjamin Wyatt's name into the search bar on her laptop, but she didn't have the stomach to follow through. Did she really want to know if he'd been released early?

Summer leaned over, pushed enter, and they watched as the search results materialized with articles and updates of the assault and resulting trial. It wasn't big news back then, especially compared to the presidential election ramping up, and numerous wildfires raging all over the state.

The banner ads along the sidebar flashed obnoxious offers. *Looking for someone? Secured Search Just $99. Truthfinder.com Sign up and Log in.* Faces, reminiscent of the old milk carton missing child ads, flipped back and forth between the same man and woman. Lucy looked away while Summer skimmed the first page of results, then the second and third.

"I don't see anything about him being released, but it does mention that Lucia Perez has not been seen since the trial."

"And Lucy Price?" She'd googled her new name only once before, just to be sure it wasn't linked to Lucia. Just to be sure it wasn't linked to who she had been before landing in Drake. Lucy took a deep breath.

"Nothing," Summer said, with relief. "So, it couldn't have been Wyatt."

Lucy held onto her doubts as she stared at the ceiling in the corner of the room, where a spider was making itself at home. She climbed onto the bed and reached, but her arm wasn't long enough. Summer jumped up beside her, collected the spider, then opened the window to release it.

"Off you go," Summer said.

"Thank you." Lucy gave her friend a heartfelt hug.

"It was just a spider."

"No, it's so much more. I don't know what I'd do without you. You keep me sane." To Lucy, Summer was the counterbalance to the California madness, the yin to Lucy's yang. Summer squeezed Lucy in reply.

"Goodnight, Lucy. Don't let Wyatt get to you. It was a false alarm and you have way more to be happy about today." Lucy raised a brow in question. "A certain Eli Moon?"

"Ah, yes," grinned Lucy. "Eli."

Summer closed the door behind her and left Lucy looking out her window just in time to see GI Joe walk up the cement steps to his front door.

Lucy feared he would turn around. It was a fear derived from being watched, pursued, and assaulted. She hated Ben Wyatt for the distrust it seeded in her. A distrust she'd set aside, however briefly, when she'd joined Eli and his son at the high school.

For the first time since she'd seen Eli's worried face that morning, it occurred to Lucy what it had meant to have him looking out for her. *I'm all right.*

But she wasn't all right, and she doubted she ever would be. Was it even possible to have a healthy relationship with a man after what had happened to her?

Lucy flipped through the deck of impressions Eli had left behind, including his interactions with the store clerk, his son, and her roommate. Summer had taken a shine to him within minutes.

Lucy turned out her light and climbed into bed thinking about what she'd told Summer years ago about leaving behind wine country for cornfields in hopes for a fresh start. It was the belief that a new town, new job, and new name could put Wyatt and all that came with that chapter in her life in the past. Unspoken was the knowledge that starting over is a fantasy, and that the past has a way of tagging along wherever you go, like an unwelcome stench.

The tattered jean jacket—a case in point. The first time Lucy had seen it, she was on the bus from one of her jobs to an evening class on campus. The odd-looking man sat across from her. He was a grad student, maybe a teaching assistant, she'd guessed. Still, his unkempt appearance, stringy black hair, filthy blue jeans, and a tattered jean jacket—unbuttoned to reveal a motheaten T-shirt— dissuaded that notion. A vagabond, she'd mused, with busfare.

He'd stared at her like he was tripping on drugs—looking through her, to a notion deep in his own head.

That was the first of many seemingly random encounters. Each time, the jacket, the stare, the stench warned Lucy of his presence.

The details never changed, regardless of how she framed them. Had it been right to move? What if she'd stayed? She shifted between alternate outcomes. What if she'd reported Wyatt before it had gone that far? What if she hadn't fought him? What if … ?

Wyatt's arrest had done nothing to quell her fears. The memory of her ordeal was enough to keep her wary, but she'd let her guard down since living in Drake. Now, for the first time in three years, Lucy felt vulnerable.

Sleep came eventually, sometime between three and four in the morning, when her weary mind found softer ground in thoughts of Eli and his son.

CHAPTER FOUR

AWEEK LATER, LUCY ROUNDED THE CORNER ON HER BIKE AND COASTED DOWN Fox Street to the Chrysanthemum House—her haul from the farmers' market swinging from the handlebars. She dismounted and looked up at the porch to find Eli sitting on the swing, unshaved and wearing a pair of thick-rimmed glasses.

"Hey, you," she said, removing her helmet and grinning ear to ear. Her heart pounded with the excitement of seeing him again.

"Hey." Eli rose from his seat and rounded the steps just as she began her ascent. His thick whiskers grazed her cheek as they collided in a quick and clumsy hug.

"The kite is cleared for takeoff," she joked. "I'll just run in and grab it."

"No rush, I … was that tree blooming last week?" Eli pointed up at a full-grown magnolia in the small yard, thick with white blossoms. "How did I miss that?"

"You weren't wearing glasses last week."

"Contacts," he said, smiling at her and lifting his glasses out of the way. "Blind without them."

She sat down on one end of the porch swing, and he sat on the other, setting it in motion—back and forth, *creak* and *groan*.

"Where's Owen?"

"My sister is watching him."

Lucy's phone rang, and she scrambled to free it from her tote. With a pained look, she answered, "This is Lucy." She took the phone and her shopping inside, embarrassed for the interruption. It was a parent who'd been told of an incident with another student. A disagreement which hadn't been fully resolved, in her opinion. It was one of the hardest parts of Lucy's job, balancing her duties as a teacher with the need for discipline.

Sometimes Lucy felt like the parents expected her to raise their children. A proxy parent. She did her best, but some parents did not like her open-minded style even though that's what they had signed up for.

Lucy returned to the porch with two tall glasses of ice water, dripping with condensation.

"I wish I had something more interesting to offer you." She sat back down beside him, sliding her worn and faded Keds off her feet and pushing them to the side.

"This is great. Thanks. Everything all right? The phone call?"

"It'll be fine, just a behavior issue with a student. That was her mother."

Eli shifted uncomfortably in his seat. "Lucy?" He glanced over at her, and she recognized the concern in his eyes. "About what happened last week ... Never mind. It's none of my business."

She pushed off with her bare toes from the porch rail. *There it was again*, she thought. The racing heart. The catch in her breath. She sensed what he wanted to ask.

"It's all right if you don't want to talk about it. I understand, but, well ..." The swing creaked and groaned as Lucy considered her options. How much to say—if anything.

"When I was in college, there was a ..." she began. Why was this so hard? "A guy who ..." She couldn't finish. Eli's eyes went wide—he was thinking the worst, she knew.

"Lucy, were you ... that's okay, you don't have to talk about it."

Attempted rape is not rape, thought Lucy, *but what Wyatt had done to her left deep and permanent scars, physical and psychological.*

"I was assaulted." Lucy thought about her face pressed against the rancid smelling dumpster as Wyatt ground himself against her, moaning, with his hand down the front of her pants.

She looked abruptly away from Eli. She'd embarrassed herself the week before, and here she was again.

"Last week I thought I'd seen him, the guy." *I thought I'd heard his voice, too*, but she kept this to herself for reasons she couldn't explain.

"No wonder it looked like you'd seen a ghost. What does he look like? Maybe I saw him too." Lucy marveled at the extent of his concern.

"There's no way it could have been him," she reassured him as she attempted to reassure herself. "It was the jacket the guy was wearing. It was …" She searched for the word. "It was a trigger, you know?"

"I do, yes."

They sipped their water, thinking about what to say or do next, when Eli pointed out the greasy neighbor peering at them from the steps of the duplex across the street. The disheveled man was dressed in shabby army fatigues, and a faded *Don't Tread on Me* T-shirt. His red MAGA hat was clutched in one hand.

Lucy followed Eli's glance and shook her head. "It's not him. Summer and I call him GI Joe. He just moved in a few weeks ago."

The conversation had gone from light and airy to divulging more about herself than she'd intended. What did she know about Eli? He played sports in high school. He has a son and a friend named Mia. Was there an ex-wife? Was it any of her business?

"Let's go for a walk," suggested Eli. Lucy slipped back into her Keds, and they meandered down the road toward St. Michael's.

They walked down Fox and crossed Golden Avenue as the church bells tolled two, three, four. But neither paid any attention. Two women stood in the doorway, whispering something that didn't concern them. A small dog, off-leash, ran up to Lucy as if they'd known one another.

"Hey, Biscuit. Where's your mommy?" Biscuit was a ten-pound mongrel that lived next door. Her owner, Shel, wasn't far behind. Lucy swept her up and handed her over.

"I don't know what's gotten into her. Sorry." Shel scolded Biscuit as she carried the little pup back to her house.

"We never had a dog," said Lucy, turning back to Eli. "My mom said she was allergic, but I think she just didn't want to clean up after one."

"We did. Grandpa had a German Shepard named Fritz. He

was a good dog, mostly." Eli laughed. "He had it in for my mom, though. Wouldn't let her near Grandpa. I remember he was hit by a car, and we had to put him down."

"How old were you?"

"Six, I think."

"Owen's age. Do you think of getting a dog now?"

"Sometimes. He's kind of dog-crazy these days, so I think about it more and more, but a dog like that," he pointed back at Biscuit, "never."

"Nothing cute and fluffy, then?" she teased.

"Not making any promises I can't keep," he laughed as they walked ahead. They both looked up at a passing jet, the contrail marking its path against the blue sky. "So, California. What's that like?"

"Oh, you know—sunshine and happiness," she joked. She recalled waking to foggy mornings that lingered all day. "My folks still live there." It broke her parents' hearts the day she left for her new life in Drake. She still felt the guilt of that. Lucy's heart ached, thinking of her parents and filled with longing for the days spent on the bay, where she would watch the sea otters play in the kelp, or fill up on free samples from the restaurants along Fisherman's Wharf with her sister.

She hadn't seen her parents in three years and often worried about her father in the strained political climate, with its cruelty to immigrants.

Eli led her up the next street like he had a destination. "Tell me about your home," he said. "Where you grew up in California."

Again, he was learning more about her than she about him. Lucy took a deep breath. She was determined to avoid talking about the obvious difference in the climate. The bone-chilling winters she had never adapted to.

"My high school had a scuba club and a hands-on marine science class," she began. Eli was visibly impressed. "And living so close to the heartbeat of technology certainly had its advantages, like one-on-one tech clinics. We had guest speakers and workshops from companies like Facebook and Google."

"Seriously?" Eli dragged his fingers through his thick hair, unable to put any order to it. He grinned. "Sounds like Drake's a real step up then." Lucy gave him a playful push.

She went on. "There are also miles and miles of farms. But instead of corn and soybeans, we have grapes, oranges, strawberries, almonds, and—"

"And everything else," he finished.

"Pretty much." She flashed her gap-toothed grin.

"What about your family?"

"Well, my dad has a landscape business. My mom is a homemaker. I have a younger sister—*blah, blah, blah*. It's not very interesting."

"Not the way you tell it, no." He laughed. Lucy thought about her father, a Mexican immigrant who'd crossed the border under cover of night at the age of seventeen. She pictured the youths currently in cages on the border, packed together like cattle. That could have been him.

She decided it was her turn to question him. "And you? Tell me about Eli Moon."

Eli smiled. "Born and raised in Drake. Our family goes back generations here. My sister and I still live in the old house."

"You live with your sister? You and Owen?"

"Mm-hmm. She's a therapist. Keeps an office in the house, but that might change soon."

Lucy imagined the cramped quarters and patients coming to the front door with a child underfoot.

"She's thinking of moving in with her girlfriend, Mia—from the toy store, remember?"

"I remember. She's beautiful. What's that accent?"

"Haitian. Or is it French? I can never get that right. She moved to the states as a kid." Eli led her across the street "Come, I want to introduce you to someone."

Lucy saw a older man emerge from the free clinic. She'd never been there herself. She hadn't been to a doctor since arriving in Drake.

"Dr. Franzki!" Eli waived the man down.

The years had been kind to the doctor, Lucy noticed. At eighty, he had excellent posture and a full head of wavy white hair. His shoe-button eyes looked sharp behind a pair of round, wire-rimmed glasses resting halfway down his nose. His tan slacks and black turtleneck, together with the eyeglasses, gave him the look of an old beatnik.

"Hey, Eli. To what do I owe the pleasure?"

"We were just passing by."

"So glad you did. Who do we have here?" Dr. Franzki smiled and held out his hand to Lucy. She took it, returning his broad grin.

"This is Lucy Price, my—new friend." Eli grinned down at Lucy for confirmation.

"Well, Lucy, it's a pleasure to meet you."

"Dr. Franzki doesn't know the meaning of retirement," teased Eli. "He delivered my sister and me, and then left private practice to open the free clinic here."

"Just doing my part," Dr. Franzki said. "Trying to keep up with the Moon family." He laughed and put an arm around Eli.

"No good reason to retire. What would I do with myself?"

"Take it easy? Travel? I don't know."

"My lesson to you, Eli, is never to retire unless you have a good hobby. Even then, well—what good is a hobby with so much work to do?"

"Fine advice, doctor." Eli looked up at the newly installed security camera. "What's that all about?"

"I had to clean off anti-Semitic graffiti from my front porch a few weeks ago. And there were picketers outside the clinic just last week." He scratched his head. "Just the notion alone..."

Something about Drake was changing, Lucy could feel it too.

Lucy looked up at the camera and thought of the type of fear that necessitates security. Her heart went out to the old doctor, who ducked inside his clinic and emerged with a recent copy of the local newspaper—a weekly publication that Lucy subscribed to, but seldom read.

"The city of Drake has been a substantial part of this clinic's success for the past twenty years, Eli," said the doctor, launching into another grievance. "But look at this." He peeled the paper open and pointed. "They've pulled their funding."

"I saw that," said Eli.

"What are you going to do?" Lucy looked into the doctor's wired spectacles and suddenly noticed the dark rings under his eyes and the deep creases of worry across his forehead.

"The only thing we can do, Lucy—reach out for more donations and lean more heavily on our volunteers. We've already cut the regular staff hours as far back as we can. God forbid we have to start charging for some of our services. That might be the last straw."

"The social service office is taking a hit too," Eli said, "but we still have State and County funding. If it's all right with you, I can reach out to my contacts there."

Dr. Franzki wrapped his arms around Eli with the strength of ten men, judging by Eli's gasp and wide eyes. "It's great to see you, Eli, and your friend here. Tell me, Lucy, do you live here in Drake? I don't believe I've seen you around."

"I moved here about three years ago."

"Well, it's nice to see a fresh face. You know, towns like Drake don't get a lot of newcomers. Most families have lived here for generations."

"Lucy lives just down a few blocks, near St. Michael's," Eli volunteered. "She runs an independent school."

"Is that so?"

While they visited, no one had noticed GI Joe working his way toward them with a fistful of fliers that he had been carefully stapling to each light post along the sidewalk.

They stepped aside in surprise when he'd reached them. He stopped, posted another flier in front of the clinic and kept walking, but not without a quick glance at Lucy. Was it her imagination, or had he nodded at her?

The doctor ripped down the flier. An organization called American Values in Democracy was announcing a rally at Drake Park the following Wednesday. The leaflet was encouraging attendance, promising "Agitation to Reclaim our Nation."

"What is happening to this town, Eli?" he asked, waving the flier. "This rally—you know what it is, don't you? It's those right-wing nuts, AVID. American Values, my ass. Just a bunch of rotten apples thinking it's their God-given right to protect the world from non-white, non-Christian individuals." He tore the flier to bits. "Eli, look after yourself and your sister. These are troubling times." He gave Eli a knowing look and shook his hand goodbye. "It's an outrage." He turned to Lucy. "You're in good hands, young lady. Eli's an honorable man." Eli was visibly uncomfortable. "I know, I know. Humble, the lot of you! Take care, kid."

They walked on in silence, digesting the doctor's words. Lucy pulled a flier off the next light post and read it.

"Who are these guys, American Values in Democracy?" Lucy asked handing Eli the flier.

"I've never heard of them till now," Eli answered, shaking his head.

Lucy wondered further what gave them the right to proclaim themselves as True Americans? The infuriating answer was simple. Democracy gave them the right. The Constitution gave them the right.

The rally on Wednesday would be an orgy of bigots, homophobes, and what Hillary Clinton had called "deplorables," thought Lucy, *all swarming the otherwise peaceful Drake Park.*

Eli led Lucy along Washington Street, past the recently constructed city hall, which also housed the police department. The merger was the brainchild of the previous mayor but suited the current one, Mayor Church, just fine.

Eli spied GI Joe cutting through the Washington Street parking lot across the street and tugged at Lucy's sleeve. Her heart skipped a beat as GI Joe made eye contact with her, then abruptly looked away. His odd behavior was disturbingly familiar. *Not again.* Ben Wyatt had stalked her for months before his assault.

They wandered up toward the outstretched arms of the Old Oak as they approached Drake Park, where folks were lying in the sun, playing with their children, and feeding the ducks.

Eli stopped on the corner, in front of the Drake Coffee Co. "I work down there," said Eli, pointing down the street. "At the social service office."

"Location, location, location." Lucy laughed. The office stood between SamSams sandwich shop and the DK Nail Salon, directly across from the park square.

"That was Beth's doing. She's my boss. She nabbed the office years ago, and the city signed off on it. That would never happen today."

"Why not?"

"This mayor has it in for us. He rejects social programs of any sort. If it weren't for the county, we would have been evicted the day after he took office."

"He doesn't have that kind of power, does he?"

"He does pretty much as he wants. Since he was elected last January, he's done nothing but cut. He's peeled back our budget to the point that we had to scale back some of our most beneficial programs and eliminate others," said Eli. "Like the food bank vouchers, and counseling for new mothers. All the hard work built up over so many years is just unraveling. Have you noticed that he hasn't actually created any new programs or policies?"

"The Dismantler-in-Chief," said Lucy with a wry grin.

"It's true," said Eli. "That's what the article in the paper is about. We have a meeting on Wednesday to learn our fate. I'm dreading it."

"That's the day of the rally," Lucy reminded him, noticing GI Joe lurking within sight, posting his fliers. She looked away and sat down at one of the café chairs outside the coffee shop, and Eli joined her. "And the meeting—what do you think is going to happen?"

"I honestly don't know. We're working on a report to validate what's left of our pet programs. Our office does a lot of good for this community. Not everyone around here has it easy." He leaned back and looked down at his lap, as if it held his next thought. "At least we still have the county on our side—and the state kicks in some too. But without the city, we'll have to reduce or cut many of our pet programs."

"Most people are oblivious to what their losing until it's gone," Lucy said, looking over her shoulder to the barista staring at them from the window. "Do you want a coffee?"

"Not really. You?"

"No, but their looking at us," Lucy whispered. Eli turned and waved.

"Don't worry about it."

Eli leaned on the table; his chin propped up with a fist. Lucy noticed the frayed cuffs of his blue sweater. It wasn't just the cuffs; the collar was shaggy with years of wear. Lucy gave his sleeve a flirtatious tug.

"This was my dad's." The sweater reflected a hint of the blue into his otherwise gray eyes. "You mentioned triggers earlier. I have triggers everywhere I look—even here, sitting at this table. I sat here with my dad just days before I left for college. We talked about my course load. He was worried I was going to burn out. He said, 'It's your freshman year. Have some fun.' I can hear his voice like it was yesterday." Eli gazed up at the clouds like it was somehow easier to concentrate.

"My dad's sweater, my dad's car—there are memories of my parents everywhere I look." He took a deep breath. "My parents died six years ago, Lucy, and it hasn't gotten any easier." He cleared his throat and looked down.

Lucy reached for his hands, pressed flat on the table, and clutched them in her own.

"Triggers," he said again, pulling his hands back and rising clumsily from the table. "They're everywhere."

His emotions were right at the surface, and she felt them as if they were her own. Lucy stood and reached for his arm, just as he had the week before.

"I was married." His voice was strained with anguish and heartbreak. "Owen's mom. She died right on the heels of my parents. I can't even look at my own son without the tremor of … what? Grief? Guilt? They're one and the same. I couldn't save them. I couldn't save her." He brushed her hand away as if he'd only just realized it was there. "I was a husband, and then I wasn't. I was a son, and then I wasn't. By the time I turned twenty-two I'd lost my wife, my parents, and my grandfather." He started walking. They crossed the street. Lucy tried to keep pace with his stride, but she was falling behind.

"Hey, wait up!"

He stopped and turned to face her; his eyes brimmed with tears while she caught up. She felt his pain and couldn't think beyond it. He was purging years of pent-up grief and regret, and the flood-gates were wide open.

Reflexively, she held out her arms, and he stepped right in, enfolding his own arms around her. She welcomed his warmth and strength as he clutched her. She indulged herself in the closeness of him, the thumping of his heart, and the wholeness of his embrace, mingled with the scent of his body.

"I love your sweater," she said finally, and felt his tremble of laughter in her arms. Eli stepped back and wiped the tears from his cheeks.

"You are something else." He brushed a loose strand of hair from her face and tucked it behind her ear. "Thank you."

"We're even now," said Lucy playfully, knowing full well she'd held back essential details from her story.

They walked back to the Chrysanthemum House in no particular hurry, retracing their steps past the clinic and the church to Lucy's front door. Eli looked up at the mid-day sun and removed his sweater, clenching it in his hand. The black t-shirt that remained enhanced his dark features.

"Have a seat, I'll get us some ice water."

"I should get going. My sister will be waiting for me," Eli said.

"Oh," Lucy said, "Hang on, I'll get Owen's kite." Lucy pulled the door open, wondering if he'd follow her in, but he strolled over to the swing. She returned with the repaired kite and handed it to Eli.

"Thanks for doing that, fixing it I mean. You didn't have to." Eli held the kite in one hand and laid the other on the back of the swing. "Owen's been talking about it all week. I was wondering, you know, if we could go again sometime."

"I would like that." Lucy watched as Eli walked lazily down the steps and back to his car. "Eli," she called after him. "Why don't you bring Owen by tomorrow evening? I'll make you dinner."

He laid the kite on the back seat and looked up at Lucy standing on the porch. "Excellent," he said. "We'll see you tomorrow then."

CHAPTER FIVE

THE CHURCH BELLS AT ST. MICHAEL'S WERE TOLLING FIVE AS ELI'S BMW PULLED up to the Chrysanthemum House the next day. He emerged with a big grin and a bottle of wine.

Owen clambered out of his booster seat and ascended the front steps carefully, carrying a paper bag which he handed to Lucy with great satisfaction. There was some heft to it. She looked in the bag and spied some pale pink tissue paper on the bottom. He studied her face with anticipation as his father looked on.

"What do we have here?" she asked with delight.

"I made it in school. It's for you." She observed him, rocking heel to toe the way he had in the toy store, watching her every move as she unwrapped the tissue paper to reveal a rough clay sculpture, painted and glazed green, brown, and red, with yellow eyes and black feet. "It's a turtle," said Owen.

"I can see that," said Lucy with a broad smile. "I love it! How did you know that turtles are my favorite animal?" Her expression of wide eyed wonder matched Owen's. "Slow and steady wins the race, right?"

"Right." Owen was pleased with himself.

Lucy knelt and hugged the boy, whose arms squeezed her tightly—his soft, curly hair tickling her neck. She was flooded with a rush of affection. "Thank you." Owen released himself and headed into the house as if he owned the place.

"Not exactly Her Highness," said Eli holding the door open for Lucy.

"It doesn't need to be." Lucy admired the small turtle in her hand as they caught up to Owen in the kitchen with Summer.

The house smelled amazing. Lucy had miraculously pulled

together her mother's shredded pork enchilada recipe, and it was bubbling away in the oven.

"How can we help?" asked Eli, pushing up his sleeves.

"There's nothing to do now except fill our plates." Lucy pulled the enchiladas from the oven.

"Just wait till after dinner, we'll put you on clean-up duty," Summer said, laughing. "I'm serious. I hate doing dishes."

Owen watched Lucy portion out the meal onto four plates. He looked half-starved with anticipation as she handed him his plate, which he carried gingerly to the table. Eli sat down beside him, and Summer sat at the head of the table, explaining that Her Highness had been demoted for the evening.

"Eat up everyone, before this gets cold." Summer already had a forkful poised in front of her face.

Lucy watched Owen eat with periodic little noises indicating he was wholeheartedly enjoying the meal. Eli hovered over him, cautioning him to pace himself, or reminding him to use his napkin. It was abundantly clear that, while Eli didn't have a wife, he certainly was not single.

Owen ate two helpings and was searching the table for more when Lucy excused herself to the kitchen. She returned with a plate of colorful cupcakes.

"Oh!" squealed Owen. "I love cupcakes!" Then, from behind her back, Lucy produced a birthday candle in the shape of the number six and fixed it to the top of one of the cupcakes.

As she set the small plate in front of Owen, the six fell over, smudging the frosting. Owen quickly picked it up and licked it off with a smile so broad he could have fit the whole cupcake into it.

"Make a wish," said Summer, lighting the wick. Owen squeezed his eyes shut tight and opened them to three expectant faces.

Later, true to his word, Eli rolled up his sleeves and filled the sink with soapy water while Owen made himself at home in the classroom.

"Thanks," said Eli, handing Lucy a dripping dinner plate. "It's been a great night, and the cupcakes—you sure have his number."

"Well, to be fair—I love cupcakes, too."

"Do you think you could get away tomorrow? I'll be working on the report for the mayor, and I could use a friendly diversion."

"So, I'm a diversion?" she teased.

"No! I … um … I would like to see you again. Sometimes I … That is, if I didn't already scare you off with the waterworks earlier."

"Did I scare you off last week?" she said. Eli shook his head, and she smiled. "I can meet you after three. Is that too late for a diversion?"

"Three o'clock is perfect."

Summer played some fun music in the living room, and Lucy felt like dancing for the first time in years.

THE FOLLOWING DAY, Summer practically pushed Lucy out the door before the students were even excused. Lucy used the extra time to walk up to the square, choosing to leave her bike behind, chained to the street sign in front of her house.

It was a bright, sunny day, and the walk gave her a chance to think about how Eli had confided in her about his parents and his wife, and his struggles at the social service office. The tables had turned. What had she given in return? Sure, he discovered her in the throes of a panic attack, and later she'd inferred her sexual assault. It was all she could do at the time. Did that make them even? Had she given as much as she'd received?

Eli seemed much more at ease, talking about his personal life. His openness was part of his charm. She wondered what it would take for her to reveal the whole ugly story. It wasn't something you drop in someone's lap like a bundle of junk mail.

Her phone rang, and she pulled it out of her pocket and answered before checking the number. The caller spit an aggressive assault in a language she didn't understand. German? Dutch? Lucy hung up and blocked the number. She'd been getting an uptick in spam calls lately. With all the blocked numbers, she had prevented a fair share of the population from ever contacting her.

She walked around the small duck pond and lay down behind

a dense wall of cattails in a patch of shade under the Old Oak, where she let her mind wander as she waited for Eli. Gazing into the broad branches, where a robin worked out how to weave an additional twig into her nest, Lucy put a few sticks together of her own. If he's trusting her with his past, she should trust him with hers. But …

She heard footsteps and flinched. Eli stepped into view and grinned down at her. "Looks like I took you by surprise," he said, sitting down in the grass beside her.

"You're early," she said, tossing a baggie of plump, green grapes at him. Eli popped off a few and threw them back. It was just before three. He wasn't that early.

Lucy opened her tote and fished out a sandwich, handing half to Eli. He examined the colorfully stacked ingredients, then gave it back. It was her favorite combination of alfalfa sprouts, cucumber, tomato, and roasted red pepper, with a smear of hummus between two fat slices of dense, fibrous bread.

"Not a fan?" She took an unladylike bite, chomping into it as hungrily as Owen had with his enchilada, and then washed it down with ginger kombucha. "How's your report going?" He took the grapes from her lap and ate a few more.

"Nearly there. Beth needs to look it over, but I doubt any of it will make a bit of difference. It's like in college when you know the professor has it in for you, but you feel a responsibility to turn in your best work anyway. Mayor Church wants to crush us, but we're not going to make it easy."

A mother duck waddled in front of them, with six ducklings lined up behind her on their way to the pond. Lucy stood with her tote and motioned for Eli to follow as she walked back and around the cattails to the murky pond. She tore off a piece of crust and flung it into the water. Chaos ensued as a dozen or more ducks scrambled, wings flapping and feet paddling toward the soggy crust.

Eli found an empty bench, and they sat down with the tote bag tucked between them. Lucy considered sharing more of her sandwich with the ducks but offered it to Eli again instead. He shook his head.

"I've eaten. Had a SamSams special an hour ago."

"I'm sure it was marvelous," Lucy teased, thinking of the dense, white hoagie roll stuffed with the nitrate-laden cold cuts the deli was known for.

"Extra mayo."

She laughed at his mischievous smile and popped the last bite of her sandwich into her mouth, wiping her hands on her denim skirt. "What's Owen up to today?"

"Well, there was school this morning. Morning kindergarten is a grind, you know. He's at daycare now. Little Ducklings over on Wilson Street. Do you know it?" She didn't. He checked his watch. "There's someone I want you to meet." He pointed to his office across the way.

Lucy looked at the rusty-red brick building that may have been as old as the city itself. The two windows on either side of the glass door had always had their blinds closed in the past, she remembered. But today they were open wide.

Eli stood and reached out a hand to help Lucy up. She stumbled upright, and he shot out his other hand to support her, holding it there on her lower back until she was balanced.

Eli was a toucher, Lucy noticed. If it wasn't his hand on her arm, it was his hand on her back, her shoulder, her knee. At first, in the park when she'd first met him, the touch was necessary. She understood that. But it had become clear that it was more a form of communication. Like, "do I have your attention?" or, "are you all right?"

Like the coffee shop down the street, Eli's office had a small table set up on the sidewalk with two plastic folding chairs. Lucy saw a middle-aged woman with brassy blonde hair and a spray-on tan stretched out on one of the chairs, a cigarette pinched between her fingers. She was overtly observing them through white-framed sunglasses.

"That's Beth, my partner. She hired me on the spot when I walked in six years ago. I guess she knew my parents and my situation." Lucy listened as she popped a grape into her mouth. "I told you Beth had opened the office?" Lucy nodded. "She was born to that job. Even after hours, she's off doing volunteer work. She's pretty amazing." Lucy looked across the street again as Beth lit her cigarette and took a long drag.

On Lucy's approach, Beth stood, removed her sunglasses, and gave her the quick once-over—an animated gesture, dramatically done for Eli's sake.

"Lucy, this is Beth Lawrence. She's the better half of our operation here at this field office." Eli grinned proudly. "Beth, this is …"

"I know, I know, this must be Lucy Price. Aren't you a pretty picture, Eli's spoken of little else for the better part of the week. It's very nice to meet you," said Beth turning to Eli. "As for you, young man,"

"Yes?" said Eli.

Beth disappeared into the office and reemerged, gripping a tiny red alarm clock in her hand. It was beeping—a piercing sound enough to drive anyone up the wall. Beth slammed the clock firmly on the table and glared at Eli who acted sheepish.

"I'm going to lose my flipping mind, Eli! Shut it off, or I'll have to kill it!"

Lucy looked from Eli to the clock to Beth, who stood before them with her hands firmly planted on her ample hips.

"I'm sorry," Eli said. "I tried to shut it off before I left. It just wouldn't."

"So, you stuffed it in the seat cushion." She shook her head in feigned disgust. "Children," she said, hiding her smile.

Eli cowered dramatically, playing to her tone of voice. Then he looked at Lucy with an impish grin.

"I've had this bugger for twenty years, and this has never happened. You broke my clock," said Beth turning to Lucy. "I lent it to him so he could relax," she said. "He'd been so preoccupied with meeting up with you today, he couldn't concentrate on preparing for our meeting with the mayor tomorrow." She glared at Eli, who groaned like a teenage boy.

Lucy picked up the little clock, turned it over, removed the cover, and popped out the AAA battery. The beeping stopped. Beth roared with laughter, which soon turned to coughing and hacking. She threw her half-smoked cigarette on the ground and flattened it with the ball of her foot.

"Damn cigarettes," she grumbled.

Eli disappeared into the office and returned with a replacement battery, which Lucy struggled to get in. She studied the clock more closely.

"There's something in there." She shook it, and they all heard the rattle. Handing it to Eli, she suggested opening the whole backside of the clock. He marched back into the office and came back with the smallest of screwdrivers. Three Vietnamese manicurists from next door stood in their window, curious about what was going on.

Five minutes later, Lucy had the clock laid out in two pieces on the table. Beth leaned in close, and the table wobbled, dislodging a tiny white disk, which rolled out and landed flat on the edge of the tabletop. Lucy picked it up and held it in the palm of her hand. She noticed a sticky substance along one side, and a tiny silver node with puncture holes sticking out of the rim.

Lucy pinched it between her finger and thumb. "It's a ... bug," she whispered. "You guys are being bugged."

This was followed by another roar of laughter from Beth. "You're messing with us."

"No, I'm serious," she whispered. "They covered all kinds of weird stuff like this in computer club." With her free hand, Lucy sorted through the rest of the clock bits. "Here, look." A hair-thin wire ran along the inside of the battery cover. "We're looking at the transmitter and the antenna, but who has the receiver? Who's listening in?" Lucy's voice was barely audible. Eli shrugged. Beth stood open-mouthed and speechless.

Lucy explained that bugs were usually triggered by sound and activated only when a conversation was loud enough, then shut off when it got quiet.

Fearful, Eli and Beth stuck the tiny device in the small office refrigerator and quietly packed up their laptops and enough of their work to finish their current projects at home while Lucy waited in the doorway.

"Eli, I'll catch up with you in the morning before we meet the mayor. You'll be ready?" asked Beth.

"I'll be ready." Eli joined Lucy at the door as Beth held it open for them. "Whatever good it'll do."

"Now don't be like that. We have to keep the faith." Beth teasingly shook her finger at him. "It was nice to meet you Lucy, and—very educational. I hope to see more of you." She smiled at Eli and waved goodbye.

"Very nice to meet you too, Beth," Lucy called after her and turned to go.

"Lucy, could I give you a lift home?" Lucy thought about this. It wasn't much of a walk home, but the ride would give her a little more time with Eli, so she nodded.

"Why would someone bug your office?" asked Lucy as they walked down the street.

"I can think of a dozen reasons off the top of my head, all relating to the mayor's office directly or indirectly. But I'd rather not think about that right now."

They rounded the corner toward the city hall and crossed over to the Washington Street parking lot. Eli knocked on the hood of a late model BMW with a broken antenna. He opened the passenger side door for her, and she got in.

The leather seats had been broken in years ago, a hairline crack ran the length of the windshield, and a coffee cup sat half full in the cupholder beside the shift. Lucy set her tote between her feet over crumbs ground deep into the carpet. It was warm in the car and Eli opened the windows as soon as he sat down.

"This was my dad's car." He gripped the steering wheel tightly in his hands. "I couldn't dream of driving anything else. Is that strange?" Lucy thought about her father's ten-year-old diesel pickup truck. If he were gone, would she love it? Probably not, but who could say?

"I get it. Cars take on the personalities of their owners. This probably brings you close to him."

"Exactly. This was his dream car. It's a little worse for wear since I've been schlepping a kid around in it. Dad kept it like new." He patted the dashboard. "Another trigger, but a good one, you know?" He started the car and put it in gear.

"I know." It hadn't been her experience as far as Ben Wyatt was concerned, but there were small things that reminded her of home, her parents, or her sister that she could consider good triggers.

Eli pulled in front of her house and shut off the engine. A soft breeze floated through the open windows. It was quiet in the car, just the two of them now—face to face. He leaned toward her and reached a hand behind her head. She flinched and pulled away. He was about to kiss her, which was not a bad thing, but the hand on the back of her head. Triggers—not the good kind.

She thought of Ben Wyatt, his hand on her head, pressing it, holding it against the dumpster, the rancid stench, the taste of rust on her lips, as he molested her in the alley.

"Thanks for the ride," she tried to say as she fumbled for the door handle.

"Lucy, wait. I'm sorry."

"It's just that—you know?" Her voice shook. No, he didn't know. How could he? He looked at her with calm understanding. His beautiful eyes. His beautiful mouth. How could she turn him away?

"I know. I overstepped. I'm so sorry." He held his hand out, and she took it. This she could do. They sat this way for a short while, their minds spinning off in different directions. Finally, Eli spoke.

"Um ..." It was a start. "How would you like to come to my house for dinner on Friday?" He squeezed her hand and met her gaze. "I want a chance to repay you for the other night."

Lucy didn't think long. "I would like that," she said, thankful she hadn't scared him off.

"Great." He looked relieved. "I'll text you my address." Lucy took his phone from the console and entered her number.

"The house is, well ..." He paused and furrowed his bushy brows, then glanced up at her with a wry smile. "No judgment."

Just what did he mean by that? She wondered.

CHAPTER SIX

THE SCHOOL-DAY EXODUS WAS ALWAYS SOMEWHAT BITTERSWEET FOR LUCY. SHE loved the daily interactions with her students but embraced the calm when the last student had gone home.

That calm was shattered Wednesday afternoon by the chants and steady drumbeat from the rally up at the park. The rant reached a fever pitch; *AV-ID, AV-ID*, the attendees shouted, the word thrumming as steadily as a heartbeat. A *lub-dub* of hatred raged an assault on Lucy and Summer's ears.

"What the hell," Summer said, gasping after the last child had been collected. "How did we get through this day?"

Lucy was just as clueless. The chanting had begun around noon. A megaphone was introduced soon after. The students, for obvious reasons, had questions. There were honest answers, and there were "honest enough" answers. Summer and Lucy chose the latter. They didn't want to interfere with how their students' parents might have explained the behavior of grown men and women who flatly disliked—no, hated—people who were not white, Christian, or straight; people who AVID believed were un-American.

What Lucy and Summer finally chose to say was that the rally on the square was to recognize a particular way of life. That didn't prevent follow-up questions, however. Lucy was afraid that she may have, through a particular lens, shown a particular bias, while trying to clarify what she meant by *particular*.

The school included children from first to eighth grade. The older kids were hip to what was going on. They read the newspaper. They watched the news. They were bright, intellectual, mature kids who would no doubt go on to be college professors, great writers, artists, or scientists. She was proud of them all—even the younger, less mature children. But she had no place telling them what or how to think of the world, other than to say, "Be honest. Be fair. Be kind. Be helpful. Be aware. And be yourself." It had become a credo of sorts for the school. They were a family at the Chrysanthemum House. Summer and Lucy took that responsibility seriously.

There was a poster on the classroom wall, mounted high where it couldn't be missed. *THINK*, it said in bold black letters. It was a message to all of them, not just the children. When Lucy walked into the classroom each morning and looked up at the word, it established her mindset for the day.

If she had more nerve, Lucy would have painted that same message on posterboard and waved it at the riotous group at the park.

Lucy's phone buzzed with another text from Eli. Now that he had her phone number, he was texting her with continuous photos and updates of the lunacy across the street from his office.

My head is about to split, he had written. *Gotta get outta here.*

Instead of texting back, she called him.

"Hi."

"Hi. Can you hear this insanity?"

"Not like you, I'm sure—but yes, we hear it."

"I wasn't joking about my head splitting. I'm about to call it a day. No one is showing up for their appointments. Too scared."

"How did your meeting go today?"

"The emojis didn't say it all?" He laughed. "It was a farce, Lucy. Church didn't even get past the cover page of our report."

"He'll make hay from it nonetheless!" Beth chimed in from her end of the office. "It'll be in the paper, just you wait and see!"

"Did you hear that?" Eli said.

"Make hay. I heard."

"She's right. He's done this before. I can't believe we fell for it." Lucy pictured him, dragging his fingers through his hair in frustration. "Are we still on for Friday?"

"Wild horses," she said.

"Remember what I said?"

She thought of the inside of his car and multiplied that by three bedrooms and two bathrooms. "I remember. No judgment."

When she hung up, Summer joked that she was getting jealous of Lucy's new best friend.

"No one could ever replace you, Summer."

LUCY'S STUDENTS PUSHED past her Friday afternoon, as they made their mad dash out the door to freedom. Summer fetched backpacks and homework reminders for the fleeing students. There were a few stragglers, as usual—the younger students, who always took their sweet time; and some still waiting for their parents to arrive.

Lucy was pulled aside by Mrs. Gates, but noticed Summer's supportive smile and the *tap-tap* on her wrist—a reminder that she needed to get ready for her dinner at Eli's.

Mrs. Gates, who held strong opinions on just about everything, was sharing some of them about the renovations to the Drake Art Museum, among other things.

"—and I told Caroline that if they raise my taxes to pay for this eyesore, they've got another thing coming. I mean, you know? And Caroline said ..." Lucy began walking toward the door, hoping Mrs. Gates would follow.

A few other parents lingered out on the sidewalk. Lucy spotted Debbie Post and waved. Mrs. Gates hurried to her friend and began her tirade all over again, as they walked to their cars. When the last parent left, Summer closed the door and locked eyes with Lucy, grinning.

"What are you wearing tonight?" Summer asked as they tidied up the classroom.

While Mrs. Gates had been going on about the museum—and before that, the new chip card reader at Gardner's Grocery; and before that, her negligent neighbor who never picked their weeds—Lucy had settled on her blue sundress, and wondered how to wear her hair.

The day had grown unseasonably warm for May, and the humidity was so thick that she nearly choked on it. When Lucy finally stepped into the battered claw-foot tub and pulled the curtain around her, she quickly succumbed to the flow of tepid water and allowed her mind to roam.

No judgment, Eli had said. What did he mean by that? Is his house a mess? Is it small? She promptly chastised herself for pre-emptively judging. His sister worked from an office in that house, which had to be presentable for patients, she assumed—so it couldn't be *that* bad.

Lucy was bringing dessert. A berry cobbler she had managed to throw together that morning—the only dessert she had any practice in making, and something she imagined Owen would devour. Should she stop for ice cream—and brave the new chip reader at Gardner's Grocery? She laughed.

A primary concern, one which she'd been dwelling on much of the day, was Eli's sister. Would she be there? Was this a meet the family kind of dinner? Maybe Lucy was reading too much into it.

She had been hasty to agree to the invitation, but her impulse was genuine. She was rather curious about how Eli lived, and she wanted to see him again.

Her attention skipped back to when Eli had sat beside her at the park, studying her with his gentle gray eyes. She remembered wanting to touch his lips—but was thankful she hadn't.

For all his physical features, it was his sincerity she was most attracted to. His expressive face was nearly as transparent as little Owen's. It's likely why she trusted him so quickly.

While Lucy seldom went out of her way to exercise, she walked and biked almost everywhere, and her young, fit body was nothing to be ashamed of. She wondered, while lathering it with the floral-scented soap, if Eli would get close enough to notice.

Her sudsy hands slid across the landscape of her legs and hips until they reached one small hiccup—the scar on the lower left side of her back. It had been left by her encounter with Ben Wyatt—a crescent of raised skin, dark and ugly. He'd left his mark on her body as well as her mind.

Eli had wanted to kiss her the other day, and she had stopped him. *I'm such an idiot*, she thought. It wasn't that he had tried to kiss her. It was that his hand had pressed so firmly on the back of her head, unwittingly pinning her in place.

Lucy squeezed her eyes tight, holding off the unpleasant memories, until Summer banged on the door with a twenty-minute warning. Lucy set the soap down and gave her hair one last rinse.

Twenty minutes later, she was posing for her roommate at the foot of the stairs, and feeling confident in her light-blue cotton, spaghetti-strapped sundress.

"You sure this is a casual dinner?" Summer teased. "You look amazing." Suddenly, Lucy felt overdressed and turned to head back to her room—until Summer stopped her. "Don't you think about it, Missy. He won't let you out of his sight."

"That's not what I'm going for here, Summer."

"Yeah, right. And Donald Trump is a saint."

THE ADDRESS WAS rural, and further than Lucy was comfortable riding on her bike, especially after dark, when she'd be riding home. So Summer elected to give her a ride. She would have let Lucy borrow the car, but Lucy hadn't driven in years

Sitting shotgun, with Summer at the wheel, Lucy gazed out of the window at the passing trees of Thatcher Wood, which went on for several miles. It had rained earlier in the day, but now the late afternoon sun blazed in the sky above. She was surprised when Google declared they had arrived at their destination. Could the app be trusted out here in the woods?

"This can't be right," said Lucy, looking up and down the road.

"There." Summer pointed to a black mailbox beside a narrow gravel road, with thick weeds flourishing between the deep ruts. The mailbox was dotted with gold stars and the word *MOON* hand-painted on its face.

The Subaru rolled slowly down the gravel road for nearly a quarter of a mile, passing overgrown shrubs and a forest of mature trees that shielded the house from the street.

Halfway down the drive, the gentle perfume of fragile blossoms drifted in through the open windows from a seemingly endless orchard, shabby and uncared-for.

Lucy's heart raced as they approached the end of the gravel road, and the grand house came into view. It wasn't formal, nor was it rustic, but Lucy thought the Craftsman Style looked warm and inviting—like something that had sprung organically from the earth.

The siding was constructed from stacked stones and thick timbers. The roofline was broken up by regularly spaced dormers and multiple chimneys, and the prominent front entry nested beneath a high arching alcove. Together it gave an impression of a past century.

"Holy Hacienda," said Summer under her breath, bringing the car to a full stop. "He's flippin' Bruce Wayne."

"This can't be right," Lucy repeated, just before Owen appeared out of nowhere, dressed neatly in cargo shorts and a navy-blue polo shirt. He held a baseball in one hand and a new stiff mitt in the other as he hopped and skipped toward the car with bouncing curls and a broad smile.

Eli was not far behind, in nice fitting jeans and a white cotton tunic with the sleeves pushed up, revealing the thick dark hair on his forearms. His damp hair was combed in place—not all tussled the way Lucy remembered it from the last few times she'd seen him. She noticed too that he was wearing the glasses she'd seen the other day. What was different? He was on his own turf.

Lucy tentatively stepped out of the car and pulled the cobbler from the back seat. Summer handed Lucy her woven, green bag. "Hope you packed a toothbrush," she murmured with a sly grin. Lucy blushed, reminding Summer that she would text when it was time to go.

As Summer headed back down the drive, Eli placed his hand lightly on the flat of her back and planted a quick kiss on her cheek, as if it was something he did every day. Owen, never shy, said, "You look pretty."

"Thank you, Owen," she answered, accepting the compliment, knowing full well that to be called pretty by a six-year-old was high praise. "You're looking rather handsome yourself," she added, glancing at Eli.

"Come on back," Eli said. "Kali's waiting to meet you. I hope you don't mind." Her uncertainties about the evening were being addressed one bombshell after another. The house was certainly not small—nor anything to be ashamed of—and the sister would indeed be joining them.

Eli leaned closer. "Your hair looks beautiful like that." Lucy looked away, embarrassed as he led her around the house to a large, partially covered patio surrounded by a waist-high stone wall, and shaded by a mature silver maple. She was faced with the enormity of everything; the solid wooden table, the outdoor kitchen, the stone pavers leading to the open French doors.

She clenched her cobbler in two hands as she looked around. Then the toe of her sandal caught on a stone. Eli quickly caught her by the elbow.

"I've got you—relax," he said with a reassuring smile. *Nothing like a graceful entrance*, she thought, newly aware of two women staring wide-eyed from the French doors leading into the house. Lucy recognized Mia from the toy shop. The other woman held out her hand.

"Lucy, this is my sister, Kali." Kali looked older than Eli, yet she had the figure of a young teen who had not yet filled out. Her long, black hair was pulled tightly back into a French braid, and the black, sleeveless blouse she was wearing accentuated her slender frame. She was a beauty with green eyes, smooth skin, and a glowing, welcoming smile.

"Good to see you again," said Mia, weaving her hand together with Kali's.

"Hi, Mia. It's nice to meet you, Kali." Lucy was self-conscious. The dress was too much, and she should have kept her hair up. She held out the cobbler. "If it's all right, I'll need to warm this in the oven."

"Come on in," said Eli leading her through the French doors with Owen bouncing all around them. "I'll show you around."

CHAPTER SEVEN

LUCY FOLLOWED ELI INTO A ROOM THAT STRETCHED LONG AND WIDE AT EVERY corner with a fireplace at one end and a broad arched doorway to the kitchen at the other. She stood in the center of the room, feeling small, as Eli took the cobbler and disappeared through the doorway.

Despite its size, everything in this room seemed designed for warmth and comfort—from the colorful Persian rug to the plush sectional sofa. Her eyes rested on a sturdy stereo cabinet. A vinyl record lay idle on the open turntable, and a stack of albums leaned against the cabinet on the floor.

Lucy admired a landscape painting mounted above the fireplace. It depicted a hill covered in wildflowers of red, yellow, pink, and orange—the same colors as the rug under her feet.

"My grandmother painted that," said Eli, re-entering the room. Lucy kept her eyes fixed on the painting, not knowing what to say. The grandness of the house was beyond her imagination. She cautiously laid her hand on the mantle and looked up into the thick beams above her head.

"They're from the cleared timber when they built the house back in the thirties. Same with the fireplace; each rock and stone was carried up from a ravine behind the old farmstead." His calm, resonating voice comforted her as he stood beside her. "It's a lot, I know," he added, apologetically. "The property was part of a farmstead established a generation earlier. Then, when my great-grandfather discovered he had more of a mind for business than farming, he proposed the family go into canning." He laughed. "Back then, that was revolutionary! He was a vanguard of his time."

Lucy had heard that Drake was established out of the canning industry, much like other towns in the Midwest. Now here she was, where it had all begun.

"Owen, get down from there before you hurt yourself." Owen had slipped into the room and was jumping on the sectional sofa. He bounced on his rear with a giggle. Eli turned back to Lucy. "Am I boring you? I'm boring you. Sorry."

"I'm not bored, just a bit—overwhelmed." She held out a hand as if halting traffic and laughed. "Not judging."

"Jeez," Eli said, looking to where Owen was sitting impatiently on the sofa. "Honestly, Lucy. I'm a little nervous." He fanned his arms around. "This is not ..."

Oddly, Lucy was reassured by his nerves. "Eli, I'm not bored. I want to know the story. Seriously. What happened next?"

"Well, the brothers rejected his proposal, so he took his share of the farm to build this house and a processing plant for canning."

"What happened to the brothers?"

"He eventually bought them out. We have over a thousand acres all together; one mile deep and two miles wide. That's how Grandpa always put it."

Owen had lost interest in the story and was walking circles around the sectional. He looked up when Eli stopped talking. "Lucy, wanna see my room?"

Lucy turned to Eli, who nodded. "All right, Little Bird, lead the way." Owen took her hand and led her to the main staircase. From the foot of the stairs, there was a long hallway that split left and right, and the entryway straight ahead, which was big enough to park a car in.

Family portraits and photographs in gilded frames lined the wood-paneled walls. Stained-glass windows flanked the heavy door, and a Tiffany-style lamp hung high overhead.

She stopped to admire a family portrait. In it, Eli was a little older than Owen, with his parents standing behind him and a pre-teen Kali sitting in a chair beside him. Lucy looked closely at Eli's father, a bespectacled man with a high forehead, whose gaze focused far beyond the camera to something or someone who had made him smile with such joy, it made her smile just to see it. His mother, with dark hair pulled back tight, looked directly into the camera with a candid smile, her head cocked as if she was just about to say something. Eli, smiling like his father, had his hands stuffed in his pockets while Kali looked like she'd rather be anywhere else. It was as if the photographer had snuck in a quick shot before the actual family portrait, capturing a real moment.

"I love that one too," said Eli.

"What were you smiling at? Do you remember?"

"Grandpa was making funny faces. That's him there with my dad before I was born, and that's my grandma. See that face?" Lucy didn't need to look very hard to know his grandmother was a serious woman. There were other pictures too, but nothing added since the accident. It was as if time had stopped.

Lucy ogled the thick, hand-crafted front door. "What's this?" she asked, pointing to a rectangular silver plate fixed to the frame. It was about six inches long and had an ornate design.

"It's a Mezuzah!" said Owen excitedly. "Mezuzah, mezuzah! You're supposed to touch it for good luck." He reached up high and brushed the bottom of the plate. Lucy ran her fingers along the length of it, studying the design more closely.

Eli smiled. "Well, Little Bird, it's a bit more than good luck, but we'll talk about that another time."

Eli explained that the front entry was seldom used, since they usually came in through the garage when they arrived home from anywhere, and when they were already home, they used the back door they way Lucy had entered that day. The front entry was for formal occasions, and that didn't exactly suit Eli and Kali.

Opposite the photographs stood an arch—like the one to the kitchen, but broader—which led to a formal dining room with seating for twenty. Eli flipped the light switch and invited her in. A fireplace with a stone hearth and thick-beamed mantle anchored one end. A sturdy sideboard matching the table anchored the other—and another stained-glass light fixture, bright with golds and reds, hung in the center.

"Like the great room, these are all materials from the property. The stone, the beams, and even the wood for the table."

"What is it?" Lucy placed her palm on the solid slab of wood, dark and rich, and dotted with an elaborate pattern of rings from the tree's knots.

"Buckeye. They used to be all over the place. Still are a few out there behind the orchard."

Eli led them from the hall to the foot of the main staircase in the center of the house. He walked alongside her up the stairs as she held onto the thick wooden banister, marveling at the craftsmanship.

At the top of the stairs, she looked down into the great room and saw Kali looking back up at her from the kitchen door. They nodded at one another, smiling a polite acknowledgement. Lucy could only imagine what Kali thought of her, and it bothered her how important it had become to make a good impression.

Lucy turned her attention down the hall to her left and then to her right, guessing there were at least a dozen doors.

"Kali's room is down that way. The south wing."

"Sheesh," said Lucy, lacking the words for what she saw.

"This is nothing, there's another floor up." He pointed to the end of the hall. "That door down there is a back staircase. It leads up to the servants' quarters."

"Servants?" This truly was a different world.

"Not now. Not since I've been on the scene, anyway. We had a housekeeper, though, years ago. She retired when I left for college. Would you consider her a servant? My mom had a guy to help in the garden too. And then there was the seasonal help in the orchard." Eli winced. "This sounds bad, doesn't it?"

"Not really. I mean, look at the size of this place. There's no way your mom could have done it on her own." Lucy was wholly aware that she was out of her league, servants or not.

Eli crossed the hall from the stair landing and pulled back a faded, floor-length drape.

"Voila!" he said, revealing an intimate alcove with two plush, overstuffed chairs. "My sister and I used to hang out in here when we were kids," he said, stepping toward a heavy glass door and opening it to the orchard below. "Telling secrets, or gossiping. She sat in that chair when she came out to me. I don't think I understood the gravity of the moment, then, but in hindsight, it was a big deal." They stood on the small balcony and looked out over the regular rows of trees. A pleasant draft floated into the alcove, ripe with the scent of apple blossoms.

"Pretty shabby, I know," said Eli of the expansive orchard. "My grandfather was still here when my folks died. He did what he could, and we helped—to a point. He kept the crew to maintain the orchard and hired some of the bigger jobs out, but after he died, the money was gone. Well, not gone, but tied up. It's a long boring story. We do our best." He sighed. "Did you notice the tree garden on your way in? In front of the house? It was, or is, a collection of specimens collected by my grandparents. Some date back to my great-grandparents."

"Yes, I noticed it. It's beautiful."

"It's looked better. There's a map around here somewhere of each and every species out there. Varieties from every corner of the world. It breaks my heart to know that this place was a paradise once upon a time, and it went downhill on our watch." Eli bowed his head as if in prayer. "Everywhere I look, I see one more reminder of their absence—the condition of the tree garden, the orchard, the house that's literally falling to pieces."

Lucy understood how he was surrounded by triggers like the photos on the wall, the neglected orchard, and dozens more she would never know.

They padded down the long hall to the north wing. Owen, in his bare feet, pulled Lucy into his bedroom. She couldn't pin down any particular theme in the room. It was a jumble of airplanes, race cars, dogs, and farm animals, all juxtaposed with a substantial *Star Wars* influence that suggested the passage of time from baby to boy.

His new kite hung from the corner, a little worse for wear. A *Star Wars* poster of the original cast from the 1970s had been thumbtacked over his bed, which was draped with an R2D2 comforter.

As with the rest of the house, Owen's room was overly spacious. Lucy loved the window seat, though, looking into the late-afternoon sun at the overgrown tree garden in the front of the house.

It was impossible to avoid seeing the picture on the nightstand of a young woman with a Hollywood smile. Owen's mother?

"Lucy, over here." Owen was on hands and knees in his open closet. "Follow me."

She glanced back at Eli, who looked suspiciously familiar with this ploy, then bent to join Owen, pulling her dress tighter around her backside.

She followed Owen into his dark closet and through a child-sized door at the far end which opened wide to where Eli stood on the other side, his hand stretched out to help her up, and a playful smile on his face.

"A secret passage!" exclaimed Owen. Lucy looked around her now, realizing they were in another room.

"That is awesome!" Lucy replied, putting an arm around Owen's shoulder while he hugged the breath out of her.

"Easy Little Bird, she's fragile," teased Eli.

Lucy looked from the queen-size bed to the matching dressers, trying to be nonchalant as her eyes came to rest on the Persian rug, the fireplace, and a small sofa and chairs beside the window seat. The bedroom had been professionally decorated at some point. She met Eli's gray eyes in the reflection in the full-length mirror. He smiled. This was his room.

"I tidied up," he said to the mirror. "Had a feeling you'd end up here." Lucy quickly looked away, and he hastened to correct himself. "No, not like that. Just that Owen would want to show the secret passage." He reached for the door. "This house has all kinds of surprises like that."

In the hall, Eli opened another door. "It's an elevator!" squealed Owen. Eli set the record straight—it was a dumbwaiter that ran from the basement up to the servants' quarters. He pushed one of two buttons beside it, and it groaned into service, slowly clicking and clacking to the main floor. Lucy could imagine how it might be used as an elevator, in a pinch, for a small person.

They took the back stairwell at the very end of the hall that Eli had pointed out earlier, and followed it down to the main floor where they emerged in another hallway. Lucy heard the *ka-thunk* of the dumbwaiter coming to rest. Eli opened the door. Owen stepped in and slid open a pocket door at the rear. There was a dark, musty-smelling tunnel behind it.

"I have no idea why this was necessary, but it leads to the tree garden."

"Gnomes, maybe?" Lucy teased.

"Or trolls," he laughed.

"Bootleggers."

"They'd have to get past the trolls, though," Eli said with a laugh. *And the spiders, and the rats.*

Owen closed the pocket door, and Lucy followed him down the hallway to an open door.

"This is ... *was* my mom's sewing room." The sewing machine was secondary to the bookshelves, which were filled with popular fiction, classics, and a small selection of famous memoirs. Lucy regarded the collection with appreciation.

"I thought you would like that," said Eli.

Owen had moved on, leaving the two alone in the small room. Lucy looked closer at the bookshelf and picked up a dusty copy of Hillary Clinton's biography, then set it down and looked into Eli's expectant face.

"I'm saving the best for last." He turned and led her out the door and across the hall to a set of double doors. Eli pulled a skeleton key from his pocket to unlock one of the doors, pushing it open.

Dust tickled her nose, and Lucy stifled a sneeze as a rush of cold, damp air hit them. A long bank of windows along the outside wall lit a room the size of her middle school gymnasium. Then Eli hit the lights, and a string of chandeliers came to life, casting a brilliant glow across the length of the elaborate parquet floor.

He reached across her and flipped a switch. Lucy heard a *click, click, click* as drapes covering the far wall opened to reveal a stage platform.

"Welcome to the great hall. It's not too over-the-top?"

"Well, yes. It's totally over-the-top," she said, laughing. "But I love it!"

"It's ridiculous," admitted Eli. "I know."

"No judgment," she reminded him with a grin. Then her

grumbling stomach reminded her why she was here in the first place. "Why do you keep it locked?"

"No reason, really. We never use this part of the house, so it's been locked up for a long time." Lucy's stomach grumbled again, and he nodded. "You're hungry. I'm sorry this took so long." Eli turned off the light and shut the door behind them.

They walked past a small powder room, to the main stairs and great room on their left and the front hall on their right.

"Just one more little thing, if you can hang in there."

"Sure." Lucy rested her hand on her grumbling stomach. "I'm not actually as hungry as it sounds."

He opened the door to another powder room with a window open to an overgrown flowering quince and the mild perfume from its bright pink blossoms. A yellow plastic stepstool was positioned in front of the vanity with the inscription, *Stand up to be Tall, Sit down to be Small.*

The laundry room was next. A mountain of clothes in various stages of cleanliness either covered the countertop or was piled high in a mismatched pair of baskets on the floor. *No judgment.*

Further down, also on the same side of the hallway, was a door to the three-car garage where Eli's BMW was parked between Kali's compact Mazda and a pale blue Prius that had belonged to his mother.

"Kali doesn't drive the Prius?"

"Nope, she like's her old beater. My car is pristine compared to hers," he joked as they crossed the hall to the last door. "Okay, this is it, I promise—then we'll get a beer, all right?" He opened the door to Kali's office. "This used to be my dad's den. She basically hasn't done anything different here except adding that door." He pointed to an alternate exit, which led to a small vestibule that opened to an outside door.

Leather furniture, a desk in the corner, built-in bookshelves, and a pair of matching floor lamps all gave the room a masculine feel. Lucy looked up at a mantle clock on the bookshelf that read eight o'clock.

"Is it really that late?"

"No—that?" He laughed. "It's been eight o'clock for ages. No one's wound that clock since I can remember." He led her back into the hall, and they rounded the corner into the great room to find Owen jumping on the sofa again. "Owen! What did I tell you?" Eli told Lucy there was an ice bucket filled with cold beer and sparkling water on the patio. He was going to get the food together and would meet her in a bit. She offered to help, but he just shook his finger and told her she could help clean up. "It's only fair."

CHAPTER EIGHT

LUCY LOOKED OVER THE SELECTION OF COLD BEER, SODA, AND SPARKLING water swimming in a tub of ice on the patio table. Without much thought, she plucked a bottle of hazy IPA from Big Grove Brewery and opened it with the UI Hawkeyes novelty opener. After a long, thirsty draw from the ice-cold beer, Lucy crossed the patio to the garden gate, tired and rusted with age, and opened it to the neglected rose garden. The roses, overgrown and tangled together, were heavy-set with young buds. The thick tangle of overgrown hybrid teas and floribundas prohibited Lucy from venturing much further, so she turned around and spotted Kali on the patio, watching her.

Kali's scrutinizing expression was calculating and thoughtful, and Lucy braced herself, acutely aware of her numerous weaknesses and shortcomings.

Just as she was putting her unease to rest, she noticed Kali's expression soften, and she adjusted her expectations. *These are friends*, she reminded herself.

"Such a beautiful day," began Kali.

"Such a beautiful house. I'm trying to get my bearings, though." Lucy pointed back toward the house. "Town is that way?" She set her bottle down on the table, and pulled her hair up and off her neck, then fastened the clip in place.

"That's west. The town is north, past Thatcher woods, that way." Kali pointed this way and that, like the scarecrow in *The Wizard of Oz*. "I can see how it's confusing. The orchard here," Kali pointed past the garden gate and beyond the roses, "is east, and it sweeps south along the driveway. It was part of the grand plan. The master bedroom faces east to catch the sunrise over the orchard and this sad little rose garden. My room's on that side too."

Kali then plied Lucy with the typical questions about how she came to be in Drake. She fished for details about the Chrysanthemum House.

Lucy answered as honestly as she could, notwithstanding the gaping oversight of Ben Wyatt. If only it were as simple as white-washing him from her mind.

"I came to teach." That was true. "I've always been intrigued by the Midwest." That was true enough. "It seemed only fitting to begin my career in the middle of the world." That was a half-lie.

Lucy recalled the long wait in her therapists office years ago after the assault. She'd picked up a random magazine with an article about Drake, Iowa. It pictured the Old Oak. *To locals, the century old tree marks the middle of the middle of the middle of the world.* The idyllic image captured Lucy's imagination, and she thought, why not? It was like a bullseye on a dartboard.

"Still," Kali continued. "Eli says you're from Monterey. It just seems like such a leap."

"Not really." Lucy did not elaborate. Her elusiveness had served her well for three years, why stop now? She didn't explain her random choice, or the job search that followed, or the half-dozen rentals she'd walked through after a job interview at Drake Middle School.

She remembered the afternoon she'd first seen the broad front porch, the swing, and the carving of a flower overhead. Her mind was nearly made up to start her own school before she had set foot in that house. When she saw the layout—the vast room occupying almost half of the lower level tucked behind wide pocket doors—the Chrysanthemum House Home School Project was born.

Lucy explained her specialized approach to education and what she hoped to achieve. Kali listened intently, as if she were trying to put it all together into a complete puzzle, despite missing a handful of pieces.

"I have a partner. Her name is Summer." Lucy sipped her beer. "She's brilliant."

"You seem so young to have your own business," said Kali.

"Do I?" Lucy didn't feel so young. She was twenty-four, independent, and aged by trauma.

Owen and Eli arrived at the patio table with their hands full. The screen door slowly squealed, then closed behind them with a loud *snap* that startled them all.

"I know," moaned Eli with a sly look at his sister. "I'll get to it this weekend."

Kali handed out the paper plates while Mia laid out the food. Owen circled the table with plastic forks and napkins, then sat down between Lucy and Eli, facing out toward the orchard. Kali and Mia, sitting across the table from Lucy were as familiar with one another as any two people could be. They joked and teased one another—a touch here, a kiss on the cheek there.

Lucy imagined what it would be like to have that kind of intimacy, as one of her spaghetti straps flopped off her shoulder. Eli reached for the strap and slid it back in place.

"Dig in," said Eli, nodding, his eyes smiling as if he could read her thoughts. It would have been a challenge, though, to catch up with her racing mind.

Dinner was not nearly as grand as the house. Pulled pork sandwiches, fruit salad, and potato chips. It was a simple Midwest spread. The beer had curbed Lucy's hunger, but she helped herself to a sandwich and a heaping spoonful of the fruit salad.

"These strawberries are delicious."

Eli laughed. "You can thank Gardner's Grocery for all of this."

"That's going to change," said Kali with a broad grin, "someday." It was a running joke, explained Kali, that one of them would learn to cook. "Eli says you make some mean enchiladas. Think you could teach him how to pull that off?"

"I'll teach you both. It's easy." Lucy reached into the icy tub beside her at the end of the table and drew out another IPA.

"There used to be strawberries out there behind the roses," said Kali. "We had green beans coming out of our ears. There are still racks of mason jars in the basement of beans, tomatoes, pickles, beets ... I could go on. Grandma used to can everything. Mom too."

"It's funny, you know," added Eli, "because that was the family business. Mom and grandma could have had all the canned veggies they wanted," Eli fished out another handful of potato chips and set a few on Owen's plate, "yet they had to make their own."

Lucy looked past Kali into the orchard, where a crow had just landed on a high branch and caused it to bend and bob up and down. She felt Eli's eyes on her. It felt good to be admired. She turned slowly to face him. His smile was sure and kind—not the mischievous grin she was accustomed to. It was as if she were the only other person at the table.

"I don't like it," Kali was saying. "It's dangerous." Lucy had missed the seed of the heated discussion across the table.

"It's not your choice to make. The motorbike is mine, and it is safe." Usually soft-spoken, Mia raised her voice.

"Eli?" Kali said.

"What?"

"Tell Mia about what motorcycles can do." Kali's scowl reminded Lucy of the photo of their grandmother.

"Motorcycles can go very fast." Eli teased his sister. "They can cut through traffic. They can ..."

"Tell her," Kali insisted.

Eli addressed the group with a mouth full of pulled pork. He held up one finger before swallowing. "I got the bright idea to fix grandpa's old Bridgestone two-stroke so I could take it to school. I was, like, what? Fourteen?" He looked across at his sister for confirmation. "The motorcycle was a relic and, well, I'm not much of a mechanic, so ..."

"Get to the point, brother."

"So, when it was all tuned up and ready to go, I sailed down the drive, going way too fast—and discovered too late that I should have replaced the brakes."

"He finally stopped by crashing into the fence that used to be across the road—then he was thrown into a tree," added Kali.

"Well, yes. That was the first and last time I rode a motorcycle. Mom and Dad had a bird."

"It's a miracle you didn't crack your head open with just Grandpa's old helmet on your head." Kali started laughing.

Lucy learned he'd broken his leg, his collarbone, and his nose in the wreck. He'd also broken his arm falling out of an old tree-house. He'd split open his chin and broken his nose for a second time playing lacrosse in high school. Later, he crashed his mom's car into a snowbank, totaling the front end, and breaking his nose for a third time.

"That last one happened when his face hit the steering wheel." Kali was laughing so hard at this point, she had tears running down her face. "All of this before graduating high school." Eli stood up and took a bow. The fact he was accident prone didn't seem like a joke to Lucy, yet Kali reveled joyfully in the accounts, and Eli went along with it.

Owen got onto his knees and studied his father's face, running two fingers along each side of his nose. "Did it hurt?" He couldn't understand why everyone was laughing at his question.

THE MEAL HAD left its mark on Owen, who wore the barbecue sauce and berry smudges from the cobbler in a ring around his mouth. Eli took him inside to clean him up while Mia quietly excused herself to clean up the kitchen.

"Wait up, Mia, I'd like to help," said Lucy rising from her seat to follow her.

"She's got it," said Kali. "Sit down awhile. Relax."

The two sat quietly, sipping their beers as a jet flew high overhead. The sun was low in the sky, and the crickets had begun their rhythmic *zee, zee, zee*—so familiar this time of year. Lucy could hear voices from the open window in the kitchen; Eli was laughing.

"I want you to know something before you and Eli get better acquainted." Lucy straightened her posture—shoulders back, hands in her lap—and thought self-consciously about how badly she needed to floss. "Eli is a good and decent man, a wonderful father, and a great brother. He's been to hell and back again, Lucy, and I need you to understand from the outset, before things get any more serious, that Owen is number one around here."

I'm aware, thought Lucy.

"If you start to feel ignored or slighted, just remember that." Lucy nodded. Kali cleared her throat and took a drink from her beer. "I'm not trying to dissuade you—just the opposite. I like you. I just want you to know what you're getting into, so nobody gets hurt. I say this because if you are scared off by a six-year-old boy, this is going to end badly for everyone."

Lucy considered Kali's caution, and for some reason, it irked her. Perhaps she was irritated by the assumptions Kali was making. Then a necessary calm washed over Lucy. It was a self-preservation tool she used whenever she was nervous—a conscious mindset to keep her voice level and her head clear.

"I understand what you're saying, Kali. I would do the same for my sister if we were in your shoes. Your situation is unique. I appreciate that. Owen, as you know, is a special little guy. He's kind and funny, and I love his confidence." Kali nodded, and Lucy went on. "I haven't known Eli long, but I have gleaned for myself what a decent guy he is." Lucy thought about the circumstances in which they met—his rescue, his patience. What, if anything, did Kali know about that day? She looked back to see if Eli was anywhere about. For now, she and Kali were still alone. Lucy reached for her beer and drank, feeling the tickle of bubbles as they ran down her throat. "I'm grateful to be his friend, and I want to know him better. I want to know them both better."

Kali narrowed her eyes and grinned. "Eli never brings women home, Lucy—that's why you need to know." The weight of those words hit Lucy hard, and it probably showed on her face.

"Did Eli mention that I'm a therapist?" *Slow breath in, slow breath out.* "Relax, I'm not a shrink, just a good listener." Kali pushed Lucy's beer closer to her—Lucy took another sip, thinking of how to respond. How much had Eli shared about her?

Finally, Lucy responded, "It's interesting that you both went into careers that similarly help people. Your parents must have been amazing role models." She hoped to take the focus off herself.

"Oh, they were!" Kali became more animated. "Our mom was a professional volunteer— the school, the library, the community hall. She even volunteered at the free clinic with Dr. Franzki. And when our dad ran the cannery, he took it to a whole new level. The operation was practically a model of socialism—full insurance, free lunch, daycare, flexible schedules. That's just what I know about. There was probably more. His employees worshiped him."

"Eli mentioned the cannery."

"Did he tell you it was closed?" Kali looked at her hands spread flat on the table with fingers fanned, and Lucy witnessed her go from a woman in complete control of her emotions to someone on the brink of tears, and then back again—all in the space of a single, deep, cleansing breath. This metamorphosis was clearly a familiar friend, and Lucy could relate. Somehow, they had leveled the playing field.

"Many of the hundred or so employees who lost their jobs are, or have been, my patients," she continued. "They depend on most of the programs offered through the social services office. It's seriously depressing."

The screen door slammed shut and Eli reached into the tub for a cold beer. He tossed a small wheel of dental floss on the table before sitting down beside Lucy. He looked from his sister to Lucy.

"Our parents' death didn't just affect us," Kali said. "The whole community took a hit because the legal succession to the company was unsettled. The assets are still tied up because our parents didn't have a clear directive. No succession plan beyond a typical next of kin. I guess my dad thought he would live forever." Kali and Eli laughed.

"Grandpa had a brother, Uncle Ernie," said Eli. "He lives on the East Coast now. Our lawyer said he and his family believed they had a say in all the family assets, including the business, and they're challenging ownership. Still, without a clear directive, we've been at the mercy of our old family lawyer to work the mess out."

"Next of kin?" asked Lucy. "Uncle Ernie gets it all?"

"No," said Kali. "Well—not yet anyway. It's all a confusing mess."

Eli scooted closer to Lucy. "So, here we are, six years later, and it's still not resolved. The company had to close its doors because all the capital was and still is tied up. There's no resolution in sight."

"On a lighter note," said Kali with a wry smile, "we did get this house and the land. Our legacy." She spread her arms wide to reveal the rich inheritance. "Eli gave you the tour?"

"Just the A tour," he smiled broadly. "I'm saving the B tour for another day." He turned to Lucy. "There's still a whole estate to explore."

Lucy set down her empty beer, gazed out into the orchard, and imagined what lay beyond as Eli slapped at a thirsty mosquito. Lucy looked over her shoulder to the house.

"Time to pack up," said Eli grabbing the ice tub and draining the melted ice. He plucked out the three remaining bottles, while Lucy collected the empties from the table. "Off to bed, Little Bird." Eli announced as they entered the house. Owen popped up from the sofa and tackled Lucy with a goodnight hug.

"Goodnight, Owen." She squeezed him and kissed the top of his head.

Once Eli left the room, the house was quiet for the first time all evening.

After a quick text to Summer, Lucy went to the kitchen to get a bottle of water from the industrial-sized refrigerator, which was filled with take-out containers, deli clamshells, and leftover pizza.

She looked around now, from the kitchen to the great room, trying to put the pieces together. This is how they lived. *No judgment.*

Eli returned to find Lucy sitting quietly, and perhaps somewhat expectantly, on the sofa. He smiled at her and stepped over to the stereo where he removed the album from the turntable and slid it into an empty sleeve, then selected another record. He held it up to her.

"Milt Jackson okay with you?" he asked. She didn't know the name but nodded anyway. "It's part of a collection left behind by my grandpa. It's old-school, but I've always loved it." Eli reverently laid the record on the turntable and slid the needle over. A startling *pop* and *crackle* were soon followed by the resonant bells of Milt Jackson's vibraphone hanging in the air as if waiting to take a breath. Finally, Eli sat down close beside her, his body relaxing into the soft cushions.

"I think that went well," he said. Lucy assumed he meant her introduction to all things Moon.

"And Owen?"

"Out like a light." Eli slowly wove his fingers through hers, and her heart raced.

"Summer's on her way." The words had no sooner left her mouth before he'd slid into position. His warm lips brushed hers, as if asking for permission, and she moved closer. The nervous flutter in her chest intensified as he removed the clip from her hair and kissed her firmly, with confidence and ardor.

His fingers ran through her loosened hair while he nuzzled her neck and throat. Lucy was intoxicated by his attention as Milt Jackson played on.

Neither of them was ready for the text from Summer, announcing her arrival.

CHAPTER NINE

AFTER MEETING ELI'S SISTER AND HER GIRLFRIEND, AND GETTING A VIP TOUR of the house, it was evident Eli was giving her a front-row view of life with the Moon family. Owen had endeared himself with warmth, youthful charm, and his cock-eyed smile. He showed her his notebook, filled with equations and copied text, and it made her *glad in her heart*, as her mother would have said.

In the days after the dinner party, Eli's attention throughout the evening and their snuggling on the sofa later was often on her mind. There were prolific texts back and forth, smiley face emojis, and late-night phone calls. Lucy learned that Eli had been working tirelessly to salvage the Mother, Infant, Child program, a supplemental plan funded by the city, and which had recently been put on the chopping block by Mayor Church.

One afternoon, after the students had left for the day, Lucy was sitting on the side of her bed, staring out the window into the branches of the magnolia, when her phone pinged with a WhatsApp text from her sister, Julia: "Are you busy?" Lucy touched the phone icon, and they were squealing and giggling in no time— just like they had when they were young, jumping on their beds and dancing to the Pussycat Dolls.

The sisters had kept in touch via WhatsApp throughout Julia's adventure. It was the only way she used it, and even then, she used a code name—CAKitten95—to stay under the radar.

Julia had extended her Europe trip to hike the backcountry in Wales. She had been filling her passport from Italy to Belgium, stopping along the way at some of the more popular hostels, and lucking out with a few homestays.

There had been a few exchanges with Julia since Lucy met Eli, but they hadn't talked yet. Now, Lucy was eager to tell her sister everything.

"Lucy's got a boyfriend," sang Julia.

"It seems that way."

"What's he like?"

Lucy couldn't think of a way to describe him without it sounding unrealistic. How could she explain his way of just being present, engaged, attentive, and sincere? There wasn't a word for the cadence of his voice, or the slight bounce in his step, or the smile that said he understood her. He was serious yet light-hearted, handsome yet ordinary, familiar yet unexpected.

Lucy had better luck describing his looks. His jet-black hair, floppy bangs that would not stay put, eyelashes that were so long they brushed her face when they kissed.

"He has a little scar on his chin he's self-conscious about. And ..." She paused for a beat. "He smells like chai tea."

"Chai? Seriously?" Julia giggled.

"Seriously. Like cloves, and cinnamon, and something sweet."

"That's what little girls are made of," teased her sister.

"He's smart, funny, kind, and his hugs ... Ugh! I wish he could hold me all day."

"Birth control?" asked Julia.

"God, Julia. I've only known him for a few weeks. We're nowhere near that stage."

"Lucy!" her sister howled. "If you're lost in a hug, you need to get realistic, think ahead, and be prepared. God, where exactly do you think that stage is?" They sat silent for a moment. "If you're not thinking about it, I guarantee he is."

"Who said I wasn't thinking about it?" Lucy laughed. "I just don't want to rush."

"Wyatt?" said Julia. Lucy's sister had put her finger on the spot. Could she blame Ben Wyatt for her reticence regarding sex?

"I don't know," Lucy answered honestly. "Catholic guilt, maybe." It was more than that. It was more than Wyatt, more than her sister knew about, more than Lucy wanted to acknowledge.

"Speaking of birth control, you said he has a kid."

"Julia! We were not speaking of birth control."

"What? Just making my point,"

"Your point being?" asked Lucy, knowing her sister was referring to unprotected sex.

"Never mind. I'm a dope," said Julia. "What's the kid like?"

"Owen? He's kind and bright and funny. It might sound strange, but there is something so familiar about him, you know? Maybe it's his smile, maybe his laugh. Owen has such a tender little heart." Any and all of what she said to describe Owen could have applied to Eli. "I can't help thinking that he looks just like Eli did when he was a little boy."

"C'mon. He's still just a kid."

"No, not just any kid—seriously. I'm around kids all day—you know that I am. But he's not like the others, you know? He's not trying to outsmart me or shock me or anything. He's just—Owen."

Lucy told her sister about the death of Eli's parents and explained the relationship he and his sister maintained with the out-of-work employees of their father's closed business. How they used their own careers to find assistance for them, and to do justice to their father's vision of the world as it should be—a vision of decent people looking out for one another.

She described the house—going over every detail, from the secret passages to the dance hall. The size and scope of that house couldn't fit into Julia's imagination, considering the size of the sisters' own childhood home. The comparison was laughable. Their whole house back in Seaside would fit in the great room.

"I'll be back in the states this summer—July sometime. But I wouldn't want to commit to that." Julia laughed.

"No, not you. Hey, have you talked to mom and dad lately?"

"Ugh, no. I'm feeling a little guilty about that."

"Plenty of guilt to go around, sister. I haven't called in months."

They talked for over an hour—finally hanging up when a call came in from Eli.

"Be prepared," was the last thing Julia said—and the words stuck with Lucy long after she got off the phone with Eli.

The only time Lucy had been with a guy was a night in college with a friend of a friend that never should have happened.

He had coaxed her into his dorm room under the pretense of studying together, and she fell for the ruse hook, line, and sinker. The sex was rushed. He was all hands and mouth, and she felt sick and used—too meek to say no, even while, in her mind, she was screaming the word.

She felt nothing but shame and embarrassment the next morning on her way to class, hating herself and avoiding him for the rest of the semester. *Me too*, she thought.

Eli, she knew, was the polar opposite of that guy. Was it infatuation that she felt for him? That panicked, anxiety rich, one-sided relationship she was too familiar with? She longed to be with him, to hear his voice, smell his skin, and feel his touch—but whether she wanted to accept it or not, the horrific memory of her sexual assault was something she needed to overcome.

CHAPTER TEN

IT WAS WEEKS AFTER HER DINNER AT ELI'S, A MONTH SINCE THEY'D MET AT THE farmer's market when Lucy kicked back on the porch swing with a fresh cup of steaming coffee, trying to ignore the truck and trailer across the street that had arrived moments earlier to disrupt her Saturday morning.

Step by step, piece by noisy piece, the two landscapers unloaded their instruments of torture—mower; hedge trimmer; edger; and, worst of all, the gas-powered blower that kicked up dust and debris, noisily launching it all over to Lucy's side of the street. It was just the first week of June and she cringed at the thought of a whole summer ahead of this. The weekly routine that was not exclusive to the summer months. Winter brought with it ice chippers and snowblowers to replace the lawnmowers and leaf blowers.

Secondary to the racket was the fact that it made Lucy acutely aware of her negligence regarding her own front yard—such as it was. The reduced rent—in exchange for discounted tuition for the landlord's children—did not include landscaping.

The magnolia blossoms had been replaced with a canopy of tender leaves. The untamed camellias, left and right of the front steps, had steadily built up an impressive layer of mulch over the years, and there wasn't much grass to deal with since the clover had taken hold.

Lucy set her guilt aside as she watched the men across the street. She thought of scenes like this playing out across the country. Brown-skinned men with Spanish names doing what they could to put food on the table. Her own father had started off that way when he arrived in the country, eventually launching his own business.

JPL—Javier Perez Landscaping—had provided food, clothing, and shelter to Lucy and her family for as long as she could remember.

Eli texted: *Ten minutes out.*

He was going to join her for the farmers' market. Afterward, they would spread a blanket on the park lawn to watch the weekly concert. Concerts on the Lawn, a weekly Summertime event, had blocked out six Saturdays with a different band each week. Today was the first concert, and it was someone Summer knew from her college days in Chicago.

Thomas was the lead singer of the Genial Disposition, a versatile band that played a wide range of music, but mostly their own up-beat blend of bluegrass, folk, and jazz. Back in Chicago, if she was lucky, Thomas would let her play her flute on some numbers. They were a couple briefly, before Summer finished her degree and joined Lucy at the Chrysanthemum House.

Lucy tossed the dregs of her coffee over the porch rail and dashed upstairs for a record-setting shower. She had thrown on a denim skirt and a linen blouse over a skin-tight tank top, returning to the porch with a mop of wet hair—still uncombed as Eli's car pulled up. He hopped out, smiling broadly. They had been seeing each other for a month, and while they often spoke on the phone and met regularly between obligations, it was rare to be face to face without the presence of Eli's Little Bird.

But Kali and Mia would be bringing the boy along for the concert, so Eli and Lucy's alone time was limited. He followed her into the kitchen where she kept her reusable totes, and before she could open the cabinet, his left arm slipped around her waist, and the right touched her wet hair as he kissed her.

"Knock, knock," said Summer, sweeping through the kitchen to grab a yogurt out of the fridge. "You two." She shook her head and wagged her spoon, then slipped out again.

"God, I've missed you," Eli said, when Summer was gone.

"You just saw me last night," Lucy said, laughing. She nuzzled into his neck, inhaling the scent of him. "The market—remember?"

"Can't the market wait? Just a bit?" He kissed her again, his fingers getting tangled in her uncombed hair. She managed to free herself long enough to fetch a brush out of her purse. She knew what Eli wanted—she wanted it too. But she didn't want it like this; rushed and a little sneaky. Their busy lives and lack of privacy had prevented intimacy beyond kissing and petting, but Lucy was determined to wait for the right moment—so he would have to wait too.

LOCALS AND OUT-OF-TOWNERS worked their way around the square, inspecting the produce and crafts laid out to best effect. The bandstand—a small platform set between the playground and the oak, was vacant for now except for a few kids running up and down the length of it, merrily playing air guitar. Lucy recognized two of them and waved.

She loved her brief encounters with students outside the classroom. These were among her few ties to a community she had otherwise felt disconnected from until recently—until Eli.

The wide-reaching branches of the Old Oak shaded much of the park from the center outward, and the four benches beneath were all occupied, so Lucy and Eli sat down on a street-side bench within sight of Eli's office.

"Isn't that GI Joe?" asked Eli, motioning to the now-familiar figure in ratty fatigues leaning on the wall between Eli's office window and the nail salon, casually watching the flow of pedestrian traffic.

"It is, but who are they?" Lucy was referring to the two heavy-set men who had stopped to speak with her scruffy neighbor. She wasn't fooled by their pretense of a chance encounter.

"They're the Hill brothers. Lamar is the one with the beard, and Harlan is the bald guy."

"Tweedledum and Tweedledee," Lucy said, laughing.

"Well, they're the mayor's number one and number two on the city council." Armed with this new information, Lucy watched the interaction more intently.

The three men talked for some time before being joined by Mayor Church. The mayor acknowledged GI Joe with a handshake.

"Did you or Beth ever find another transmitter?" Lucy asked thoughtfully.

"Nope. I looked but didn't find anything. Think those guys have anything to do with that?"

"I wonder if we should look again. They look like they're up to something," said Lucy. "Maybe there's a new one."

"After the concert, maybe," said Eli.

They completed their circuit around the square, holding hands like teenage sweethearts, and stopping periodically to shop.

Eli suggested they take the perishables to the office before the band began to play. There was a small fridge there, and the other things would be just fine in the air conditioning. He took Lucy's hand and led her across the street to where the men had been camped out earlier.

Eli held up the office key dangling from a bright red carabiner and slipped it into the lock. They stepped inside and were struck by how warm it was despite the closed blinds.

"Fridge is in the back there." He pointed to a makeshift kitchen with a compact microwave, a dorm-size refrigerator, and a Keurig coffee maker set on a small chest. Lucy appreciated the womanly touch of a colorful cloth draped across the chest, and the seascape that hung above it.

The office was comprised of a waiting room with a small two-seater sofa and three chairs. Beth's office was to the left. Eli's office was to the right. The kitchen, as Eli called it, was against the back wall beside a bathroom with a door wide enough to be handicap accessible.

Eli stepped up behind her as she closed the refrigerator. He stood so close, she thought he'd hear the pounding of her heart. His hands glided to her hips as he kissed her neck, and his breathing slowed as he rocked her gently from side to side. Lucy closed her eyes, transfixed by his nearness, when his warm fingers slipped into the front of her skirt, and an alarm sounded in her head.

"No!" She pulled away abruptly, as she straightened her shirt with trembling hands.

"I'm sorry. God, Lucy, I'm so sorry."

His apologies broke her heart as she looked into his eyes. It was the afternoon in his car all over again. He didn't understand, and she was frustrated with herself for not being able to explain. *It's not you*, she wanted to say. *It's Wyatt's phantom still haunting me.*

Eli crossed the room and opened the door for her to the street. He looked confused and hurt.

"Eli." Lucy approached him and stopped just short of the door, reaching for his hand. She pulled him toward her and kissed him. "I'm the one who should be sorry."

"No rush, Lucy. It's fine." He stroked her hair, then led her out the door.

The park across the way was filling up with a patchwork of concert chairs and colorful blankets. They found Summer spreading out a blanket of her own, staking her claim to a sweet patch of grass just beyond the zone which had been set aside for dancing. Eli and Lucy sat on the blanket while Summer placed another, smaller blanket beside the first.

"Are you okay?" Lucy asked Summer, knowing her friend was nervous about seeing Thomas again.

"Nervous as all Hell," said Summer. "I haven't seen him in years. Wonder if he'll even recognize me." That struck Lucy as funny. Who wouldn't recognize Summer? As if the long red hair wasn't enough to distinguish her, she stood a head taller than most of the women there.

Tweedledum, whose round, piggy face was obscured by a poorly trimmed beard, walked in front of them on his way across the park. He looked critically from Eli to Lucy. It was unnerving.

"What is his deal?" asked Summer.

Lucy spied Owen running toward them, his curls bouncing, a plastic light saber clutched in one hand. "Dad!" he called. "Dad!"

"Yes, Owen. Over here," said Eli. Owen plopped into Eli's lap; his toy lightsaber held high.

"Hello there, Little Bird," Eli said, giving his son an affectionate hug.

"Hi there, Big Bird," Owen replied in a funny voice, attempting a wink and squeaking out a little giggle.

"Looks like we boys are outnumbered."

Mia, her mass of curls held back with a bandana, complained about the parking, and Kali spread out on the second blanket. Kali and Mia had brought some chips and little turkey sandwiches from the deli to add to Lucy's trail mix and fresh strawberries.

Beth swung by to say hello, holding an unlit cigarette between her fingers. The no-smoking policy for the park had been lifted, thanks to Mayor Church, but Beth wasn't going to give him the satisfaction. Lucy slid over to make room.

"You're a peach, but we have our own claim over there." Beth waved toward her daughter, standing like a sentry further out from the bandstand. "Eli, Mr. James wants to see you Monday morning. Do you have time for him?" Mr. James was a boomerang client. Just as soon as they'd taken care of one issue, he'd be back with another. He'd worked for Moon Harvest, the cannery owned by Eli's father who'd hired him with the condition he attend Alcohol Anonymous meetings. Mr. James cleaned himself up and was steadily promoted from general maintenance to floor manager, supervising twenty employees. He was lost without the structure of Moon Harvest.

Eli looked up at Beth from his blanket. "I'll make time." Owen slid into the space between him and Lucy.

"That's my boy," said Beth waving her cigarette and turning to go.

"Hey, Beth?" Beth stopped and kneeled beside Eli while he described the scene outside their office earlier in the day. "Lucy and I are going to take a closer look after the concert, if that's all right with you."

"Of course, Eli. Let me know what you find." Beth stood and rejoined her daughter.

The Genial Disposition was gathering on the platform, and a few of the members were warming up their instruments "Check, check," said the lead singer looking out at his audience, and promptly recognizing Summer. "Hey folks," he announced. "It's Summertime!" He jumped off the stage, and Summer practically threw herself at him.

So this is Thomas, thought Lucy.

Thomas was an olive-skinned man with sparkling blue eyes and thick, wavy, black hair, which made Lucy think of a Greek God. He had all the markings of the hipster musician he was, with a smudge of soul patch on his chin, and tattoo sleeves up to his elbows.

"We're playing tonight at The Gypsy. You should all come," said Thomas. "Bring the flute!" he added with a heart charming smile, then dashed off to re-join his group on the stage.

They ate. They danced. Lucy reveled in the company of her friends. Eli caught Summer sitting out a number and joined her on the blanket while Lucy and Owen let loose.

From the corner of her eye, Lucy noticed Eli and Summer in deep conversation and wondered, self-consciously, if she was the topic.

Owen's hair was drenched with sweat, and when the band closed with a slow song, he laid himself out on the blanket.

Nearly the whole time the band played, Thomas had his eyes on Summer. When the group wrapped up, he pulled her aside to remind her they'd be playing at The Gypsy.

Eli came back to Lucy, who was packing up their things, and told her Owen was going home with his sister, while Mia may join them all at the club to hear the band again.

Summer then informed Lucy, with a wink, she had every intention of being out all night.

Eli took Lucy's hand, and they headed back to the office to collect their things and do a quick sweep for another bug.

The office was warmer than it had been earlier, so Eli stepped over to the thermostat, popped open the plastic cover, and, just like that, found another bug.

"Lucy," he whispered, peeling it away from the electrical tape that was holding it in place. He pinched it between his fingers the way Lucy had with the first one. "This must be new. The air conditioner worked yesterday."

"We should take it to the police," whispered Lucy.

"I want to make sure there aren't more, first," he whispered back.

They started in Beth's office, opening each drawer and pulling each book and binder from the shelf. They turned over each item on her desk—and if it could be opened, they opened it. She had a picture frame on her desk with a photo of her three daughters when they were small and innocent. Lucy felt like she was in a spy novel, taking the back off the frame to loosen the picture.

They pulled a framed picture off the wall and did a thorough search, just as they had done with Beth's state license, mounted beside the door in a cheap plastic frame. They found another bug with a wire taped along the top of the frame.

"If there are three bugs, and two were both in Beth's office, does that mean she's the target?" Lucy whispered into Eli's ear, the bug pinched between her fingers. "The clock was hers, remember?"

"But there was one in the waiting room," he whispered back.

"So, keep looking?

"Keep looking." They doubled their efforts, turning over Eli's office thoroughly. Lucy realized how impersonal it was, compared to Beth's. The books and binders on the shelf were all job-related. The walls were bare except for an outdated calendar swinging from a thumbtack beside the door. She was secretly hoping to find something like a photo of Owen, or Eli's parents, or … his wife. But as she sifted through a random collection of pens and paper clips in his desk drawer, she found no photos. She also found no bugs. Then she stepped up to the window and stood on the orange chair, looking for something up around the frame or attached to the blinds. She flipped the chair over and ran her fingers around the trim. When she set it right, she sat with a sigh, collecting herself.

"Zippo here. How about you?"

"Nothing." Eli had explored the door frame, the bookcase, and the underbelly of his desk. He stood and rolled his desk chair back in place.

Lucy lifted herself lazily from the chair, and noticed what looked like a phone charger plugged into an outlet on the wall, nestled between the corner and the bookcase. A tiny green light blinked on and off. Ordinarily, a listening device would not be the first thought to occur to her, but for the task at hand.

Lucy crossed the small room and got down on her knees to take a closer look, then pulled it carefully from the outlet. It was another bug.

"Now, we go to the police," she whispered, holding the device cupped between her hands.

"Monday," said Eli. "I want to take them directly to the chief."

Eli called Beth to tell her the grim news, while Lucy stashed the collection of bugs in the refrigerator. She exchanged them for the items she'd left in there earlier, and turned to see Eli holding the door open for her.

"I wish I knew how long those bugs had been there," lamented Eli as he locked up the office. *Whatever good that would do.*

"What would be the worst thing anyone could learn? How could they use it against you?" Lucy followed Eli toward the coffee shop, taking two steps for every one of his.

"You have a devious mind," said Eli. He peered at her before crossing the street and slowed his pace. "Beth thinks it's the mayor looking for dirt."

"Maybe. Or finding out what your favorite projects are, so they can sabotage you." Lucy handed her tote bag to Eli, then removed her hair clip as they walked past the ice cream shop toward the toy store. Her fingers combed through her tangled hair, and the afternoon breeze felt wonderful on her scalp.

"Either way, it's the mayor." Eli watched her pull the hair off her neck and refasten the clip.

"Either way, there's something fishy."

CHAPTER ELEVEN

AS LUCY AND ELI APPROACHED THE CHRYSANTHEMUM HOUSE, THEY FOUND Summer on the front porch, chatting with a middle-aged couple.

Summer introduced Lucy to Mrs. Lancaster—a thirtysomething woman wearing a crisp, name-brand pantsuit and a small fortune in jewelry. She swam in a toxic cloud of perfume, feigning what she probably believed was a warm, sincere smile. Lucy resisted judgment.

Mr. Lancaster, kicking back on the porch swing as if he owned the place, was decked out in Tommy Bahama—an outfit Lucy imagined the wife set out for him that morning, complete with stiff white deck shoes.

Summer was indulging them. A pitcher of iced tea sat untouched and weeping with condensation on the small table by the door. The wife held a glossy Chrysanthemum House Home School Project folder filled with credentials, school philosophy, and a basic application.

"So nice to meet you." Mrs. Lancaster scrutinized Lucy and extended a cold bony hand with manicured nails and a Pandora bracelet dripping with flashy charms and baubles. Then she fanned herself with the folder and said, "We found your sweet little website. Adorable. We just didn't find what we were looking for."

Adorable? Thought Lucy. She'd designed the site herself. Everything included in the folder Mrs. Lancaster held in her skeletal hand was available on the website, as well as a lengthy FAQ page and numerous testimonials. The criticism hit a nerve as was the likely intent. Just as showing up on a Saturday without an appointment was obviously meant to catch Lucy and Summer off guard.

"What are you looking for?" asked Lucy.

"Well, dear, um, what is your name again? Lucy? We're looking at the platform of the school. The model, you know, to replicate."

"It's an original model, approved by the state. We have no intention to replicate it at this time," said Lucy.

"That's what Summer told us." Mrs. Lancaster tucked the folder under her arm. "We won't take any more of your time."

After a hasty goodbye, the couple set off in their shiny red Lexus, which was parked across the street. They left a fog of perfume in their wake.

"What in the world?" Lucy stared at Summer, dumbfounded. Summer held up one finger and ducked into the house. She returned with a bottle of lemon vodka and immediately spiked the iced tea.

"That's more like it," said Summer after drinking from her glass and filling two more. Eli reached for them and handed one to Lucy, then sat on the swing while Lucy stood face to face with Summer. "So, we have been made an offer. Mr. and Mrs. Fancy Pants want to invest in our school and open three more."

Lucy's mouth fell open.

"Are we—celebrating?" asked Eli.

"I feel sick," said Lucy, who promptly sat down on the swing beside Eli. After a few sips of her tea, she found her voice. "This wasn't the plan, Summer."

"It's just a proposal. Let's wait and see what Mrs. Fancy Pants says. I'm pretty floored, too, for what it's worth."

Lucy thought about how unwelcome this new development was to her newfound bliss. She was just starting to feel normal again. Now she would be under a whole new level of scrutiny. She'd buried her identity so long and so deep that she didn't even know how to deal with this situation. Any simple investigation would reveal her real name. A deeper look would reveal her whole story. And if either came to light, Lucy would be in danger of being discovered when Ben Wyatt was finally released from prison.

"What exactly did you tell the Lancaster's?"

Summer looked a touch surprised—but she considered the question and answered. "Well, I didn't say much. I handled it like we handle the parents of prospective kids. Maybe I was a little heavy-handed with the sales pitch. I don't know. Before you ask—they had heard of us through some friends, though they didn't say who. And they wanted to know if there was any kind of formula that could be duplicated."

"There isn't. You know this. It's just you and me." A subtle tremble resonated in Lucy's voice.

"That's roughly what I said. But Lucy—if they want to invest, we could do so much more. Think of the field trips and memberships we could get—not to mention some new materials. I feel like all we have is our best intentions and great imaginations. Is that enough?"

Eli, reached for Lucy's hand. She resisted the urge to push it away, knowing he meant well.

"They're not going to invest without researching us—you and me. You know what that means?" Lucy glared at her friend. She had confided so much in Summer, but it appeared it hadn't made any difference.

Summer's hand flew to her face. "Oh my God! Lucy! I wasn't thinking!" She looked from Eli to Lucy. "I'm an idiot!"

Summer knew that Lucy needed to keep a low profile. They'd talked about that a million times. It was one thing with local parents who were satisfied with the folder like what Summer had given Mrs. Lancaster. Most didn't look any further.

"Lucy, what's really going on here?" asked Eli.

Lucy's mind was a turnpike of options as to what or how much to tell Eli. He knew of the assault, though not every detail, but he didn't know she used an assumed name. He didn't know she was in hiding.

Summer stepped inside the house to refresh the pitcher, giving them a moment of privacy. Eli took Lucy's hand and brought it to his lips, putting an arm around her. Lucy tried to focus on the soothing, gentle motion of the swing." He always seemed to know just what to do.

A fresh pitcher of spiked iced tea dripped across Lucy's lap as Summer reached over her head to refill their glasses. It roused the couple from their quiet contemplation.

"Pizza's on its way." It was welcome news. Lucy was famished.

They followed Summer into the house where the table was set casually with leftover Halloween paper plates.

"Really knocked yourself out," Lucy teased.

Eli answered the rap on the screen door and brought the veggie pizza with extra cheese to the table.

"More tea?" Summer topped off their glasses.

"I'm way past being able to drive," Eli confessed, reaching for the pizza.

"Looks like you'll have to stay the night," Summer said, laughing as she stacked two slices of pizza, sandwich style.

"Summer!" Lucy was horrified. "Eli, I'm ..." Before Lucy could finish her sentence, Summer had grabbed her purse and made for the door; the pizza sandwich clutched in her other hand. "Thomas is already at The Gypsy," she said, "and I don't want to miss a note. You can thank me in the morning." With that, the screen door snapped shut, and they heard the clickety-click of Summer's flats tripping down the porch steps.

They stared at the door. "Well," said Eli.

"Well."

They avoided eye contact as Eli topped off Lucy's glass. The silence lay like a chasm between them. Why was she hesitant? She'd prepared for this. It was the whole reason she'd endured the humiliation of an annual exam at Planned Parenthood, and the invasive questions about past and present relationships. The emotional discomfort was surpassed only by the placement of an IUD, with cramps that rivaled anything she'd experienced before.

"Lucy, it's all right."

"What is?" she asked, avoiding eye contact.

"I hope you don't mind, but I asked Summer about what happened to you. What he did."

"And?" *Damn you, Summer.*

"She said I need to ask you. But if you don't want to talk about it, I understand."

"Eli." Lucy met his eyes. "I can't. I can't go there right now. I won't."

"You don't need to. I'm sorry." He laid a hand on her

shoulder—then abruptly pulled it away, as if afraid he'd overstepped again. She had done this, she thought. She had made him fearful to touch her.

"I have an idea." Lucy took his hand and led him up to her room, where she stood him beside the bed and closed the blinds. She could do this, but it would have to be on her terms. "Take off your shirt." He obliged. "Close your eyes." He closed them.

"Ah—"

"Shh." Lucy laid a finger to his lips, and stood back, admiring the soft hair fanned out across his chest like angel's wings, and the thin black line of finer hair that led below the belt.

"What—"

"*Quiet*," she whispered. He stood still, hands at his sides, biting his lip to keep from speaking as she unfastened his belt and allowed his jeans to drop to the floor. Eli nodded. He understood now what was happening. She was in control of the situation, the pace, the progression. She would have no surprises. He listened to the shuffling sounds of Lucy removing her clothes and dropping them one by one on the floor.

Naked now, Lucy placed her hands on his chest and ran them down to his belly and around his waist. She tucked her thumbs into the waistband of his boxer briefs and delicately removed them, then circled around and examined his broad back as her fingers explored the scars, moles, and contours of his body. Eli remained silent but for his breathing, which accelerated with each touch. He bowed his head, chin to chest, resigning himself to her examination.

She laid him down across the bed and slid over him, running her fingers through his thick hair, then began to kiss the lips she found so irresistible. Gently, he kissed her back, and they vanished into the sensual abyss of new lovers.

CHAPTER TWELVE

THE TOLL OF SUNDAY MORNING CHURCH BELLS BROKE THROUGH THEIR BLISSFUL sleep. Lucy opened her eyes to find Eli gazing at her. She beamed. "Good morning." The smile was fixed. She couldn't have wiped it away for all the riches in the world.

"Mm." He reached around her and drew her to his bare skin. "Good morning."

The room was bright despite the blinds being closed, and the church bells had just informed them that it was ten o'clock. It was nearly eleven when they finally decided to get up and dressed—before Summer returned to interrupt their spell.

They moved slowly, never missing an opportunity to touch, kiss, or nuzzle. Lucy noted her contentment. She wanted more than anything to never let it go.

They were in the kitchen pouring the first of the coffee when they heard the snap of the screen door—a bookend to last night's departure. Lucy reached into the cabinet for a third cup. Summer appeared around the corner and stood, beaming at them.

"I'm in love!" Summer said, taking the cup and filling it, before pulling some almond milk out of the fridge to lighten it up. "Did you hear me?" she asked. "I am in *love!*"

They were bemused by the sudden declaration and encouraged her to go on.

"So, we're at the club, right? The Gypsy? Genial Disposition had just finished the first set. Mia and I had a little table—you know, the kind that's high, and where it's more comfortable to stand than sit? In walks this yahoo—we saw him yesterday. Fat dude with a beard, you know?"

Lucy nodded, thinking of Tweedledum, who Summer now dubbed *Dum Beard*.

"Dum Beard sees us sitting together and makes some crack about lesbians being freaks of nature. Like how did he know she was even gay, right? Mia, she's small, right? Even standing in three-inch heels—who dances in heels? And she says, 'At least I know what it's like to be loved.' Then she said something in French, which was probably not very nice, and he decks her! I'm serious! She flies back, knocking me over—and the guy at the next table to boot! And then—you'll never believe this—Thomas steps right up to him and punches him in the face. *Boom!*" She pantomimed the punch. "Just like that, Dum Beard is bleeding out of his nose, and then, *bam!*" She wheeled her arm around. "Thomas socks him in the gut, and Dum Beard drops to his knees. All this takes like a minute, right?"

She paused to catch her breath.

"Then Thomas helped Mia up and apologized for the clientele. He picked me up off the floor and asked if I was hurt. Like, he was really concerned—seriously. I'm not used to that. Two of the other bandmembers picked Dum Beard up by his armpits, which was a job—he's a pig—and dragged him out the door. It was awesome! The place practically exploded in cheers!"

"Well, good morning," said Lucy. "And congratulations. Here's to love."

"To love," all three toasted with their mismatched coffee cups.

ELI WAS GONE by noon. He had to get home to spell Kali and get Owen ready for his first T-Ball game at the high school.

The rest of the morning, Summer wouldn't shut up about Thomas. Thomas was fine, sweet, strong, talented, kind, tough, fill in the blank. Thomas was it, as well as a great lover, and a gentleman. Oh, and smart. Thomas was the image of perfection.

Secretly, Lucy was glad of her friend's effusiveness—it meant she didn't have to share anything about her own incredible, beautiful night.

Owen had the most prominent cheering section at his T-ball game that day. Eli, Lucy, Kali, Mia, and Summer all spread out on their blankets, hooting and cheering him on. He was playing second base and waving at them throughout the game. His mass of curls spilled out from under his lopsided cap.

The other players were amusing enough—the crotch scratchers, the nose pickers, the daydreamers, and the few who were engaged, looking like little men already securing their future high-school varsity status.

The mayor was there, looking every bit the televangelist in his black suit and stiff shoes. His thin gray hair was perfectly combed, and hair-sprayed in place. His well-fed gut spilled over his belt like a Salvador Dali clock. His grandson was on the opposing team—a nose picker.

"How could such a fool have become mayor?" asked Eli, rhetorically.

Summer flipped a quarter in the air, and they watched it drop to the ground. "Heads or tails? That's how engaged our Drake voters are," she said.

"That's about right," Eli said, laughing.

"And the city council. All male," said Summer.

"Well, the town is called *Drake*, after all," added Kali, pointing to the banners along the road. The male mallard city logo and high school mascot was also the profile on every T-Baller's back, whether their team sponsor was the Drake hardware store or the Drake Coffee Company. Drakes abounded. "It's a male, male, male, male world."

Kali pointed to the mayor, who was handing out little cards to certain people. He looked over at their group and promptly away. "We are not worthy," teased Summer under her breath.

Lucy looked toward the mayor, his small entourage surrounding him as he doled out the cards, but her attention was drawn away by a passing motorcycle. The driver, hidden behind a full helmet, pulled over and turned his head toward the field as if interested in the game.

The game ended with a tie, and Owen was delighted. Impulsively, Lucy tried to snatch him up in her arms, but barely got him off the ground.

"Oof, you're heavy," she said, satisfied with a hug.

"Good game, Little Bird," said Eli, swinging him up onto his shoulders.

"Dad, is Lucy coming home with us?"

"Sorry, kiddo," she answered for him. "I have to get ready for school tomorrow." She looked up into two crestfallen faces. Eli set Owen down and told him to get in the car. Lucy thought about her last visit to Eli's and smiled as Kali handed him one of the cards the mayor had been passing out. He held it out so Lucy could see.

City Council Budget Committee
Recommendations on Health and Social Services
For Special Election
City Hall, Room 206, Tuesday, June 12th, 7pm
Agenda includes budget appropriations vote
for the coming fiscal year
All Welcome

"This is his idea of transparency," said Kali, red-faced and livid. "I'm going."

"I'm going too," said Eli.

"No—the mayor knows you, and you'll get shut out. I'll give you a full report."

"I need to argue in favor of the social service office. I should, by all rights, have been invited." Eli pushed his hair out of his eyes, visibly frustrated. "You read the card. *All Welcome.* I'm going, and I'm bringing Beth."

"I'll call the Drake Register. See if Tina can cover it." Kali reached for her phone excitedly. Tina Reynolds was a writer for the local weekly paper.

Eli turned to Lucy as the others walked on ahead. He took

her hands in his and drew her close. "Are you sure you can't come home with us?" Lucy thought about what the rest of the day would look like at Eli's. It wouldn't be what she wanted, with Owen hopping about and Kali watching her every move. On the other hand, if Eli were to come home with her, they would have to contend with Summer's love-struck serenade.

"I'm sure."

"I'm going to take in the bugs tomorrow after work."

"I'll go with you."

"No, this is my fight."

"I'm *going*," she said. Eli groaned an agreement and gave her one last kiss, releasing her to join his son, who was growing impatient, waiting in the car. "Tomorrow," Lucy called after him.

"Did I mention I'm in love?" declared Summer. Eli looked back with a burst of laughter.

CHAPTER THIRTEEN

T HE FOLLOWING AFTERNOON, LUCY ARRIVED AT CITY HALL WITH A BIG BEAU-
tiful smile on her face.

"I love that smile," said Eli. Lucy looked down in embarrassment. The space between her teeth could have been remedied
with braces, but when she was a kid her father considered the
expense extravagant, and she had learned to live with the minor
imperfection.

Eli leaned down to give her a quick kiss on the cheek and
then led the way through the modern building. The clock was
ticking, and there was no time for indulgences. They didn't have
an appointment—an unfortunate oversight.

"Wait there." The receptionist, whose hair dye had left its mark
on her forehead, pointed to a row of stiff plastic chairs.

Lucy grumbled something about how ridiculous it was to have
business hours for police, since community safety was a twenty-
four-hour thing. Eli pointed out that the emergency lines were
open twenty-four hours, with an exception for the chief. That only
solicited more grumbling.

The idea of merging the city hall and the police department
had come from the previous mayor, Mayor O'Sullivan, who put
it up for a community vote. It passed without a word of dissent,
which was either a testament to O'Sullivan's popularity or the
lack of voter engagement. Lucy assumed it was the latter, but was
impressed with the new building, nonetheless.

The old city hall was subsequently converted to an antique
store, and the police department plowed down to become the
municipal parking lot across the street.

The new building was well underway when Mayor Church took

office and made some of his own recommendations, extending the schedule and ballooning the budget. That was something he had developed a name for, despite his denials, his self-aggrandizing, and his promises of belt-tightening.

They waited for forty minutes. It was nearly five o'clock, and the office was about to close. Eli was in the middle of texting Kali, pleading for her to pick up Owen from daycare, when Mayor Church and the stodgy Chief Donoghue finally emerged from the office, shaking hands enthusiastically. The chief was clearly engrossed in an obtuse effort to ingratiate himself.

"We'll just watch and wait then," said the chief, clearing his throat.

The mayor looked down at them and briefly acknowledged Eli. "Mr. Moon, I hope you're well." Eli stood, and they shook hands as the mayor's head pivoted to Lucy, who was rising from her chair.

"I'm Lucy Price. I run the Chrysanthemum House on—"

"I'm aware." Lucy watched his face contort as he considered her extended hand, then spun on his heels and headed down the hall.

"Yes?" The chief quickly interjected. Chief Donoghue was a tall, odd-looking man. He resembled a tortoise with a clump of gray fluff on his head and a drape of flesh hanging in rings from chin to chest. He was unshaven and missing the eye patch he usually wore to cover the result of a botched surgery—which had left his eyes looking in different directions, and had effectively removed him from the field, landing him behind a desk with the mayor's blessing.

The chief brusquely ushered them into his office. They had three minutes to make their case. Three minutes to explain the magnitude of Eli's office having its private and confidential conversations violated. Start the clock.

Despite his outward appearance, the chief still projected the image of a fearsome man. With surprising courage, Lucy took the bag of listening devices from Eli, held it out to the chief, and shook it at him, while his lazy eye looked somewhere over her shoulder.

"These four listening devices were found in the social services office on Park Street. Were you aware the office was being surveilled?" Lucy was unsure which eye she should be addressing.

"What is this?" The chief chortled under his breath in a slow Kentucky drawl that made Lucy furious. "Are you interrogatin' me? Who would wanna surveil that office?"

"We don't know," Lucy said. "That's why we're here." She struggled to suppress her frustration and set the bag on his desk.

He glowered with condescension and disgust, clearing his throat with a repulsive, guttural croak. "I know nothin' about this." He picked up the bag and turned it over in his hand. "And I'm afraid, little girl, that we are short-staffed and don't have a single man free at this time to look into it."

Eli stepped up. "I'm sure you'll think of something."

"Listen, kids," he drawled. "I don't know just what you think I can do. Fingerprints? No, you've been handlin' 'em. Set up a sting? Like I told you, I have no one to help." He shook a finger at Eli. "And don't you get any stupid ideas. There's no call for Hardy Boy heroics."

Lucy's heart was racing, her mind buzzing with fury. *Slow breath in …*

"We have our suspicions about two men who've been snooping around the office," said Eli. "I believe you know them."

"Right. Well. If you see 'em snoopin' again, let me know. In the meantime, I got nothin' for you."

Lucy snatched the bag back from the chief and stuffed it into her tote.

"You can let yourselves out."

They kept their heads down as they passed Miss Clairol on their way out to the street.

"What the fuck?" hissed Lucy as a black Denali motorcycle slowly rumbled by. Its driver, cloaked in black leather and a full helmet, looked at them through a darkened visor. Lucy watched as the bike turned the corner. She remembered seeing it yesterday at the T-ball game. Chills ran up her spine as she fought off a recurrent notion, something left behind by having had a stalker. Would she always feel like someone was following her? "Let's get Owen."

WHEN THEY ARRIVED at Lucy's with Owen, they were horrified to find her mailbox stripped from the house and laying in two pieces on the sidewalk. Lucy picked it up with trembling hands and carried it up to the house.

They plunked Owen in front of the most recent episode of *Droid Wars* with lemonade and a slightly burned grilled cheese sandwich. Lucy had often criticized parents who used the TV as a babysitter, but now she was hip to the necessity.

She opened a beer and handed it to Eli, taking a drink from her own bottle before pouring the remainder into a tall glass.

"This is all the mayor's doing. You know it is. Did you see the way he looked at me?"

"The mayor vandalized your mailbox?"

"No, of course not. It's obvious, the mayor planted the bugs. The chief is covering for him. What's to stop them from doing it again?"

Eli suggested a security system for the office. He called Beth to let her know what had transpired with Chief Donoghue and received her wholehearted approval for the security system idea.

Lucy looked over at her mailbox and considered her own line of defense as Eli and Beth joined the ranks of Dr. Franzki. Perhaps she and Summer should entertain a similar solution.

CHAPTER FOURTEEN

A WEEK LATER, THE WHOLE GANG ARRIVED AT LUCY'S FOR A PRE-CITY COUNCIL dinner of chicken tacos and a fresh green salad. The house was warm and bright. All the windows stood open, but there was little breeze to provide relief. Fortunately, no one seemed to mind.

An abundance of salsa and guacamole, compliments of Summer, was spread out on the dining room table. This was the first time Owen had tried guacamole, and he nearly made a meal out of that alone. Kali and Mia joked about how they might be over for dinner every night, and Eli declared that he was going to learn how to cook.

"Praise God!" exclaimed Kali, taking her plate to the kitchen sink, and adding it to the stack of dirty dishes. She looked at Lucy apologetically.

"I believe Summer is going to give Owen a lesson in domestics." Lucy pulled a chair up to the sink the way her mother had done for her when she was young. She handed Owen a dry towel and he accepted it with an amiable shrug.

"Excellent," Kali said. "My brother can cook, and my nephew will clean. Why would I ever want to move?"

"Everybody out!" Summer was practically pushing them out of the tiny kitchen. She grabbed Owen by the shoulders and pointed him to the chair, while the rest filed out of the house. "Not you, bud—you're all mine."

"We won't be too late Little Bird. Be good for Summer, eh?" said Eli. Owen smiled at his father, waving his towel. He climbed up on the chair, ready for what was next.

"We'll have a great time, won't we, Owen?" said Summer. Owen nodded. "Now off you go, you guys. Don't be late." Summer gave Eli a push out the kitchen door.

Eli climbed into the driver's seat of his BMW and waited while the others got settled. Lucy sat beside him, with Mia and Kali cuddled in back.

They had gotten as far as the church on the corner when Lucy observed a small man walking toward them. He peered into Eli's car as it passed, his face partially obscured by the brim of a baseball cap. Lucy felt a wave of nausea as Eli drove on.

The days were long. The sun still hung bright in the clear blue sky. Lucy couldn't blame her uncertainty on poor vision. It could have been anybody, but her mind locked onto the morning at the farmers' market just over a month earlier, the voice, the jacket. Her sense of panic spiked.

Eli and Kali were talking or not talking. It might have been the radio. It might have just been the pounding of her heart. With a jolt, Lucy was abruptly revived by car doors opening and slamming shut. She was aware of the sharp sting of anxiety as her fingers tripped over the buttons, locking and unlocking the door as she struggled to close her window. *Slow breath in...*

"Lucy?" Eli opened the door and held out a hand. "What's wrong?"

"Nothing," said Lucy, digging deep for the armor she had developed years ago in the hospital, to fend off repeated attempts to make her talk. *Slow breath out...*

Dr. Stewart, the hospital therapist assigned to Lucy after the attack, had helped her start to put that armor away, with meditation and deep breathing exercises. But those techniques were not enough to put her armor away for good.

Lucy spotted GI Joe standing just outside the city hall with his MAGA hat firmly in place, as her small tribe approached from the parking lot across the street. He locked eyes with her for a split second as she and the others passed through the doors. She wanted to believe he was harmless—but to her, and to many minorities, MAGA was code for hate.

Lucy held onto Eli's hand as they ascended the crowded stairs to the meeting room which was filling up quickly considering the meeting hadn't been published.

Tina Reynolds, a journalist from the *Drake Register*, was the first person they saw in room 206. She was dressed in snug skinny jeans and a flimsy peasant top, and she was armed with a high caliber smartphone to capture the event in real time and turn it into editorial gold.

"Well, look what the kittens dragged in." Tina looked up from her phone just in time to see Eli squeeze through the crowd with his sister and Mia.

Eli squirmed. "Hi, Tina. How've you been?"

"Great, just great." She gave him a quick hug and laughed. "The mayor is keeping life interesting." Her smile was genuine, and Lucy wrestled with an unfamiliar emotion, waiting for an introduction or some type of explanation for Tina's affection.

"Good to see you, Tina," said Kali, grabbing Eli by the shoulders and pushing him into a chair. Lucy quickly took the free seat beside him.

Lucy looked up at the four committee members, two on either side of Mayor Church, sitting at the arc-shaped table facing the room full of mismatched folding chairs—some dating back decades.

The frugality of this city appeared in the most unlikely places. This mayor slashed the budget where the need was greatest, while collecting the highest salary of any prior mayor from Drake or its surrounding communities. His office, under construction when he was elected, had been enlarged by knocking down the wall to the adjoining room, just as staff salaries were cut and the retirement plan nixed.

There was nothing the prior mayor had initiated, Lucy had discovered, that Mayor Church hadn't tried to do away with. Plans to build a new sports park on the east side—with soccer fields, basketball and tennis courts, and a dog run—were now on permanent hold. Science and math scholarships were annulled, and plots in the community garden, revoked. It's no wonder Mayor O'Sullivan, after watching his hard work disassembled, moved to Vermont under the protective umbrella of Senator Bernie Sanders. Lucy wondered if her neighbors ever regretted their ill-informed votes.

Lucy hadn't voted. She never registered with the state; the risk to her anonymity was too high. But she'd liked O'Sullivan and thought most Drake residents liked him as well. It's one of the reasons she and Summer were so baffled by his loss. It was almost as if Frank Church had—cheated.

Lucy gave Eli a nudge and pointed at the four-member council with one finger while covering it with her other hand. Tweedledee and Tweedledum, aka the Hill brothers, were looking smugly across the crowd from their council seats. Kali gave him another nudge and whispered, "That's Roy Bird—remember him from the cannery?"

Roy Bird had been the CFO for Moon Harvest, the Moon family business, and one of their father's best friends. He was now the third member of the city council—the last being Alex Bridges, who was a big name locally among the NRA crowd, and the mayor's stiffest competition for the next election. Roy sat at full attention two seats down from the mayor. His wire-rimmed reading glasses rested near the end of his nose, and he was wearing a shirt and tie, looking like the only professional at the table.

The mayor stood briefly to introduce the council, making a quick opening statement before calling the meeting to order with his pint-sized gavel.

"The primary purpose of this meeting is to vote on the budget cuts as it pertains to all things related to social services. What will stay and what will go." The mayor straightened his posture, thrusting his shoulders back with the smug confidence of a small-town potentate. "We intend to follow the lead of the federal government in trimming the fat of government handouts. This socialist agenda ends now in Drake." He gaveled in, grinning, and stepped back as if waiting for an arena of fans to explode in adulation. The response was disappointing.

Behind the mayor was a projected image of the bullet points for the "proposed cuts and the possible benefits to taxpayers". Beth whispered to Eli that "possible" was the operative word. She trusted the mayor as far as she could throw him.

The mayor read from the bullet points, adding nothing new, but holding off the inevitable question/answer segment of the meeting. Eli and Beth hadn't been mentioned by name, but the implication was clear. Each and every bullet point was a direct shot at the social service office.

Hands were quick to rise when it came time for open questions. People shouted over one another to be heard. "What about the food bank?" "Will my child-care credits be taken away?" "How soon do these cuts take effect?"

"Enough!" The mayor slammed his little gavel, emphasizing his tantrum. "I will not hear another word about the cuts to your blasted liberal programs! The citizens of Drake voted for thrift, and I'm damn well going to give it to 'em!"

The room went silent. Eli turned to see Kali shrugging her shoulders. The look on his face said, *What the hell was that?*

Beth did not give in so easily. She remained standing, hands on hips, and let him have it. "The citizens, sir, voted for you by the slimmest of margins!" She turned to the crowd. "They expected you to keep their quality of life while only spending what was necessary! They did not explicitly say they wanted less help with mental health care, putting food on the table, or less access to the free clinic!" She was just getting warmed up and the crowd was with her, to the horror of Mayor Church who blustered and waved his arms. "They did not vote for less security or funding for special education! They did not vote for your ridiculous raise or the refurbishment of your home office, which includes, by the way—listen up you all,"—she gestured dramatically to the crowd—"your home renovation." The room rumbled with mixed reactions to Beth's rant.

"Lies!" He was livid. "If you value this community at all, you will shut your big mouth, woman, and give a little thought to your slanderous words here!"

"I will not! Not as long as you hold office." The rumble of voices grew. "You are a menace to this community. A royal joke foisted upon us with lies masquerading as insincere promises." Some people began to stand and cheer for her. Those who didn't sat silent.

"Shut up!"

"I will fight you. We—will fight you!"

Tina Reynolds stood. "Mr. Mayor. Tell us about the home remodel. How was that funded?"

"Meeting adjourned. All in favor?" The committee members sat mute, stunned into silence by the spectacle. Unsure how to respond.

Lucy had been so engaged in the drama that she had not noticed Mrs. Fancy Pants in the front row. But she noticed her now. She was the best-dressed woman in the room, of course, with her shoulder-length blonde hair straightened to silky perfection. She and the mayor would make a perfect match.

"All in favor?" The mayor's eyes cut like knives into the stunned committee.

Tina Reynolds was not ready to give in. She asked if this meeting would re-assemble at another time, since there was not a resolution.

"There most certainly was a resolution." The mayor stood straight, shoulders back, chin up, and arms spread—it made him look even more like a Televangelist than usual. "If you didn't catch it, then you're a pathetic journalist. If you report otherwise, I will deny it. You will write what I say you write. Anything less is Fake News!" The mayor's voice had grown to a shriek, and he was red-faced and sweating profusely.

His delicately combed coif had not budged despite his fury, giving testament to his brand of hair spray as he flung the door open. Apparently, he intended to slam it behind him to make his point, but the slow release hinges wouldn't cooperate, and his exit fell flat.

There was confusion in the room as people tried to figure out what had just happened. The council members clustered, with Tina hovering nearby. Lucy and the others were joined by Beth, fidgeting and desperate for a cigarette.

Once Tina realized there was nothing more she could glean, she entered the hall, where Mrs. Fancy Pants caught up to her. Lucy followed Eli into the hall, but they were stalled at the stairs by the logjam of meeting attendees also trying to leave. She watched as Mrs. Fancy Pants approached Tina and stopped in her tracks. She feared when she'd met the Lancaster's that they were up to something. Is this when Lucy's story becomes public knowledge? Lucy split off from Eli and squeezed down the stairs. She needed air. She needed perspective.

"Lucy!" Eli called after her. "Lucy, wait!" She had a full minute to get her head together before Eli caught up to her on the sidewalk. "Are you okay? What happened up there?"

"I'm fine now. Just needed some air," she said, planting a smile on her face. "Really." Eli put his arm around her shoulders and walked her across to the car. It was still light outside, but the sun was sinking fast and the sky was lit up as if it was on fire.

ELI WAS FIRST in the door when they returned to the Chrysanthemum House, and Lucy followed him up to her room, where they found Owen snoozing on her bed with *The Wind in the Willows* open to an illustration of Mole and Ratty on a river adventure. They stood quietly in the dark hallway, listening to the muted voices of the others down below. She felt much calmer now.

Eli's hands slipped up the back of her shirt as he bowed his head to kiss her. She felt his fingers explore along either side of her spine and stop. The scar. Again, it was the scar.

It wasn't fair to make him wonder, especially since she had an account of every scar and broken bone he'd ever suffered. She would tell him the whole story, she decided. Soon.

"OWEN," WHISPERED ELI as Lucy watched from the bedroom door. "Owen, time to go home."

"Dad?" Owen rolled over and looked sleepily at his father. He'd only just fallen asleep according to Summer, who'd read to him from *The Wind in the Willows*.

"Time to go home, bud," said Eli.

"I want to sleep here." Owen rolled over and scrunched the pillow under his head. Eli looked over at Lucy and smiled.

Eli was eventually successful in luring his son down the stairs once Lucy promised him that he could take the book home. "I think I like Badger best," said Owen.

"Yes, Badger is an interesting fellow," Lucy agreed, handing the book to Eli on the porch. "Goodnight, Owen."

"Goodnight, Lucy," he said sleepily.

Eli leaned into her with a kiss on the forehead. "Goodnight. I'll call you later."

Once they had their house back to themselves, Lucy and Summer retreated to the kitchen, where Lucy produced a quart of strawberry ice cream. She gave her friend a quick rundown of the chaotic meeting, as she filled two small dishes. She especially relished describing the mayor's public mental breakdown.

"I thought his head was going to explode. No kidding." Lucy thought it was encouraging that the community stood up for themselves considering the mayor's goals to strip the city of its social safety net and AVID's burgeoning movement, Drake was going to need the community to rally.

"I missed all the fun," Summer pouted, sitting on the counter with her empty bowl on her lap. "Do you think the budget cuts would have passed if the vote had taken place?"

"Absolutely. You should have seen the city council." Lucy noted the exception of Roy Bird, explaining that Roy had worked for Eli's dad. "Mrs. Fancy Pants was there too. I saw her with Tina Reynolds, and they looked pretty cozy."

"God, Lucy—I'm so sorry."

Tina seemed to know Eli well, but Lucy remembered watching Eli and Mia in the toy shop and look how that turned out. She stared into her bowl wondering if Tina was friend or foe.

"It's not your fault, Summer. It was inevitable." Lucy's mind was racing: where she would run next, what she would take with her, and what—or who—would be left behind. It was a tough pill to swallow.

"Don't allow Wyatt to control you like this."

"Why do you say that?" Lucy thought about the man she'd seen earlier from the car. Wyatt was in her head so deep she believed he was everywhere. He was still stalking her beyond the prison walls.

"About Wyatt? You don't know what's going to happen there, do you? Mrs. Fancy Pants probably doesn't know anything worth publishing and you're letting it ruin your night. You are not a victim. You are a survivor, my friend. A survivor with people who love you." But the scars ran deep, and Lucy struggled to acknowledge her friend's words. "Say it," Summer insisted.

"I am not a victim," Lucy said, unconvincingly, a spoonful of ice cream melting on her tongue. Summer glared at her. "I'm a survivor," she emphasized to satisfy her cheerleader—but was rescued by the buzzing phone in her hand.

"Hey, you," she said, fleeing the kitchen and climbing the steps two by two, breathless at the joy of hearing Eli's voice.

"Are you alone?"

She closed her bedroom door and flopped on her bed, then pushed her back against the headboard and tucked her feet under the covers where Owen lay not so long ago.

"Yeah, I'm all yours."

"What a night," Eli said.

Lucy agreed, thinking back to the man she had seen in the street, GI Joe at the doors, Eli and Tina Reynolds embracing, Mrs. Fancy Pants at the meeting, and, of course, the mayor's tantrum.

"Eli?"

"Yeah?"

"Who is Tina Reynolds?" asked Lucy, wondering if she was better off not knowing.

"You know, she writes for the paper."

"That's not what I mean. Is she—was she a friend of yours? You just seemed so ..." Lucy wasn't sure how to put it into words. "She seemed so friendly with you."

"Oh, that." Lucy imagined Eli dragging his fingers through his hair like he did when he was thinking or worried.

"We dated in high school," he sighed, "then later, briefly, after Eva, when Owen was about three. It was, well," Eli paused. "It was a colossal mistake; on many levels." He spoke in a calm and quiet manner that made Lucy feel as if he were lying beside her, talking in the dark. It made her wish she could roll over and touch him. "Tina wanted to just pick up where we left off and …" Eli took a breath. "I wasn't ready. Not ready to date, and not ready for her. I handled it badly, though. It's not something I'm proud of. Does that make any sense?" Eli asked. Lucy thought about Tina's embrace and his awkwardness. It made perfect sense. "Lucy, you know this is different, though, you and me," Eli said softly, "don't you?"

"Yes, I know. I didn't mean to pry."

"You have a right to pry. I'll tell you anything," he said. Lucy had told him so little.

"Eli?"

"Mm-hmm?"

"You're thinking about my scar."

"I am yes. You can tell me when you're ready. It's just that I have a pretty vivid imagination, and not knowing is driving me a little nuts."

"I'll tell you soon. I promise."

Eli cleared his throat. "Change of subject. I made dinner reservations at Bistro 88 for tomorrow."

"You did?"

"Just the two of us. Kali will watch Owen."

"That sounds wonderful." Lucy paused. "Can you—stay the night?"

"I'll keep an open mind." Lucy could hear the smile in his voice.

They said their goodnights, and Lucy reclined deeper into her pillows, holding her phone for a minute or so, thinking about the evening and looking forward to the next.

CHAPTER FIFTEEN

LUCY WAITED FOR ELI ON THE PORCH, WEARING HER BLUE SUNDRESS. SHE PRAC-tically tumbled down the stairs in excitement when his BMW rolled up to the curb.

As an extra treat, Eli had purchased admission to the Drake Museum of Art an hour before their dinner reservation. The museum had grown significantly in size since Eli had first visited as a young boy. "Back then, it was the size of the social service office and had two employees," he'd told her. After years of fundraisers and dona-tions, the museum had grown to many times its original size.

Lucy was curious about the latest renovations Mrs. Gates, so disgruntled by the expense of it all the previous month, had referred to as they made the rounds through the permanent collec-tion, and on into the hall of photographic art.

The photo collection had four contributors reflecting life from the four corners of the United States. The photographer from Maine had been in the museum the previous week to sign his book, which was on sale in the gift shop. Lucy lost herself in the photographs from the Pacific Northwest, which included the natural splendor of the Cascade Mountain Range. She pictured herself tucked away in a cabin in the woods where Wyatt could never find her.

They climbed the stairs, where one hall was draped off with a dusty plastic sheet. The other side held a small collection of Turkish textile art spanning five centuries, on loan from the University of Chicago. This was the exhibit they enjoyed most, and they had to resist the temptation to touch some of the more luxurious items. The beadwork, the stitching, and the design of elaborate vests and tunics stood beside formal military uniforms and ornate tradi-tional wedding costumes.

They listened intently to one another as they shared their impressions of the art, their voices bouncing off the walls, sounding soft and malleable. They were wholly absorbed with one another as they moved around the space in tandem, always within arms' reach. Lucy would sweep her fingers along his arm. Eli would touch her hair, as it flowed loose over her shoulders.

The renovation was extensive and, no doubt, just as costly as Mrs. Gates had suggested. Membership prices had gone up fifty percent, less the special renovation discount.

The backside of their tickets listed notable supporters. The City of Drake was listed as a Premiere Supporter and Gold Label Donor despite the notoriously tightfisted mayor. Also on the supporter list were the *Drake Register*, the Wine Splendor tasting room, the expanding Grand Mallard Hotel with their doormen in spiffy uniforms, and St. Charles University.

The University was a small, private, liberal arts school that boasted of their equestrian team and Christian values in equal measure. The tickets also listed the administrative staff, with Nancy Church—presumably the mayor's wife—in bold print as the Museum Curator.

"Well, that explains quite a lot," said Lucy thinking how easy it was for the mayor to turn his back on charity when it came to his own citizens, yet forked it over for his wife's benefit.

"Isn't there a word for that?" asked Eli.

"Hypocrisy," said Lucy. Eli laughed and she joined in. Their explosive laughter ricocheted off the high ceilings attracting the scrutiny of an elderly docent. They let their laughter fly as the doors closed behind them and walked the short distance to Bistro 88.

It was the only restaurant in town that had been rated by the *New York Times*—suggesting that though small, it was a hidden gem in the middle of the world. Apparently, the critic had read the plaque at the foot of the city's beloved Old Oak. The restaurant had also hosted dozens of presidential hopefuls over the years—as attested by several photos hung throughout the space.

Lucy and Eli were led through the restaurant and out a side

door to the patio, where they were seated at a quiet and cozy table for two.

They were enclosed on two sides by an ivy-covered garden wall and low hedge, and overhead by an umbrella that kept the sun off their table.

Lucy regarded Eli across the table; the creases in his shirt, the fresh haircut, and the hint of cologne all pointed to the effort he'd gone to. But that was just the beginning.

Upon sitting, the pair were immediately brought a small charcuterie of craft cheese, fresh honey, and homemade crackers. A bottle of champagne was chilling in a quickly melting ice bucket. Eli had planned ahead.

Of course, the inevitable happened. Lucy was carded before the waitress would open the bottle. She produced her driver's license, and waited as the waitress, not any older than Lucy, scrutinized her ID and placed it on the table, where Eli was quick to pick it up.

"Eli, no." Lucy reached for the card, but he smiled as he looked it over, teasing, flirting, Lucy wasn't quite sure. She held her breath. She wasn't ready for this. Their waitress popped the cork and filled their glasses as he studied the card, and then laid it back down.

"I was just looking for your birthday." Lucy watched the bubbles in her glass as they released their grip and soared to the surface with a pop. Then she saw the hurt in his face. He'd seen the name, and Lucy ached with the guilt of it.

"I meant to tell you. I should have. There's so much I want to tell you." She picked up the card and tucked it back into her purse hanging on the side of her chair.

"Lucy, do you trust me?"

"I do trust you. It's not that. Here, in Drake, I am Lucy Price. I have to be. It's just easier—no, safer to be Lucy Price."

"Do you honestly think that guy is going to look for you? Maybe it's none of my business, but I'm not blind. I see you looking over your shoulder. You're afraid. I'm asking you, is that what you're so afraid of?"

Lucy took a swallow from her glass. "The short answer is yes.

The long answer is too much for me to get into right here." Her voice choked, and her eyes went glassy with tears. "I'm sorry, Eli."

They sipped their drinks, allowing the moment to pass—determined not to let it ruin their evening. But she'd hurt him with that secret. Moving on was not easy. *What will he think when I tell him the whole story?* thought Lucy, as the waitress interrupted their silence to take their order.

Lucy ordered the farro salad, a meal she could eat with delicacy. Eli ordered a bottle of Chardonnay and the chicken piccata. His mother used to prepare it, he explained, and it was his favorite meal, which he ordered whenever he could.

"I'm going to learn how to make it myself someday. I'm serious about learning how to cook."

"I have a neighbor down the street who used to be a chef. He gives cooking lessons. I can look into it if you want." Lucy looked at him for approval.

"Maybe we could go together." Was forgiveness always so easy for him?

Eli started describing the security system he was looking at, but ultimately found it easier to pull it up on his phone and let her read about it herself.

"Look, it's got three cameras, and you can see everything on your phone."

She scrolled down, "Ooh—it's motion activated."

"I thought you'd like that," he said, as she handed his phone back. "Should I order two? Would you feel safer with something like this?"

Before Lucy could answer, the waitress arrived with the Chardonnay. She set two wine glasses in front of her and peeled the foil away from the bottle. As they sat quietly, waiting for their wine to be poured, another server arrived with their meals and cleared away the empty cheese platter.

"Price is actually my mother's name," said Lucy once they were left alone. She looked across the table for his reaction, but he gazed back, unflinching. "My full name is Lucia Mariela Perez. Mariela is a grandmother I've never met." She picked at the salad.

"Elijah Solomon Moon." Eli held out his hand. "A pleasure to meet you." They were starting over. "Elijah was my grandfather, and Solomon was my dad's name. My ancestral name is Mondschein. My great grandfather changed it to Moon years ago." He lopped off a piece of his chicken and dredged it through the lemon caper sauce.

"Mondschein? But it's a great name. Why change it?"

"Moon is a bit less conspicuous than Mondschein. Being a practicing Jew in this little town has its challenges." Lucy rolled the new information around in her brain like the soft bits of farro in her mouth.

"Like?" She waited while he finished his mouthful and stabbed another bite.

"Well, it was the twenties when he changed it, and the climate wasn't so friendly toward Jews. The climate has never been great, but then there's the stereotype—you know? The biggest business in town was owned by Jews. Truth is, we went to temple maybe twice in my lifetime. We acknowledged the holidays for the sake of tradition. I think it bothered my grandfather, but he didn't speak up about it. Early on, though—long before my time—that dining room was witness to some serious worship. The house served as the de-facto temple for the few local Jews, like Dr. Franzki. That all ended when my grandpa's brother, Ernie, moved east. Grandpa was never the Zionist his brother was." Eli already managed to eat a good portion of his meal, speaking between each mouthful.

"This salad is amazing! I have to tell Summer, she loves farro." Lucy finished another mouthful while Eli grinned at her. "What?" she said. He put his finger to the corner of his mouth, and she had to laugh at what had become their first inside joke. She wiped the smudge away with her napkin and continued. "I'm Catholic, but my sister and I basically walked away from the church when we left home. It crushed my father. He lives by the Catholic doctrine." Lucy recalled her first communion, confirmation, Ash Wednesday, and Lenten fasts. Church each Sunday was mandatory. It was all at his insistence. "Can't tell you how liberating it was to have Sundays to myself." She laughed.

"So, you didn't join the Jesuit club in college?" he joked.

"No interest, and no time. I was either working, in class, or studying. I had to make it work. It was a small school, and after the first year, they kick you out of the dorm. You either live at home or find a place. I found a little studio apartment—basically, a dorm room that cost twice as much and didn't come with a food plan. So, I worked three jobs in addition to the work-study position in the library I was immensely fortunate to get, to supplement some limited scholarship money and a grant."

"That sounds exhausting," said Eli.

"No kidding. Add classes to that, and you'll know why I was frazzled. You should have seen my calendar." Lucy laughed. "I finished in three years, though."

"Like a champion. Nobody deserved that degree more than you." Eli chuckled. "Now, here you are, all grown up with a business of your own. Your parents must be proud."

"Yes, of course. My dad has his own business too. Landscaping." Lucy decided to share one more layer of her story. "He's an immigrant. Slipped across the border from Mexico when he was seventeen."

"You are full of surprises."

"He has a green card now, and my mom is a US citizen. She went to a private catholic school in Monterey, and took the bus every day from her home in Salinas. Their love story began there." Lucy sipped her water. Thinking of her mother's account of the scrawny boy who smiled at her each day on his way to the nursery where he worked. "You will never meet a more passionate American than my father. But some think that just because he wasn't born here, he can't love this country. That is simply not true."

"This country can be challenging. I'm optimistic, though." Eli looked down at his empty plate.

"More challenging for some than others, Mr. Mondschein." Lucy lifted the last of her wine in a toast.

"Miss Perez." Eli tipped his glass to hers, and they polished off the wine.

"On a more pleasant note," she said, lifting her glass as if to make another toast, "Summer is at Thomas's tonight." She smiled sheepishly, and he gave her hand a squeeze.

"I thought he lived in Chicago."

"Nope, moved to Drake last week. Summer couldn't be happier."

"Did she mention she was in love?" Eli flashed his award-winning smile.

"Like, a hundred times." Lucy laughed at the memory along with the expression on Eli's face. "Don't order dessert, we'll have ice cream at my house."

"Is that what we're calling it now?" Eli grinned and placed his credit card on the table for their waitress. *Make that two inside jokes*, she thought.

"MONDSCHEIN." ELI POINTED up at the full moon rising like a halo over the Old Oak as they walked back to his car.

"So you said," replied Lucy looking up at the moonlit tree.

"It means *moonshine*."

"Sounds intoxicating." Lucy giggled at her little joke, feeling a little intoxicated herself.

It was a short drive to the house, and Lucy was happy to see that Summer had left the porch light on. But she was alarmed by the unlocked door. Summer should have known better.

"I need to get these contacts out—they're driving me nuts." He started up the stairs.

"I'll be up in a sec."

After a quick visit to the kitchen, she went up after him, holding two small bowls of strawberry ice cream. She found him sitting at her desk—his shirt unbuttoned, and his thick glasses perched on his nose.

CHAPTER SIXTEEN

BISCUIT'S RAPID-FIRE YAPPING WOKE LUCY EARLY THE NEXT MORNING, HE WAS riled about something. She gazed up at Eli, sitting on the side of the bed, staring at a spot on his shirt. The clock on her nightstand read 6:08.

"Have you been up long?"

"No, but I have to go. It's a workday, and I need to get Owen off to school." She read the apology in his voice. It was part of the package. She thought she had blown it the night before when he read her driver's license. *Don't you trust me?* He'd asked. She did, and was a step closer to telling him all about Ben Wyatt.

When he lay back down beside her—fully clothed but for his shoes—she rolled over, looked into his face, and removed his glasses.

"I wish I had the time," he laughed as she kissed his lips. She loved his mouth—the soft, full lips that smiled so readily and kissed so tenderly. "Lucy, I can't," he moaned, reaching for his glasses. "Really." Lucy watched as he replaced his glasses and returned to his sitting position. Eli picked up his shoes by the desk, where two bowls of melted ice cream sat untouched. Then he bent to kiss her goodbye and walked out of the room, the door squeaking as he pulled it closed.

She lay there in bed, listening to the *crick-crack* of the floorboards in the hallway, the groan of the front door, and the turn of the engine from his father's BMW. Moments later, she was fast asleep.

AN HOUR LATER, the weekly paper landed on the porch with a *ka-thunk*, pulling Lucy from her warm bed. She padded down the stairs dressed in a T-shirt and baggy jeans to fetch it off the mat.

She peeled it open on the spot and scoured it, heart pounding, for anything about her school or the people who operated it. Tina Reynolds' byline was only accompanied by a play-by-play of Tuesday's city council meeting, and the aftermath. The mayor had since formed an independent budget committee, which did not go over well. Three members would occupy the seats of this new committee, which was designed to affirm the mayor's passion for cutting out what he called *waste* from the city budget.

The photos in the article showed two faces that Lucy had come to know well in recent weeks: Lamar and Harlan Hill. The third committee member was identified as Eddie Baxter—whoever that was. One photo showed the mayor shaking hands with Harlan Hill in front of the city hall, as his woolly-faced brother stood a step behind him.

The article read, "Roy Bird, who has sat on the council for the last twelve years, resigned in protest upon hearing the announcement, and Alex Bridges had also threatened to exit, leaving two positions open. The mayor was delighted with the pending resignations and stated he is looking forward to filling the positions as he pleases until a special election can be held."

Although Lucy was relieved that her name did not appear in the *Drake Register* this week, she was wary for whatever surprises were yet to come—fearing that she would never again be free from the paranoia of being found out. It was bad enough that Eli knew her full name, though he posed no threat. Mrs. "Fancy Pants" Lancaster and Tina Reynolds were different.

For a while, Lucy entertained the idea of just going to Tina and telling her what was at stake. Throwing her mess out there and meeting the consequences. *Such consequences.*

The screen door snapped shut. Summer was home. Lucy set the paper down on the kitchen counter and poured her coffee. Then she got herself ready for a busy day with students.

THAT EVENING, OWEN let himself into the Chrysanthemum House, skipped back to the kitchen, climbed onto the counter, and lifted the stash of graham crackers from behind the year-old Betty Crocker cake mix neither Summer nor Lucy had admitted to buying.

She was surprised to see him, and more alarmed when Eli snuck up behind her with a firm embrace.

"Hey there! Didn't think I'd see you so soon," Lucy said, whirling around to face him.

"Wild horses, and all that," he grinned. "Hope I didn't scare you. Owen was ahead of me at the door, and..."

"We brought you dinner!" Owen proudly announced with a graham cracker in each hand.

Eli stepped out onto the front porch and came back in with a bag of groceries. "Tacos. Hope that's all right."

Lucy handed Owen a copy of *Magic Tree House*, and sent him on his way to find a quiet place to read—knowing he was not quite ready for the small chapter book, so it would occupy him to distraction.

While Eli unpacked the groceries, Summer and Thomas sailed into the kitchen, holding hands and giggling.

"What do we have here?" Summer asked, laying two cold six-packs beside the sink.

"Tacos. Plenty to go around."

Thomas threw a bag of chips on the counter, and the doorbell rang. Beth did not wait to be invited in.

"Did you all see the paper today? We have serious work to do!" She tossed two footlongs from SamSams on the counter beside the chips.

Eli's phone rang. "Hey, small detour. We're at Lucy's. Beth, Summer, and Thomas are here too—wait, I'll ask."

"Lucy, is it all right if Kali and Mia swing by?"

"Kali?" asked Lucy.

"And Mia," he laughed.

"The more, the merrier."

"The more, the merrier, she says. Grab something at Gardner's. Salad or something," Eli said, pulling Lucy close. Lucy thought of the moment they had after he told her about his parents; the emotion, the embrace, the sound of his voice, and his scent. She nuzzled into him and inhaled the mingled aromas of cinnamon and cloves.

"Owen is having a sleepover for his end-of-the-school year party this weekend."

"That sounds like a blast," Lucy answered. "I love sleepovers."

"He thinks you should come." This was not what she expected. She raised her eyebrows and tilted her head. Eli leaned in and whispered into her ear, "It's a start. We'll figure out the details later."

Eli mentioned the night before that he'd wanted her to stay over, but was worried about Owen, who was accustomed to having his father to himself. He'd said that Kali thought it would confuse Owen's young mind.

Lucy brought a bottle of sparkling water to Owen, who took a swig and handed it back, tucking his nose back into the book.

Kali and Mia arrived with a stack of deli containers, saying they couldn't make up their minds. Potato salad, bean salad, broccoli salad, and something called *superfood* that looked questionable. Kali was all smiles. That's how it was when she and Mia were together.

Someone had opened a window, and an evening breeze flowed through the house from the screen door. Lucy felt grateful for the fresh air but more grateful for her small collection of friends who had multiplied significantly since knowing Eli.

The group gathered at the dining-room table, demoting Her Highness to the bookshelf. Beth made sure everyone had gotten enough to eat and a few beers in their bellies before launching into the state of city affairs, and proposing they formulate a plan of action. It was only the beginning of something more organized.

"At least one of us should attend the city council meetings," declared Beth, standing tall at the end of the table. "Ignorance is not an option."

"Agreed," said Kali. "We should speak with Roy Bird and that other guy."

"Alex Bridges," offered Beth.

"We should talk to Roy and Alex Bridges, to find out any inside scoop about the plans for the budget. They may be on the outs now, but they've heard things."

Summer stood tall and raised her hand to speak. "Who wants to bet the budget cuts will just result in padding the mayor's pockets?" Many laughed. "That's not really a joke."

"I think we should plan a rally of our own," Lucy called out from the kitchen. She sat back down at the table with a second helping. "A peaceful rally to show the mayor that Drake citizens do care about the programs. We need to push back."

"I'll second that," said Beth. "You should see my mailing list!"

"Push Back for Justice!" hollered Summer. "I like it."

"PBJ?" said Thomas, who up to this point had been silent.

Summer laughed. "Let's just leave it at Push Back. Drop the J." She smiled at Thomas and kissed him on the cheek.

"Is anyone paying attention to these AVID folks?" Eli snitched a corn chip from Lucy's plate. "I mean, who *are* these guys?"

"No one I know," said Beth.

"Me neither," added Kali.

"Well, the Hill brothers have got to be part of that tribe. And I wouldn't count out the mayor." Lucy knew Eli was speaking from the few encounters they'd had recently. "Remember the bugs in the social service office?"

"How about the police chief?" she asked. The group bandied that possibility around the table, and Lucy's agitation grew at the difficult circumstances they'd been placed in. Were all city governments this corrupt? Did every mayor milk the city coffers with cover from the chief of police and city council? Lucy didn't want to believe it.

To relieve some of her distress, she left the table and joined Owen, who scooted over and made room for her in the beanbag chair.

"What's this word?" he asked as the hum of conversation continued in the background.

"Prob-lem-at-ic," she said, breaking it down into syllables. "It means difficult—something that makes life challenging. Like not knowing how to read." She looked down into his determined face.

"I can read." He proved his point as Lucy listened, waiting patiently through the long pauses and clumsy pronunciations. She was filled with pride at his progress.

She felt Eli's presence behind her and looked up into his eyes. *Problematic:* devising a plan to outwit an organization that feeds on hate, creating a future while coping with the past, or falling in love when you're most vulnerable.

Eli knelt in front of them, his knees grazing the beanbag. If he could have, she thought, he would have climbed in with them.

"We have to say goodnight, Little Bird," he said, his voice soft and caring. "Go put your book away and wait for me at the door."

Owen closed his book and slid from his seat without dissent, while Eli took his place. It was snug. They were exceedingly close as Eli took Lucy's hand and kissed her open palm. She had fallen in love and didn't own a parachute. Problematic.

CHAPTER SEVENTEEN

THE NIGHT BEFORE ELI ARRIVED AT HIS OFFICE TO INSTALL THE NEW SECURITY system, DK Nails, the nail salon beside Eli's office had been broken into. Whoever had done it had trashed the place, but taken nothing. Instead, they left behind a wall painted with racist epithets referring to yellow skin and slanted eyes.

Lucy and Beth comforted the women and helped them report the incident to the police while Eli and Thomas unpacked and read up on how to install the cameras. Eli was torn between his contempt for the vandals and his excitement about the new equipment when Lucy and Beth returned from the salon to give him a hand.

"How did that go?" asked Eli.

"They're pretty shook up. The police acted as if this happens all the time," said Lucy.

"Does it?" asked Thomas.

"No!" answered Lucy, Beth, and Eli in unison.

"Is Chicago any different?" asked Lucy.

"I'm no expert, but Chicago has its share of discrimination. It's different though, I think, than what's going on here." Thomas scratched his head and picked up the first security camera. "Eli, let's get this mess together, shall we?"

Eli was giddy as a little boy with the latest video game, as he unpacked his new security system. Lucy and Beth, after marking the prime locations for the cameras, sat back to watch Eli and Thomas mount them in place.

But as excited as Eli was to install the cameras, it was nothing compared to the joy he felt after installing the app on his phone. He and Beth played around with their new toy for a while before they were comfortable with the app and satisfied with the set-up.

There were three cameras, one from Eli's office targeted toward the waiting area, one from Beth's office targeted toward the rear, and one above the door targeting the entry and sidewalk outside.

The next morning, while Eli and Lucy made their rounds at the farmers' market with Owen in tow, Eli excitedly showed Lucy his phone. "Just got the first ping on the app. Check this out." Lucy looked down at an image of the tops of two heads and laughed. Then Eli scrolled to live footage of Dum Beard gawking at the camera placed above the door.

Lucy reluctantly set down the jar of fresh honey she was about to purchase, and they stepped out of line to where they could see the Tweedles waddling from the social service office, and toward the corner coffee shop.

"Now what?" she asked. Eli looked down at Owen. She could tell he wanted to follow them, but Eli wasn't about to involve his son.

Lucy took Owen's hand. "Let's go get that honey." They stepped back in line as Eli dashed across the street.

As an added distraction, Lucy allowed Owen to select a half-dozen honey sticks. He plucked them out of the display one by one, considering each choice.

They joined Summer, who had already spread out in front of the bandstand and was waiting for them as the Gin Jam Jug Band set up for the weekly concert.

Lucy pulled a thin blanket from her tote bag and handed it to Owen, who by now had finished the first of his honey sticks. He took great care to straighten each corner of the blanket with his sticky fingers.

Eli reappeared with Thomas, who had been in the coffee shop when the Hill brothers walked in. Eli gave his son a big hug.

"What's this?" he asked, turning Owen's hands over.

"Honey!" Owen reached into his back pocket and produced the remaining five sticks. "Lucy let me have them."

"Isn't that sweet," Eli said as Lucy pulled a wet wipe from her tote bag and handed it to Owen. Eli sat down with Thomas and Summer and invited Lucy to sit.

"So, what happened?"

"I was already there when the slobs walked in," said Thomas sitting down beside Summer. "Caught a little of what they said before Eli showed up."

"Well?" urged Summer.

"They were grumbling about Eli's surveillance camera. Said, 'He's not going to be too thrilled,' or something."

"Is it enough?" Lucy scooted over to make room for Owen.

"Probably not. Catching rats takes time and patience." Eli snitched one of Owen's honey sticks. "We need a trap."

"I don't think they make rat traps big enough," said Summer. She laughed and took Thomas's hand as the first notes played from the stage. "Let's dance!"

CHAPTER EIGHTEEN

THE NEXT MORNING, THE CLATTER OF FOOTFALL ON THE FRONT STEPS ALERTED Lucy to her guests' arrival. She folded up the newspaper she'd been reading and anchored it with Her Highness as Eli and Owen let themselves in.

"Hey guys!" she said excitedly, rising from her chair. She'd been expecting them. It was a gusty afternoon, and they were going to walk back to the high school so Eli could try out the kite he'd ordered online. Eli stepped up to her for a quick kiss.

"Are you ready?" asked Owen rising up on his toes and rocking back to his heals.

"I just need a minute." Lucy dashed upstairs to grab her kite, then slipped into her Keds and they were off with Owen leading the way toward St. Michaels.

The closer they came to the football field, the more difficult it was to keep up with Owen, who only stopped long enough to retrieve his kite from Eli.

They had only just gotten their kites in the air when their fun was cut short by the loud rumble of thunder. Lucy reeled in her kite as the first drop of rain hit her head with a heavy splat. *Here it comes.*

The clouds overhead shifted to a strange shade of purple as the first drop became a deluge, and the drum of thunder grew closer.

They gathered their kites and splish-splashed across the field to take refuge beneath the announcer's box in the top row of the bleachers.

Owen perched on the edge of his seat until a crack of lightning unleashed a deafening *boom* of thunder over the stadium. He clung to his father as all three pressed against the wall. Anything they wanted to say had to be shouted over the assault of lightning and thunder on all sides.

It was a half-hour before the storm gave way, leaving just a light pattering of rain in its wake.

"Let's head back," Eli said.

Lucy looked up, considering leaving the shelter of the announcer's booth overhead, somewhat reluctant to leave it behind. She nodded and collected her kite. The storm had passed, and the residual rain was warm.

West coast gales didn't seem to carry the same hit and run assault as the midwestern summer storms with threats of tornados and flood. As children, Lucy and her sister would hunker down for a day, maybe two, waiting it out until the winds shifted or the clouds parted, and life returned to normal.

Eli climbed down the aluminum bleachers with Owen and Lucy not far behind.

"Dad!" Owen pointed up to the announcer's box from the foot of the stands, eyes wide and worried, and tugged on his father's damp shirt. "There's a man in there." Lucy and Eli looked up but saw no one.

"He was watching us."

"I'll bet he's nice and dry," Eli said, ruffling Owen's damp curls. "Let's get you back, Little Bird. We all need to get dried off."

Lucy stepped down out of the bleachers, turned and looked back up toward the announcer's booth. *It couldn't be.*

Owen pulled his kite closer to his body, following closely behind his father. Lucy caught up to them and laid a sympathetic hand on Owen's shoulder, wondering about the man watching them.

When they got to Lucy's house, Eli immediately put Owen into a warm shower. He emerged from the bathroom, his hair still damp from the rain, with a ball of wet clothes for the dryer and a towel wrapped snug around his waist. Lucy stood, waiting outside her bedroom door in a striped T-shirt and denim skirt. She took the damp bundle from his hand with a playful tug at his towel.

"Oh no—no ice cream for you, madam," joked Eli. Lucy laughed at the reference with a more vigorous tug before she marched off to the dryer in the basement.

OWEN AMUSED HIMSELF by untangling the kites, wearing one of Lucy's T-shirts, as they waited for their clothes to dry. He looked up as Summer walked into the house with eyebrows raised at Eli's towel. Her long red hair was as much of a wet, tangled mess as the kite strings.

"What have we here? Am I interrupting again?" She grinned.

"We were flying kites," said Owen.

"Is that so?" Summer kneeled on the floor beside Owen to help with the kites, when the dryer buzzer sounded from the basement, and Lucy fled downstairs to retrieve the clothes. "Party over so soon?" she giggled.

CHAPTER NINETEEN

JUNE WAS COMING TO A CLOSE, AND SUMMER BREAK WAS WITHIN GRASP. THE students were restless—aware that conventional schools had been excused weeks ago. But as much as these kids yearned for their carefree summer days, it was nothing compared to how Lucy and Summer felt.

Lucy was about to wrap up the final unit at table three with instructions to open their workbooks to the vocabulary quiz, when she heard something hit the porch with a clatter. She took a step in that direction just as the picture window shattered and the front door was blown off its hinges.

"Out, everyone!" Summer yelled, tugging open the old door to the garden as the reek of sulfur wafted through the classroom. The doors were barely closed behind them when they heard the muffled blast of a second explosive—this time detonated inside the house.

Lucy imagined a war zone, with armed troops about to descend upon the school. But her own terror was secondary to the welfare of the students, as they crouched, shocked and confused, in the far corner of the side-yard. Somehow, she managed to stop her hands from trembling enough to call 911.

THE CHRYSANTHEMUM HOUSE was crawling with first responders by the time Eli arrived.

Lucy felt disconnected from reality as she studied the responders from the top of the stairs, like a child fascinated by an anthill. In and out, they traveled, murmuring to the students, calling to one another, collecting debris, or offering a hand.

Slowly she descended, and from her vantage point at the foot of the stairs, she saw Tina Reynolds emerge from the kitchen just as Eli was passing.

"Elijah Moon, you show up in the strangest places," Tina said.

"What? Oh—uh, have you seen Lucy?"

Lucy watched as Tina's fingers brushed along the length of his arm. "She was here just a minute ago."

Summer emerged from the kitchen and glared at Eli. Lucy was thankful for her friend's good timing.

"Where's Lucy?" he asked Summer.

"Right there." Summer pointed over his shoulder and moved on, with Tina in pursuit. "Could I ask you a few questions?" the reporter asked, but Summer only looked back with disgust before hurrying out the busted front door to the sea of first responders and frantic parents.

Eli led Lucy up to her room and closed the door, then sat on the edge of the bed beside her with a compassionate sigh. "I feel numb," she murmured. Eli's arm reached across her shoulder, as she added, "It's like I'm not even here." The odd sensation of detachment was familiar, and she was thankful for the mysterious biochemistry responsible for preserving her sanity.

"I know, I know." The resonance of his voice calmed. "You're in shock."

"Keep talking."

"I remember sitting outside Eva's hospital room when my grandpa stepped off the elevator. I looked at his face and thought *this is what devastation looks like.* I remember his struggle to find his voice. When he did, it was like someone had picked up a hatchet and started chopping off one limb after another. My mind filled with a dense, black fog of pain and confusion. They were gone— dead. I would never see my parents again. That anguish still sneaks up on me, slaps me across the face and knocks me cold with— what? Reality? Truth? For that moment, I am confronted by both. Awake, asleep—it doesn't matter. That slap breaks my heart. I struggle to break free from the sting. The pain overtakes me, and I can't breathe."

Eli pulled Lucy closer.

"He left it to me to tell Kali. I don't know where I got the strength, but I told her what had happened. It was like I was someone else, repeating his words, dismembered and blind."

Lucy squeezed his hand and leaned into him. He understood trauma, the aftershocks which follow, and the determination to forge ahead.

Eli led her downstairs, and she stopped cold at the sight of the classroom, an unrecognizable disaster. They stared transfixed at the scene beyond the broken window of the swing, which dangled with one end resting on its side like a fallen soldier. A broom, left behind by a well-intentioned parent, leaned against the collapsed railing beside a mound of glass shards and splinters. The parents and students were gathered in the street among fire trucks and police cruisers.

"I need to go out there. The parents are waiting to talk to me." Lucy stepped through the mangled door to see Summer flitting from child to parent like a butterfly unable to land. She stood at the top of the porch steps and clapped twice. The students looked up, recognizing the signal for attention.

"Let's take a minute to thank the Drake fire department for their quick response." They turned to the heavily clad firefighters and uniformed EMTs lingering beside their trucks. The EMTs took a playful bow, as Lucy checked a text message on her phone. Then she looked back into the expectant faces in the yard.

"We all feel a little—shaky. It's perfectly natural. The free clinic is offering to counsel anyone interested. Just mention the Chrysanthemum House when you schedule your appointment. We are a family here at the Chrysanthemum House, and we can count on each other for support." Lucy looked at Eli, who hadn't budged from her side.

"Parents, you have questions. We should have some answers for you in the next few days—but every effort will be taken to clean up this mess and be back to business as usual for the next term.

Students, grades will be online in two weeks, and registration will open on the first of August. The high school transition is Monday morning at nine. We'll meet at Drake High this year." The students looked at Lucy, waiting for more. "Enjoy your summer break." It was remarkable how that last statement changed the atmosphere, erasing the collective fear and anxiety. Even Summer and Lucy felt some degree of relief.

The police were the first to leave, having only interviewed Summer and a few of the students, promising to return. Lucy and Eli watched as the last firetruck rolled off, followed by the EMTs. One by one, as the students and parents disbanded, Lucy found it a little easier to breathe.

"I've got some plywood back at my house to patch up," Lance Kirsch said, frowning at her as if this was her fault. "It'll take me a while to get it." He scratched his beard and looked over her shoulder at the mess. "I'll tack it up tonight, but you're on the hook for the rest. Hope you have renter's insurance." Lucy wanted to slap him. He acted like she had thrown that bomb herself. Instead, she nodded as he turned to leave. Up to this point, Lucy had always believed her landlord was on her side.

"He's an ass." Summer leered after him in disgust. He never used to be like that, thought Lucy. He and his wife had always been supportive of their school.

"I just don't understand it." Lucy stood beside Summer on the sidewalk and gazed up at the disaster. Eli tucked the loose strands of her hair behind her ear, then wrapped his arms around her. She closed her eyes and succumbed to the security of his embrace.

The feeling was just coming back into Lucy's body with a new resolve, when Tina Reynolds emerged from the wreckage.

"Hello, Lucy—or should I say, *Lucia?*"

Lucy stared up at Tina. "So, you know my name. Good for you."

"I know more than you realize—but I could always know more. It's my business."

Summer stomped up the porch stairs toward Tina, as Eli took Lucy's hand. "I'm just trying to get the facts before going to print,"

Tina said, adjusting her shirt. "If you want me to write a story with the facts, you'll help me out, okay?"

"Tina, she's just been through hell, can you back off?" Eli stepped in front of Lucy, but she skirted his protection, moving aside so she could confront Tina on her own. She fastened her armor and led the reporter away from the steps. Tina's tall, lean frame towered over Lucy as they faced one another under the magnolia.

"Just want to set the record straight, honey." Lucy saw through the tough-girl charade, which was likely for Eli's benefit. Since Eli was now out of earshot, Tina dropped the act.

She explained that she heard from Mrs. Lancaster, aka Mrs. Fancy Pants, that the business license listed Lucia Perez, which was the original red flag, and that her Mexican father was illegal.

"My father is not illegal." Lucy huffed in exasperation.

"Of course, I didn't just take her word for it," Tina said, rolling her eyes. "There is a journalistic code, after all." Lucy shook her head in disbelief. A journalistic code from one accustomed to covering high school sports and city council meetings. "It's why I suspect the house was targeted," said Tina.

"AVID? Do you think Mrs. Lancaster is part of the organization?" asked Lucy. She thought about the strange vibe Mrs. Fancy Pants gave off when they'd met. The way she treated Lucy with a superiority beyond social/economic status.

"She could be."

"She stopped by with an offer to invest in the school. I turned her down." Was the offer a ruse? Lucy wondered. An excuse to get in the door, or shut down the business Lucy had worked so hard to build?

Lucy could clearly imagine the smug expression on Mrs. Lancaster's face when she believed she was handing over a defamatory scoop. This situation was precisely what Lucy had feared. That, and the possibility that Ben Wyatt would find her, using the news story as a roadmap. Now, with the Chrysanthemum House under a microscope for the bombing, Lucy feared she had no hope of anonymity.

"I'll try to find out if Mrs. Lancaster is part of the AVID movement. Would there be any other reason to target the school—or you?" asked Tina expectantly, waiting for Lucy to say something.

Lucy shook her head, not wanting to face the prospect she'd been sweeping under the rug since May. "Are you sure about that?" Lucy wondered what Tina was driving at. "I plugged Lucia Perez into an online database. It's easy. Anyone could do it," Tina said.

"Anyone?" *Not just nosey journalists?*

Tina nodded. "It's cheap, but I had to fork over some contact information, and now I'm being inundated with more spam than you could possibly imagine."

Lucy didn't care about Tina's spam. "What else did you learn?"

"You and your sister were born in California, and your mother was born in Oregon and now lives with your father in Monterey, California, where you grew up. Does that sound, right?" Lucy nodded. "Your dad's questionable history, including the fact that his green card is expired. Did you know that?" Lucy shook her head. She thought he was a citizen. "A litany of articles about your encounter with Ben Wyatt, and the trial that followed. Were you aware that Ben Wyatt was released from prison?"

"What?" Lucy gasped. "When? I did a Google search back in May and it didn't show up." Was this what Tina had been eluding to this whole time? Lucy's armor crumbled.

"Three months ago. April. I found it by searching his name in public records. You wouldn't have seen it on Google."

It was a jolt—a slap, as Eli had said earlier, that caught in her chest. Lucy dashed inside the house to the bathroom and closed the door behind her.

Minutes later, Summer found Lucy on her knees before the toilet, struggling to keep the loose strands of hair from her face.

"Crap!" Lucy raised her head, and Summer handed her a cold, wet washcloth.

"You can do better than that," said Summer, tilting a glass of tap water toward her friend's lips. Lucy closed the toilet lid and sat down, wiping her chin. *Three months. Why didn't my lawyer say anything?*

"He's here, Summer. I can sense it."

"Lucy? Who's here?" Eli was hovering outside the door. She would need to tell him everything, and soon.

"No one, Eli," said Summer, eyes locked with Lucy.

"Tina took off. She's going to the police department to get more info." Eli waited. "She's going to call when she knows more." Lucy's heart ached.

"We'll be right there." Summer helped her friend up, and they looked at their reflections in the small mirror over the sink. "Are you feeling better?" Lucy nodded, and Summer pushed open the door, where Eli stood expectantly, his brows knitted more deeply than Lucy had ever seen them.

"Lucy, you're coming home with me. You're welcome too, Summer. Neither of you should be alone tonight."

"Thomas is headed over to help patch things up. He's very handy that way." Summer grinned. "I'll stay at his place." She handed Lucy the full glass. "Don't worry about the mess, Lucy, we'll deal with it. Our mighty landlord will be here in a bit. You two should go." Summer gave Lucy a hug. "I'll call you if I learn anything." Then she headed out to welcome a distressed Thomas into the disaster area.

LUCY SLIPPED INTO the passenger seat of the BMW and looked back at the house, wondering what lay ahead. The consequences of this attack not only affected her, but Summer, the school, the students, and Eli, who was visibly worried about her. She needed to pull herself together. She needed to wake up. But her mind was a jumble of disconnected thoughts and fears.

"Do you want to talk about it?" asked Eli.

"I don't know what to say. It's just too much to process."

"Are you all right with coming home with me? I didn't even ask."

"More than all right." *Where else would I go?* The steady hum of the idle engine had a calming effect, and she stopped him from putting it in gear. "Eli, Tina told me things. Things that ..." She swallowed painfully, her throat still sore from the earlier purge. "She said my father's green card had expired." Saying it aloud made the revelation that much more real. "All these years, I thought he was a citizen. I had no idea."

"What does that mean, exactly? Will he be deported?"

"I don't know. I've never had to consider it before." Eli nodded. She went on, "But that's not all. That man who assaulted me, he was in prison." Eli stared at her. "But Tina said he was released in April."

"So, the man at the farmers' market—that could have been him?" Eli rubbed the palms of his hands along the steering wheel with increasing friction as the full impact of this revelation hit its mark. "He's here, in Drake?"

Lucy looked into his worried gray eyes, reddened and tired. "The attacker knew me," she began. "Or he thought he knew me. It started months before the attack, the stalking." Eli listened intently. "He'd be on the bus with me, or outside my apartment, or waiting around for me to get out of class."

"A stalker? Did you tell anyone?"

"For reasons that I don't understand, I told no one except a friend who I stayed with for a while after I found out he lived in the next apartment. It was right around graduation, and I just had to put up with his—what—strangeness? Just a few more weeks, then I'd be out of there."

Lucy recalled that night vividly—one week before graduation, with final exams in full swing, she was scheduled to work until closing at the coffee shop. It wouldn't be late, but it would be dark. The notion that he could be waiting for her out front compelled her to leave through the back-alley door, with its twin set of foul-smelling dumpsters and a set of plastic chairs for the employees who still cared to smoke.

It had been a long day, week, month. She was tired, her feet hurt, and she wanted to get home without the anxiety of seeing that creep. She felt shrewd about outsmarting him as she locked the heavy steel back door. With that click, she began thinking about everything she needed to do before graduation like selling her books back to the University Book Store, and the importance of trying on the cap and gown which had arrived in the mail.

She turned from the door toward the pair of smelly dumpsters, and then looked ahead down the alley, where a light glowed brightly at the street.

"Hello there, Lucia Perez. Remember me?"

His face was obscured in the dimly lit alley. She noticed him open a pocketknife, then snap it closed. He had her full attention, staring at her with a focus she'd never seen. The blade popped open again. Terror struck her, and she started to run toward the street, but he quickly stepped in front of her, so she jumped to the side with her eyes trained on his hand, repeatedly opening and closing the pocketknife as he stepped closer to her. *Shook, snap, shook, snap.* Her heart pounded with fear.

She would have to move quickly, because he was getting uncomfortably close. She jogged to the left, then quickly shifted to the right, trying to outwit him. But he had anticipated her attempt to escape and caught her arm. He hissed with hatred and drew close to her face as she fought to free herself.

His stench rivaled the sour reek of the dumpsters. "My name, Lucia. You know it. Say it."

She just shook her head as tears spilled from her eyes and made one more attempt to pull her arm from his grasp. His grip tightened as he dragged her around and forced her against the first dumpster, pressing his body up against her back, her face flattened to the cold steel.

She was trapped and terrified. "Leave me alone!" She had tried to scream the words, but they were muffled by the dumpster.

"Hush!" His sweaty hand pushed Lucy's face harder against the cold surface, and she struggled for breath as his free hand wrestled with his belt, followed by a whip as he pulled it off and threw it to the ground. He tugged at her pants and unfastened the button. *NO!*

She squirmed as his fingers undid her zipper and he thrust his hand down the front of her jeans, grinding himself against her. Lucy's muffled cries fell on deaf ears while he groaned in triumph.

Where was the knife? He was distracted, and she took advantage. She pulled his hand, and he tightened his hold.

"Fucking Mexican whore!" She had no idea where the strength came from, but she pushed him back until he hit the closed door with a gasp. Simultaneously, she felt the cold blade rip into her lower back, the force of it slashing angrily through her flesh.

Her senses were acute. She could hear, feel, and smell his rancid breath on her neck, and was aware she was about to throw up.

"Serves you right," he whispered into her ear. "You're a tease, a fraud. You thought you'd fooled me. You didn't."

"Hey!" called a stranger's voice from further down the alley. Wyatt pushed her away and she dropped to the ground, hearing nothing but his footsteps as he fled. She turned her head toward the streetlight at the end of the alley and passed out.

He had punctured her kidney—coming short of the renal artery, which would have killed her in seconds. She was lucky the stranger had been there and was quick to call 911.

Lucy spent weeks in the hospital after the surgeons stitched her up, Dr. Stewart taught her how to breathe, and the public legal counsel built their case. All the while, her sister, Julia sat vigil by her bed.

The string of doctors' appointments, therapy, and lawyer meetings dominated her life for months before the trial brought the whole incident front and center.

"ELI," LUCY SAID, looking over to him in the driver's seat, and trying to blot out how painful that period had been. "*I'm* the reason he was in prison. I always thought that when he was released, he'd come after me."

"The scar on your back, that was him?"

Lucy nodded.

"He stalked you, molested you, and nearly killed you. Why didn't you say anything sooner? Why am I just learning this?" He pushed his hair back unnecessarily.

"I don't know, Eli. I didn't want you to worry about me more than you do. I needed to put that behind me. It's why I'm here in Drake. I ran away. It's what I do."

Eli gripped her wrist, as if the small restraint could keep her in

Drake and in his life. She looked at him, her eyes brimming with tears from the incomprehensible situation in which she'd found herself. Her heart was heavy with self-blame, self-hatred, and frustration at not having control of the events or her emotions.

"If it is him ... if it is Ben Wyatt, then you could be in danger, too. You, Summer, Kali," she turned her head to look out her window at the carved flower above the door, thinking the worst, "and Owen."

"I won't let that happen," Eli said. He removed his hand from her wrist, and when she turned to him, he kissed her. "I won't." Lucy wiped the remaining tears from her eyes and smiled weakly, warmed by his reassurance, fearing it wasn't enough.

Eli reached for the stick, and Lucy felt the gears shift as the car pulled away from the curb.

Eli's phone rang and he answered it on speaker phone. "Hi, Tina—what's the word?"

"Police are corrupt as hell, that's the word. I can't get anything out of them. Can you believe this? What the hell?"

"Why would they pick the Chrysanthemum House?" asked Eli.

"I know why," said Lucy. "They learned my real name, didn't they?" Lucy thought back to the crushed mailbox.

"Looks that way. Peggy Lancaster has been on my case about you for weeks and wanted me to publish your lineage. I never really saw the point until now. But these radicals are freaking nuts."

"No shit," said Eli.

"Tina, how long have you noticed AVID in Drake?" asked Lucy, gears turning.

"I don't know, a few months ago. April, maybe?"

"About when you say Ben Wyatt was released from prison?" Lucy looked at Eli and saw that he understood what she was getting at.

"Yes," said Tina, "about then. You think Wyatt is part of AVID?"

"It's possible. Either that, or a strange coincidence," said Lucy.

"It sounds like a great story. I'll look into it."

"It's more than a story, Tina." Eli glared at the phone as if Tina could see his expression. "It's Lucy's life."

CHAPTER TWENTY

WHEN THEY FINALLY ARRIVED AT ELI'S HOUSE, OWEN WAS ON HYPERDRIVE, wanting to know all about the explosion. How big it was. How loud it was. If it had broken the swing. All things that were important to him. He was too innocent to realize what a terror the day had been, and the possible implications, but Lucy did what she could to placate him. It was oddly therapeutic, breaking the incident down into a child-sized frame.

Lucy was thankful that Kali had the foresight to plug a frozen lasagna into the oven. The kitchen and great room were filled with the comforting aroma of bubbling cheese, tomato sauce, and spicy sausage, which made her acutely aware of her hunger. What was it about a trauma that kills an appetite? If they could put it in a bottle, someone could make a fortune.

To keep Owen busy, Kali sent him to set the table in the dining room—but he wouldn't go without Lucy, who followed along obediently. On her initial tour of the house, they had passed by this grand room, which was bursting with warmth and style.

A stained glass light fixture hung above the solid wood dining table, framed by multiple high-backed chairs on either side and an armchair on either end. An area rug of reds and greens mirrored the colors in the lights, and a large fireplace with stone chimney and hearth, topped with a mantle like that in the great room, filled much of one wall.

Owen reached into the built-in sideboard and pulled out four white linen placemats.

"Not those, Little Bird—your auntie will have a fit," said Eli when he entered the room. Owen was visibly disappointed. Apparently, he was planning to get out the Spode china as well.

"But we never get to eat in here." It was the first time Lucy had heard Owen complain.

"We'll have to fix that, but tonight isn't that kind of dinner. It's more of a no-fuss dinner. Do you understand?"

Eli found a set of four woven placements, more appropriate for everyday use, and Owen pointed Lucy to the silverware drawer while he squatted down for the plates in the bottom drawer of the sideboard. Apparently, he'd understood.

"It's been years since we actually had a meal in here." Eli dragged a finger through the tabletop's layer of dust.

"Eli!" Kali scolded, just as he'd lifted his finger. She held a damp rag in one hand.

"Sorry—I didn't mean to upset you, Kal, but it's just how it is. This room gets ignored." Eli turned to Lucy and whispered, "Much to Owen's disappointment. He would eat in here every night if we let him." Owen overheard, and his broad smile served as confirmation.

"The napkins are top right, Lucy." Kali nodded at the sideboard as Lucy was busy placing the silverware. Then Kali disappeared for a minute or so—returning with the lasagna, which was promptly served. The aroma whetted Lucy's appetite—the sight of it practically had her drooling.

The four of them sat at one end of the table—Owen with Eli, Lucy with Kali. A bagged salad dumped unceremoniously into a wooden bowl divided them. Hungry as she was, Lucy's stomach clenched when she lifted a cheesy forkful of lasagna to her mouth.

Kali nudged her gently with her elbow—encouraging her to eat, but not making a big show of it.

"Eli—do you remember when Old Uncle Ernie was visiting, and he threatened to paddle you because you sat on his new wool hat and crushed it?" Lucy appreciated Kali's attempt at normal conversation. It was a shame, though, that all her childhood stories always involved Eli getting into trouble.

"I hid out in the basement," Eli said, "and no one could find me. I finally got so hungry I had to sneak back upstairs to steal something to eat. I got caught in the kitchen with a fat dinner roll in my fist."

"They went nuts, remember?"

"I got that paddling—then another from dad for disappearing."

"There were welts on his butt, Lucy. I kid you not. I actually saw them."

Owen watched the conversation like a tennis match, his eyes pivoting from one to the other. Lucy tuned it out. She was mulling over Tina's words, reliving the explosion, and trying to come to terms with the fact that her father's green card had expired. All the while, her gut was telling her that the jean jacket, the rider on the Denali, and the man she'd seen on their way to the city council meeting were one and the same. *A quick and easy search,* Tina had said. *Anyone could do it, for a price.*

IT WAS LATE by the time the table was cleared, and the dishes done and put away. Eli dried his hands on Owen's damp dish towel.

"Time for bed, Kiddo."

"Can Lucy put me to bed tonight?"

Lucy was exhausted, but the plea warmed her heart, and she hoped Eli would give his blessing. She needed Owen's sweet ignorance. She craved it.

Eli regarded her hopeful face and gave her a thumbs-up, so she escorted the little boy upstairs.

While Lucy waited for Owen to brush his teeth down the hall, she reached over and picked up the photo beside his bed. Eva, Eli's wife, had been everything Lucy was not. She was tall, fair, and blonde—with a spattering of freckles across the bridge of her nose, and a voluptuous figure.

The photo, Lucy noticed, was taken on the patio. The sky was blue, with snow stacked on the stone wall and flocked trees in the orchard beyond. Eva's white sweater and black leggings accentuated her figure, but the UGGS on her feet humanized her as she looked into the camera eagerly—almost daringly. She wondered if Eli had taken the photo.

Lucy was sickened by the pang of jealously she felt, but also sad that Eva had been robbed of knowing her son—her Little Bird. It was all so wrong.

Before this moment, Eva had just been a concept. The photo made her real. But that reality—a person who lived, laughed, and loved; a daughter, wife, and mother; a living breathing human being—had been extinguished by cancer so ruthless it resulted in Owen's premature birth, then quickly overtook her. She had been there—and then she wasn't.

Owen plopped on the bed with his borrowed copy of *The Wind in the Willows*, and she read her favorite passage at his insistence.

Lucy looked at Owen's face as he lost his grip on wakefulness and slipped into the peaceful world of Mr. Toad, Badger, and Ratty, which would doubtless color his dreams.

What would color hers? She dreaded sleep and the images that haunted her. She gazed at the picture of Eva once more before turning out the light and closing the door behind her.

ELI AND KALI were sitting on the sectional, chatting, when Lucy entered the great room and sat down in the club chair across from them.

"Am I interrupting?" she asked.

Eli waved it off with a dismissive hand and smiled at her. "No. Not interrupting. How did that go with Owen?"

Lucy was exhausted and yearned to go to bed and turn off the lights—but she returned the smile. "Great. The best half hour of my whole day."

"How are you holding up?" Kali pierced Lucy with her green-eyed stare.

"I'll be all right. I'm just tired." *What had Eli said while she was busy upstairs?*

Kali turned to Eli, "Remember when Mom and Dad died, and everyone kept telling us we were strong? Did you feel strong? I know I didn't. I thought it was just a bunch of shit—just more babble we were growing deaf to along with the other platitudes people throw around when someone has died, like, "so sorry for your loss." And, "everything happens for a reason." But now that the dust has settled and years have passed, I think about that, and you know, we were damn strong."

"I disagree," said Eli. "It wasn't strength. It was—I don't know ... necessity? Is that it? I mean, we were brain-dead, confused, and powerless. In fact, so much of that time is just a blur, lost in a haze of temporary madness." Lucy was startled by Eli's impassioned reply. "I hadn't even come to terms with their deaths yet, with Eva so sick and her parents hounding me for details, and Owen in an incubator. Think about that! Don't you remember? I didn't sleep for weeks. Thank God Grandpa was here. We were incompetent, ignorant, and distraught. That is not strong."

"It was replaced by strength in the end, and we got through it, right? Look at us now," said Kali. "We're okay. Yes, it's tough. In many respects, we're in over our heads, but look at Lucy."

Leave me out of this, thought Lucy. She tried to relate their grief to her situation. But all she felt at that moment—beneath her exhaustion, horror, and rage—was the determination to make it right. Was that strength? She needed sleep and a clear head.

"Lucy, I can't talk to you professionally, as much as I wish I could. But these issues need to be resolved for you to feel safe again. How do you feel about therapy?" asked Kali.

"You think everyone needs therapy," chided Eli.

"Everyone *does* need therapy. Me, you, Lucy—everyone."

"I'm all right," Lucy said. "Really." They looked at her skeptically, but she understood what Kali was driving at. Dr. Stewart had been a critical factor in Lucy's healing after the attack. Therapy works—but in the days immediately following Wyatt's attack, it was action that saved her, giving her a modicum of control. The lawyer provided by the state had met her in her hospital room, and she had found strength in the system.

"This is how I see it," said Lucy. "I plan to call my lawyer in the morning and get the real scoop on Ben Wyatt. Also, I have a Skype call with my parents tomorrow, and I'll bring up my father's citizenship then." She sighed. "As for the bomber, I'm going to wait to hear back from the police. I can't immediately assume that it was personal."

Lucy sat quietly, looking at her lap, surprised by her rising emotions, the tightness in her throat, and ringing in her ears. She recalled her announcement that afternoon to the students and their parents, playing the role. It wasn't strength Kali saw in Lucy, it was her armor, and that armor was failing her now.

Lucy picked up a throw pillow from the floor and hugged it in her lap. "I have it under control." Her voice cracked, and she began crying. She was too tired to pretend.

"Lucy," Eli said, going to her. He took her hand and drew her to the sofa, where Kali waited with arms outstretched. She heaved with emotion for the events of the day, the events of the past, the affection she received, and the affection she gave—for Eli, his sister, and his son. Fatigue played its part, she knew—but her feelings and tears were genuine.

Eli took her hand and led her upstairs, and she followed him down the hall toward his room, with her backpack slung over her shoulder. He pushed open the door to the bathroom as they passed.

"Go ahead, I'll use the one down there." He pointed to the other wing past the alcove.

She entered the large and comfortable bathroom, with its generous walk-in shower, partially submerged tub, and marble vanity set with twin sinks. The luxury was a stark contrast to what she was used to.

The water ran cold from the faucet as she brushed her teeth, warming enough to wash her face with the bar soap beside the sink. She didn't feel prepared to climb into bed with Eli. It wasn't that kind of night. She stared at her red-rimmed eyes in the gold-framed mirror and released her hair from its clip with an attempt at making herself presentable.

When she entered his room, illuminated by the light of a single bedside lamp, Eli was straightening the covers on the bed. She side-stepped a mound of clothes beside the door, piled there as if he had just kicked everything from the floor in that direction. The small sofa she'd seen the first time she'd been in the room had vanished beneath a mountain of unfolded laundry. A stack of newspapers fluttered before the wide-open windows of the window seat.

Lucy stood beside the bed, stripped down to her underwear, and slipped between the sheets, which smelled of him. The last thing she was conscious of was Eli's arm pulling her close, as they fell into a deep, exhausted sleep, with the warm night breeze flowing over them.

LUCY OPENED HER eyes early the next morning to a small child dressed in nothing but an old Drake High School T-shirt and Spiderman underpants, wedged between her and Eli. She jumped in alarm and scrambled for the bedsheets to cover up. The commotion woke Eli, who sat up with a start.

"What!" He gasped—then promptly noticed his son and murmured, "Sorry, sorry, sorry."

"I had a bad dream," Owen said to his father. Eli took his son in his arms. "I dreamed it was raining, and we were playing baseball, and Lucy was there." He gazed up into his father's face. "Then we were at Lucy's, but Lucy's house wasn't Lucy's house—it was in a tree, and that man was there. He said he was a friend, but he was really scary, and I thought he was going to push me out of the tree. Then I woke up."

"What man, Owen?" asked Eli.

"You know, that man—at the school."

Eli shook his head. "Sorry, Little Bird—I don't know."

"Yes, you do," insisted Owen. "When we were flying kites, that day it rained really hard, that man in the window. He's scary."

"I'm sure it's just a coincidence. But the next time you see him, you point him out, okay?"

"That's what I was trying to do."

Lucy sat quietly, her heart racing. "Have you seen this man often, Owen?"

"Sometimes."

"What did he look like?"

"He was ugly." Owen twisted up his face as if he were sucking on a lemon.

"Anything else? What color was his hair?"

"Black. And his face was white like this." Owen held up a corner of the bedsheet. "He looked like an evil wizard." Lucy looked at Eli with a sudden shock, then collected herself.

Owen," Eli said, his eyes wary, "you're safe. I'm always here, and so is your auntie, and so is Lucy. We won't let anything bad happen to you."

Lucy decided it was time to shut down the conversation. "Okay, guys—it's a beautiful day. Let's have some breakfast, and you can show me around the property." But even as she tried to move them along, her panic rose to the surface. After the bombing the previous day, she didn't believe in coincidences.

FOR THE SAKE of his son walking near them through the orchard, Eli kept his calm, but Lucy knew how he felt, the fear, rage, and confusion that accompanies a life threatened by Ben Wyatt and where that could potentially lead. If she were him, she'd break all ties with the damaged Californian who attracted such a danger to her family and the previously sleepy town of Drake. She'd cut her losses if she were him, but Lucy didn't believe Eli was that guy. He wouldn't make a decision like that, so she would have to do it.

She dreaded the notion of starting over in another town, carving out another life. She dreaded the potential loneliness and solitude of living off the grid, like a social outcast, or an unwelcome immigrant.

They came upon a field beyond the orchard filled with Queen Anne's lace and blue cornflowers. Eli plucked an early black-eyed Susan and tucked it behind his ear for a cheap laugh, which both Lucy and Owen provided. Then he removed it, tucking it into her hair instead.

They went along quietly for a time, Owen exploring some distance ahead of them, their twisted thoughts accompanied by the buzzing insects, the warm sun, and even the crows squawking overhead, while Eli and Lucy struggled with the notion of the man from Owen's dream.

"You sent him to prison."

"I did." She didn't want to think about it. She didn't want to acknowledge the weeks of preparing to testify and the emotional tax she'd paid sitting on the stand to put him behind bars. But this was part of the process of coming clean, and she would answer any of his questions, if it would help to get this behind her.

"He stood trial for attempted murder, assault with a deadly weapon, sexual assault, and attempted rape. They downgraded the predatory stalking to a misdemeanor, even though it qualified as a felony, because that's how California law rolls." Bitterness rose from her gut.

"Lucy, he's a madman." She nodded, and her heart ached for bringing this to his doorstep.

"He pleaded innocent to all charges, which would have added up to more than twenty years. He was only convicted of assault with a deadly weapon. A four-year sentence—the maximum." Lucy started walking again, trying to bridge the growing gap between them and Owen.

"The sexual assault," he began. "They didn't charge him?"

"His word against mine." Lucy's heart was fluttering with anxiety, remembering the trial and how her jeans, soiled with his semen, were deemed inadmissible for reasons beyond her understanding.

She lifted her eyes from the orchard floor and looked into his horrified face. "The jury couldn't deny the gash or the doctor's reports—but for some reason, they disregarded the greater violation. The one that left deeper scars than the arc on my back." She laid a gentle hand on his chest and took a moment to collect herself. Eli covered her hand with his and pulled her so close she could feel his heartbeat in the palm of her hand.

"This is going to sound stupid," Eli said softly into her ear.

"Please don't take it the wrong way, but I need to ask. Why you?" He took a small step back and watched for her reaction.

"Why me?" Lucy pulled her clip, combed her fingers through her hair, and brought it all together again, buying time while she refastened her clip. She looked away from him down the path toward Owen skipping along far ahead. "The police interviewed me for hours, asking me the same thing." She wiped a bead of sweat from the side of her face. "As if I had provoked him in some way." The police, her lawyer, the jury, her therapist, her parents, now Eli. She wanted to kick him.

"I didn't mean it like that—you must know." He reached for her and she stepped away. *Must I?* she thought. She walked ahead, putting some distance between them, and was thankful he'd given her the space. Once the noise died down in her head she turned around and faced him.

"He told the police he was in love with me—that all he'd wanted was for me to talk to him, to notice him." Lucy stood straight and strong in front of Eli; her fists clenched at her sides. "I did not encourage him, Eli."

"Lucy," Eli stepped toward her and she backed up. "I wasn't suggesting that."

"Listen, Eli, he was an odd, lonely guy with an obsession for a girl he believed was like him. But when he saw my full name under my employee photo at the coffee shop, it was like I'd deliberately tricked him. Like I'd intended to make a fool of him. He told the police he never meant to hurt me. He said it was an accident. Eli, I saw his face that night he assaulted me. He was out of his head with anger. He had every intention of punishing me."

"Because of your name," said Eli plainly, stepping forward. "Perez."

She'd been surrounded by Hernandez', Guzman's, Castro's, and Suarez', but she was the chosen one because her skin was a shade lighter, because a single gene led him to believe she was white, like him. He'd disregarded her dark hair, brown eyes, the set of her chin, and the high cheekbones inherited from a proud ancient culture.

"Yes—in a way, the attack was because of my name. And it's not just Ben Wyatt. Now it's the filth who call themselves AVID, and hundreds of groups like it." Lucy tried to keep her voice level and controlled, but her passion broke through. "I see how they look at me, Eli. It's that same deluded rage I saw in Wyatt's eyes. That blind hatred. Their banners that say 'Go Back.' I can't help that my dad is a Mexican immigrant. I didn't push him over the border when he was seventeen. I am just as much an American citizen as any of those creeps—maybe more, because I still believe this is a country for everyone."

"I see them too, Lucy. The xenophobic men who hate women, needy children, brown skin, and any sexual orientation other than what they believe is right. I've dealt with religious prejudice my whole life. You changed your name to Price. My grandfather changed his name to Moon. It didn't change anything. We are who we are. I know what hate looks like. I was brought up knowing what hate looks like. These guys from AVID are the worst of the worst. And Ben Wyatt deserves to be in prison."

They took a moment, standing still in the shade of the trees to collect their thoughts and their emotions. Lucy's racing heart slowed, and she reached for Eli's hand. He wove his fingers with hers and she rested her head on his shoulder. At this moment, they understood each other completely.

They caught up to Owen, who was sitting patiently on an old stump. His shoes were off, and he was gleefully wiggling his toes. Eli bent to get them back on, explaining that old farms have lots of sharp things to step on.

Stiff resistance from Owen led to a compromise, which was to put the shoes back on, but no socks. Owen relented and ran on ahead as Eli tucked the tail ends of the socks into his rear pocket.

"There used to be a barn here, years ago. Long before my time." Eli's voice lacked its usual pride and enthusiasm. Lucy wondered what was going on in his head. Was he processing the story? Was he concocting an exit plan? "That field over there was for horses and some cattle." He bent down and picked up a rusty bracket. "Stuff like this is everywhere—little bits of barn or machinery." Lucy thought of Kali's stories. There was bound to be one regarding tetanus.

They rounded the field and made slow, lazy progress back

through the orchard. Owen was climbing on some rocks outside a small stone building.

"This is the old pumphouse." Eli lifted the rusty latch and opened the door. It was just big enough for the three of them, and just tall enough for her to stand at full height—but not Eli. He stooped as he showed her the old mechanics of the pump, which took up more than half the space—explaining how it drew from a well dug nearly a hundred years ago. On the far wall, there was a short stack of shelves, with old tools and tins of rusted nuts and bolts.

Owen wrinkled his nose. "It stinks in here."

Eli tossed the rusted bracket into one of the tins before closing and latching the door behind him. They walked the rest of the way back to the house, with Owen skipping along ahead of them.

Eli held her hand. "How are you doing?"

"Still rattled. I hate thinking about it," she said. "I can still see his twisted face, hear the squeak of his voice, feel the blade ..." Lucy had to stop, and Eli pulled her close to him—his arms wrapped tight, her cheek pressed to his heart. "I wanted to tell you the story from the first day. I just—couldn't. Now I'm afraid he's coming after me—to punish me."

"You think Owen's guy is Ben Wyatt?" She heard Eli's voice resonate through his chest.

"I honestly don't know, Eli. Jesus, I hope not. But either way— if a man is spooking him, we need to find out who he is."

"He's spooking all of us." Eli was stating the obvious. She wanted to cry, scream, or hit something—so great was her guilt.

Benjamin Lee Wyatt. She shuddered just thinking of his name, remembering the trial—how the jury had stared at her, as if she had some blame of her own. Why would anyone bother with her unless she'd encouraged them?

When Owen said he saw "the man" sometimes, it thrust her back in time to the random sightings of this creep. Watching. Always watching.

Was he watching her now?

CHAPTER TWENTY-ONE

WHEN THEY'D RETURNED TO THE HOUSE, KALI WAS WAITING FOR THEM ON the patio with the French doors wide open behind her as she scooped Owen up in a robust hug. She set Owen down and he dashed through the open doors while she waited for Eli and Lucy. She had something on her mind, thought Lucy. What kind of caution or advice awaited her? Go home, she supposed. The very thing Lucy told herself—yet she couldn't take that first step. Where *was* home? The house in Monterey belonged to her parents, and the Chrysanthemum House belonged to her students. Where did she belong?

"You two all right?" asked Kali. Eli nodded, holding firm to Lucy's hand. "Eli?" Kali followed them into the house. "What's going on?" Eli looked at Lucy, eyebrows raised, asking what to do next.

"Owen had a bad dream last night," said Eli. He left it at that.

Owen pulled out a jigsaw puzzle, and spread it across the coffee table. Lucy helped for a while, letting the tonic of Owen's company fortify her for whatever might come next.

Her phone had been ringing and buzzing with well-wishes from students and parents. "We love you, Teacher Lucy." "Hang in there, Lucy, we've got your back." "You're the best." "Call me if you need to talk." She appreciated Mrs. Gates' offer, but she knew who would be doing the talking in that case. The thought brought a fleeting smile to her face—and for a moment, she felt hopeful.

Lucy sent out a group email to the families letting them know that the investigation was underway. *She hoped*. And repairs to the school were pending. She thanked them for their well-wishes and promised to keep them up to date with future developments.

Finally, Lucy went up to Eli's room, to Skype with her parents. She invited Eli for the first few minutes, to introduce him.

They sat shoulder to shoulder in the window seat, with her laptop turned away from the unmade bed and general untidiness—which lingered despite Eli's small attempt at cleaning up.

It took a minute or so for Lucy's parents to get situated, shoulder to shoulder, at their kitchen table. Lucy's heart soared to see them, and she made a mental note to Skype more often.

"Hey there!" she said excitedly.

"Hey, hello," said her mother. Elaine, Lucy mother, wore her hair pulled back, like Lucy, and had Lucy's lighter skin, but otherwise they looked nothing alike. "Oh, sweetheart it's wonderful to see you," she sighed.

Javier, Lucy's father, pointed at the screen as if to touch her. "Ah, we've missed you, Kitten." He broke into a smile that stretched from ear to ear. His exuberant nature was more than Skype could capture. Lucy wished Eli would get a chance to meet her father and get the full impact of his personality.

"Kitten?" said Eli turning to Lucy, who gave him a playful push.

"Mom, dad, this is Eli, my," she grinned, "my boyfriend." Lucy loved saying that and relished her parent's delighted reaction.

"So, there he is!" said Javier. "So good to meet you, Eli." Lucy had mentioned Eli briefly in a phone call several days earlier, before the madness, before her world had been turned upside down with Tina's revelation that Wyatt was on the loose.

"Likewise, Javier. A pleasure to meet you too." Eli leaned into Lucy, grinning. She longed to know what he was thinking.

They visited like this for a short while, comparing weather, discussing Javier's landscape business and a mole he'd had discovered on his chest. Eli asked to see the mole, and Javier was more than happy to unfasten the top two buttons of his cotton shirt and spread it open. The mole was impressive, but Lucy cringed at her father's forthcoming nature. Did he ever say no? True, he was pleased by Eli's curiosity, and his antics, such as showing off his muscular chest, always made her mother laugh.

Owen slipped into the room through the secret passage in the closet, and tapped on his father's arm, peaking at the two new faces on the computer. He often spoke with Eva's parents this way.

"Who do we have here?" asked Elaine.

"Owen Alexander Moon," said Owen proudly. He looked over at Eli and smiled.

"Owen, these are my parents, Javier," Lucy pointed to her father, "and Elaine. They live in California." She'd shown Owen where California was on the map posted in the classroom back at the Chrysanthemum House.

"Such a good-looking young man," said Javier, beaming. "Like your father."

Lucy studied her parents on the monitor and noted their intimate body language and animated facial expressions as they gushed over Owen. They were one person.

Eli took Owen from the room to give Lucy some privacy with her parents. Explaining what happened at the school was going to be difficult, and she appreciated his sensitivity.

Eli made an excellent impression. Lucy knew he would, and long after he had left the room, they were still talking about him.

She neglected to mention that she was staying at Eli's primarily because she wasn't sure how long she would be there, but also because she was sensitive to their old fashion Catholic values. Of course, from her parent's perspective, after seeing Eli and her together and meeting Owen, Eli and Lucy were as good as engaged. The fact that he was a widower and single parent, struggling to make a living from a notoriously low-paying job, and living in an unconventional family, was, in their opinion, no obstacle at all to love. Perhaps not—but Lucy had a greater obstacle.

"Just think of the hurdles your father and I had to jump through before we could get married," said her mother. "Now, that was not an easy thing." That was Lucy's segue into the subject of immigration.

The topic was immediately brushed off, but she persisted. She described the right-wing extremist movement that was growing in town, and her belief that this group unjustly targeted her because of an unfounded innuendo regarding her father's immigration status.

She described, in detail, the events from the previous day, and watched their pleasant expressions shift into looks of concern and unease.

Up to that point, her parents believed that the attack on the Chrysanthemum House had been random. "Unfortunate," Lucy's mother had said. They were hesitant to believe that her previous encounter had been racism either. Lucy's sister, Julia, accused their parents of wearing rose-colored glasses.

Lucy reminded her parents of the incident with Ben Wyatt, how she'd been a victim of racism. She'd hinted at AVID's influence on Drake and shared her fears of the possibility of a cross-over between the two. They listened closely as she spoke. Then her father reluctantly told his side of the story.

Javier had been born in Sinaloa, Mexico. He spoke no English when he arrived as a teenager, but when he met Lucy's mother, he dove in headfirst—taking classes in language, history, and culture. He knew what was going to be on the citizenship exam and had begun studying long before he was even eligible.

Her father explained, with difficulty, that back then, he had been in the country too long already to be eligible for a green card through marriage. He had to go back to Mexico for a while. That's why it took so long before they could get married. Finally, when the paperwork was complete, the priest signed off, the city hall signed off, and they became Mr. and Mrs. Perez at last.

Javier had discovered, after he was unable to renew his driver's license, that his green card was expired. Since that day, he too had been harassed—almost as if his name had been added to a target list.

"Why didn't you say anything?" said Lucy.

"We didn't want you to worry, Kitten," said Javier.

"Well, this is worse." Lucy scowled. "Finding out the way I did. What are you going to do? Do you have a plan?"

"We hired a lawyer—a young kid right out of law school, which was all we can afford," said Elaine. "He said that the papers to renew the card had not been filed. They had been completed, approved, and paid for—but the clerk had never recorded them. Your father even had a receipt."

So, through no fault of their own, her father's resident status was now in limbo. Some might see that as undocumented, but they assured her it was temporary. Their lawyer was working things out.

They educated Lucy about the complicated green card process. After getting married, the immigrant spouse files for a two-year residency—and if, after those two years, the marriage and personal character of the spouses prove legitimate, a so-called "permanent" green card is granted. But it must be renewed every ten years.

It is not against the law to let a green card expire, they assured her. "It's just very inconvenient." This last word they said in unison, and then laughed.

"That's why I'm skipping the renewal this time, and going for full-blown citizenship," said her father proudly. "I should have done it years ago."

"Why didn't you?"

"Your sister isn't the only procrastinator in this family," said her mother with a grin.

"And the documents were very confusing," her father added in his defense. "It's all being taken care of, though. Don't worry, my Kitten." He reached out to the computer screen, as if attempting to pinch her nose like he did when she was younger.

"Oh, Dad, don't call me that," she said, shrugging it off. "I'm a full-grown cat now." The three of them had a good laugh. "Dad, should I come back?" Lucy held her breath.

"No, no, you stay put. You're in good hands." They asked if she'd heard from her sister, and Lucy filled them in on Julia's vague plans to visit.

"Let us know when, Kitten, and we'll come to you," said her father.

"And, Lucy," her mother eased a few loose strands of hair behind her ear. "Be careful."

"I will. Like you said, I'm in good hands."

Lucy closed her laptop. She missed her parents, but the thought of going back was unrealistic. They were right. She was in good hands.

The trek through the orchard had brought clarity to Lucy's fears. But questions remained. Where was Ben Wyatt? Was he here? Should she be afraid?

She fished out the old number for Nathan Weil, the public attorney who handled her case, and dialed. The call went directly to voicemail. "Leave a message." That was all. It wasn't even the attorney's voice.

Eli opened his bedroom door with caution and poked his head into the room. "Everything all right in here?"

Lucy filled him in on her conversation as best she could, and told him the lawyer's call had gone directly to voicemail.

"Should we be concerned?" He sat down beside her in the window. *Yes,* she thought, but couldn't say it aloud. He had enough to worry about. "You'll stay?" he asked. It was a loaded question—one she wanted to echo. *At the house, or in Drake?* The notion of running away—again was never far from her mind, but the invitation to stay under the same roof was appealing.

"Yes—if it's okay," she said at last. "At least until the school is patched up."

"Of course," said Eli, putting his arm around her shoulders. Lucy turned to face him and leaned in against his body. "Kitten."

CHAPTER TWENTY-TWO

ELI DROPPED LUCY OFF AT DRAKE HIGH SCHOOL MONDAY MORNING TO MEET three of her students for the Annual Transition.

"Do you want me to pick you up when you're done here?" he'd asked before she stepped out of the car.

"No, the walk back will be good for me. I'll see you in a couple of hours." She leaned back in and kissed him, hoping it was enough reassurance. "Really, I'll be fine." But as soon as his car was out of sight, she wasn't so fine, and she dug deep for the strength to keep moving.

The Annual Transition was a rite of passage for her students to shift from the homeschool atmosphere of the Chrysanthemum House to the more structured format of a public school. The high school gladly accepted this annual passing of the baton, since the Chrysanthemum House provided them with some of the brightest students on the rolls.

It had been four days since the bombing. Lucy was glad to see that these students had not let it affect their outlook. She couldn't say the same for herself but kept her feelings well-hidden for their benefit.

Lucy and Summer had always dreamed of keeping their students through high school but lacked the training and expensive materials needed. Someday, they dreamed, they would be able to remedy that. It's one of the things Summer believed would have been possible with the investment Mrs. Fancy Pants had offered. Mrs. Lancaster's xenophobic nature, premeditated or not, blew up any notion of going into business together. The thought made Lucy's heart ache.

The transition began with a quick tour of the building. It was a small high school, but they had a top-notch chemistry lab, and an art room with all the materials the kids could want.

The meeting was held in the teacher's lounge. Lucy and her students sat side by side on a dingy plaid sofa while an overhead fan wobbled precariously over their heads. Counselor Warren reviewed the registration process and graduation requirements, and then expounded on the breadth and depth of their athletic program.

After the students had been dismissed, Lucy lingered to visit with the counselor and discuss the particulars of the new students.

"You probably noticed that Logan is a little shy," said Lucy. "She'll be all right though, once she has her new routine down. And Emily, on the other hand, will need more help adjusting." They bounced ideas off one another for a while before Mrs. Warren asked about the bombing and what the police had learned.

"I spoke with the insurance company this morning. That's settled, thank goodness. I can't say that the police have been as cooperative. I just don't get it. Why aren't they interested in finding this guy?"

"You're sure it's a guy?" asked Mrs. Warren. It was the first Lucy had considered otherwise, but, why not? Racism wasn't restricted to white middle-aged males like the Hill Brothers.

Mrs. Warren was old enough to be Lucy's mother and her maturity was evident in her calm, nurturing personality. She didn't hesitate to wrap Lucy in her thick arms and tell her that everything would be all right. "If there is anything I can do, dear, you just let me know."

"Thank you. I appreciate that."

Lucy walked alone back to the main entrance. The halls were quiet, with only the *click-clack* of her stiff flats on polished floors and the *swoosh* of a custodian's damp mop. She stepped around the "Caution—Wet Floor" sign to admire the trophy case, which held championship trophies going back to 1960.

Lucy didn't know how old the building was, but guessed its vintage was about the same. She found Eli's name on multiple Mighty Mallard trophies, for district and regional championships in football and basketball, starting in 2007. He'd gotten four MVP awards for lacrosse, and two plaques boasted more lacrosse accolades. Lucy amused herself, searching for Eli in the photos beside the case.

It shouldn't have surprised her to discover that he had been homecoming and prom king for two years in a row. There was a picture of him on the 2010 homecoming float—according to the inscription, the queen that year was Tina Reynolds.

"Of course," Lucy said to herself. "I should have known." She stared at his teenage face, aglow with confidence, and considered how drastically his life had changed for him in the years since. He was a twenty-eight-year-old widower with a young child and a massive estate to care for.

There were other photos of Eli, too. In one, his toe was on the finish line, a competitor just inches behind him. In another, he posed in his full lacrosse regalia, helmet under his arm and stitches knitted across his chin. She noted the same enigmatic smile and untamable hair. There was also a trophy with Kali's name for volleyball—the varsity team had been 2005 Regional Champs.

The custodian was behind her now. It was time to move on. She left the stark hall for the glare and burn of summer sun. It was just a few days until July, she thought, when Julia would be visiting, could be visiting. Lucy didn't hold her breath. Julia was known to change her plans on a whim.

As Lucy ambled up to the Chrysanthemum House, she flashed back to the emergency vehicles, frantic parents, and confused students from the other day. It struck like a dagger to her heart and shattered her sense of liberty.

Lucy climbed the battered porch steps, still shaken and thoughtful. She acknowledged with wonder, the repaired and freshly painted swing and front door, then stepped inside the house.

Eli, Owen, Summer, and Tina were gathered in the classroom. Thomas, she learned, was in the basement, washing out the paintbrushes and rollers, and had instigated the dramatic transformation.

Since the bombing on Thursday, the front door and porch swing had been repaired, the window had been replaced, the classroom had been repainted, and Thomas had installed the video doorbell the landlord reluctantly supplied. The transformation was miraculous.

Lucy decided there was something strange in how the four of them were standing around the classroom—especially the proximity of Eli and Tina to one another. Tina was standing directly behind Eli with her arm hooked through his and a Cheshire grin. Lucy's heart flipped, and she searched Summer's face for clues as to what was going on.

Owen saved the moment by running over to her. He grabbed her hand and turned her around to see a beautiful mural on the opposite wall—a Chrysanthemum in various shades of white against the freshly painted blue walls. She looked back at Eli to see him shake off Tina's arm. He sauntered toward her.

"It was Thomas," he said, with a glance at Summer. "Some of your kids and their parents helped out over the weekend too."

"I did that part," said Owen, pointing and touching one of the petals, leaving a fingerprint in the fresh paint. "Oops," he added sheepishly.

"Well, it wasn't quite finished without your mark." Lucy gave Owen a hug and admired the artwork. "This is amazing, you guys."

"Don't look at me," said Tina. "I just got here."

Eli looked anguished as he pulled Lucy into the kitchen, while Summer took Owen into the bathroom to clean him up. "I have my own stalker," he whispered.

"So, you're not rekindling your high school romance?" she whispered back, half in jest. Eli was about to respond when Thomas came up from the basement with paint-splattered pants and a smudge on his trendy, retro glasses.

"Well, if it isn't the Chrysanthemum herself," he joked. Lucy's eyes brimmed, and she flung her arms around him. "Hey," he added. "I didn't mean to make you cry."

"Just—happy," she said. "How can I thank you?" Lucy worked to gain control of her emotions.

"Adorable," said Tina, slipping into the moment uninvited. "Lucy, when you get a minute. I need to ask you something." She turned and left the room.

"I'll tell her to go away," said Eli.

"No, don't. I'll deal with it." Lucy gave him a peck on the cheek and followed Tina to the front porch.

The pair settled on the top step, taking in the mood of the street. The neighbor chef walked past with his fluffy dog strapped into a pretty pink harness. Lucy popped down the steps to talk to him about cooking classes, and he invited her to stop by to talk about it further. He didn't mean to rush off, but his little pooch was straining at her leash in a futile effort to get a sniff of Biscuit, who stood next door with his front paws against the chain-link fence.

"Cooking class?" asked Tina when Lucy returned to the porch. "Awfully domestic, isn't it?"

"Hmm? Oh, yeah. So, what did you want to say?"

"I have a shortlist of AVID members. Just the ones I could confirm. I was wondering if you have encountered any of them."

"That kind of seems like something the police should be asking, not you."

"Always stay a step ahead, that's what I say. Besides, the police are worthless."

"I'll look at your list, but I still want to talk to the police. Why aren't they more involved?"

"Well, honey, they think this is a one-off—or a two-off, if you count the Planned Parenthood."

"What do you mean the Planned Parenthood?"

"Some freak blew the door off the building there too. Just like here. Not only that, but last night that little shack out on Minnesota Avenue they use for day laborers was hit. It sent two of the fellas to the hospital in Preston; one kid was shot while running away. They didn't find him until this morning. Awful."

"What?"

"He was dead."

"They killed him?" Lucy was horrified.

"Seems like it."

"And the police?"

"They say it's unrelated to you and the Planned Parenthood. The mayor is giving a press conference out by the shack for the five o'clock news. Should be interesting."

"Seriously?" The police were useless. What was the chief thinking? Lucy thought back to the day she and Eli brought in the bugs, and it made her blood boil. This wasn't just incompetence; it was willful negligence. "Who's on the list?"

Tina pulled a folded piece of paper from her back pocket and handed it to Lucy who practically pounced on it. Two names stood out: Lamar and Harlan Hill.

"I might know more by sight, but I only recognize those two names," Lucy said, pointing. "They're buddies with our mayor."

"Right. City council and all. Thanks."

"You would probably recognize more, having grown up here and working for the paper," Lucy added.

"I've been through it already. I only know the two you've pointed out. Have you spoken to your dad?" Tina cut to the question that Lucy guessed had been on her mind from the start, but she was done with this conversation. She looked over her shoulder through the newly replaced front window, compliments of their disgruntled landlord, and saw Eli heading for the doorway.

"Time's up, Tina," he said, placing a possessive arm across Lucy's shoulders.

"Looks like it." Tina shook her head and collected her things, leaving Lucy spinning with the revelations of two more bombings.

As they watched Tina's car pull away from the curb, Lucy invited Eli to sit. He listened with horror as Lucy relayed the news of Planned Parenthood and the day laborer facility. Their privacy didn't last long—soon, Owen arrived to announce he was hungry.

"Oh!" said Lucy. "I spoke with Nikko, the chef. He wants us to stop by."

"Nikko Stark?"

"I don't know his last name. Maybe. He's dark-skinned, and a bit round."

"I'm sure it's Nikko Stark. He used to work at the cannery. Remember, we told you my father fed everyone? It was Nikko who prepared all that food. He ran the kitchen. I wondered what had happened to him. Cool, a cooking class from Nikko. This is awesome."

"Will I have to learn to cook too?"

"No, Owen. You're off the hook." Eli grabbed Owen and flipped him upside down, laughing. "For now," he added.

Lucy stepped up to Owen and gave him a hug. He held her

tightly around the waist. Eli's expression was clear. He was not comfortable with her being in that house without him.

"C'mon. Pack a bag, Summer too. There's plenty of room. You two can have the dining room to spread out your work." He kissed her softly, leaning over Owen who still had her in his clutches. "What do you say?"

"Summer too?" asked Owen, releasing Lucy and running to find Summer who was still in the kitchen with Thomas.

Lucy nodded at Eli, "Fine, I'll ask Summer, but you know what she's going to say." They knew Summer would go back with Thomas, but Lucy was still warmed by Eli's invitation. Lucy's phone rang. They walked on into the house as she answered.

"Hello?" She looked at Eli.

A man's voice, deep and gruff said, "Lucia Perez?"

"Who's this?" asked Lucy. She stopped in the dining room and sat down at the table. Eli pulled out the chair beside her so she put the phone on speaker and laid it on the table.

"My name is Richard Flack. I'm a clerk at Elliott Johnson's office in Santa Cruz." Richard cleared his throat. "Nathan Weil no longer works here." Nathan Weil was Lucy's attorney at the Ben Wyatt trial.

"Where is Nathan?" asked Lucy. She saw Owen gallop from the kitchen into the newly painted classroom.

"I'm sorry to have to tell you this, but Nathan Weil's license was revoked two years earlier."

"What? Why?" she asked as Summer and Thomas sat down across the table, Summer's brows raised in question. Lucy put a finger to her lips. *Shh.* Summer had filled Thomas in on the story after Lucy told Eli. It was all out in the open now.

"I can't say. It was quite a surprise to us all. We're very sorry for the inconvenience."

"Inconvenience?" declared Lucy. "That's what you call it? Are you familiar with the case?"

"Lucia Perez, yes." Lucy heard papers shuffle. "Right here."

"Why wasn't I informed of Ben Wyatt's release?"

There was a long pause, as more papers were shuffled. Finally, a heavy sigh. "Our apologies, Miss, um, Perez. The release papers were, um ..." *Spit it out*! "They were never transferred from the penitentiary. The parole was an internal decision, our office was not notified since Nathan is no longer licensed."

"Where is Wyatt now?" Lucy struggled to control her temper. "Doesn't he have to report to—someone? A parole officer?"

"Usually, yes. I can't tell you where he is now, Miss Perez. I mean—I don't know, exactly." The clerk was as clueless as Lucy. Why even bother returning her call. Across the table Summer rolled her eyes and Thomas mouthed, *Oh my fucking god.*

"Can you find out?" Lucy stared at the ceiling, impatient and incensed. They were either incompetent, corrupt, or both.

"I can look into it. Again, we're so sorry for the inconvenience."

Lucy rose from the table and stomped upstairs with Eli in close pursuit calling after her. She threw herself on her bed and slammed her fist into her pillow.

"Idiots!" she screamed. "Every one of them!" Eli sat down next to her and swept her up in his arms, holding her tight and murmuring softly something about how she'll be okay, and they would figure things out. Whatever he said was lost in the rage she felt at the moment, rage and, to some extent, abandonment. The system failed her. She should have been warned. Wyatt should be behind bars. The whole country was a cesspool of haters and incompetents.

"Idiots," agreed Eli. "Every one of them." He held her, stroked her hair, and spoke softly until she calmed.

A knock at the door announced Summer's arrival. "I'm sorry to interrupt, you guys, but the national news is on and they're covering the mayor's press conference."

CHAPTER TWENTY-THREE

THEY GATHERED AROUND THE TELEVISION IN THE SMALL SITTING AREA BY THE front door. Lucy cozied up on the loveseat with Owen on Eli's lap, while Summer and Thomas pulled up two chairs from the dining room. By the time the actual story came up, live footage from Drake had shown the AVID protesters at the day labor site as Mayor Church took to the podium. The screen was split with footage of satellite press vans lining the streets outside the Planned Parenthood.

Lucy was horrified when her phone whistled an alert as reporters approached her front door.

She turned and lifted the blinds behind her and counted four network vans, and a host of local affiliates lined bumper to bumper along Fox Street.

"What do we do?"

"Don't answer. Pack a bag, your computer, whatever you think you'll need until this blows over," said Eli calmly. Owen looked around from face to face.

"What's happening?" asked Owen. "Where are we going?"

"We're going home, Little Bird. Get your shoes." Eli hoisted Owen from his lap. "Summer? Are you going with Thomas?" Summer turned to him and nodded, then ran upstairs with Lucy to pack.

"What the hell, Lucy?" said Summer as they stood in the hall outside Lucy's room. "What the hell?"

"Let's just get out of here." Lucy looked down the hall, then turned to her friend. "Are you going to be all right at Thomas'? You're welcome at Eli's. There's plenty of room."

"I'm great at Thomas'. I just wonder how we're going to get out of here. Maybe we should just hunker down until they leave."

"It's stressing me out like you have no idea. I have to get out of here." Lucy thought about Owen and how confused he must be. It helped to focus her energy away from herself.

Lucy tossed a jumble of clothes into a backpack and grabbed her laptop. She passed Summer in the hall as she doubled back to the bathroom to get a few more things, and they all met at the front door. Lucy was terrified to leave the house. She checked the porch, it was going to be crazy, but if she focused on Owen, she'd be all right. Eli lifted Owen in his arms and Lucy locked eyes with the boy.

"One, two, three, GO!" said Eli opening the door.

She and Summer locked the front door behind them. They hadn't even stepped off the first step before a camera was thrust in their faces, as reporters charged in, barking all at once. Lucy was grabbed by the shirt sleeve, and a microphone hit her in the chin. The jumble of words tumbled around her as they pushed through the throng to Eli's car; *bomb, school, tell me, can I ask*, and the last thing she heard was, *why you?*

While Eli lifted Owen into his booster seat, Lucy jumped in beside him, worried about how this mob would affect him. At least she could hold his hand while Eli navigated back to his house in the country. Summer and Thomas ran their own gauntlet to his van and followed the BMW down the street.

The car forged ahead through the crowd and turned east where it was blocked by traffic. Eli made a U-turn and headed west, searching for a route out of town, but stymied at each turn. Finally, with Thomas still following, he turned up toward the square, where a growing mass of picketers had congregated. He parked, Thomas too, and they all ran for his office with Owen clinging to his father like a baby chimp to its mother. Eli tossed the keys to Thomas who ran ahead and unlocked the door. Quickly, they filed in, locked the door behind them, and closed the blinds. Eli set Owen down behind his desk and took a deep breath. Maybe Summer had been right, thought Lucy, they would have been better off waiting out the crowd at the house. Now they were prisoners, with a different kind of crowd pinning them in.

Beth arrived soon after, and they streamed the stories online, just in time to see Chief Donoghue interviewed at the day labor site, insisting that the department had full control of the situation. But the longer it went on, the more direct the questions got, and eventually he stormed off and over to a waiting podium, where he made a few prepared remarks.

The noise in the street intensified. A-VID, A-VID, they chanted. Eli laid his phone on the desk where they could all watch the security footage of the street. He didn't dare pull up the blinds to see what was going on outside. The crowd was growing.

The group forming at the park waved signs and placards while chanting at the tops of their lungs. There was no sound for the camera, but they could hear the rhythm of the chant through the building. "Make America great again," the protestors shouted, and "We want our country back!" All the while A-VID, A-VID thumped in the background.

Owen, curious, leaned over to look at the activity on Eli's phone just as one sign holder standing directly across the street, waving his cleverly designed red, white, and blue American Values in Democracy sign, lifted the placard high. Owen jerked back as if he'd just felt a jolt of electricity.

"Owen?" said Lucy, reaching for the boy.

"Dad," he said, quiet at first. "Dad." He tried again, screaming: "Dad!"

"What, Owen?" Eli snapped. Lucy looked at him in shock, as if to say *watch yourself* the way her father would have. "I'm sorry, Little Bird. What do you need?" The stress seemed to be getting to him.

"That man," the boy said, pointing at the phone on the desk. "That man—he's here." Lucy put her arms around Owen and swept the curls from his face. *That man.*

Eli picked up the phone and didn't see anyone, then opened the blinds.

"Show me."

Owen looked and saw the sign on the ground. Lucy braced herself. The man was gone. "That's his sign."

Eli and Lucy both made for the door; it was impossible to hold her back. They ran across the street to the abandoned sign and scanned the crowd. He could be anywhere. Out of the corner of her eye, Lucy saw someone in a baseball cap take off, running. From behind, she couldn't tell if it was Ben Wyatt, but she was determined to find out. As Eli chased her, a body slam came out of nowhere, knocking the wind out of him. Lucy looked back and saw him on the ground. She stopped, torn for a split second between the chase and going back to Eli—and in no time, she was at his side.

"Was it him?" Eli choked.

"I don't know—I lost him." In the excitement of the chase, they had lost sight of the crowd in the dusky shadows of the Old Oak, whipped into a frenzy. Now Eli and Lucy were surrounded, and as much as they did not identify with their Jewish or Mexican heritages, they were quite aware of the possibility that others could or would only see the invisible stamp minorities were often assigned in such situations.

GI Joe stood like a camouflaged stone pillar in front of Eli, reached out his hand to help him up, then told them they needed to get their asses out of there. It was a very confusing moment, but they didn't argue. They ran back to the office, dodging the riotous men and women waving and chanting their racist slogans. Thomas held the door open, and they collapsed, breathless, on the stiff sofa in the waiting room.

It didn't take long for the press, vans and all, to catch up to the mob-scene at the park. They were like hyenas, sniffing out their prey.

Lucy wouldn't be going home anytime soon, though, and the memory of her college terror was now forefront in her mind. Whether or not the man Owen had seen was Ben Wyatt, Lucy faced the fact that his elusive spirit haunted her. Would she ever be able to shake the fear of her silent stalker?

CHAPTER TWENTY-FOUR

I T WAS AFTER TEN AT NIGHT BEFORE THE STREETS WERE SAFE ENOUGH TO FLEE the sanctuary of the office. Summer and Thomas walked Beth to her car, while Lucy and Eli stumbled over the littered sidewalk to theirs, Owen's head bobbing on Eli's shoulder.

Owen woke partway home and grumbled that he was hungry; so was Lucy. Her stomach had been in knots for hours, but the quiet drive along the country roads effectively calmed her, restoring her apatite.

Kali stood in the driveway as they finally pulled up to the house. She approached them with a pair of keys swinging from a ring. She dangled them in Eli's face when he emerged from the car.

Owen stumbled into the house, and Lucy followed him into the kitchen, where he helped himself to a box of cereal from the pantry. She opened and closed several cabinets, looking for the bowls and spoons, and placed three of each on the kitchen table. She looked up when Eli stepped through the door, and her heart sank.

"What's wrong?" It was a ridiculous question. There was so much that was wrong. He shook his head and reached for the milk in the refrigerator.

"I'll tell you in a bit." His tone was somber as he poured milk into Owen's cereal bowl. "C'mon Little Bird—eat up, and let's get to bed."

"No bath?" Owen asked.

"Not tonight. You're off the hook."

Their hunger satisfied, Eli walked Owen upstairs, leaving Lucy alone to clean up. She was glad at first to have the time to herself as she rinsed the dishes and loaded them into the dishwasher, but Kali interrupted her peace.

"I need to show you something," Kali said, motioning for Lucy to follow.

Kali's office was lit by a single dim lamp centered on the antique desk on one side of the room. She followed Lucy's eyes to the tall cabinet in the corner. The partially open door struck Lucy as a tease. Was this a test?

She was invited to sit on the black leather loveseat to her right. Kali sat across from her in an upholstered wingchair and crossed her legs as if she was waiting for Lucy to say something. *Really?* thought Lucy. *Therapy? Now?*

"You are welcome here, Lucy," Kali said. "We are all happy to have you. Especially Eli. But ..." She stood and walked over to her desk, turning the light one notch brighter.

"All right, Kali," Lucy said. "What is going on here? Is this, like, an intervention or something? Do you want me to purge my feelings? My defenses are down. Do your worst."

Eli entered the room and looked from Lucy to the corner cabinet. "Kal, you weren't supposed to start without me," he huffed, clearly annoyed. He quickly slid onto the couch beside Lucy and took her hand.

"Okay, this is so strange," Lucy said. "Maybe I should just go back home."

"No, Lucy—hear us out." Eli squeezed her hand tight as Kali crossed the room to the open cabinet and swung the door wide to reveal a shotgun strapped to its support along the inside of the door. Kali removed a small black handgun and handed it to Eli with the muzzle pointing away. It looked like a toy in his hand. He checked the chamber and placed it in Lucy's lap.

Lucy was horrified.

"No!" She pushed the pistol to the floor, like a hot potato. "This is ridiculous. I don't want it. I don't even know how to use it." A wave of nausea rose in her throat. "This is so wrong." Lucy's heart raced and her face went hot with a mixture of anger and fear.

"It's just to keep you safe." Eli placed his hand on her shoulder, likely meant to comfort her, but made Lucy feel like he was trying to keep her in her seat. "I'll teach you how to use it."

"No way!" She stared wide-eyed at the pistol now lying at her feet. She kicked it away. "Never!"

"It's not loaded," said Kali, stooping to pick it up. "Lucy, relax. This is just an option. We thought you would …"

"I don't." Lucy fled the room in a panic and bolted upstairs to the only place she could think of to be alone—the small alcove at the top of the stairs. Just as she pulled the curtain shut, Eli flung it back open. She shook her head. "Just give me a minute, Eli. I need a minute."

"Lucy, I'm so sorry." He stepped out to the veranda and stood with his back to her as sparks fired inside her head like Pop Rocks. She dropped into one of the chairs and waited for calm. It was challenging, with Eli standing just five feet away. Therapy? That was within reason. A gun? Not reasonable at all. She dreaded the prospect that he would again try to convince her to put that little gun in her hand.

Lucy had seen a gun just one other time in her life. When she was twelve, the neighbor boy showed her where his dad kept his pistol in the bedside table. It was much larger than the Colt Mustang Eli and Kali showed her. The neighbor let her hold it, and she recalled the heft of the cold metal in the palm of her hand. Two days later, while showing it off to another friend, that boy had accidentally shot himself. It was the only funeral she'd ever been to.

She finally pulled herself together and joined Eli on the veranda. He stayed quiet, likely humbled by his misstep.

"I may have overreacted, but my answer is the same. I just can't, Eli. It's not me."

"I'm sorry. It was thoughtless. We just want you to feel safe." He turned to her, and she saw the distress in his eyes. Lucy leaned into him, and he wrapped his arms tight around her.

"*This* is what makes me feel safe," she whispered, and he held her tighter still.

CHAPTER TWENTY-FIVE

THE NEXT MORNING, KALI GREETED LUCY AT THE KITCHEN DOOR WITH A FRESH cup of coffee.

"I'm sorry, Lucy. Our hearts were in the right place."

"I know. It's fine. I just …" Lucy took advantage of Kali's sympathetic ear. "Kali, I hate guns. I hate guns and the culture that goes along with them." Then she proceeded to tell her about the neighbor. Kali bobbed her head as she listened with the occasional mmm-hmmm or ah-ha.

"He was a child, Lucy. It was an accident. I understand that accidents can happen to adults, too—but we'll teach you. We'll go to the shooting range. You can practice." Lucy marveled at Kali's persistence.

"That's not the point," said Lucy. "I have no intention of ever using it."

"And my point is, you might not have the choice. Just think about it. We care about you. I hope you understand that much." She picked up the coffee pot. "Here—let's top that off." With that, Kali dropped the subject. Lucy appreciated that she knew when to back off.

They had a point, Lucy acknowledged. But she would need to overcome a decade or more of bias, and it wasn't going to be easy.

"Mornin'," said Eli, sauntering into the kitchen with Owen two steps behind gripping a butterfly net in one hand. Kali swooped down to give Owen a giant hug.

"Good morning to you, Little Bird."

"Aunt Kali, can we collect butterflies today?" He stood in the doorway, swinging the butterfly net high over his head.

"Of course! Anything for my favorite nephew." Kali took Owen's hand and led him out of the kitchen.

"Nothing like a little ice cream for breakfast," Eli whispered, nuzzling Lucy's ear. He filled a cup with the steaming coffee and set it down on the island beside Lucy. "I called Beth. Thought it was best to take the day off."

"You took yesterday off," Lucy said.

"Yes, I did. She understands."

Lucy grinned. She was glad to have the time with him, but couldn't expect him to put his life on hold. "Summer called this morning. She's planning on going with Thomas on his tour. Getting out of town."

Eli gazed into his cup, deep in thought. "I'm sending Owen to Wisconsin, to stay with Eva's parents. He usually goes for a few weeks during the summer, but it might be a good idea to send him off a little early." Eli took a cautious sip of the hot coffee. "Just— you know, be safe."

Lucy's heart lurched. Eli and Kali were removing Owen from harm's way and shining up the small arsenal in Kali's office. All because of Ben Wyatt. Because of her.

The squeak and slam of the screen door to the patio alerted Lucy to Kali and Owen's departure. "I can't let you do this."

"Do what?" Eli left the kitchen and reached for the TV remote on the coffee table.

"Eli, stop." She followed him, and he froze as if he knew what was coming. She sat on the sectional and pulled him down beside her. "We need to talk." He shook his head. If he were younger, he might have put his fingers in his ears.

"Guns?" she said. "Sending Owen away? I'm putting your family in danger. Even if it's not Wyatt, you guys are preparing for the worst, and it's my fault. I'm responsible for this, and it's tearing me up. I shouldn't be here."

Eli adjusted his glasses and reached for her. She held him off. He'd learned that holding her made her feel safe, and now he thought it was the cure-all. "Who am I to you that you have to go out of your way for me?" she asked. "Rescuing me from danger, or the hint of danger? You hardly know me."

"You remember the day we met?"

"Of course."

"I was standing in line there at the farmers' market, trying to keep Owen from bouncing all over the place and knocking into people. He was such a nut that day. I was losing my patience and was just about to leave when I noticed this girl about to collapse right there on the spot."

Lucy hadn't realized he'd been standing there all along. But it was coming together now. She did remember Owen—his little voice, and that crown of dark curls.

Then she heard another voice. The high-pitched squeak she'd heard in the coffee shop in Santa Cruz, ordering a ridiculous coffee morning after morning. His stare so intense she believed he was looking right through her.

Eli broke through the ugly memory. "I don't know why exactly, but the instant I took your arm, I felt responsible. You seemed so vulnerable." Lucy winced, but he pushed on. "Don't look at me like that. I couldn't just leave you there on the bench. You might have wandered off into traffic or something. So, I sat there and waited for you to … come around."

He sighed. "Kali thinks it's because I couldn't save Eva. Maybe so at first, but it's more than that now. That pretty girl who nearly fell at my feet is now a part of my life. Owen's too."

"Stop, Eli. It's too much. I can't …" *I can't stay.* She thought of the sanctuary of her parents' home, the cabin in the woods— anywhere Wyatt couldn't find her. She wanted to get far from the heartache she felt for putting people she cared for in harm's way. Her gaze drifted from his pleading eyes to the painting above the mantle. She studied the vivid colors of the meadow blurring through her tears.

"You're right," he said. "We are going out of our way to keep you and Owen safe. I want to be safe too. By now, you must realize that I am one of two. It's Owen and me. But now you are very much a part of this little tribe. Even Kali likes you—and she's never liked anyone I've been with."

"Eva?" Lucy looked away from the picture and into her lap, unable to meet his eyes.

"She liked Eva, all right. But she knew that Eva and I were totally wrong for each other. We were so young." Eli shifted in his seat. "School was over. She got a job. I got a job. We were ready to go our separate ways when she told me she was pregnant. I stupidly proposed, and she stupidly accepted. If Owen hadn't come along, she could have …" He stopped. The thought of what might have happened if Owen hadn't come along hit Lucy at that moment too. Eva might have lived.

"But here we are: you, me, and Owen. Before that day at the park, I was resistant to a new relationship. You changed that. You needed me. You and your black eyes. Your beautiful smile. Your compassion." Eli swept the escaped wisps of hair from her face and smiled tenderly. "And your flyaway hair."

"But at what cost, Eli?"

"It will work out, Lucy. Trust me. Please don't go. Please." He'd read her mind. This time, when he reached for her, she didn't resist. That trust, that security—it was like a drug, and she was hooked.

They could hear Owen and Kali on the patio in an animated conversation. His little voice telling a story about his friend at day-care. "Let's go for a drive," said Eli.

TEN MINUTES LATER they were speeding along the county highway towards town with the car windows rolled down and Lucy working futilely to contain the wild strands of hair that had again escaped her trusty clip. It wasn't yet noon, but the heat and humidity were already intolerable.

"Where are we going?" asked Lucy as they turned from the country road to another.

"The cannery." He pointed, unhelpfully, in the general direction of their destination, as a cornfield opened to a string of small subdivisions and a strip-mall. "This used to be the middle of nowhere," Eli said, raising his voice over the roar from the open windows. "Now the middle of nowhere has a 7-Eleven and a liquor store. Most of the small farms who sold their crops to the cannery sold out to developers. The funny thing is, with the cannery closed, no one can afford the houses, and most of them either stand empty—or else they're owned by families from Preston or Ashville, who don't mind the commute."

A half mile further down the road, Eli pointed to a sprawling complex to their left and slowed as they approached. "There it is," he said. "Moon Harvest."

With clenched teeth, he gripped the wheel and turned into the vacant lot of the abandoned facility. He parked in front of the first and largest of four brick buildings, with a heavy chain draped through the door handles. It was secured by a thick padlock. White paint was peeling on the window frames.

Lucy stepped out of the car into the weedy, gravel lot, and followed Eli around to the side of the building, where he peered through a window crusted over by years of grime.

Heat radiated from the brick facade as they moved on to another building, also secured with a lock and chain. Eli cleared broken glass from a low windowsill and helped Lucy up and through. Her wine-colored tank top and denim skirt, while fine for the heat of the day, was not the best choice for this adventure.

Lucy brushed off her skirt while Eli clambered in behind her and they waited for their eyes to adjust. Once she had her focus, she was awed by what had been left behind six years earlier.

The equipment, now still and covered in layers of dirt and dust, filled a building the size of a football field. Motionless conveyors looped through the facility. A can of blue lake green beans stood alongside a pair of brittle work gloves on a wooden cart. Cobwebs hung from the rafters like moss dripping from a Georgian Elm.

Lucy realized by Eli's silence that this sight must be very painful for him. She put a reassuring hand on his arm.

"My dad was planning to transition into frozen food, and maybe even distribution of fresh produce. He said the market was changing, and the company needed to keep up."

"Could you ever see yourself filling his shoes?"

"Hmm. Well, it wasn't ever my intention," he said thoughtfully.

"But now that I'm here, I think maybe that was his plan for me. I think it must have hurt him when I went into social work."

"I doubt it. If your dad was anything like you, he probably just wanted you to be happy. Besides, I think, based on what you guys have said, that he would be proud of you, and ..." Lucy turned around abruptly, startled. "Did you hear that?"

A loud rumble outside the building was soon followed by another. Lucy followed Eli back out the window, where two diesel pickup trucks were now parked at the loading dock. Lucy was afraid they were vandals, or opportunists planning to load up some of the old equipment. Then she recognized the man from the city council. It was Roy Bird, and he was with a younger man.

"Eli, it's just you." Roy pulled off his John Deere cap and wiped the sweat from his deeply creased forehead. His hair, what was left of it, was mostly gray and clipped short. He was an inch or so taller than Eli, with a strong, handsome face and kind eyes. "We saw a car pull into the lot. Thought we should check it out." As it turned out, Roy and his family lived in one of the new subdivisions. Roy had become the cannery's de-facto security guard since the place closed six years earlier.

Eli reached out and shook Roy's hand.

"This is my son, Benjamin," Roy said, proudly—nodding at the tall, broad-shouldered kid of about nineteen or twenty with a tobacco plug tucked under his lower lip. "He's been studying to be an engineer. Nearly there, eh, Benny?" Benjamin nodded, removed his hat, and offered his hand to Eli.

"We actually met once," Eli said. "Company picnic, out at Stinson Quarry. We were kids."

Roy laughed. "And now you're not?" Roy turned his attention to Lucy. "So, who do we have here?"

"Lucy Price," said Eli as his fingertips brushed against hers. "My girlfriend."

"You're the little lady who runs that school. The one blasted by that pipe bomb."

"Yes. I am." Lucy wondered about her notoriety.

"Shame, isn't it?" Roy said, as both Lucy and Eli nodded. "And those poor folks at the labor place down there." Roy and son took off their hats, wiped their brows, and shook their heads in tandem.

He stepped back to his truck and came up with a massive ring of keys. After sorting through them for a minute, he produced a key to the padlock on the office door and removed the chain. Eli opened the door, and the four of them stepped in.

Dust and grime covered everything from forgotten desktops and the old Dell computers that sat upon them, to the windowsills and file cabinets against the far wall.

"Shame, isn't it?" Roy said again. "I mean, you know." *Shame this place had run down like this? Shame it put so many people out of work? Shame his parents died?* Thought Lucy, *or all of the above?*

Eli nodded.

"He was a hell of a guy, your dad." Roy stuffed his fists into his pockets, as did his son standing beside him.

"Mind if we poke around here a while, Roy? I haven't seen the place in years."

"Course not. We'll just be around the corner."

Lucy accompanied Eli to his father's office, but remained quiet while he walked over to the dingy old desk. He stood in front of it, as if his father still sat there in the cracked, leather swivel chair. With a deep sigh, he walked over to the wall and stared at some old photo in a tarnished frame. Then he picked up a notebook from the top of a file cabinet, blew the dust off, and opened it.

Lucy watched Eli flip the pages one by one. There were hand-written notes, small to-do lists, and reminders. Tears welled in his eyes and he turned his face away in embarrassment. Just as she had once before, Lucy held his trembling body until his sobs turned into whimpers, and the whimpers turned into sniffs. The tissue she drew from her pocket was insufficient for the job, but it was all she had. A few minutes later, Roy appeared in the doorway.

"Well, Eli, we'd better lock up here. You let me know if you need anything, all right? Your dad was a decent man. He and your grandpa were really good to my family and me for all those years." Eli's red-rimmed eyes could not have escaped the attention of Roy and his son as they all strolled to the doors. They stood awkwardly in front of Eli's car.

"Roy," Eli said, clearing his throat. "Would it be possible to get together sometime soon? We have a few questions about the city council and the budget issue."

"Don't get me started on that, Eli. I have a few choice opinions that would take the better part of a day to download." Roy and Benjamin laughed. "But, sure, Eli—I'd be happy to. Just name the day."

Benjamin proceeded to his truck, tipping his hat as a goodbye. Roy turned toward his own vehicle when he thought again and spun around to face Eli and Lucy.

"You know, Eli, I saved all the files from this place. They're stored in my garage for safe keeping. If there's anything you want, you just let me know." Eli nodded. "Oh! And it was a pleasure to meet you, Lucy. Best of luck with the school!"

"Thanks, Roy. It was nice to meet you too." Lucy turned to where Benjamin was getting into his truck. "And you, Benjamin." The young man smiled shyly and nodded.

When they'd returned to the car, Eli told Lucy that Roy could very likely be an enormous help with the estate. He hadn't spoken with the family lawyer in too long, and maybe this was the break they needed.

"Would it be okay if we swing by Nikko's?" Eli asked. They hadn't yet scheduled the cooking classes with the chef. "Let's get on his calendar."

"Sure. When was the last time you saw him?" Lucy asked.

Eli started the car. "The memorial."

"What?" Lucy was amazed.

"I haven't seen a lot of people since the memorial service. It's like everybody moved on but me and Kal. I wonder if it's like that for everyone?"

Lucy thought about her situation. She hadn't stuck around to find out. But Eli was here under the noses of old family friends and acquaintances who hadn't bothered to follow up after his parent's final send-off. Besides Beth and Dr. Franzki, who did he have, outside of Kali? Tina? Lucy didn't want to go there.

ELI WAS THRILLED when Nikko Stark opened the door. "Elijah Moon!" Nikko boomed in his gruff, gravelly voice. He reached out and wrapped his arms around Eli, his protruding belly flattened against Eli's. After the long embrace, Nikko brought them both directly back to the renovated kitchen and poured them each an iced tea, teasing about the pimple-faced teenager who had worked on the loading docks during the summers

"It's been far too long, my boy, and I'm sorry about that. There's no excuse."

"I'm partly to blame, Nikko," Eli conceded. Lucy wondered how difficult that was for Eli to admit.

"So tell me, what's going on?" Nikko put his arm around Lucy's shoulders. "You meet this sweetheart, and suddenly you want to cook? The fastest way to a woman's heart and all that?"

Eli laughed awkwardly.

It had taken Nikko years to build up his reputation as a teaching chef. To get his license, he had to take a few extra classes himself and then intern for two years, "like a goddamned rookie," said Nikko. As with Lucy's school, word of mouth was his best marketing tool. He also ran a small catering business, but it was not taking off as quickly as he'd like.

The class Eli and Lucy wanted to take would meet on Tuesdays at seven. They would be joining another couple, who were taking a refresher course, so Nikko could have more time for the neophytes. Nikko handed Eli a course description, which included information about the few things they would be expected to bring with them.

Eli and Nikko caught up further while Lucy played with the little dog—a rambunctious brown and white Havanese mix named Lupita.

They all said their goodbyes, with promises to see one another the following Tuesday, then Lucy and Eli strolled up toward the Chrysanthemum House to have a look around.

They stood on the sidewalk looking up at the house in horror.

Profane and racist graffiti covered the steps and front of the house, including the freshly painted and repaired front door.

"Who would do this?" Lucy gasped, rushing up the steps with her heart racing and her mind spinning. This was not an attack on the house, it was an attack on her.

"Assholes," said Eli.

Adding insult to injury, an envelope was taped beside the door, which contained a fine from the city: five hundred dollars if the mess was not cleaned up within a week.

"Lance will have a conniption." The Chrysanthemum House was on borrowed time if they couldn't get the upper hand on the situation. It was bad enough to be a victim, but to be blamed for it was heart-wrenching.

Lucy texted Summer a photo. "Did your alarm go off? Mine didn't."

"We should call the police," Eli said.

"Why bother," Lucy mumbled. She unlocked the door and they stepped in. The smell of fresh paint and lumber still lingered.

Lucy turned and looked out at the street just before closing the door behind them and noticed the blinds snap closed in one of the windows in the duplex across the street.

She checked the app on her phone, looking for the event that it apparently missed. The event was there, stamped 4:55 am.

"Look at this." Lucy handed her phone to Eli. The video clip showed a tall, thin person dressed in black, with a hood cinched tightly over a baseball cap, tromping up the porch steps and standing there for a moment before pulling a can of spray paint from a plastic shopping bag and painting over the doorbell. It was impossible to tell if they were a man or woman—the only visible body parts were their hands and chin.

"This is outrageous," said Eli, handing her phone back. He pushed his hair from his face with both hands, revealing his frustration.

"Did they know I wasn't home?" Lucy looked at the still image of the vandal again. The fact that her house had been vandal-ized—twice—was impossible to ignore. The bombing was in a class of its own.

"We need to go," Eli said. "Kali's going to want a break."

"I should stay."

"Absolutely not." Eli's face hardened. "Not when you have a safe place to go. It's ludicrous."

"Eli, this is my home." She should have stayed home last night. The door was locked. No one had broken in.

Angry and at a loss for words, he confronted her, gripping her by the arm and yanking her close. He stared into her face, eyes narrowed, and lips pursed. His expression caught her off guard. *He's just trying to protect me*, she thought. But the situation was disconcerting. Stay or go? Independence or dependence? Bravery or cowardice?

Lucy broke eye contact with Eli and pulled her arm free. The phone, clutched tightly in her hand, buzzed with a text from Summer, which she ignored for the meantime. She needed to put Eli's fears to rest first.

"I'll get some things." Lucy stuffed the citation from the city into her back pocket and went up to her room to pack.

Eli waited for her on the porch and turned toward her with a weak smile. "I'm sorry, Lucy." He took a step toward her. Lucy reached for her forearm, remembering his grip. She said nothing, but looked over at the duplex across the street.

GI Joe's blinds were still closed, but one slat was cocked up just enough to see through. She tried to shake the notion away, but it kept coming back like a pesky fly. *Stalker?*

OWEN WAS WAITING for them when they pulled up the drive. He had his butterfly net in one hand and a magnifying glass in the other. Summer's car was parked in front of the garage, and she appeared right behind Owen. She hadn't mentioned the visit in her text earlier, just a kneejerk reply to Lucy's text, "Holy Crap!"

"Mind if hang out a while?"

"Come on in," said Eli. "Are you hungry?" He led the way back to the patio and through the French doors, then sent Owen to wash up.

It hadn't occurred to Lucy until that moment how late it had gotten. The cannery, Nikko's, and the stop at the school had taken hours and they'd missed lunch. It was now dinner time, and she was famished.

This was the first time Summer had been inside the house, and Lucy watched as she absorbed the wonder of the great room and general splendor of Eli's ancestral home before bringing up the assault on their school.

Summer had been just as surprised as Lucy that the app had not alerted either of them. She followed Lucy into the kitchen and laid her laptop on the table, then got online to see if she could figure out what had gone wrong. Before she got far, Lucy handed her the notice from the city.

"You are flipping kidding me!"

"We have a week to clean it up. Do you think Thomas could give us a hand?"

"He left for the tour this morning," Summer said. "Now I need a place to crash for a few days. The thought of sleeping at the school still creeps me out."

"Thank you," said Eli, approaching the table from the kitchen archway. "I feel validated." Lucy gave him the stink eye, but he gave her hair a playful tug. "There you are, Little Bird. How about a bite?" Owen had slipped into the room and pulled out a chair, looking from face to face as Eli kissed the top of his head and reached into the pantry for a loaf of bread and a half-full jar of peanut butter.

Lucy smiled, thinking ahead to the cooking classes she'd signed up for and the little boy who would benefit.

It was decided between mouthfuls that Lucy and Eli would take the video to the police the next day.

"Beth and her daughter, Rachel, asked if they could help with the cleanup," Eli said.

"We're going to burn out our friends. It's too much."

"It's just a little paint," Eli said. "She's happy to help."

"What about next time, and the time after that?" Lucy stopped herself.

"Beth told me the city council is meeting this Friday," Eli said. It was only Tuesday. They had time to prepare.

"Great," said Summer. "Check it off the list." Lucy recalled the action plan they'd come up with before the last city council meeting they'd attended. Attending city council meetings, speaking with Roy Bird and Alex Bridges who left the council, and planning a rally were all ideas that were tossed around. "Maybe we can bring up the vandalism then. It couldn't just be the school, could it?" Summer asked. Lucy thought about that. The graffiti on the school seemed personal to her, but she widened her scope considering AVID and what damage they could do as an organization.

"Dr. Franzki was vandalized back in May. He added a security camera too."

"Security cameras, city council, check and check." Summer stood and stretched her arms. "What are we missing?"

"I asked Roy Bird if he'd be willing to talk," said Eli.

"Push Back for Justice!" Lucy's spirited declaration made everyone laugh. She wasn't usually so boisterous.

"Ladies and gentlemen, the formidable Lucy Price," Eli announced. Lucy stood and took a bow. She was feeling much better after eating, and happy that Summer was moving in for a few days.

"What does 'formidable' mean?" asked Owen, wiping a smear of peanut butter from his face with the hem of his shirt.

CHAPTER TWENTY-SIX

THE NEXT MORNING, LUCY SPIED THE MAYOR SLIPPING AROUND THE CORNER TO the stairs when they arrived at city hall to speak with Chief Donoghue.

"I think the mayor is hiding from us," whispered Lucy.

"Running from the formidable Lucy Price, no doubt," Eli said, grinning. Lucy had to admit the new moniker did give her the courage she needed to confront the police chief. *Formidable.*

They waltzed right past reception and invited themselves into the chief's office with their fists clenched. Chief Donoghue, dressed in a rumpled uniform and practical shoes, sat behind his cluttered desk and sipped coffee from a Styrofoam cup. He was alone. Lucy was happy to see that his eye patch was firmly in place as he scanned her from head to toe.

"Yes?" He sneered at having his morning interrupted.

"We want you to take a look at something."

"Again?" His drawl was thick. "Did you two not hear a word I said?"

Lucy set her phone on his desk and pressed play. There was no audio—the landlord had been too cheap. But the police chief gazed down at the video of the vandal climbing the porch stairs and producing the can of spray paint from a plastic shopping bag. The chief was unfazed—as if he were waiting for Lucy to say or do more. She leaned over his desk and pressed play again. "*Look* at it," she insisted. *Formidable.*

"You don't think I have something to do with this, do you?"

"Perhaps you do. Perhaps you don't. But you do have the power to do something *about* it." Lucy spoke calmly; her voice measured to avoid misunderstanding. She looked at Eli, who stood to her right, ready to step in.

"May I suggest the obvious solution?" His exposed eyebrow bobbed up and down with the inflection in his voice. "You can always leave."

"Look again." She pressed play. He looked to Eli now, as if there would be some intervention. As if Eli would remove this annoyance from his office. "Look what they wrote," she said, pointing to a still photo of the messages that had been hastily painted across the door, siding, and windows. "Go Back Mexican Whore." "Beaner Go Home." "American Values Are Not Your Values."

The chief grinned as if she was a precocious five-year-old, and Lucy dropped her calm facade.

"Stop and consider this," she said, standing firm. "We have been coming to you for months with bits and pieces of harass-ment—the listening devices, the front porch bomber, the picketers outside Eli's office. Now I have a video of the person who violated my house, and you still dismiss us." She looked to Eli for support, then back at the chief. "If I didn't know better, I would think you *did* have something to do with it." The four walls of the already small office were closing in.

"Now you settle down there, before you embarrass yourself," said the chief, just as the mayor walked in, dressed in his Sunday best. He looked surprised when he saw the visitors and took one step back.

"Good morning Mr. Moon, Miss, um, Price," said the mayor.

"Mayor," Eli said before launching into the reason for his and Lucy's visit.

Mayor Church responded, "You could always move."

"You're missing the whole point," said Eli. "It's not about the house."

"Then what's your problem?" asked the mayor.

"I'll be right back, sir." The chief got up and marched out of the room, leaving them alone with the mayor, who was profoundly uncomfortable.

"Terrible times. Terrible times," said the mayor, like Piglet wringing his hands.

"You two sure are cozy," said Lucy, looking him in the eye. "It seems that whenever we come to see the chief, you're always around."

"We have a meeting. To discuss, um, city matters," said Mayor Church, looking down at his shiny black shoes.

"I imagine you're working on what to do about the serial bomber?" asked Lucy, taking a step closer. Mayor Church stared blankly. "What are you doing about the racism, bigotry, and overall anger from economic frustration? What are you doing about crime, drug abuse, and affordable housing?" Eli put his hand on her shoulder, and she shook it off. "What are you doing about this gang of thugs taking over our town?"

"This is not the time or place," said the mayor, coolly.

"We'll be there at the time and place. You can count on it," said Eli. "We'll see you Friday." The mayor scowled. Apparently, he remembered too well how he had embarrassed himself when he was confronted at the last city council meeting. The chief reentered the office and handed Eli a stack of complaint forms.

"Wouldn't want to be accused of not doing my job," he said with more than a hint of sarcasm.

They left the office and filled out two of the forms while standing at the receptionist's counter. One form complained about the lack of police supervision over AVID, the other complained about the lack of response from the chief and his police force regarding this latest vandalism and the trashed mailbox from a month earlier. Lucy took a picture of the completed forms, just in case they needed proof later, and handed them over to the nervous receptionist. Lucy stood in front of the counter, waiting to see what would happen to the forms. What good was this action, when the chief himself would be the recipient?

Eli looked over at Lucy with his fists clenched. She was overheated. her face, neck, and the palms of her hands were damp with sweat. It wasn't the heat of the day, but her anger. Her blood was boiling.

Eli stormed across the street to his car while Lucy jogged along behind him. He was undoubtedly as angry as she was, judging by the flow of colorful language he usually kept in check.

"I don't know who's worse, the mayor or the chief," he fumed.

"Can we sue the city for negligence?"

"We can vote." Eli slammed his door. Three more years of this? Drake will be forever changed, thought Lucy. That log cabin was looking pretty good. She tried to picture Eli and Owen living in the forest—hunting and foraging. Maybe not.

By the time they'd arrived at the Chrysanthemum House, the graffiti had been scraped from the window, and Summer was repainting the door. Beth turned to them and waved a soapy scrub brush.

Lucy was slow to emerge from the car. She was tired. Through the open window she heard Eli vent as he stormed up the porch steps. "You will never believe what that SOB said." Eli was still venting as he climbed up the porch steps—but had cleaned up his language for Owen's sake. "He told her to … *move*. That was his grand suggestion."

Eli marched into the house with Beth to give her the rest of the story.

"Come on," said Summer, coaxing Lucy out of the BMW. "Tell me all about it."

Lucy climbed out and embraced her dearest friend, awash with gratitude for Summer's loyalty and friendship. It outweighed the racist graffiti and stood firm in the face of the changing climate in Drake. This wasn't Summer's fight. It wasn't Eli's fight either. In fact, thought Lucy, the same went for Kali, Mia, the ever-gleeful Owen, Beth, and her daughter Rachel.

They got comfortable on the porch swing and listened to the creak and groan as Lucy pushed off the rail.

"Summer, what am I doing here? Maybe the chief and the mayor were right. I need to go."

"What? Are you kidding? And leave me behind?" Summer grinned and leaned into Lucy. "Listen—for what it's worth, this place is my home, and you are my family. You're not about to abandon your family, are you?"

"I did it before."

"Okay, so that was a bad analogy. What about the school? What about Eli? Lucy, you have too much to lose by leaving—so just put that out of your pretty little head, or I'll have to lock you up like a princess in a tower."

"I know that story," said Owen emerging from the house. "Lucy, are we going now?"

"Going?" Her mind raced. How much had he heard?

"No, munchkin," said Summer. "We'll be right in." Owen nodded uncertainly and went back into the house.

"Summer, I'm so sorry. The bomb, the graffiti—this is our home, and because of me, you've been displaced." Lucy gave the swing another push.

"It's not because of you. You're ridiculous. It's AVID. You know it is."

"It's more than that. More than the vandalism. I think Ben Wyatt is part of all this. I think he's following me. I think he's the guy Owen has been seeing."

"Lucy," Summer gasped.

"It's good you're getting out of town. Owen is going to stay with his grandparents in Wisconsin. But what about Eli? If I'm in danger, so is he. It's selfish to stay."

"It's selfish to go." Summer gripped Lucy's hand so tight that her knuckles were pinched together. "I was talking to Kali last night. Do you know what she said? She said you were a life raft for Eli." Lucy shook her head. "I'm serious. She said that—other than Owen—there was no joy in Eli's life. His flame had gone out after their parents died, and you reignited it." Summer released her grip. "Like I said, it's selfish to go."

There was a *tap, tap, tap* at the window behind them. "C'mon," said Owen through the glass.

"Ready?" asked Summer.

"Ready." Lucy walked into the house just as Eli was saying goodbye to Beth and Rachel. She wrapped Beth in a warm hug. "Leaving already? I haven't had a chance to say thank you. Honestly, you guys didn't have to clean up that mess."

"Nonsense. That's what friends do, and we were happy to help out."

Eli's phone rang. "Hello? Oh, hey there." Eli's thick eyebrows furrowed. "I'll check it out right away. Thank you." He looked at Beth. "Feel like going to the office?"

"What is it?"

"That was Doctor Franzki. He said there's picketers outside the social services office—but not just the ones we're used to." Eli opened his app to see just what the doctor was talking about. "Dr. Franzki said he has a dozen at the clinic too and heard there are more at Planned Parenthood."

"Holy Jesus," said Beth. "I vote to steer clear."

"You should call the police, mom," said Rachel. Eli was already on the phone, and the others chatted nervously until he was done.

"They're sending an officer over," he said after hanging up. "I said I would meet him there."

"And you believe them?" Lucy said. "After the meeting we just had?"

"They should be supervising this demonstration. It's a shot in the dark, but I want a call-in for the record."

"I'll go with you," Lucy said.

"Guess I'll go too," Beth chimed in, despite her vote to steer clear.

Summer and Rachel stayed behind with Owen. They closed the blinds, locked the doors, and stayed busy in the classroom playing a card game Rachel knew.

THE NAIL TECHNICIANS from DK Nails, all Vietnamese, were outside their salon, scrubbing something dark and sticky from their windows as Eli, Lucy, and Beth pushed through the wall of picketers, who were furiously waving their placards, with the usual messages: "Socialist Radicals OUT," "Right is Might," "American Values in Democracy," and "AVID Voters Will Decide." The chants were in the same vein.

Lucy couldn't see the Tweedles through the mob of protesters, but she suspected they were nearby.

While they waited for a uniformed officer to show up, Eli referred to his security app and scrolled back to daybreak, when

Harlan Hill was seen sitting in his car for an hour, chatting on his phone until his brother showed up. They were soon joined by others, one by one—like ants appearing from cracks in a wood floor.

Lucy sat in the orange chair in Eli's office and peeked through the blinds. She watched the crowd grow. She was looking for the Tweedles among them when she noticed a young, blond, and unnaturally tall officer push through the throng, trying to get the picketers' attention.

Many of the assembled backed off with the officer's arrival, disgruntled but not discouraged. Those who remained became more vocal and aggressive, and the officer was pushed this way and that before finding his way to the door, which Eli held open until he came inside, before quickly locking it behind him.

The officer introduced himself as Danny Bradley and explained that he was new to the department.

"Thank you for coming. We appreciate it," said Eli, leading Officer Bradley into his office.

"Could you tell us what the hell is going on here?" asked Beth, standing firm, hands on her hips, while Lucy looked on from her chair at the window.

"The way I understand it is that this AVID movement is against every little liberal issue." Officer Bradley spoke slowly and had just a hint of a southern drawl.

"You could say that again," said Beth.

"So, if you support any social causes—as I imagine you do here—you will get picketers. This group is strong in Drake. I don't hear about these disturbances taking place in Preston, Ashville, or Jefferson."

"Where are they coming from?" Eli asked.

"Well, that's a good question." Officer Bradley drew back the window-blind to see if the group had diminished. "They're not local. We've pulled a few of these guys over—you know, speeding and the like, and they're from back east, some of them. Others are from the south, like Florida and Alabama. I don't want to say anything, but back when the national press was here, I think some of these guys saw it as, like, a call to arms or something."

"Could I show you something?" Eli took out his phone and

showed Officer Bradley the video from his app. "Harlan Hill and his brother have been snooping around here for a while. I believe they planted the bugs we found."

"You found bugs? Like surveillance?"

"We went to your chief. He never told anyone?"

"Nope. But that may have been before I was hired." Officer Bradley took one more look at the video.

"I have another video of the Chrysanthemum House, added Lucy. "It was vandalized the other night. There's footage of that, but it's tough to see anything conclusive."

"Can I see that?" Officer Bradley watched it through twice. "Is there any way we can see this on a bigger screen? My eyes are struggling here."

Eli set up his laptop, and they watched them both again and again. The officer asked Eli to send him a copy, and he would get some help. Not long after, his radio squawked, and they all heard that Dr. Katz's house was being picketed.

"Dr. Katz," said Eli. "He's a professor at the University."

"That St. Charles University out there off the County Highway?"

"No, God no. The State University. He teaches Genetics, I think," Eli said. "He's Jewish." The officer nodded, knowingly.

"Well, I have an interesting day ahead of me." A determined Officer Danny Bradley left the office, brushing past Beth, and out the door.

"Looks like we have an ally," said Eli.

Tina Reynolds phoned Eli, and he put her on speakerphone. Lucy listened in as Eli got Tina up to speed about Officer Bradley and the news of Professor Katz.

"Katz wasn't the only one, Eli," Tina said. "Your friend, Dr. Franzki, at the free clinic, was beaten up too. I heard it was pretty brutal."

"Franzki?" Eli gawped. He pulled his chair up close to the desk and rested his head in his hands. Beth entered the room with two cups of hot tea and set them down on the desk. It looked as if she was going to speak, but Lucy placed a finger to her lips. It was juvenile, but she didn't want Tina to know anyone was listening in.

"And there were protests outside the homes of a few liberal

politicians. You know Frank Schroeder and Carol Clifford? We were hit here at the *Drake Register* too."

"This is messed up," Eli said. "What did they do there at the paper?"

"We were hit with red and black paintballs. Target practice, and they missed the target."

"What?" Eli asked. Beth pulled up a chair.

"It seemed they were aiming at the sign up over the door." Lucy had seen the sign. It was white with black letters and spanned half the length of the building. How could they have missed it? "They hit the door, the roof, the tree by the street, but they missed the sign altogether." Tina laughed. "Boneheads."

"These boneheads are beating people for their race." Eli glared at the phone and looked up to see Beth and Lucy equally upset.

"True, true. Sorry, you're right, but hell of a news day," said Tina. "Maybe we could meet later to talk about it a little more? They have a great happy hour at The Gypsy."

"I don't think so." He rolled his eyes and grinned across his desk at Lucy. "Will you be at the city council meeting on Friday?"

"With bells on," she said, laughing. "Maybe we could meet after?"

"Tina, I ..."

"I know. You have a girlfriend." She laughed again. "See you on Friday."

Eli put down his phone and took another look at the security footage on his laptop. "Is that who I think it is?"

Lucy could nearly make out someone at the park on the other side of the street. GI Joe?

CHAPTER TWENTY-SEVEN

FRIDAY MORNING BEGAN WITH THE DRUM OF APPROACHING THUNDER. THE weather radar predicted it would be passing overhead within the hour.

Despite Eli's protests and Lucy's anxiety, she and Summer decided to spend the day at the Chrysanthemum House going through the school materials and setting up a curriculum for the next term. It wasn't something they could do at Eli's, and it needed to be finished before Summer left to meet Thomas, but Eli made sure Lucy wouldn't be alone, and that she had Officer Bradley's contact information.

"If anything happens—anything—call Bradley first, then call me."

The school was sweltering when they arrived. It had been buttoned up for days, and the heat and humidity had been trapped. Lucy wanted to open some windows, but with the rain and wind, Summer cautioned her against it.

From the classroom, they heard the gate squeal open to the little side yard, then slam shut. "That latch should have been fixed after the bomb," grumbled Summer, closing the blinds in the room.

"Can't we open just one window?" begged Lucy.

"We won't be that long, relax." Summer followed Lucy into the dining room.

The reading list was on the dining room table, under the watchful eyes of Her Highness. Lucy thought that the little statue would make an excellent weapon if need be, as she and Summer worked out how they were going to afford the new editions, and debated whether or not to use the materials they already had.

"We'll make two lists. One for a budget based on full enrollment, the other for less," Lucy said. Lightning flashed and thunder followed seconds later with a deep rumble.

"We could always raise tuition. Five percent would go a long way, and we wouldn't have to skimp." Summer always suggested higher tuition as the solution to budget issues, but Lucy was afraid that even five percent would drop enrollment. Then they'd be back to square one. She didn't want to gouge the parents who were scraping together the tuition as it was.

"Will Owen be joining us next term?" asked Summer. Owen was home with Kali and Mia that day, even after pleading to come along.

"We've been talking about that. Eli wanted Owen to go to the same primary school he and Kali had gone to. Also ..." Her voice trailed off.

"Also what?"

"Well. What if it doesn't work out? Eli and me. It would be so awkward."

"Are you joking?"

"I'm not."

"All right, well, odds are that it will work. I see how Eli looks at you. And remember what Kali said about you being his lifeboat?" Summer said. Lucy remembered, and thought, *who saved whom?*

A big gust of wind slammed the house with a roar, and they both jumped at the sound of something hard hitting the dining room window. The storm had arrived with a vengeance.

"Jesus Christ!" Summer yelped. They were both skittish. It was raining sheets outside, and the street was black as night. Lucy had never experienced a tornado but thought this might just be the day. She opened her laptop and began looking for the budget spreadsheet, keeping an ear open for the warning siren.

"I hope I'm not cramping your style at Eli's." Summer fanned herself with a small paperback and set it down. "I haven't overstayed my welcome, have I?"

"Absolutely not. Jeez, Summer, it's been three nights." Lucy looked over her shoulder at the printer, waiting for it to spit out her document. Summer got up, grabbed the copies, and sat back down beside Lucy.

"I'll be out of your hair soon enough."

"I know," Lucy frowned. She would miss her friend greatly,

even with Eli and Owen to help fill the void. "Hopefully, the crazies will have moved on before you get back."

"You'll be just fine without me. You, Eli, and little Owen playing house in that castle."

"It's pretty great." Lucy flashed her gap-toothed smile.

"How can you even think that it might not work. It's working. Don't question it."

"I'm really going to miss you."

They nearly leaped out of their skins at a sudden *thump!* in the basement that came on the heel of a thunderclap.

"Holy crap!" shouted Summer. "I just about peed my pants." They laughed nervously as the house creaked and moaned, resisting the assault of the storm. Then a *thud* from the basement alarmed them both.

Lucy rose slowly from the table and stood nervously at the top of the basement steps, listening and waiting. Just as she was about to close the door, they heard it again.

"Ignore it," urged Summer. "Let's just finish this up and get out of this place."

But Lucy was determined. She turned back to the table, grabbed Her Highness by the neck, and descended the steps.

"Lucy, don't be crazy!"

Midway down, she peered through the dim light to where she heard the *thud* again. An open window above the dryer swung free with each gust of wind. That window had never been opened since she'd moved in. Why would it be open now? The window wasn't large, just big enough for a fat raccoon. *Or a scrawny man with a squeaky voice.*

Lucy tried to ignore the ripple of fear surging through her body as she set down Her Highness, climbed onto the dryer, and shut the window, fastening the latch tight. She hopped off the dryer and picked up a box of detergent from the floor beside a damp towel and reclaimed Her Highness with a firm grip. There was another flash of lightning, and she bolted up the stairs, heart racing.

🌿

THEY WORKED THROUGH lunch, and the storm finally let up around three as the sun peeked through the clouds, steaming up the streets and sidewalks. Lucy decided to walk into town to meet Eli, refusing Summer's offer to drop her off.

"You shouldn't be out on your own," Summer cautioned as she got into her Subaru.

Lucy shrugged it off. "I need the fresh air." She couldn't stand being bottled up any longer. She was hot and uncomfortable, and her nerves were shot.

Lucy turned her face to the sky as she strolled down her street toward the church. She quickened her pace when she turned the corner to the square, excited to see Eli. The Old Oak soon came into view.

The tree was a symbol of strength to Lucy. Season after season, it endured, regardless of heat wave, ice storm, or civil unrest. It could be counted on to wake up each spring to begin its cycle anew. Starting over. Sometimes a little worse for wear, marred by broken limbs or hungry caterpillars, but persisting all the same.

As she approached Drake Park, she realized she was being followed. She stopped at the corner, opened her bag, and pretended to search for something while she glanced behind her. It was GI Joe. He caught her eye and nodded a hello, then crossed the street to the park. She kept track of him as she made her way to Eli's office, where two picketers clad in full rain gear held their boards high as she passed. "Go Back," and "Homosexuality is a SIN," the signs said, standing side by side in unity.

From the sidewalk, Lucy saw Eli sitting at his desk and waved. He met her at the door.

"I don't understand you, Lucy. It's not safe for you out there. You know this, so why?" She followed him into his office.

"I can't live like that. I won't." She thought about GI Joe, wondering if he was someone she should fear.

"You're right. Absolutely—but why take the risk?"

Why *had* she taken the risk? She didn't know. Was she trying to prove something to herself? To Eli? To the world?

"Hell of a storm, eh, Lucy?" Beth said as she bounced into Eli's office. "It chased off most of the picketers, Thank God."

"They'll be back," Eli added with a shake of his head.

"Should we grab some dinner before the city council meeting?" Beth asked. Lucy smiled. She was hungry. When Beth left them to get her purse, Eli pulled Lucy close.

"I'm sorry—I just worry," he whispered. Lucy remembered Eli sitting beside her on the sectional, telling her why he felt responsible for her. It was something she would need to get used to. But it wasn't the worst thing to have someone looking out for her.

EVERY SEAT IN the room was full when the meeting began at the stroke of seven. Mayor Church stepped up to the podium and began his nonsensical speech about "American values." Lucy half-expected him to finish the phrase with "in democracy." Instead, he went on about what a brilliant mayor he was, giving himself an A+.

Eli, Beth, and Lucy sat lined up in the second row. Tina looked at Eli and rolled her eyes. The mayor was on a roll.

"Drake couldn't be in a better position to prosper," said Mayor Church. "With the savings from our new budget and the fees we've proposed, our fair city will be the envy of Iowa."

The fees he was speaking of were as good as taxes imposed on services like the free clinic, the food bank and the emergency shelter. Instead of helping those programs, Mayor Church was devising a way to starve them out of existence. Tina caught the whole historic con job on her phone. There were two reporters from out of town doing the same. Lucy looked from them to the mayor, whose reddened face dripped with sweat as he spoke.

Mayor Church had accepted Roy Bird's resignation after the first budget meeting debacle, and had replaced him with none other than Mrs. Lancaster. In a Ralph Lauren pantsuit and shimmering necklace, she darted her eyes, heavy with dark makeup, here and there, often settling on Lucy.

The mayor found a more straightforward way of dealing with the public than he had during the previous meeting. He took no questions from the citizens and no questions from the press. He stood before them all to unveil the unanimously agreed-upon budget. It wasn't the clean sweep Beth and Eli had expected, but that would undoubtedly be the next shoe to drop.

He thanked everyone for coming and promptly exited the room, ignoring the explosion of questions as the door closed behind him. The rumble of voices in the room was reminiscent of the storm earlier that day. Beth watched the spectacle with her jaw agape and the list of unanswered questions still sitting in her lap. The two visiting reporters looked at one another quizzically and started laughing.

"I didn't think it could get any stranger, and then he does this," said Beth, turning to Eli.

They watched the exodus from the room as many of the citizens hoped to catch up with the mayor on the other side of the door. Eli and Lucy waited it out. It was like getting off the airplane before the doors to the gate have opened.

Roy leaned over a row of folding chairs and tapped Eli on the shoulder. "Do you have a minute?"

Eli and Lucy joined Roy in the back of the room. "Did you see this coming?" asked Eli.

"It's been his whole mission from the start. That's what I want to talk to you about, Eli. I'm going to make a run for mayor this fall, and I could really use your support. You too Lucy. It would mean a lot to me."

"That's excellent news, Roy," Eli said. "You have it. I'll do what I can—just name it."

"We need to expose this a-hole. I've already spoken with Miss Reynolds. She said she would work with you on a plan."

"That's news to me." Eli cringed.

"We'll be happy to, Roy," Lucy said. "We'll do whatever you need."

"Within reason," Eli joked, grinning at Lucy.

WHEN THEY ARRIVED at Eli's, Lucy shared the news of the city council's "meeting," and Roy Bird's run for mayor. Summer, Kali, and Mia all wanted a piece of that action.

"Democracy, my ass," said Summer, who was quickly shut up with a look from Eli—Owen was just in the other room. "DMA," she said, more quietly. Mia and Kali laughed, holding hands at one end of the sectional while Lucy and Eli sat cozied up together at the other.

Eli received a text from Tina. "When can we meet?" He held the phone out for Lucy to read.

"Lucy and I can meet you next week," answered Eli—making it clear, he hoped, that he and Lucy were in it together.

A long pause, then: "Great."

Eli gave Lucy's shirt a gentle tug. "Are you sure you really want to be part of this? Politics isn't exactly your thing."

"Well, I'll do anything to get rid of Mayor Church—even if it means working with Tina Reynolds."

"Formidable," said Eli, with a twinkle in his eye.

CHAPTER TWENTY-EIGHT

THE FOLLOWING MORNING, SUMMER PACKED HER BAGS AND LOADED THEM INTO the back of her Subaru. She was leaving for Chicago to catch up with Thomas. Before she pulled out of the driveway, she made Lucy promise to stay in Drake. This was something Lucy struggled with regularly—but the longer she remained at Eli's, the less willing she was to leave Drake, her school, and especially Eli.

"I promise. I'll be here when you get back," Lucy said as she hugged Summer. "There's too much to lose."

"You know it." Summer tightened her embrace, then stepped back. They looked at one another, smiling.

They planned to reopen the school in August, when Summer returned—but it really depended on what AVID was doing, and what kind of help they could get from the police.

Lucy had never felt more defeated than when the chief rejected her claim of harassment in his office the previous week. He was unconvinced, even with the video footage. Fortunately, Eli had formed a bond of sorts with Officer Bradley—the only reason Lucy had any hope of salvaging the Chrysanthemum House. Otherwise, her lease was up in September, and she would have to walk away from her school. She wasn't going to put herself or her students through the stress of waiting for the next inevitable strike, however it may manifest. The thought was overwhelming. *Walk away from the school? I'll rebuild, but where?* If not AVID, some other group would shut her down, vandalize her building, unravel her life. Why? Because she had brown skin? The notion was ludicrous.

Eli, Owen, and Kali joined Lucy in the driveway to say their goodbyes and wave farewell to Summer, then returned to the house one by one.

She added ice to her coffee and stepped out onto the patio, where Eli stood staring out into the orchard.

"So hot," complained Eli. Lucy knew he was struggling with the expense of repairing the air conditioner. The problem was getting more difficult to avoid as the summer heat intensified, with its oppressive humidity. But the cost of the unit, the service, and the electric bill would be prohibitive.

Lucy had never gotten used to the Midwest summers. She hadn't adapted to the winters either, for that matter—despite Owen's proclamations of how fun it was to play in the snow.

Owen appeared behind them with his butterfly net. Without a word, the three walked past the unruly roses and out into the shade of the orchard. Lucy watched Owen's mop of curls bounce as he bounded down the first row of trees with his net held high.

"Don't wander off too far!" Eli called.

"Okay!" The reply was faint, but still within hearing distance. Eli relaxed, stripped off his shirt, and surrendered himself to a soft patch of grass in the shade.

A veneer of condensation wrapped Lucy's mug of ice coffee. She held it against the back of her neck, shivering as the drops trickled down her spine.

They were alone now, among the chatty birds and buzzing insects. Eli looked up at her from his bed of soft grass, his eyelids at half-mast. *Bedroom eyes*, she thought with a knowing smile. She stepped up to his prone body and placed a foot lightly on his belly.

"You wouldn't," he dared her playfully while tensing in response to the weight. As she gazed down into his gleeful face, she thought of how much she cared for him. How could she even put it into words? Whatever it was, it was mutual—his broad smile said precisely what she was feeling.

Kali caught up to them, holding four frozen fruit bars, still in their colorful wrappers. Lucy removed her foot, took two, and handed one down to Eli.

"Where's Owen?" asked Kali.

"He's exploring," said Eli. "Owen!" he yelled. "Owen! Popsicles!"

A moment or two passed. No Owen. Eli popped up and took a few steps deeper into the orchard. "Owen!"

"Owen!" called Lucy and Kali. Still, there was no answer.

They fanned out into the orchard, calling after him, with growing anxiety. Eli's panic was adopted by Lucy and his sister, who called for him in a chorus of worried voices.

Lucy rushed in the direction she'd seen Owen last, but then veered off toward the old farmstead. He'd been so preoccupied with that site on an earlier walk, she guessed that would be the first place he'd go. She was just at the edge of the orchard looking out into the meadow when she heard his little cry from only a few yards to her right—the old pumphouse directly behind him. He was trembling. Tears rolled down his round cheeks and dripped onto the weeds surrounding his bare feet. Her heart filled with relief at finding him, and compassion for his distress.

"He's here! I have him!"

Lucy knelt and wrapped her arms around him. His crushing grip on her relaxed once he caught sight of his father. Eli caught up to them and was soon joined by Kali. Lucy stepped back to give father and son their moment. Owen continued to tremble. His eyes welled with tears that spilled onto Eli's shoulder. Lucy promptly knelt back down at their side.

"What is it, Little Bird? What's wrong?" Eli's soft, calming voice did not deceive Lucy, who focused on his trembling hands.

"It was him, Dad," said Owen in his little voice, quiet and shaking. "That man. He's here."

"It's fine, Owen. We're here. I've got you." Eli looked past his son, toward the pumphouse, and then back at Lucy; his jaw set decisively. He rose and yanked open the door. The building was empty—but a can had been toppled, and rusty nuts and bolts were strewn across the dirt floor.

The group hurried back to the house, with Lucy bringing up the rear. She was as transfixed as Eli was terrified; her senses acute to every sight and sound. Twigs snapped under her feet. Gnats and flies pestered her as she ran. She nearly jumped out of her skin when a sandal strap popped free, and she threw it off, not daring to take a chance on fixing it.

Owen was hustled up to his room for some much-needed comforting. Eli and Lucy said what needed to be said to ease the boy's fears. Then, after leaving him to his toys, they said what needed to be said to ease their own.

"Kal?" called Eli when they returned downstairs. They found Kali in her office, standing in front of the open gun safe, staring blankly at the weapons.

"I just left a message with Mia," Kali said. Then she slowly shut the heavy door and locked it tight. "She would know what to do." Lucy understood. Sometimes it takes two. Whether Summer or Eli, she felt stronger and more self-assured with someone dear beside her.

"Give me the keys, Kali. I need to go out there and look around," said Eli.

"No," said Lucy. "Call that policeman who came to your office."

"Officer Bradley?" Eli sat down in Kali's chair and placed his phone on her desk. They all listened in on speaker as he explained what had happened.

TWENTY MINUTES LATER, Officer Bradley sat in the center of the sectional, with Owen beside him, ogling his badge. He allowed Owen to hold his radio and touch the badge during a light conversational interview, before stepping out into the orchard.

Lucy took Owen upstairs to distract him. She watched as he absentmindedly put together and took apart his Lego pieces, while she sat in his window seat and stared out into the tree garden.

After more than an hour, Eli and Officer Bradley returned to the patio with nothing but Lucy's broken sandal, and the possibility that whoever it was, they'd likely been hiding out in the pumphouse. Officer Bradley dusted the door and latch for fingerprints with the small hope that he'd find something usable.

"I don't have anything conclusive, Lucy," said the officer, handing her the broken sandal. "We'll have to wait for the scans." He turned to Eli. "Would it be all right if Owen helped us out a little more?"

"What do you mean?" Eli asked.

"There's a sketch artist I know who could speak with him."

Eli stuffed his hands into his pockets, thinking. It occurred to Lucy how stressful this could be for Owen to have to recall the man he saw in such detail. She imagined Eli was considering the same thing.

"I'll get back to you," Eli finally replied.

"It sure would be a big help, Eli." Officer Bradly nodded and walked back to the driveway. Eli and Lucy listened as his patrol car turned around and drove back to the street.

ELI AND LUCY had had only one cooking lesson to date, and dinner that night was Eli's first attempt at using the grill at home. The shish kabobs were stacked with chicken, red peppers, mushrooms, and pineapple chunks. But as far as little Owen was concerned, it was all about the pineapple.

As they sat around the kitchen table, Owen was happy to learn that the officer wanted him to come into the station the next day, so they could get an official sketch of the man in the orchard.

"I can draw a picture of him myself," said Owen proudly, with a mouthful of grilled pineapple.

Kali's phone buzzed from the kitchen counter, and she leaped for it. "Hey." Her face fell in obvious disappointment. "Mr. Lang—hello." She left the room to speak with her patient, leaving Eli and Lucy with Owen at the kitchen table.

"What's going on?" Lucy picked at the food on her plate.

"She's been waiting for Mia to call her back. She's M.I.A.," Eli said. The he leaned into her and whispered, "Trouble in paradise." She turned to face him. He grinned and placed a finger to the corner of his mouth. It had become more than an inside joke. It was an endearment—a touchstone to the day they met. Although that day had been fraught with anxiety and fear, they had both reached to the time after leaving the park which sparked their friendship. They hadn't yet declared their feelings with the golden *three little words*, but this gesture was a close second.

When Kali returned, Lucy cleared the table, and they set to rinsing the dishes while Eli took Owen upstairs for his bath.

"Do you want to talk about it?" asked Lucy. Kali turned the water off and opened the dishwasher, then stopped.

"I think Mia is seeing someone else." The confidence stunned Lucy, who thought the girlfriends were a committed pair. "We've been talking about moving in together for a while, but whenever I bring it up now, she acts like it was never on the table. The other day she denied ever discussing it, and I … gave her an ultimatum."

"You're getting the silent treatment."

"Probably."

"It doesn't mean she's seeing someone."

"No, but it doesn't mean she isn't." Kali turned the water back on and scraped the last dish into the sink. "I'm overreacting, aren't I?"

"You're asking the wrong person." Lucy filled the soap dispenser and turned on the dishwater. They sat back down at the kitchen table. "But, for what it's worth, I don't think she's playing games, if that's what you're getting at." Lucy had no way of knowing what Mia was up to, but she'd read the signals between the pair and couldn't fathom Mia cheating on Kali. Kali shifted in her seat and locked onto Lucy's eyes as the dishwasher chugged noisily in the background.

"Did she say something to you?"

"No. No, nothing like that. I watch you two; probably like you watch Eli and me, right? You move in sync. The way she looks at you is enviable. I think she just might be nervous about the commitment."

"Who's the psychologist now?" joked Kali. "I'm glad you're here," she added.

"I'm not in the way?" Lucy recalled what Summer had shared about Lucy being a lifeboat. She was nearly confident of her standing with Kali, but she wanted to hear it for herself.

"Just the opposite. I know you didn't choose to move in here; circumstances being what they are. I understand. But this house needs people. Does that sound strange? It used to be my grandparents, my parents, me, and Eli." Kali stood and fetched two bottles of beer from the fridge. She held one out to Lucy, who nodded. "The house was full of activity—company coming and going, Mom's book group, Eli's bazillion friends playing video games or blasting music from his room, Grandma and Grandpa's many vocal disagreements, and the little squabbles between Eli and me." Kali poured the beers into two glasses and brought them to the table.

"Eva joined us right after grandma died. The house flexed with the addition, and held its breath for Owen's arrival. Then—*poof*—it was all gone. The house has been in mourning ever since—but with you here, it's like a fresh start. I can feel it." Kali was relaxed now.

"I'm glad you feel that way," Lucy said, "but I'm afraid."

"Of what?"

"What am I adding, in light of Ben Wyatt? In light of sending Owen off for the summer? In light of ..." She couldn't finish her sentence. There was too much static between her ears—things she didn't want to say. It was entirely within her power to stop what was going on with Wyatt, and Eli was making it too easy for her to ignore the best solution.

"Owen will be fine. He'd be headed to Madison anyway. And you talk about Mia and I being in sync—but I've never known Eli to be this content. Don't think that he is your responsibility. He's a big boy. But he is committed to you. We both are."

"But Owen. He ..."

Kali's phone rattled on the table, and Mia's name appeared on the screen. They both sighed with relief.

As Kali took the call, Lucy wandered upstairs to find Eli. She peeked through a crack in Owen's bedroom door and heard Eli saying goodnight to his Little Bird. No doubt, there was a lot of love in this house, but it was still difficult for Lucy to believe she had anything to contribute.

She was pulling the covers down on the bed when Eli walked into the room. Exhausted, they spoke little. Eli pulled the heavy curtains closed over the open windows, restricting airflow while allowing them to hear the night.

"Do you think he's out there now?" he asked.

"I don't know."

"I locked up downstairs."

"All right." They lay face to face in the dark, listening to the crickets, and speaking in hushed voices. Lucy was startled by a small hand on her shoulder, then moved over so Owen could fit himself between them.

Without another word, they all fell asleep.

CHAPTER TWENTY-NINE

OWEN CLUTCHED A HOME-DRAWN SKETCH IN HIS HAND AS THEY ENTERED THE interview room. The drawing had a strong resemblance to Darth Sidious, and the police sketch artist, who had been brought in from Iowa City, complimented his skill but said he was eager to make his own attempt. Owen politely agreed, and the two were left to this task as Eli and Lucy looked on anxiously from the window of an adjacent room.

A door squealed on the other side of the room, and Officer Bradley stepped in, followed by the ominous figure of GI Joe, in full costume. Lucy stared into the man's cold blue eyes.

"Eli, this is Agent Bob Marshall," said Officer Bradley. GI Joe reached into one of the many pockets of his fatigues, and produced an official-looking badge.

Lucy was stunned. GI Joe was an agent for the Federal Bureau of Investigation.

"Just call me Bob, okay? We need to talk." It was as if the world had flipped. Up was down, down was up.

"Okay, this is just plain weird," said Eli.

"Not to worry, man," said Bob. "You're not in any trouble."

Why would we be in trouble?

Officer Bradley stepped over to the water cooler, filled two cups, and handed them to Lucy and Eli, as if he knew their throats had gone dry with the revelation.

Lucy thought back to the man who posted fliers all over town and loitered outside Eli's office as she and Eli exchanged looks of disbelief. They glanced over their shoulders into the examination room, where Owen chatted with the sketch artist. Agent Bob

Marshall strolled to the water cooler and pulled another cup from the dispenser.

"Accept my apologies, Lucy. We don't have much time here." Bob filled the cup and drank it dry—then refilled it as if he'd arrived at a desert oasis. "Just listen for now, all right? I'll make this quick, but we'll need to meet again soon to fill in the blanks." He waited a moment for their acknowledgment. "It is not a coincidence that AVID is here in Drake. They were drawn here by the leader of their organization, Ben Wyatt."

"He *is* here," said Lucy. She hadn't been imagining, and her suspicions were now confirmed. But the idea that he was the leader of this organization? That was unbelievable. No, not unbelievable. She believed it.

"Yes, Ben Wyatt is here. It's just been challenging to get eyes on him."

"How do you know he's here if you haven't seen him?" Eli said.

"Chatter. Social media—not your typical Facebook stuff, but something much darker. It's also how the FBI identified Wyatt as the kingpin of AVID a year ago, while he was still in prison. Organizations like that pop up all over the place. Most fizzle. Wyatt seems to have lit a bonfire under this crowd. I'll explain more another time." Bob Marshall looked past them, into the next room where Owen was still engaged with the sketch artist, perhaps checking to see how much time he had left to speak with them alone.

Lucy's phone buzzed in her hand, she looked down at the security alert. Lance Kirsch, her landlord, was standing at her door.

"I was sent here because of you, Lucy," Marshall said, as she tucked the phone into her back pocket. "He's a slippery little weasel, and our best guess was that he would try to track you down."

"I thought I'd seen him a few times, but hoped I was wrong. But after the bombing and learning that he'd been released, that hope was pretty thin."

"When did you first see him?"

"May. At the farmers market," said Lucy. Eli took her hand.

Bob nodded. "The guy you were chasing in the park." Bob

slugged back what water remained in his paper cup. "In the park, you remember that?"

"Yes," they answered in unison.

"It was Wyatt. I had just finally set eyes on him when you two came out of thin air." He shook his head. "Man, can you ever run! I had a hell of a time catching up to you. Wyatt is a dangerous man—hear me? A very dangerous man. If you'd caught up to him, who knows what would have happened?" Bob articulated these last few words carefully.

"Is Lucy safe? Are we safe?" Eli looked over to his son.

"For the moment. We think Wyatt's just watching Lucy for now. Your son is not a target." Bob walked back over to the water cooler and refilled his cup. "He's obsessed." Lucy cringed. Here she was again, but now there was collateral damage. *Poor Owen.* "He's hiding out somewhere, but I haven't managed to find where. That's why it means so much to us to know he's been spotted."

"In our orchard?"

"Or squatting with a supporter, or—" He looked over Eli's shoulder and nodded. They were finished with the drawing. The artist held it up for Bob, who confirmed that it was indeed Wyatt.

"I've embedded myself into the organization. That's where you've seen me. I'm staying in the duplex across from Lucy's place, trying to keep watch as much as I can. Damn sorry I missed that little bomb and the shithead graffiti artist, but I can't be everywhere at once."

"She's staying with me now. I thought she would be safer there." Eli put his arm around Lucy. "And it wasn't just a little bomb." Bob shook his head and looked away like he knew the difference.

"See these fatigues? Afghanistan—two tours. I know a bomb when I see one," Bob said. Lucy didn't get the feeling he was being snarky. He was just giving them some reference.

Lucy thought about whether she was really safe, given the fact Wyatt was confirmed to have been in the orchard. He made it his business to know where she lived, where she went, and who her friends were. There was no such thing as safe unless Eli believed he was enough protection—Eli, Kali, and the small arsenal in her office.

"Why didn't you say anything sooner?" Eli asked. "Why deceive Lucy like you did?"

"I didn't intend to deceive Lucy. I was only protecting my cover. But now," Bob shrugged, "the time seemed right to reveal myself. You two can keep this between us, can't you?"

Owen stepped cautiously into the room, keeping a watchful eye on Bob, and effectively shutting down any private conversation. Bob handed Lucy and Eli each a business card with his contact information. He placed a hand on Officer Bradley's shoulder. "My right-hand man, understand?" Eli nodded. "I'll be in touch." With that, Bob slipped out a side door, narrowly escaping view from Chief Donoghue.

CHAPTER THIRTY

THE BMW ROLLED UP TO THE CHRYSANTHEMUM HOUSE JUST AS LANCE PULLED away. Lucy was supposed to meet him a half-hour ago, but the sketch had taken too long, and she was late.

They walked through the house and looked around. A note, written in magic marker on a folded scrap of yellow construction paper, was taped to the kitchen door.

"I'LL CALL YOU."

Lucy sighed with the guilty tug of schoolgirl shame, then wandered out to the back garden to water the few vegetables resolved enough to survive—noting that some of them had up and vanished altogether.

She handed the watering can off to Owen, and he happily doled out water to each plant while she stepped back inside.

"It's an oven in here," said Eli, just as the doorbell rang.

Lucy peered through the screen door, but saw no one, and was just about to walk away when she heard a squeal and "Hey, sista'!"—followed by Julia flinging open the screen door and wrapping her arms around her.

Lucy was speechless for a stunned moment, before the squeals of joy from both women filled the front door and were pulled into the house.

Eli and Owen looked on with eyes wide and mouths open as Lucy and her sister, simultaneously hugging and jumping up and down, finally fell into the sofa, laughing so hard that tears ran down their faces.

"What are they doing?" Owen stared at Lucy as if she was a stranger, fingers in his ears.

Julia wore knee-length black tights with an oversized sleeveless shirt. She resembled Lucy in the face and jaw, and broad smiles that were strikingly similar. But Julia's hair was coarse, black, and boyishly short, and her skin was a deep golden brown to Lucy's lighter complexion. She was loud and confident, and her personality seemed to fill the room.

"I know who you are," said Julia, pointing to Owen with a twinkle in her eye.

"You do?" Owen's eyes grew wide as saucers.

"I have a little something for you." She reached deep into her giant pack and produced a pair of small, colorful maracas from Spain. Julia stepped up to Eli and hugged him around the middle. "And you must be Eli. Lucy's told me all about you." Her smile implied intimacy, and Lucy caught the surprise in Eli's face. Julia stood back and started giggling. "Well, where's my room? Or are we sharing?" Lucy looked at Eli, who was grinning from ear to ear. Julia had that effect on people. She would have made a perfect Midwesterner.

"Not here, and *not* sharing," Lucy said. "I'm staying at Eli's, and there's plenty of room." *The house will thank me*, she thought.

Eli needed to stop at the office before going home. Lucy suggested they wait for him at the park. The sisters could visit while Owen played.

Owen shook his new maracas all the way up to the square, and Eli parked the car in front of his office. Just as Lucy reached for the door handle to get out, he grabbed her other hand.

"Julia, would you take Owen to the playground? We need a moment," said Eli, pointing to the other side of the park, which was unusually busy for a weekday. Summer vacation brought out children and parents in numbers seen only on weekends or holidays during the rest of the year.

Julia and Owen weren't halfway across the street before Eli's lips came to rest on Lucy's, in a series of kisses, which began small and finished in a lingering exchange that blocked out the rest of the world. Eli had a way of transporting her into another dimension where time stood still, and life was nothing but love and kindness.

They stepped out of the car and met on the sidewalk. "I won't be too long," he whispered. Lucy laid her head against his shoulder, her arms fastened around him. It was all she could do to peel herself away. "Julia, remember?" he laughed, looking out into the park where they could see Julia helping Owen onto the tire swing.

Crossing the street, Lucy heard Owen's delighted cries as Julia spun him wildly around and around, back and forth. His eyes were closed, and his head tilted back with the inertia of the swing. It was tough to interrupt their fun, but it was the first time she'd seen her sister in over a year, and they had a lot of catching up to do.

Lucy looked around, noticing the wear and tear on the park lawn and the litter left behind by regular stampedes of picketers and protesters. She sat down on a bench beside the playground which was cast in the shade of the Old Oak's protective outer limbs.

It didn't matter to the tree what had transpired here in the past few months. Just as in the century which had preceded AVID's arrival, the oak would produce its acorns, drop its leaves, and revive from dormancy on schedule, regardless of conflict or time-eclipsing kisses.

Julia left Owen to play with a friend from school as she joined Lucy on the bench. Lucy told the whole ugly story about the bombings in town, the graffiti, the demonstrations, and the events of the previous day that led to Owen sitting down with a sketch artist at the police department that morning. Julia listened closely. She already knew about Ben Wyatt—she sat with Lucy in the hospital for days and skipped school to go to the trial. She knew it all.

"So, you're saying I couldn't have shown up at a worse time," said Julia, kicking at the dirt under her feet.

"Oh my God, no. I'm happy you're here. I need you." Lucy clutched her sister.

"And Eli?" asked Julia. "You two are living together now? Sharing a room? Lucky you." Julia winked. "Am I going to be in the way?"

"No, you won't. Just wait till you get to the house. This place is …"

"I know, I know—you told me. It's a palace." The sisters started giggling and drew some attention from an elderly couple passing by.

Lucy shared the latest detail—the FBI agent living right across the street. It still seemed like a crazy dream.

"What? Did he think, like, Wyatt was just going to go up and ring the doorbell?" asked Julia. "What kind of agent is he?"

"I know, it sounds weird, but there's so much more to the story."

This issue was bigger than Lucy or scaring a little boy or disrupting the pace of life in a small Midwestern town. This was FBI big.

Lucy left off there, in favor of hearing about her sister's trip—like some of the more "adventurous" adventures, also known as "things Mom and Dad will never hear." Julia regaled Lucy with stories about the diverse group of friends she met along the way, often finding herself a week-long guest, or just roughing it along with some other trekkers.

Owen was playing now with several friends he knew from school and came over to introduce one of them as Anika. Anika smiled, exposing a missing tooth, then ran back to the playground.

"Anika has a dog," whispered Owen, as if revealing an intimate detail—before running along after her.

"Maybe now is not the best time to let you know, but Mom and Dad are on their way." Julia winced.

"Whoa. Okay. Now, there's that." Lucy thought for a moment. "What do you think they'll say when they find out I'm staying with Eli?" Their parents were staunch Catholics.

"You still have your own house, Lucy. Just go back there for a while."

"It's not as easy as that."

"Just pack your bag," said Julia. "What's the big deal?" Lucy shook her head. Julia still didn't get it.

"He's trying to keep me safe," Lucy said.

"Sounds to me like he's trying to keep you close."

"Well, that too." Lucy giggled.

She hadn't sorted out her feelings on that. She really wasn't safe anywhere. Ben Wyatt cast a dark cloud over everything. And she was acutely aware of her role in drawing Wyatt to Eli's house.

They were interrupted by Lucy's phone.

"I have to get this," she said. She answered as Julia made her way back over to the playground.

Lance was one of her first loyalists. He and his wife were eager to sign up their two kids and helped spread the word about the Chrysanthemum House.

That's why it hit her like a ton of bricks as she sat in the dappled shade of the oak, and he told her that when the lease was up in September, he would be putting the house up for sale.

"To be honest," he said, "I had considered evicting you, with all of the trouble and attention the house has been getting. That way I would be able to sell the house sooner. But my wife talked me around." Lucy made a mental note to thank the wife, bewildered by his cold treatment. He didn't used to be like this.

In a long-winded account of everything *he'd* been through and the unwelcome attention *he* was getting, he finally got around to telling Lucy he was giving her first option to buy.

"Classes start the end of August," she explained to him, feeling as if the rug had been pulled out from under her. "There isn't much time, and I'll need to get in touch with Summer, who's traveling right now."

"That's what cell phones are all about," he said, chuckling.

Having his kids as students muddied the waters. His son, Maxwell, would be one of her oldest students next term, and if they left, he would likely transition well. But she worried about Macy, the shy ten-year-old who was one of her favorites.

ALL OF THIS was explained to Eli later that night, after Julia had gone to bed. The two lingered on the patio lit by porch lights on either side of the French doors. They stretched out on their respective lounge chairs, and stared up into the shimmering white underbelly of the silver maple fluttering in the breeze.

"Thank you for letting Julia stay." She reached out for his hand across the small gap between their chairs. "But there's more." Eli raised his brows. "My parents are on their way."

"Oh." He squeezed her hand, and then pulled it toward him. "All right. That's—awesome."

"Seriously, it's too much."

"No, it's not. There's plenty of room, and I'd like to meet them, Kitten." He pulled a little harder, and she couldn't ignore the suggestion—one more tug and she would be on the ground. She got up to join him, straddling his lap. He drew up his knees to hold her upright.

"We can go back to the Chrysanthemum House. My dad is more protective than you, if you can believe that. And I have my very own FBI agent, right across the street."

"Lucy, I want you here. Not against your will, of course, but—this is working, isn't it? Don't you like it here?"

"I love it here. You and Kali have made me feel nothing but welcome. But it's not my home."

He kissed her sweetly. "It is for the time being. Can we agree to that?" She was glad he wasn't going to pressure her.

"And Owen?"

"Well, I think he's your number two fan." He grinned, Owen-like.

"But you're sending him away, right? Because of me."

"He'd be going anyway, just not for so long. We do this every year. I hate it. But they're his grandparents, and they have a right to spend time with him. We made this arrangement long before you came along."

"Hmm." Lucy rolled over, so they were sitting hip to hip, and he placed his arm across her shoulders. "My landlord called. He's selling the house."

"What! He can't do that, can he? Don't you have a contract or lease?"

"It's up in September. Summer and I have the first right of purchase, though."

"We'll figure something out."

"No, Eli, this is my problem."

"No, no—not like that. I don't have a cent to spare, but Jasper, my roommate from college is a lawyer, and he might have some free advice. Would you allow at least that?"

"Fine, yes." They sat quietly for a minute digesting the eventful day. One development stood out; GI Joe was an FBI agent.

"What about Bob?" asked Lucy.

"I love that movie."

"You know what I mean. There he was the whole time, and what good was he?"

Lucy was vexed that he had been that close and still unable to prevent either event at the Chrysanthemum House.

"He's not your personal bodyguard," Eli reminded her, but that only elicited a frustrated groan from Lucy. She gazed up into the maple branches, collecting her thoughts.

Eli climbed out of the chair and offered a hand to Lucy. "Let's go to bed." He shut and locked the French doors behind them—as he'd done every night since Lucy had begun staying there.

The heart-to-heart was overdue and extended until well after midnight while they lay in bed, working out the more delicate points. Sleep eventually overcame them, despite a rogue mosquito they ineffectually tried to wave away.

"A swing and a miss," said Eli.

CHAPTER THIRTY-ONE

BOB MARSHALL CALLED LUCY TO ARRANGE A PLACE TO MEET WHERE THEY wouldn't draw attention. She suggested Nikko's and told him she would set it up. As it turned out, the other couple they usually met with would be away in Italy for a month.

When Lucy and Eli arrived at their cooking class the following Tuesday, Nikko poured wine and set a platter of fresh fruit and cheese on the coffee table, as if this were a social event.

Nikko was nervous. It wasn't every day an FBI agent came to visit. Lucy sat down beside Eli on the leather sofa and sipped her wine, hoping it would quell her own unease.

Eli checked his watch. Bob was late. Lucy joked about the traffic, just as Bob slipped in through the kitchen door and sat down across from them. He looked tired.

Eli led the introductions. "Bob, this is Nikko Stark." Bob and Nikko shook hands. "I've known Nikko since I was a boy."

Bob nodded. "Thank you, Nikko, for allowing me to crash the lesson." He looked at the spread on the coffee table. "Looks more like a party."

"Yes, well …" muttered Nikko. "Sir, would you like some wine?"

"Thank you—whatever you have is fine." He looked across the table at Lucy. "We arrested another key member of AVID today." He didn't sound happy about it.

"And?" Eli leaned closer to the table dividing him from Bob.

"And we interviewed Wyatt's last known foster parents." His voice was flat, considering this progress. "It's crystal clear where Wyatt got some of his ideology. His foster father proudly took credit for helping Wyatt form American Values in Democracy. The guy is a real piece of work."

Nikko arrived with a glass for Bob, then topped off Lucy's and Eli's. He wasn't quite sure what to do with himself after that.

"Please, sit," said Bob. "There will be more of these meetings, and you should be in the know. Are you comfortable with that?"

"Well, yes. Do I need to sign anything? Take an oath?"

"No, Nikko. You're fine. Just sit down." Bob reached for some cheese and sipped his wine. "Back to the foster father. His name is Stan Carter. With the help of the prison warden, he smuggled promotional materials in and out. AVID began as one cancer cell in the bowels of that prison with Wyatt's warped view of the world. Prison is already rife with bigotry and hate, but Carter's xenophobic propaganda in Wyatt's hands turned one man's obsession into a full-fledged movement. Wyatt was the perfect example to the other like-minded prisoners, considering he'd been put in prison unfairly."

"Hey!" Lucy pushed up her blouse, to where Bob could see the scar.

"*I* didn't say it was unfair," Bob said, "but Wyatt and his kind thought it was. You know what I mean? I'm just telling you what I learned, all right?"

Bob reached for a fat strawberry and bit into it before continuing. "So, here's where it gets personal. AVID has a social media page on a platform that Carter runs, called Weissmacht. It's filled with propaganda and illicit suggestions. Think of Facebook, but it caters to white supremacists." Lucy remembered Bob mentioning the dark site. "One such suggestion was to find Lucia Perez. It was a contest, and they pounced on it. Within hours, your whereabouts and family history were on the site."

"How is that possible?" asked Eli. "She changed everything." Lucy thought about Tina Reynold's earlier search.

"Even if she'd changed her name legally through the courts, it wouldn't have mattered. That's public information—as is her driver's license, business license, each previous address, current address, and phone number. Even her financial records can be found for a price. And to some of these nuts, it was worth that price to be in Ben Wyatt's good graces. These folks follow him blindly. He's like a god to them."

"A god." Eli stared at Bob. "Why?"

"I suspect because he brought AVID to life," Bob said. He turned to Lucy, as Nikko was refilling her wine glass. "I could have found you through one of those websites, but, well, the FBI had you pretty well fleshed out. I know where you went to primary school, that your eighth-grade teacher was arrested for tax evasion, that your father was investigated after marrying your mother, that Summer's brother was a high-school dropout. And don't get me started on Eli."

"What!" Eli almost choked on a slice of melon.

Bob laughed. "Just kidding, man. You're golden." Eli glared at him. "Lucy, I have a thumb drive filled with your life story. There is no such thing as privacy in America. But I have just as much on Wyatt. Everything but a current address."

"Revenge." Lucy stared at Bob. "That's why he's in Drake. That's why AVID is in Drake."

"Yes. They already had your address. They've been watching you and reporting to Wyatt through Carter and the dark social media site, Weissmacht."

"My phone number," Lucy murmured.

"I mentioned that—yes, they have your phone number."

"I've been getting so much spam! Voice usually, but text sometimes. Some are the usual scams you hear about. But some are in German, I think."

"Save any of these?"

"I block them and report as spam. You know the drill. But my email cache is loaded."

"I'll need to look into that."

"Do you want my email address?"

Bob laughed, took a long draw from his glass, and said, "No, thanks—I have it."

"So, Bob—how long has Wyatt been in Drake?" Eli reached for Lucy's hand. She'd been wondering the same thing.

"We can't be sure, but he was last seen in California on April 21."

"He was supposed to be in prison for four years. What happened?"

"Early release. Like I said earlier, Carter had an in with the warden—who, as it turns out, is a white supremacist. With his help, he got time off for good behavior if you can believe it. Also, his lawyer swung a deal where he could get credit for time served awaiting trial." Bob stood up and stretched his arms.

The wine bottle was empty, but Nikko was already opening a second when Bob said he had to go.

CHAPTER THIRTY-TWO

THE EXPECTATION OF OWEN'S GRANDPARENTS GAVE EVERYONE A PURPOSE ON the day of their arrival. That morning, Eli welcomed a contractor into the garage to have a look at the air conditioner. They had not switched it on for years, and it needed a bit of work. By lunchtime, after tinkering with the unit on the other side of the garage, and replacing the filters, the potbellied repairman had proclaimed success, and cool air blew out of every vent.

Lucy wondered if Eli would have gone to so much expense if Nana and Papa were not planning to stay the night. But it didn't matter. The house had become an oasis from the unrelenting heat and humidity, and she was grateful.

To Owen's delight, he was asked to set the dining room table for eight, with Kali crossing her fingers that Mia would make an appearance. She hadn't replied to the invitation, but Kali wasn't giving up hope. They had aired their concerns about moving in together, and while it wasn't off the table, it wasn't imminent either.

"I see them together, Eli—they adore one another," said Lucy when they'd discussed his sister the previous day.

"I know that, and you know that. But Mia grew up in a pretty messed up family, and I don't think she'd recognize a welcome mat if she were standing on it."

"What do you mean?" asked Lucy.

"It's kind of a bizarre story, but it ends with her living on her own with her step-brother when she was still in high school. She's super independent because of it."

"Abandonment issues," suggested Lucy.

"Well, listen to you." He laughed.

Lucy hoped, for Kali's sake, that Mia would show up—but for

Mia's sake too. It had become glaringly apparent what a privilege it was to live under this roof.

After Owen set each plate, flanked with forks and knives as Lucy instructed, he dashed upstairs to change his clothes. All his favorites had been set aside already, sitting in two little towers beside his new suitcase. Lucy found him standing in front of the mirror in Eli's room, looking himself over.

Eli had shared a story of Owen admiring himself in the mirror at the barber the day before, as if no one was watching. As she thought about that, she picked up a brush from her dresser and ran it through his hair. The barber had cut most of his curls off, and that changed his looks considerably. She had to admit that without the mass of hair, he looked less like his father, and it made her a little sad.

Julia and Lucy worked on making their mom's enchiladas while a blackberry cobbler bubbled in the oven. Eli and Owen spent hours shopping for new clothes and getting haircuts. An R2D2 roller bag was purchased, and Owen was now, after days of moping, excited about his Wisconsin adventure.

Lucy, Julia, and Kali cleaned the house top to bottom while Eli was at work. When he returned, Julia began issuing orders from the rose garden. From the moment she had stepped into the yard and discovered the shed full of "toys," she staked her claim.

Julia had studied horticulture in college and spent her summers working with her father on various landscape projects. She was well-trained and thrilled with the prospect of revitalizing what she could with the tools at her disposal—and no one was happier about it than Kali. She had always felt guilty about letting the garden go—but neither she nor Eli knew a thing about it.

Owen took his raking seriously, reaching deep into the shrubbery to get every dry bit. But when it came to picking it all up and loading the wheelbarrow, he found he was best suited as a supervisor.

"Mom would love this," said Kali. Not just about the rose garden being reclaimed, but about having a houseful of family, unconventional as it was.

Nana and Papa arrived late that afternoon with robust hugs for everyone. They were probably the most beautiful people Lucy had ever met, and it was awkward, considering how she had been quietly hating on them the past few days for taking Owen away.

It was understood that Nana and Papa wanted to be called such by all. As for their real names, Lucy was sure Eli knew them, but Nana and Papa they were, and Lucy and Julia just went with it. Even after Mia showed up, just in time for dessert, they were introduced as Nana and Papa.

Lucy learned that evening that they had had their first grandchild nearly twenty years earlier. Owen was number eleven. To date, there were thirteen grandchildren, and they were eagerly awaiting the day when they would be great-grandparents.

THE NEXT MORNING, Eli and Owen packed his little suitcase with his new clothes, a swimming suit, and some "grubbies," as Nana put it, so he wouldn't always be so worried about getting dirty—especially since they had a camping trip planned with all of his cousins.

Eli felt envious. He never had that family connection himself, and wasn't able to provide the extended family for Owen that Eva's family could.

Before climbing into his booster seat in Papa's car, Owen gave Lucy a monster hug, and like a little gentleman, wiped her tears away and asked her not to cry. She cried anyway.

Nana said goodbye to Eli with a hug and a wink.

Lucy watched Papa pull Eli aside. "She's a keeper."

"I'm aware," answered Eli glancing at Lucy who grinned back at him.

As they watched the minivan roll down the gravel drive, Lucy tickled the back of Eli's neck. "So, I'm a keeper, am I?"

"You know it."

NOT LONG AFTER they'd said their goodbyes to Owen, Lucy's parents texted that they were two hours out, and would see them soon. Julia teased that they were running a bed and breakfast as she and Lucy changed the sheets on the bed Nana and Papa had used.

They rolled up on schedule, in their 2008 diesel Chevy Silverado. Lucy was relieved that at least her father had left his equipment trailer at home. Her mother climbed out of the truck and stretched her long arms high into the air. Her white capri pants and short-sleeve blouse were wrinkled, and her lipstick had worn off, leaving a pink stain on her mouth, as if she had just finished off a cherry popsicle. Lucy's mother pulled a clip from her hair and refastened it one, two, three.

Lucy's father, Javier, was a short man with stubby legs, muscular arms, and an endearing smile. He immediately made a beeline for his daughters. Then, after the hugs and tears were out of the way, he made himself available for introductions.

He remembered Eli from the Skype call weeks earlier, and practically collided with him in an exuberant embrace.

"Finally, we meet the man who is taking such wonderful care of our little girl. I'm sure it won't be long now till it's official, am I right?" said Lucy's mother, Elaine. Eli blushed. Lucy shook her head and pulled her mom aside to set the record straight, while her father embarrassed her further.

"Oh, Kitten, don't be so hard on your mother. She's a dreamer."

"Kitten?" said Kali, waiting to be introduced.

"Dad, this is Kali, Eli's sister."

"Well, hello there, Kali." Javier stepped over to Kali who didn't seem quite prepared for him, but he swept her up in a hug. "Lucy's been my Kitten since before she could walk," he said, delighted to share this familiarity. "Meowing to be picked up and held." Javier laughed a big belly laugh, turning to Lucy and giving her a squeeze. "Now that one," he said, pointing to Julia, "she's my little brown Peanut." The laugh exploded from Javier's pint-sized body. It said everything you needed to know about the man. Julia gave her father a little push and picked up his suitcase.

"Goodness you're tall!" Elaine craned her neck as she wrapped her arms around Kali's waist. Kali looked over at Eli, overwhelmed. He smiled at her and she grinned back.

"Follow me," Lucy said, and the group set off to the back patio and into the coolness of the house.

Elaine was heartbroken to learn they'd missed Owen. They had picked up a cowboy hat from a gift shop they stopped at on their trip and were sorry they wouldn't be able to give it to him themselves.

"He'll love it," said Eli. "We'll be sure to send you photos of him when he tries it on."

"Oh, you're wonderful," said Elaine, squeezing his hand. "Isn't he wonderful?" she asked Julia, who nodded wholeheartedly. "Now, let's see what's going on in that kitchen." And just like that, the Moon household fell under the influence of Mr. and Mrs. Perez.

CHAPTER THIRTY-THREE

ELAINE BUZZED WITH EXCITEMENT WHEN SHE DISCOVERED THE FULL-COLOR INSERT in the weekly paper of listed events for the Independence Day festivities: parade, hot dog boil, doggie fashion show, and the Whisky Boys Jazz Band.

Lucy and Eli had not planned on attending, but not going was out of the question for Elaine, who had infected Javier with her enthusiasm.

That night, after Lucy and Eli climbed into bed, they spoke in hushed voices about their memories of the event as they had attended it in previous years.

"When I was little," Eli said, "my dad would hoist me onto his shoulders to see the passing firetrucks and classic cars." It wasn't difficult for Lucy to look at the man and see the boy. "All the local businesses would use the event for advertising shamelessly. Moon Harvest did it too. Every year the employees threw together a parade float with their take on that year's theme. It took months of planning." He thought a moment. "I remember riding on it once before my great-grandfather died. Four generations of Moons collected to wave at the town and toss candy as we passed. Mostly what I remember is the candy." He grinned.

This event, as an adult, held no interest for him. "It would be different," he confided, "if Owen were here. But he's always in Wisconsin this time of year, spending the holiday watching a different parade in a different town with different people."

Lucy, on the other hand, had attended the event on her first summer in Drake—and then vowed never to return. It was festive, colorful, lively, and peppered with a certain Midwest charm—but watching the families, friends, and couples while she stood on the side of the road by herself made her lonelier than she could imagine. This year would be different. She was part of a couple, and her family was there. But Eli was right—it would be better if Owen was there. She sighed.

Regardless of how they felt, at eleven o'clock the next day, they piled into Eli's car and set off for the event. Even Julia was now curious to take in this Midwestern show of national pride.

It was an embarrassing spectacle. The parade itself was predictable. There were the fire trucks and the classic cars Eli remembered from his youth, along with the traditional floats cruising up Golden Avenue from the high school, around Drake Park, down Wilson, and past the city hall. Red white and blue dominated the floats with balloons and loudspeakers.

"Tell your friends about the Grand Mallard Hotel. Right here in the heart of the city."

"Watch out for great deals—they're going to get you at Drake Hardware and Appliance."

"Ladies—remember Dorothy's Dress Shop when you need to freshen up your wardrobe, and don't forget a new pair of shoes to make it extra special." Lucy and Julia rolled their eyes.

The toy shop, the coffee shop, the museum, and the independent grocery on Jamison and Flint all had their turn to boast—but the worst was the lead float. The preacher man himself, Mayor Church, touted his own greatness through a cheap microphone, with the Star-Spangled Banner as accompaniment.

Elaine ate it all up. Javier wasn't so sure about the parade, but he got a kick out of the doggie fashion show. His belly laugh could be heard a block away.

There were plenty of familiar faces. The Hill brothers walked beside the city float, waving their miniature flags. Eli joked that it was likely the most exercise either of them had gotten in recent history. GI Joe, aka Bob Marshall, dressed in his classic camo, was leaning up against the bandstand, keeping an eye on things while the Jazz Band set up behind him. He looked utterly unapproachable, with a grim expression and tightly folded arms.

Beth intercepted their little group, and introductions were made while her middle daughter, Rayanne, made eyes at Eli.

Lucy said hello to many of her students from over the three years she'd been teaching in Drake, and Eli shook hands with multiple clients from the social service office, past and present.

An old high school friend approached Eli with an invitation to go out some night and catch up. He was back in town for a few weeks and was trying to get a few guys together for old time's sake. Eli wondered which high school friends were in town, since he'd neither seen nor heard from any of them in six years.

Despite the many familiar faces, there were many more they didn't recognize. Rough-looking men, making the rounds, studying the population. Bob had his work cut out for him.

Lucy had been on the fence about whether to be on her guard or not. If Ben Wyatt wanted to hurt her, he would find a way. Was having Bob Marshall around going to make a difference? She glanced back to see Bob looking in her direction.

By the time Elaine gave them all the go-ahead to leave, they were tired, and their feet hurt. Their bellies were full of hot dogs, kettle corn, and a fry bread that Javier thought was the best thing he'd eaten since being home in Mexico. Lucy thought she was going to be sick.

They were approaching the Washington Street parking lot when Lucy sensed they were being followed. As she opened the car door, an arm reached out and grabbed Javier's shirttail. He was a young man, twenty or so, with a pug-nose and a ponytail. The assailant gave it a good yank and tried to pull him to the ground— but they underestimated him. He stood firm and pulled his shirt from him. Two more guys joined their friend, bigger and older, his father and uncle perhaps.

"Back off!" said Eli.

"We don't want any trouble," said Javier. Julia jumped in surprise and rubbed her arm where someone had just pinched her. Alarmed by the aggressive encounter, Lucy, Julia, and Elaine quickly climbed into the car, while Eli and Javier worked things out.

Lucy listened to the muffled voices outside the car. "You don't want trouble?" The assailant looked from Javier to Eli. "I'll back off as soon at that Beaner goes back to Mexico, you fuckin' Jew." One of the men threatened Eli with a ready fist, but Eli brushed him off as he helped Javier into the car and made sure everyone else was accounted for.

Eli put the car in gear as the men spit and yelled racial slurs. "Unamerican, all of you!" hollered one of the older men.

He sped down Washington and turned east, quickly putting distance between the men and his car as he drove out of town.

"I'm sorry," said Eli, once he was in the clear. "Lucy told you about these guys, right?"

Javier leaned forward enough to be heard and gripped the back of Eli's seat. "Yes, Eli. No need to apologize. That sort is everywhere."

Lucy and Eli hadn't shared the latest news with her parents or Nana and Papa; that Ben Wyatt was the ringleader of this ugly tribe. Nor had they told them about Bob Marshall. They thought it was best to keep things simple.

CHAPTER THIRTY-FOUR

TWO WEEKS INTO THE PEREZ VISIT, LUCY TOOK HER MOTHER ON A WALK through the orchard and asked how long they intended to stay. Elaine was caught off guard.

"Have we been a burden? Are we in the way?"

"No, of course not," said Lucy. "I wouldn't even ask if we were all staying in my own place."

"Why aren't we at your place?"

What was she going to say? It's not safe there? I'm being racially targeted and haunted by my attacker?

"It's complicated."

"Nonsense, there is nothing complicated here. You prefer Eli's bed. I get it. I wish you had a ring on your finger, but I get it."

Lucy wondered if it really was that simple. At some point, she imagined, the zealots would pack up their signs and go back home to their jobs and families, the FBI would capture Wyatt and lock him away, and she would be free to return to the Chrysanthemum House--if she wanted.

"Sweetie, we've tried to pull our own weight. I do what I can, and your father, well, your father has really turned that orchard around with Julia's help," Elaine said.

"Mom, I told you—you are welcome here," Lucy insisted. "Neither Kali nor Eli have said anything. It was just a simple question."

Having her parents around had its pros and cons. She'd missed them terribly, and the extended stay gave them a chance to reconnect. But Lucy had grown accustomed to the Moon house and the subtle patterns that had formed in the short time she'd lived there—including Owen's bedtime ritual and the unspoken rules that revolved around Kali's appointment schedule.

Kali had to come out from her office on more than one occasion to quiet Javier's booming voice, or the racket from the kitchen. She had started staying over at Mia's more and more too.

Lucy believed she had calmed her mother's anxiety by the time they'd returned from their orchard tour to the comfort of the great room.

The air-conditioned house was a sanctuary, not just from the summer weather, but from the bonfire Javier had started behind the orchard, near the foundation of the long-gone barn. The wind had switched, and instead of blowing out into the meadow, it was now drifting toward the house. He and Julia had been working hard toward this day, pruning away the deadwood from the long-neglected apple trees.

Lucy left her mother to think about their conversation and rode her bike into town to see Eli. It wasn't a challenging ride; it was flat most of the way, but it took nearly an hour to go the seven miles, navigating the rural roads. The faster she rode, the better the breeze, which was welcome on this steamy day.

Black-eyed-Susans, cornflowers, and Queen Anne's lace were joined occasionally by a poppy here and there along the side of the road.

Lucy detoured past the Chrysanthemum House, the impulse too tempting to resist. She planted one foot on the curb across the street to look at what she was likely to lose, and an ache lodged itself in her chest.

"It really is a beautiful house." Bob Marshall walked down his porch steps to the sidewalk. "You know, Lucy, there is no reason you shouldn't be able to move back in. You have that security camera, and I'm right across the street. Officer Bradley has been keeping an eye on the place too." He stood in front of her bike, now looking up at the large, faded blue carved flower on the face of the house. "I think your school is brilliant. You shouldn't give up on it." His voice was deep and steady.

Lucy watched him gazing at the house and wondered how she could not have trusted him.

"It's more than that," she confided. "If I can't come up with the money to buy it, my landlord is going to sell it out from under me." Bob looked at her in disbelief.

"What's his name?"

"What, you gonna turn him in for being an asshole?" she said, laughing, and he smiled for the first time since she'd seen him. The stern, rough-cut GI Joe now spoke like an uptown, educated man.

"If that were all it took, Lucy, I would. Actually—I just thought he may be part of AVID. I was going to see if his name was on the list."

"How long is this list?"

"Too long. There are more members now than ever. It's expanded beyond Drake. And it's not just AVID, there are organizations just like it all over. You would never believe how many xenophobes there are in this country. They call themselves nationalists, and they are more than small clusters of extremists—they are a serious national threat."

In her limited TV-based experience of the FBI, Lucy had never seen an agent confide in a civilian. "What are you actually doing here in Drake, Bob?"

"Well," he said, laughing—another first. "I am supposed to track the movements of Ben Wyatt, but the directive has expanded. There are a handful of agents here now, not just me. We can't apprehend anyone until they break the law, however—and to date, they are mostly out of our reach."

"How can I help?" Lucy surprised Bob and herself with the question.

"Lucy, you've helped plenty already. You led us to Wyatt, and the security footage from you and Eli has helped us identify two members of the group—not important members, but we've made two arrests."

Lucy looked confused. "You have?"

"Well, yeah. The two arrests helped us to fill out the list—with a little encouragement." Bob laughed. "So, that was you too. I'm not about to put you in any danger for more. This is beyond anything you could do."

"What if we could prove the Hill brothers bugged Eli's office?"

"They didn't," said Bob. "Not themselves anyway. It was the

same guy who bombed your school, doing their dirty work. That dumbass would do anything to please them."

"This guy planted the bugs and bombed my school for the Hill brothers." Lucy was trying to get it straight.

"Yes. He's admitted to as much. His admission is not enough to arrest the Hills, but it will help us hold them when the time comes."

"Oh." Lucy was disappointed. "So, why did the Hill's bug the office?"

"It's one of the fringe issues here. The Hills have had it in for the social service office for years. Ever since Planned Parenthood moved in. They've been trying to prove that Beth and Eli want young women to kill their babies."

"What? That's ridiculous." Lucy had heard of similar stings on the news, but to think that they thought abortion was encouraged was insane.

"Once Officer Bradley learned about the bugs, they packed up their effort."

"And the bomb? That was directed by the Hill brothers?" asked Lucy.

Bob nodded. "Which was probably directed by you know who."

"Ben Wyatt."

"Again, no proof. We need more information. We need more AVID members willing to spill the beans."

"I'd like to be more help, Bob. Think about it."

Bob shook his head. "I'm thankful to have two of Wyatt's loose-lipped associates. They're now in federal prison—where he should be." *Amen*, thought Lucy. "Come to mention it, have you ever filed a restraining order against Wyatt?"

"No."

"Say he does get close—it might be enough to get an arrest. The FBI would take care of the rest."

"I'm bait?"

"We're watching for him, Lucy. You have nothing to worry about."

Bob also said he'd yet to find the person or persons who funded this whole movement.

"Donations?" asked Lucy.

"If so, then where was the money trail? I need a trip to DC to meet my senior officer. That would help me create a road map—but I'm afraid it won't be enough. I needed more feet on the ground, more eyes and ears. I've requested two more agents." Bob went on. "Everything okay with you otherwise? Was that your family at the parade?"

"Oh, yes, that was them, with their open-ended departure date." Lucy laughed.

"I get it. I remember falling in love. I remember it well." He smiled at her. "Must be hard to have your folks around." The words "falling in love" flowed into her ears and did a lap around her heart. "Say hello to Eli for me—and don't hesitate to call if you need me. I mean it."

"I will." Lucy pushed off and cruised around the corner toward the square.

"HEY, WHAT ARE you doing here?" Eli's broad smile greeted Lucy when she walked into his office.

"I needed a distraction," she laughed. He popped out of his chair and went to her.

"So, I'm a distraction now, am I?" Eli laid his hands on her hips, grinning.

"Get out of here!" Beth shouted from her office. "The two of you! Eli, I'll take your last appointment—you're worthless to me now anyway, moonin' over your sweetheart like that."

Eli held the door open. "Let's go to the park."

The playground was full of children and their watchful parents as the couple strolled leisurely around the square. They sat on their favorite bench under the Old Oak and watched the ducks with their juvenile offspring, looking every bit as gawky as teenagers. Lucy started naming them when Eli stopped her with a tender kiss. The park was far from private, but at that moment, they felt every bit as alone as if there had been four walls around them.

Eventually, Lucy got around to telling Eli about her conversation with her mother. He would not admit that they were wearing out their welcome, but he did acknowledge that he was longing for a little privacy.

"Your dad meets me every night when I get home, giving me the progress report for the orchard." Javier and Julia had cleared the dead limbs and pruned what they could. They also cleaned up the tree garden in front of the house and revitalized the roses. "The turnaround is remarkable, but I wish *you* were the one running to meet me—you know?"

"I don't know how long they plan to stay, Eli. I'm thinking— well, I think it's too much to expect you and Kali to put up with so many outsiders for as long as you have."

He laughed. "It's not like they've moved in permanently, have they?"

"No—they can't. I mean, my dad has a business to run. But it got me thinking—you know, the living arrangement. We've practically taken over your house." She didn't want to say it. She didn't want to *do* it. But what choice did she have? "Maybe it's time to go back to the Chrysanthemum House. I just saw Bob. He said it should be safe with Officer Bradley and him and the security camera."

Eli looked stunned. "Lucy, you know ..." His voice trailed off and he regrouped, laying a hand on her arm and nervously giving the hem of her T-shirt a little tug. "You know how I feel about that. How I feel about you." Lucy's heart flipped. Eli shifted in his seat as a duck waddled up to their feet, hoping for a fallen scrap of food. He looked down at it, then up into the tree as if searching for the right words. "What are you so afraid of?" he finally asked.

"Eli." Lucy turned his hand over and began massaging his open palm thoughtfully.

He leaned in close, laying his forehead against hers, and whispered, "Can't you see I'm in love with you?"

"Eli." Lucy took a breath, then pulled back slowly.

"I have been from the start."

Lucy had known. She loved him too, but the words had never been said aloud. The duck wandered off to the pond. He'd given up on them. She wasn't going to give up on Eli. She wasn't going to reject the best thing in her life or turn her back on what she was feeling. She was devoted to Eli, his son, his history. She looked into his gray eyes, glistening with emotion. The long dark lashes that brushed her face when they kissed. His full lips which gave her so much pleasure. She took a deep breath, her heart pounding as if she teetered on the edge of a cliff—and she jumped, knowing Eli would catch her. His sentiment lodging itself in her heart.

"I love you too." *There it is.*

They sat quietly, stupidly grinning at one another. Disregarding the watchful eyes of a small group of mothers standing nearby, Eli kissed Lucy with such desire, she completely lost herself to it.

Eli pulled Lucy up onto her shaky legs, and they staggered love-drunk to the Chrysanthemum House, where they tripped hastily up the stairs to her room, undressed and were just getting into bed when Lucy heard a voice from downstairs. She realized just then that she'd accidentally left the front door open

"Hello?"

From her bed, naked and flushed with lust, Lucy and Eli froze.

"Kitten?" It was Javier.

Panicked, they scrambled to get their clothes back on and walked, step by step, down the stairs to find Lucy's mother peering at them. Julia looked mortified beyond belief. Her father went back outside.

"So, this is the place you've been talking about," said her mother, glancing around at the dust and clutter, seemingly oblivious to the intrusion. She explained that they were going to hole up here for a few days before heading home. Javier had gone back out through the front door to collect the luggage.

"No, Mom, really. This place is not ready for company." Lucy looked pleadingly at Eli. The house reminded her of the last days of Pompei. A shoe here, a plate there. Lucy and Summer's hasty exit was glaringly evident to everyone in the room.

"Seriously, you are all welcome at my house," Eli said. "There is plenty of room, and you are the easiest company anyone could hope for." He was still buttoning up his shirt.

"God, Mom—this is so embarrassing," moaned Julia. "Lucy, I'm so sorry."

Lucy saw her father out the front window. He pulled two suitcases from the back seat of his pickup and bumped the door closed with his hip. Exasperated, she rushed to meet him on the front porch, where they sat down together on the swing.

"We just wanted to come out to see you, Kitten—and your sister, of course." He still clutched the handles of the twin black roller bags. "We've missed you both so much. The house just isn't the same without the two of you."

"Empty nest syndrome," said Lucy, and he laughed.

"We should have had more kids," he joked, and let go of one suitcase to put his arm around her. He looked over his shoulder into the house and cocked his head, smiling. "Seems we interrupted something." Javier winked.

"Um … well—you should have called, maybe?" She kicked off against the railing and set the swing in motion.

"Julia sent you a text. We thought that's why the door was open." Her phone was where? The bedroom floor? It was awkward, this acknowledgment of her sex life with her father, but Lucy could only smile when she looked into his eyes. He understood, and she was thankful.

Lucy noticed Bob Marshall standing on his front step, pretending to have a cigarette. She nodded at him discreetly, and he went back into his apartment.

Suddenly, a van sped down the street and pulled up onto the curb in front of the house. The side door flung open with a rumble as a brutish masked man, dressed in blue jeans and a camouflage jacket, sprang out and sprinted up to the porch. He grabbed Javier aggressively by the arm—but he had underestimated Lucy's father.

Javier, with his solid, muscular arms, hoisted the roller bag, still gripped in his dominant hand, over Lucy's head, and it collided with the assailant's. The latter lost his balance, falling head over tail down the steps. The mask was pulled to the side, making it impossible for him to see through the eyeholes.

Another man, wearing a blue T-shirt and no mask, shot from

the van—not to collect his friend, but to finish the job with a baseball bat. He scrambled up the porch steps and swung, missing Javier by a hair. Lucy screamed, frantic to stop the assault.

Eli appeared behind the man with the baseball bat, trying to wrestle it from his hand—but the man's hold was too firm. Bob Marshall popped his head out his door to see what was going on and ran to Eli's aid.

With a firm hand, Eli pushed Lucy into the house and she closed the screen door. From there, she watched him jump down the stairs toward the first man. He grabbed hold of the camouflage jacket and pulled the mask from his face.

They looked on with horror at the man with the blue T-shirt, who had regained full control of his weapon and was now whaling on Javier. "Dad!" Lucy cried. "Papa!"

"Lucy—all of you—stay inside!" shouted Bob, leaping up the steps. He yanked the bat away with one hand, while Javier rolled out of the way.

"Stop it!" Lucy shouted as her mother fought her for the door handle.

Lucy, Julia, and Elaine looked on anxiously, while Bob quickly turned and grabbed the man with the T-shirt, then flung him down flat on the porch floor, knocking him unconscious. He tossed the bat to Eli, who held it high, ready to strike at the first assailant. The man scrambled, undaunted, to his van, and sped off without his partner in crime. Bob was not bothered. He had the plate number, and the footage from Lucy's security camera would seal the deal.

The whole melee took no more than three or four minutes, but to Lucy, it felt like twenty. That's how it was for her in the ally that day with Wyatt, yet those few minutes were the most memorable, and the most vivid of her whole life.

AN HOUR LATER, emerging from the urgent care clinic in the medical building shared by the Planned Parenthood, Lucy, Julia, and their mother escorted Javier to the truck. He was newly sleeved in a white cast, set at a perfect forty-five-degree angle from wrist to bicep. A bruise was developing on the side of his face.

Eli was waiting by the pickup with an eye on them and an eye on the surprising number of picketers still pacing in front of the building. They had taken a stand earlier in the spring, and every day there was a minimum of five picketers, marching back and forth, shouting, "Baby Killers, Abortion is Murder, and God Hates Abortion." The irony was that this Planned Parenthood didn't even perform abortions.

They drove by the park on their way to Eli's office and passed the bench where he and Lucy had been sitting just hours before. That bench was now surrounded, swept up by a growing crowd around the bandstand, seemingly waiting for something or someone to appear on the bandstand. Some had signs like, AVID Rules, and Join the Movement for Righteous Democracy, most did not. They were mostly men, but not exclusively—Lucy was surprised to see women and teenagers among the throng. *Where are the police?* Lucy wondered.

Eli and Lucy got out of the truck, loaded her bike into the back, and sent the others ahead to his house in the truck, promising to catch up later. He had called Beth earlier and gotten her up to speed, but it took some doing to convince her to close it up and get home before things got out of hand. Eli promised to keep an eye on the place with the security app. They locked up, walked Beth to her car, and caught a glimpse of Bob Marshall just as they were getting into Eli's car. Bob cocked his head in the direction of the road, and they took his meaning: it was time to get out of there.

Once safely out of sight and well on their way to his house, Eli pulled the car over onto the gravel shoulder.

"Just thought we should take a minute to catch our breath," he said. Lucy was thankful. They sat in silence with their fingers intertwined, ruminating on the events of the last few hours.

Their solitude was interrupted briefly by an incoming text from Bob. "Incident at the school wrapped up. Both men in custody. Thought you both should know." Lucy showed it to Eli, then began chuckling.

It turned from a *heh-heh-heh* to a *tee-hee-hee*—and finally a torrent of uncontrollable laughter, with tears dripping down her cheeks. "I'm sorry," she stammered, still laughing. "It's just so funny." Eli looked at her as if she'd gone mad—but such laughter is contagious, and soon he began laughing too.

"*Kitten?*" she said, remembering that afternoon. "My dad—oh, God. His face when he saw us!"

"*His* face? I wish you could have seen *your* face!" Eli sputtered between breaths. "I thought you were going to have a stroke."

Lucy leaned into him, shoulder to shoulder, separated by the emergency brake, and smiled. "I do love you."

WHEN THEY FINALLY got home, Lucy's parents were up in their room, unpacking, and the smell of something delicious was wafting from the kitchen. Kali was planted firmly on the sofa, watching TV. Without thinking, they sat down with her and were promptly sucked into the fallout from that day's string of presidential tweets.

What was the world coming to? The television had been set to cable news for days. While the five of them sat eating their Hungarian goulash, Eli, channeling his father, made a "new rule," limiting news to one hour a day.

Kali laughed. "Yeah, right."

"I'm serious. At some point it all becomes meaningless."

It brought them all back to stark reality. The sky was not falling. They didn't need to know the details of Stormy Daniels and Donald Trump or the never-ending tensions in Syria. Other than the coverage of sanctuary seekers at the border being locked up, there was little interest in the day-to-day drama at the White House. They had enough going on in their own universe with the AVID organization growing by leaps and bounds under their noses, and Ben Wyatt on the loose.

"A toast!" said Kali, raising her glass of water high. "To family."

"To family," they all chimed in.

"Owen leaves us each summer to spend time with his grandparents in Wisconsin, but I wish he were here, now, with us. With you two." Kali nodded at Javier and Elaine.

Elaine teared up as she lifted her glass. "To Owen."

Tina Reynolds stopped by after the dishes had been cleared. She wanted to give Lucy a heads up about a plot to bring ICE into her father's otherwise comfortable life.

"This is nuts!" said Lucy. *Immigration and Customs Enforcement in Drake? Really?*

"How do you know this?" asked Eli. Julia and Javier approached and listened in.

"We got a call at the paper. Not a warning. It was a tip. I think they want to make sure the *Drake Register* covers the event. They're looking for attention."

"So now they want your help. It's a far cry from the paintball onslaught," Lucy said.

"Sure is. It's madness, but I just wanted to give you all a head's up."

"Thank you, Tina." Lucy did not consider Tina a friend, but she wasn't an enemy either.

Javier's cast had been signed by everyone in their small universe, and Tina was no exception. After signing, she took a moment to visit with Lucy's parents. At some point in their conversation, Javier proudly revealed his citizenship card.

"You're a citizen!" cried Lucy. "Why didn't you say anything earlier?" She was hurt that he had kept such important news to himself. He handed the card to her, beaming.

"I'm not exactly known for my good timing," he mumbled, and Lucy blushed at the thought of the interruption earlier that day.

"I love you, dad. And I'm so proud of you."

When Eli turned out his bedside lamp that night, it was as if a spell had been cast. The events and sentiments of the day swirled about and settled into their tangled arms and legs. "I love you," he whispered as his soft lips sought her mouth and neck. "I love you," he whispered as his eyelashes brushed her face. "I love you."

Lucy absorbed the words into her pores until they were part of every cell in her body.

CHAPTER THIRTY-FIVE

A WEEK AFTER JAVIER'S BEATING, HE AND LUCY WENT FOR A TWILIGHT WALK IN the orchard where he explained to Lucy that he and her mother would be leaving for home the following day. But they would be back later in the winter when it was time to prune the apples.

"Winter? Really?"

"I'm afraid that's the season for it. Need to prune when their good and dormant."

"I'm not sure a Midwest winter is your thing, dad." Lucy knew what she was talking about. As a California transplant, she still had not adjusted to the layers of clothing required by the bone-chilling temperatures. "Cold fingers, cold toes, cold nose ..." she began.

"Warm heart," added her father. "Warm bed." He winked.

"Well, call first the next time, okay? Owen also goes to Wisconsin for a while in the winter, and I don't want you guys to miss him again." Lucy reached for a low-hanging apple, still unripe and hard.

Javier rubbed his cast as if his arm was hurting. "So, Kitten, we haven't talked about the obvious." Lucy cocked her head. "What about Ben Wyatt? Are you safe?" Lucy hadn't mentioned Wyatt to her parents since they'd arrived, but she should never have underestimated her father's keen sense.

"I feel safe." She didn't. "His days are numbered." She hoped.

Her father's concern was coming from a very real place, she knew. His was the first face she had seen waking up in the hospital after the stabbing. He was at the trial, holding her hand through the worst of it. And it broke his heart when she moved away.

"I'm safe here, with Eli." She had resolved herself, happily, to living in his house. She no longer felt like an imposition—especially knowing in her heart where she stood, and how deeply she cared for Eli. Then Lucy's father took her hand and swung it like he had when she was a young girl.

"A ring, my little Kitten, does not make a marriage," he said. "Love and respect, that's what makes a marriage."

Ever since she and Eli had shared their feelings, she wondered if she should be expecting more, and chastised herself for putting any stock in such an old-fashioned belief. Of course, he was right. She was proud of this staunch Catholic for having such an open mind. It wasn't what she had expected.

Eli was at the kitchen table with Kali when Lucy and her father returned to the house. He came to her and led her around the corner into the hall, away from curious eyes and ears.

"Hello Kitten," he whispered with a sly grin.

"Stop it."

"How about—" His phone rang before he could complete his sentence. It was Beth. Eli put her on speaker phone.

"You heard it from me first," said Beth on the other end. "Our distinguished mayor has single-handedly stripped our office of all city funding." Beth had been to that evening's city council meeting. "The meeting was all business as usual until he dropped this bomb. You should have seen the smirks on the Hill brothers' faces. I could have slapped them both."

"We saw this coming, so why am I still surprised?" Eli shook his head. "Now what?"

"We call the county in the morning. Conference call. You need to be on the call. I'll text you the number."

"Sounds good. Thanks, Beth."

"Don't thank me yet."

Beth's news was chewed on at dinner that night, as thoroughly as the rib-eye steak Eli had set on the grill under the sharp supervision of Javier. The only thing preventing Javier from taking the tongs himself was that darned cast.

News of the Perez family departure the following day was also on the table. Julia said she would join her parents as far as Denver, where she planned to meet up with some friends from her European trek. Javier and Elaine had been mapping out their route home to include Las Vegas and Zion National Park. Elaine had visited the latter as a child and had always wanted to return.

"All I really remember about Zion is the color. It was beautiful—the red bluffs and that brilliant blue sky. My father said it was his idea of heaven." Elaine reached out to Javier and set her hand on his good arm. They had always been openly affectionate, Lucy recalled warmly.

"We'll be waiting for your return in the winter, Javier," Eli said. "You've really turned that orchard around, and I can't tell you how great it's been to have another man in the house."

"There's only room for one man of the house, Eli, and you've been generous enough to humor this old one," said Javier. Lucy smiled. Her father was still in his forties.

"It will be an adjustment, getting used to the quiet around here," said Kali.

"Not for long," Eli was quick to point out. "Owen will fill the void when he gets back."

"Ah, Owen. We're so sorry we missed him. Be sure to send those photos!" Elaine teasingly shook her finger at Eli.

"Hopefully, these AVID folks will be long gone by your next visit," Kali said. "I feel like we need to apologize for the assault. It's just embarrassing, you know? These idiots."

"Don't mention it. You couldn't keep us away. And think about a trip to Monterey. We would love to return the hospitality," offered Elaine, who pulled her loose hair up off her neck and clipped it. Eli and Lucy exchanged looks.

"Eli's never been to California."

"Never? Well, you don't know what you're missing."

Julia mumbled something under her breath that only Lucy could hear. "Forest fires, mudslides, earthquakes ..." The sisters stifled a snicker while Javier lifted his beer glass in a toast to a future visit.

LATER THAT NIGHT, propped up in bed with a mountain of pillows, Lucy Skyped with Summer, telling her what was going on, while Eli said goodnight to Owen in Wisconsin. At one point, they turned their laptops to face each other so that Owen and Summer were looking at one another. Owen was very excited to see Summer and started the chronicle of his exploits from the top until Eli managed to cut him off.

"Goodnight, Owen McMowen," said Summer.

"Goodnight, Summer McNummer." Owen giggled uncontrollably, and it warmed Lucy's heart.

In their conversation, Summer suggested that she would be back in town earlier than expected. She and Thomas had split up, and she recalled why their relationship had been so short-lived the first time around. Thomas had a wandering eye.

"I'm going to swing by my folks on the way back to Drake. Haven't seen them in ages."

"Sure—you have a place here when you're ready."

"Lucy, as far as the Chrysanthemum House is concerned, how about we go in on the loan together? You know, a fifty-fifty partnership. How do you feel about that?"

"I love it!" It was music to Lucy's ears.

"You are the best, Summer." Eli inserted himself into the conversation. "No one better."

"Oh no, Lucy's the best."

"Well," he winked at Lucy, "she's in a whole different class altogether."

"Agreed."

"Shut up, you guys." Lucy was embarrassed but appreciated the kind words. "Goodbye, Summer." Summer waved goodbye and Lucy closed her laptop.

"I told you it would work out."

"It hasn't worked out yet. Where will the money come from? Have you heard back from Jasper?" Lucy had been waiting to hear what Eli's old college roommate had to say.

"He suggested you buy it as a business—not personally. That seems to work into what Summer is thinking. We can call him tomorrow to tell him about the partnership idea. He might have some thoughts on that." Eli stacked their computers and set them on the window seat, and a mischievous smile spread across his face. "I have a sudden craving for ice cream."

"Of course you do," Lucy said, giggling.

CHAPTER THIRTY-SIX

ELI FINISHED THE CONFERENCE CALL WITH THE COUNTY SERVICES TEAM JUST IN time to see Lucy's family off, he strolled out to Javier's truck while they stood around in the driveway, saying their tearful good-byes. Finally, with Elaine at the wheel, the truck rolled slowly along the drive. Eli and Lucy walked alongside, listening to the crunch and pop of the gravel under the moving tires. The pickup came to a stop at the end of the driveway, and Javier stepped out to give his daughter one last hug, laughing heartily at what an emotional family they had.

Just as he let go, a black, windowless Sprinter van pulled up. Remembering the beating he had received the last time a van appeared, Javier jumped back into the truck, and Elaine put it in gear.

The van backed up to block their way, and a tall, husky man with a poorly trimmed goatee jumped out, wearing a black uniform with ICE stamped in gold letters across the chest and back. He was followed by a less threatening female agent with a bullet-proof vest stamped similarly. She approached Elaine's window and flashed her identification: Agent Stephanie Nix, United States Immigration and Customs Enforcement, Department of Homeland Security.

"Shut it off!" she ordered. "You!" She pointed directly at Javier. "Step out of the vehicle. Hands behind your back!" The goatee translated into Spanish.

"What's the matter?" asked Javier, clumsily stepping out of the truck. They demanded his documents, and he turned to reach back into the pickup. The goatee leaped and grabbed him, roughly twisting Javier's arms behind his body. Elaine hurried around to the other side of the truck with Javier's wallet. He winced with the pain—but his small groan only excited the agent, who seemed nearly twice the girth of Javier, and who pulled at the cast with more relish.

"Let him go!" screamed Lucy. "He's done nothing wrong!" She was beside herself. She pulled her phone out of her back pocket and texted Bob Marshall.

He texted back immediately. Officer Bradley was already on his way to set things right.

Eli asked the female agent to explain the situation, as Elaine handed over the citizenship card. Agent Nix studied it, rubbed her thumb around the edges and along the surface, then asked to see his driver's license. She took her sweet time scrutinizing each piece of identification, thumbing through the various credit, gift, and rewards cards—trying to find something they could use against him. Finally, and reluctantly, she told her counterpart to release Mr. Perez, with their apologies. Her words lacked any sincerity that Lucy could distinguish.

With all the excitement and focus on Javier, they hadn't noticed the small group forming in the street. For a somewhat rural and remote road, a traffic jam had developed behind a group of five or so people standing in the street yelling racial slurs. Tweedledee, with his thin wisps of gray hair blowing in the breeze, picked up a fistful of gravel from the side of the road, and some of the others followed his example.

As Elaine walked back to the pickup, a glutinous glob of spittle hit her shoe. She shook it off frantically.

Agent Nix approached the small group, who were incensed by the lack of an arrest. They became more vocal and aggressive, insisting Javier be thrown out of "their" country. Lucy stood, silent now, stunned by the raging exchange. She noticed a red Lexus parked on the other side of the street with Mrs. Fancy Pants—Mrs. Lancaster—in the driver's seat.

The pickup was blocked from leaving the driveway by the ICE van—and then, once it pulled away, by the growing crowd. Over twenty people now were screaming and jeering. A shot rang out, but no one was sure where it had come from. Javier was frightened, Elaine was terrified, and Lucy was relieved to see Officer Bradley arrive. He was responding to a radio call he intercepted from an AVID member for an occupation outside Eli's house. He'd been on the phone with Bob when Lucy's text came through.

The group was supposed to be further up the drive when ICE arrived, but the timely Perez family exodus had taken them all by surprise. Now, a large black sedan rolled up with two men dressed in street clothes. A tall, lean black man wearing a Chicago Cubs T-shirt, and a burly redhead with elaborate ink sleeves and holes in the knees of his Lucky Brand jeans. Lucy suspected they were the agents Bob had told her about.

The three newcomers jumped into action and opened a path for the pickup to exit, with a helpful suggestion of a less obvious route out of town.

Once the truck was gone, it was left to Lucy and Eli, together with the three officers who remained, to remove the threat. Lucy's fervor to arrest the individuals responsible for her father's humiliation was shared by Bradley and the other men.

Many of the crowd slipped away when the agents arrived. The fleet of cheap, out-of-state cars and clunky SUVs slithered off. Lucy watched, disbelievingly, as Mrs. Fancy Pants slowly pulled onto the road, and urged Officer Bradley to go after her.

"She's the one who set this whole mess in motion!" Lucy screamed.

Bradley sent the slender black man ahead to pull her over, since he had his hands full detaining the remaining protesters, four of whom were already on the ground, their hands zip-tied behind them. Two more sat in the back of his cruiser. He'd made quick work of it.

The redhead zip-tied three others and then pinned the fourth between him and his vehicle, peppering him with questions. Lucy knew the last man standing as Lamar Hill. His brother sat in the cruiser.

She ran down the street to the now-detained Mrs. Lancaster, who's perfect hair was now not so perfect, and the meticulously applied makeup now not so meticulous as she struggled to free herself while spitting a tirade of racial slurs at her captor. Her husband looked mortified as he attempted a quiet escape. He didn't get far before Lucy circled around the car and stuck her leg out to trip him.

The Cubs T-shirt caught up to them and dragged the escapee back to his car. "A regular Batman and Robin, you two," he said, referring to Lucy and Eli. Lucy laughed, remembering Summer's crack about Eli being Bruce Wayne.

Once things had settled down, the Lexus was towed away. Officer Bradley introduced the Cubs T-shirt as Agent Thompson and the redhead with tattooed sleeves as Agent Fitzgerald. Lucy and Eli thanked them both.

After the agents made their exit, Lucy and Eli walked wordlessly up the drive to the house, still dazed by the frenzy as they contemplated the alternate universe of the far-right contingent that had infiltrated their little town.

"Kal!" called Eli as Lucy closed the French doors behind them. Kali appeared from her office, and they filled her in on the drama.

"How did I miss that all that? I should have been there!"

"It wouldn't have helped," Eli assured her on his way to the kitchen.

"Well, it couldn't have hurt, either." Kali looked at her watch. "I have a patient in ten minutes, and I've got to prep." She hugged her brother, clinging to him in solidarity. "You guys all right?"

"Peachy," he said, smiling. Kali released him and roughed up his hair before she returned to her office to await her patient.

"How was your conference call this morning?" asked Lucy. She reached high into a cabinet for a pitcher, standing on the tips of her toes. Eli reached over her head, grabbed the pitcher, and set it on the counter.

"It looks pretty grim. We need to present a revised budget to the county and refer clients to a sister office in Preston once we determine which programs will stay or go. It wasn't the doom and gloom it could have been, but it wasn't what we wanted either." He set a box of crackers on the island.

"Crap. It's all so maddening." Lucy tossed a few tea bags into the pitcher and filled it with hot water.

"It's frustrating, I know." Eli pried open the crackers and

handed some to Lucy. "I hate how dependent we were on the city, but we'll figure it out."

Lucy received a text from Bob asking to meet at Nikko's later that afternoon. She texted back, "We'll be there with bells on."

CHAPTER THIRTY-SEVEN

LUCY LOOKED UP FROM STRIPPING THE SHEETS OFF JULIA'S BED AND SAW ELI standing in the doorway, watching her with a sly grin.

"I know what you're thinking," she said.

"You would be right," he said, laughing. "But we have to go. They're waiting for us at Nikko's."

"We need a break," said Lucy with a dramatic sigh. July had flown by with her parent's visit and they had marched right into August without a breather.

"Tonight. I promise. It'll be just you and me. Kali said she's staying at Mia's." Lucy walked over to him, placed her head on his chest and breathed deep as he wrapped his arms around her.

It was difficult to leave the air-conditioned house—vacant of all visitors and quiet for the first time in weeks.

Kali was waiting for them in the driveway. Her mother's light blue Prius sat parked in the open garage beside the BMW, just as it had been six years earlier. It was as if some intangible part of their mother lived on as long as the Prius remained. While Eli had adopted his father's car, Kali was reluctant to drive their mother's. Instead, she drove the same pint-sized Mazda she had bought secondhand from a patient, a year or so before the tragedy.

NIKKO'S HOUSE HAD cars parked around the corner. His house was buzzing with excitement. The seed Lucy had planted regarding a rally of their own had turned into a full-fledged movement. The Push Back for Justice movement was gaining traction. Word had spread with Beth's help and the addition of Roy Bird who had staked his reputation on it.

Bird, who recently resigned from his civic duties, had begun his mayoral campaign, doling out buttons and flyers to those interested. "Together we shall soar above," they said. "Roy Bird for Mayor." Looking around the room, Lucy recognized many familiar and friendly faces from all walks of life packed into Nikko's living room, dining room, and kitchen. Beth, Officer Bradley, and a curious Tina Reynolds, among many others, were there to fight for their little town of Drake.

Lucy was full of ideas for their rally and hoped she would get some say in how things would go. She wanted a peaceful march, with banners and placards, and a broad representation of who AVID was up against. She wanted those bastards to see themselves as the intruders they were. But before they could get to any ideas for their own rally, Alex Bridges spoke up to announce that the mayor had signed off on a date for an AVID Rally. It was complete with a march route and a dozen porta-potties. Facebook had a confirmed two hundred and fifty attendees, with dozens more uncommitted.

"Not enough potties," mumbled Beth.

Lucy stood. "I suggest we hold our rally on the same day." A rumble of voices surrounded her. Alex and Roy whispered to one another. They took a vote with a show of hands, and it was agreed. They would meet AVID face to face and Push Back for Drake.

Alex added that the AVID rally had applied for and was granted a twenty-four-hour open-carry permit. The group gasped in astonishment.

As a proud NRA member Alex was particularly interested in making sure everything was on the up and up. He had called the city to confirm that the open-carry permit was legitimate. He was assured by the mayor himself that it was.

"Now, I want you all to know," said Alex, "that I'm no liberal. I carried my weight in Vietnam, as did my four boys in Iraq and Afghanistan. I believe in the right to bear arms and I'm a responsible gun owner. I *do not* advocate for violence, which brings me to the following question. How many of you have a licensed firearm?

Show of hands." Many hands shot up, including Kali and Eli. "How many of you know how to use a firearm?" Ten more hands were raised. Lucy held her hands tightly in her lap.

They split up into smaller teams, at Bob's suggestion. He counted them off in teams of five. Groups any larger made communication difficult. They would vote on a team captain who would keep track of the others. Eli, Lucy, Kali, and Beth wanted to work together, and just as they were looking for a fifth member, Mia arrived—late, as usual. Their confidence rose significantly with her arrival, and they made her captain.

"Why me?" asked Mia.

"You have the most experience." Kali placed a hand on Mia's shoulder the way Eli often did when he wanted to make his point. Mia didn't argue.

The Push Back was to gather in the park while AVID marched. One team would bring in the rear. This team would include Bob, since AVID already recognized him as their own, and it wouldn't arouse suspicion.

Bob crossed the room to get Lucy's attention. "Wyatt will have no way out." As far as anyone in that room was concerned, the Push Back was all about AVID. Capturing Ben Wyatt was first and foremost only to a select few.

"But he has to break the law," Lucy said. "They have the right to assemble. They have open-carry permits, and the city's blessing."

"Wyatt is the leader of a domestic terrorist outfit. We have that, and more. Don't worry, Lucy."

All the captains met to exchange cell phone numbers and create an active group text for any changes or additions to the plan. These group texts would include Bob, agent Thompson, and agent Fitzgerald.

Lucy considered all the loose ends. What if things didn't go according to plan? Trapping AVID like a wild animal might induce anarchy. As she saw things, they needed numbers to drown them out. She raised her hand, and Roy gave her the floor.

"You have this," Eli whispered, as she stood to speak. Lucy smiled at him. She'd never thought of herself as a confident public speaker, but today she had something to say and couldn't sit silently by while everyone sat around thinking that the solution was to meet violence with violence.

"Our greatest weapon is not our guns," she began, with a nervous glance toward Alex Bridges. Lucy took a deep breath and continued. "Our greatest weapon is our character, our reputations, our tight-knit families, our dearest friends, and our community." Lucy's voice boomed with confidence. "Tonight, your greatest weapon is your phone. Call your family. Call your friends, coworkers, neighbors. We will meet their two hundred and fifty, and together we will outnumber them!"

Beth stood and cheered, saying loudly, "Today we gather to defend a community under siege. *Your* community. *Our* community!"

Lucy had lit the fire, but Beth had fanned the flames. That night, each person tapped into the resources they had all along. They were empowered. They were emboldened. And they were formidable.

Lucy led the charge with the first call. "Hello, Lance?" Why not start at there? "There's a new movement in Drake to Push Back on AVID. We're planning a rally..." Lance Kirsch, Lucy's landlord, redeemed himself that night by adding his name to the movement and agreeing to help however he could.

Beth called Mr. James to invite him to their rally. Eli called Dr. Franzki. Nikko's house was a buzz of voices, a rally for righteousness ... and quite likely a cell tower overload.

Their teams multiplied, and six hours later, they all drove, walked, or cycled home, knowing the following week would be a show of force.

They were pushing back, and for the first time since the rise of AVID in their small town, they felt empowered.

WHEN LUCY AND Eli got back to the house, the quiet they had left behind, and the privacy they were looking forward to, was shattered by the arrival of Summer. She was sunburned from head to toe, and had gotten her long, flowing, red tresses cut off in favor of a short, blunt, trendy style. She quickly revealed a tattoo on her shoulder of a vibrant, multi-colored sea tortoise, and magically produced a pair of joints from her coin purse.

"Who are you?" asked Lucy, amazed at the transformation.

"I am reborn," Summer answered with a firm nod. "The summer Summer."

Eli and Lucy, still buzzing with excitement from the meeting at Nikko's, described the details of the Push Back for Summer, who thought they should celebrate. They all stepped onto the patio and sat down at the table. Summer lit up the first joint and passed it to Lucy, as Eli popped the tops off three beers.

Summer's pit-stop at her parent's house had yielded enough for a down payment. Lucy couldn't believe her eyes when she saw the check. "Summer, you're a lifesaver!" She leaped out of her seat and hugged Summer, kissing her on the cheek.

"Thank my parents. They practically forced it on me when I told them what was going on."

"Three cheers to that!" cried Eli, lifting his beer.

"We are the proud owners of the Chrysanthemum House," Lucy said excitedly. It almost seemed too good to be true. Lucy clinked the mouth of her bottle with Eli's and Summer's. "We have to celebrate!" Summer handed her the joint, laughing.

"I told you it would all work out," said Eli, grinning at Lucy. Maybe it was the pot, but Lucy felt so full of love, she thought she might burst.

Summer described the comedy of errors that had been her trip. "These guys didn't know up from down, and I became the de-facto manager—which was fun for a while. They were marching to my beat, and, honestly, I kind of liked the power." She flexed her arms—a pose of hers Lucy was quite familiar with. "And Thomas—jeez, he's adorable." The joint had gone full circle and she took another hit before passing it on. "He's so damn adorable, the skinny little bitches couldn't leave him alone, so I hooked up with Brad, the drummer, who ended up tattling on me. But—what the hell, right? I mean, Thomas wasn't exactly the model of fidelity, right?" She reached for the joint. "So I left." Something in that last bit made her laugh.

"Fidelity." Eli drew out the word out, syllable by syllable, stretching it slowly into an elastic strand. They waited, looking at him expectantly.

"That's his thinking face," said Lucy.

"I have a thinking face?" Eli's languid words barely contained a question.

"Yes—and that's it. There you go again." Lucy giggled, with tiny eruptions like bubbles rising to the surface of a champagne glass.

They struggled to make dinner. The eggs burned, the soup boiled over, the bread was moldy, and it was all hilarious. Lucy was thrilled to see Eli laugh with such abandon.

They ended up just eating popcorn and ice cream, joking about how much Owen would have liked it. *Eli seems to like it, too,* thought Lucy, with a giggle.

Summer lined up three lounge chairs under the silver maple on the patio, and they rehashed the events of the evening. Eli was thoughtful—now even more than earlier, with the pot wearing off.

"You should have been there," said Eli. "Lucy was amazing."

"Lucy rocks." Summer was about to light the second joint, and Eli stopped her. "God, I'm tired. Think I'll just crash right here." The evening was warm and muggy. The crickets had long ago stopped their chirping, and with no breeze, there wasn't so much as the rustle of leaves in the trees.

"No, you won't." Lucy stood and reached out a hand to Summer. "C'mon." She didn't want to say it, but the idea that Ben Wyatt lurked in the orchard had never left Lucy since the day Owen had spotted him. A rush of goosebumps traveled up her arms and down her back. It wasn't a ridiculous notion.

Eli locked the door behind him as the girls walked ahead.

"I love you, Lucy," said Summer, with a warm hug at the top of the stairs. Then she turned to Eli with a peace sign. "Love you too, Thinky-Face."

Eli and Lucy turned down to the other end of the hall and

dropped into bed. "Don't you dare call me that," said Eli, with mock indignation.

"Wouldn't dream of it, Big Bird."

"Kitten."

"Meow."

The giggles had not quite worked their way out of their systems as they drifted into a deep and peaceful sleep.

LUCY AWAKENED WITH the sun filtering through an open gap in the heavy drape. She gave Eli a nudge, but got no response. She slipped downstairs to the kitchen and made a pot of strong coffee.

The sunlight beamed through the house. The window placement was such that, whether sunrise or sunset, it shone clear through from the front hall to the great room and vice-versa. It was one of Lucy's favorite features of this beautiful home.

When Summer appeared in the kitchen doorway, half asleep, she found Lucy standing in front of the rear window, gazing into the orchard, deep in thought. "Where's Owen?"

Lucy laughed, without taking her eyes from the trees. "Really? You just figured out he's not around? He's still at his grandparents." Lucy lost herself in a chain of thoughts—beginning with Owen and skipping to Wyatt in the orchard, and then to the gun safe in Kali's office.

The two friends wandered into the kitchen and sat at the small table. "What were you thinking about?" asked Summer.

"War," answered Lucy, staring at the *drip, drip, drip* of the coffee maker.

"With the grandparents? A little drastic, much?"

"No. It's those monsters; AVID. And that fucking gun safe in Kali's office." Lucy looked over her shoulder to see if Eli was up and about.

"A gun safe?"

"Yeah—a small arsenal left behind by Eli's dad and grandpa.

Those things scare the shit out of me." Summer retrieved coffee cups out of the dishwasher while Lucy unburdened herself. "They actually handed me a pistol."

"No shit? Did you take it?"

"Of course not. Would you?"

"If I thought it would save my life—yes. I would."

The friends worked out Lucy's reluctance to use guns at the AVID march, despite Alex's urging their group to bring out the hardware.

"AVID applied for the open-carry permit. Our little band doesn't have that. I don't know what Alex was thinking." Lucy had been tempted to shut down the Push Back then and there. She didn't. She had been embarrassed to say anything in front of Mia, or Kali, or even Eli. Eli—who understood her feelings more than any of them, and would have tucked her into a secure cell to protect her.

Summer filled their cups, as well as a third. "Take this up to Eli. Tell him what you told me."

So, after pushing the drapes open, Lucy sat down on Eli's side of the bed, closest to the window. She set his coffee down on the table and rubbed his back until he rolled over and looked at her.

"What time is it?" His hair was sticking out in all directions, he had a day-old beard on his face, and he was waking from a marijuana hangover. He looked blissfully disconnected from reality, and Lucy wanted to climb in beside him and share the momentary ignorance. When he reached out to her, she handed him his glasses. "Do you still love me?" he asked, groggily.

"More than anything." She bent to kiss him and waited while he took his first sip of the coffee. "Eli, remember that night you showed me the gun safe? Do you remember what I told you?" She thought back to their conversation in the alcove, standing on the veranda.

He brushed his fingers along her arm. "I remember."

"This rally. All those guns."

"Lucy, you don't have to carry a gun. You don't even have to be there if you don't want to." He rubbed the sleep from his eyes. "But I would feel more comfortable if you would at least let me show you. It might help, you know." She didn't know, but she guessed he wanted to demystify the deadly weapon. Back then, in the alcove, she'd said that she would think about it. She hadn't. Now here she was again.

"You can show me, but I don't have to like it."

THAT AFTERNOON, ELI led Lucy into the orchard for a little target practice with the Colt Mustang she'd been handed back in Kali's office. She held the pocket pistol tightly in her hand as he showed her how to load, cock, and fire at the red ribbon he'd tacked up to a dead apple tree fifteen feet away.

She had been prepared to hate the experience. Instead, she enjoyed the thrill and rush of adrenaline she felt each time she took aim at the dead tree.

"Not so bad, eh?" said Eli. She was reluctant to give in that easily, but he was right.

"There's a difference between taking aim at a dead tree and taking aim at a person."

"Let's hope it never comes to that," Eli said as he loaded a fresh magazine into the little pistol. "One more round."

She continued to shoot at the ribbon until she was slipping on the bullet casings at her feet.

CHAPTER THIRTY-EIGHT

LUCY DASHED UP THE STAIRS TO UNLOCK THE DOOR TO THE CHRYSANTHEMUM House. As a team, they all helped Summer carry in her belongings, everyone laughing and joking. Lucy popped back out to look up and down the street, then closed the door.

Summer had insisted on moving back into the school. Eli thought she was nuts, but Lucy understood. She missed the house—its little quirks and noises—and the sisterhood she'd shared with Summer. But school would be starting soon—fingers crossed. Then she would see Summer every day.

Inside, Summer and Lucy took stock of all that had been neglected. There was a distinct funk in the house, so Eli threw the windows open as they began to empty the refrigerator and clean up the dishes that had been left in the sink. Still, the smell persisted.

The floor beneath their feet was smeared with something dark and sticky. "I'll mop the kitchen floor if you get the bucket," Summer offered. "I hate going into that basement."

"So do I. Maybe Eli will go." Lucy looked over her shoulder to see Eli already on his way.

"Thank you!" called Summer. Lucy followed him to the door, and when he opened it, the stink was unimaginable.

The stair light flicked off, then on, then off again, so Eli used the flashlight on his phone. Against her better judgment, Lucy climbed down the stairs behind him. They found the same dismal basement she had left earlier that summer. It was quiet. The old oil furnace with its asbestos-laden tentacles of hose and ducts loomed just as large.

Lucy stepped back, and her heel landed on something soft and slippery. Eli turned his flashlight on the floor to see the dead mouse she'd stepped on. Her skin crawled as she shrieked.

"It can't hurt you," Eli teased.

"Says you. That stink is enough to knock anyone out." Eli flashed his light on an open window over the dryer. Lucy remembered fastening that window in the storm. With heart pounding, wondering if Wyatt could possibly fit himself through the small window, Lucy climbed back on the dryer and shut it, locking it tight.

WHILE ELI WAS gone to buy mouse traps, Lucy and Summer cleaned up the rest of the house and took stock of the school supplies. The next term would be starting soon thanks to Summer's parents.

Eli returned and unpacked the mouse traps, Lysol, and ingredients for chicken piccata. Of course. Eli gave her a knowing smile, and she couldn't help but wrap her arms around him. She would never get tired of his strong embrace, and the security she felt in his arms.

"That's just great, Eli," said Summer. "Now that the kitchen is clean for the first time in, like, forever, you're going to mess it up again."

"I'll clean up," offered Lucy, still locked in Eli's arms.

Summer laughed. "I see nothing has changed in that department. You're both still as lovey-dovey as ever."

They cooked, they ate, and they cleaned up to music chosen by Summer because she trusted no one else's taste. At dusk, they all went out onto the porch and drank beer on the swing, wondering what had happened to the second joint as the sunset finally gave way to darkness.

Lucy was thinking about the long days of summer when a van pulled up across the street and sat parked for a minute or two. Her heart raced with dread, and she braced herself for what might happen next. It was hard to see, but Summer finally realized who it was and leaped from the porch swing.

"Thomas!"

"Got a room for rent?" he joked, stepping out of the van.

Eli whispered in Lucy's ear, "Didn't they break up?" She shrugged, took his hand, and they joined Summer across the street.

Thomas and Eli shook hands. Lucy caught Bob Marshall watching from his window.

The foursome went into the house, each carrying something from the van, a duffel with a broken zipper, a battered suitcase, a leather backpack, and of course, his guitar.

Lucy held onto Eli's arm as she kicked off her rigid flats. The new shoes had left a painful blister on her heal.

"Are you hungry?" asked Summer, in a suddenly domestic tone. Thomas followed her into the kitchen, leaving Eli and Lucy on their own. Eli smiled and pointed up the stairs, and Lucy grinned. Before they made it to the landing, though, Eli's phone rang from the dining room.

"Let it ring," she laughed. They had deliberately left their phones inside when they'd all gone out to the porch earlier. Peace and quiet were harder and harder to come by, but Eli couldn't resist the temptation.

"It might be about Owen." He dashed downstairs and picked it up. "Hello?" Pause. Eli frowned. "You're kidding." Another pause. "How long ago?" His shoulders slumped as he listened. "Did you call the police?"

"What is it?" asked Lucy, "Is it Owen? Is he all right?"

"That was Beth. The office is on fire."

"No!"

Eli scrolled down the security app alerts he'd missed and cursed.

In a rush, Lucy stepped back into her uncomfortable flats. Adrenaline blocked the blister pain.

BY THE TIME they piled out of Eli's car in front of the toy store, both the sandwich shop and the nail salon were ablaze, glowing orange and red against the night sky. The firetrucks had trouble getting to the scene through the mob of rioters blocking the road.

Eli found Beth while the others stood in disbelief as the office windows exploded, and the upper level collapsed. By some miracle, the dazed occupants had managed to get out safely and were standing in the park wrapped in blankets, surrounded by caring neighbors.

Officer Bradley was busy trying to clear the way for the firetrucks. He had burned his hand while rescuing one of the residents, and his face was smudged with soot. But the other police officers just stood around enjoying the show.

Tina stopped in her tracks when she saw Eli and Lucy.

"What do you know, Tina?" asked Eli.

"The Hill brothers were just released from jail!" she shouted over the noise. "AVID supporters have completely gone nuts!"

This wasn't the typical AVID protest, noted Lucy, this was a frenzied mob.

The riot grew loud. The mob demanded to be heard over the sirens and the roaring flames—but still, it was hard to understand what they were saying. A group of them rushed toward the bandstand. Lucy looked to the stage, where the mayor stood, front and center, smirking. Steps away from the mayor, standing boldly at the corner of the stage, was Ben Wyatt, staring directly at Lucy.

Lucy was stunned—immobilized by fear. She couldn't look away. It was the first time she had seen Wyatt since watching him being escorted out of the courtroom in handcuffs years earlier. She stared now at his face, white as parchment with two black holes for eyes. His hair seeped from a baseball cap in black snaky strands. He was as thin as an anorexic, small enough to fit through a narrow basement window. Despite the heat from the raging fire behind her, Lucy felt ice cold.

As she came to her senses, she instinctively felt for the scar on her back, then looked around for Eli. She saw him surrounded by the horror of the emboldened horde and mesmerized by the flames which devoured the building and consumed the city block.

She pulled herself from Wyatt's gaze and ran toward Eli. Out of nowhere, pain tore through her shin, and the next thing she knew, she was on the ground with her wrist crushed between her hip and the trampled earth. It was not her own clumsiness that had tripped her up. Lucy was coordinated, quick, and focused. Harlan Hill looked down on her, the light of the fire reflecting off his head.

She knew that look in his eyes, and instinctively jumped to her feet and ran. The pain in her leg and wrist burned like the flames licking the night sky. Harlan thundered behind her for a few yards—she thought she'd lost him. She gasped as smoke filled her lungs—she heard someone cough nearby. It was Eli—he was within reach! Harlan Hill gripped her injured wrist and squeezed.

With a shriek, she kicked at him. "Run!" shouted Eli. Despite the noise and chaos, she heard him and kicked again until Harlan released his grip, cursing.

She took off again, with Eli right behind her. They ducked into the cattails beside the pond to catch their breath. "Lucy, we need to get out of here. Do you remember where the car is?" She nodded. He handed her the keys. "I'll be right behind you."

"All right. On three." She counted down, staring into his eyes, then ran. She got as far as the playground when she was spotted. It wasn't just Harlan this time—he had company. Three large men she'd never seen before looked at her like a pack of hungry hyenas.

Lucy ducked behind the slide and emerged on the other end of the playground. She spotted the car in front of the toy shop and waited for Eli to catch up with her.

The flames raged on, casting an eerie orange glow over the park. The firelight made everyone's faces look red and devilish. The smoke made it difficult to breathe, and Lucy's eyes stung as she peered back at the stage. Wyatt was gone.

She heard gunshots and dropped to the ground. Where was Eli? Just then, something struck her head. She turned and quickly rolled out of the way just as a heavy boot landed an inch from her nose.

Lucy didn't recognize the man standing over her like an ogre, but that didn't mean anything. The behemoth, wearing a tight-fitting MAGA hat, glared down at her and kicked her in the leg. "Fucking Mexican bitch!" The sharp pain shot from her thigh to her foot, and she struck back with the other leg, the toe of her flats to his soft fleshy calf. "Filthy whore!" He kicked again, and she gripped her stomach. The pain was intense, but the instant she caught her breath, she kicked up to his crotch. He grabbed her by the ankle and laughed. "Two can play that game." He drew his foot back, readying a boot between her legs when someone pushed him hard from behind.

The ogre's MAGA hat flew from his head as he fell with a thud beside her. He twisted, throwing a fist toward her face, but Eli stepped in and quickly pulled her out of the way.

Eli looked nearly a hundred pounds lighter—but he was fueled by the adrenaline and rage necessary to beat the oaf to a pulp. He was outnumbered, though—and after two well-placed kicks to the ogre's prone body, an AVID gang surrounded him. One man threw him to the ground like a sack of potatoes. Another stomped on his leg. He was kicked, punched, and kicked some more.

Summer and Thomas appeared from nowhere. "Does no one see what's going on here!" screamed Summer, picking Lucy up from the ground. Her face was smudged with soot and streaked with tears. A pair of arms pushed Summer, and a large, freckled hand grabbed Lucy away. Its owner held her arm so tight she imagined it snapping in two. Though hampered by her injured wrist and the pain in her chest, Lucy did not give up trying to get away. Violently, she kicked at her attacker's legs, scratched at his face, and then finally bit his hand—breaking through the skin. He released her with some colorful words.

Thomas and Summer found Lucy, trying futilely to get to Eli through the gang of men encircling him.

"Stop it! You're going to kill him!" A wave of nausea rolled through her as she spit dirt, sweat, and blood into the grass. Tears welled in her eyes and streamed down her face, blurring her vision.

Bob Marshall pushed into the throng dressed in the camo pants and MAGA hat Lucy recognized as GI Joe. "That's enough!" he shouted authoritatively. "You've done enough damage here, boys—move along." They weren't so eager to follow his command, but when the mayor took the stage, they fled to hear what he had to say. Bob lifted Eli's limp, unconscious body from the ground, and the riot quieted to hear the rant of a rogue mayor from the stage.

"Citizens of Drake," bellowed the mayor. "I come to you

tonight with a simple request." The men and women surrounding the bandstand cheered as he went on about his efforts to clean up the city. These people aren't even *from* Drake, thought Lucy, looking around her. She tuned it out. She could only think of Eli.

A raindrop landed on Lucy's head. A fleeting memory of flying kites raced in and quickly out of her mind. Soon, the sky opened, and the dirt that had been kicked up in the riot swiftly became a sea of mud.

Thomas took over for Bob and loaded Lucy and Eli into the back of the BMW—now minus a rear window due to an encounter with a baseball bat.

The back seat was a lake, but it didn't matter to Thomas, who drove the BMW as if it were on the Autobahn to the county hospital. The driving rain made visibility poor, and he narrowly missed hitting a motorcycle speeding out of town.

When they arrived at the hospital, Eli was taken away promptly to be cared for by a team of doctors and nurses. Summer sat with Lucy in the emergency room as her more minor injuries were attended to. One young nurse stood by, not knowing how to help, until she noticed Lucy's open blister, and decided to give it her full attention. Lucy wanted to cry for the small kindness. She felt overwhelmed and exhausted. Her own injuries didn't concern her. But Eli had been beaten within an inch of his life.

"Where is he?" she rasped. "I need to see him." Summer shook her head sympathetically. "No! No! He can't be!" Lucy shrieked. Her stinging throat clenched, her stomach churned, and her heart thundered in her chest. "Take me to him!"

"Lucy—no. It's not that. He's just, um—getting patched up. He'll be fine. The doctors say he'll be fine." Lucy's eyes pierced through Summer's calm veneer. "Cross my heart."

Summer leaned over to retrieve the cotton blanket Lucy had kicked to the floor, and draped it over her. Then she nodded to the nurse, who took over while Summer hovered nearby.

The injection of lorazepam took hold immediately. As Lucy's body warmed, her muscles relaxed, and her mind drifted. "I need to see Eli." Her voice was barely audible, and her request went unheeded.

ELI WAS IN the hospital for the better part of the week. When they brought him in, his shirt was in tatters, his shoes were missing, and his pants were embarrassingly soiled. He was treated for a broken nose and eye socket, a leg fractured in two places, a dislocated shoulder, a gash on his head, a punctured lung, two broken ribs, a ruptured spleen, and numerous cuts and scratches over his back and chest.

Lucy was treated for a cracked rib and a broken wrist, but was otherwise all right--physically. The haunting vision of Wyatt staring at her from the bandstand clung to her like shrink wrap. It was suffocating. *Look what you've done, Lucia Perez*, she thought, gazing at Eli's bruised and broken body. If it hadn't been for her, Eli wouldn't be in this hospital bed, Owen wouldn't be terrorized by Wyatt, the entire town of Drake wouldn't be the command center for hatred. AVID had followed Wyatt, who had followed her.

She was curled up in the recliner beside Eli's hospital bed, trying her hardest to conjure a happy moment to displace her fear. They filtered in, one by one. The warm sun on her face. Dancing with her sister. Eli's mischievous smile. Owen's contagious giggles. Each thought was promptly replaced with a dark haze and Ben Wyatt's intent stare. *No—stop. Think of something pleasant.*

"They're letting me go home today," said Eli groggily. The drugs made him docile, like a small child. Lucy climbed out of the chair and leaned over him. "Come closer." It was painful to see him try to smile through his swollen split lips. "I love you, Lucy," he whispered.

KALI SORTED THROUGH their father's dresser to find a pair of shorts that could fit over Eli's full-length cast and came up with a rumpled pair of basketball shorts with crumbling elastic and a drawstring.

He had no choice but to wear them home, where he contented himself with keeping the couch warm in the great room.

It was difficult for him to breathe with his chest wrapped so tightly, and his leg itched within the cast, which extended from heel to mid-thigh. The bruises covering his body ranged from purple to orange and yellow. An eye patch covered the broken socket while it healed.

"I look like a monster," moaned Eli. Lucy brushed the thought aside and kissed his swollen knuckles.

"Beauty and the beast," called Kali from the kitchen.

"Hilarious, Kal." Eli could not be consoled.

His spleen had been saved, but he was under orders to take things easy. The orders were hardly necessary—as confined as he was, it wasn't likely he could do much. It would be months before full recovery.

He had long given up on his unrealistic rule about rationing their steady diet of news. He flipped from one channel to the next, gorging himself on political pundits, White House scandals, and election updates. Hate crimes were on the rise. It wasn't just Drake, but too little was being done about it. The motto of the day was "Flip the House," as if that would make the difference.

He turned to the local channels for a dose of floods, tornados, shootings, and pretty much anything that could be caught on a police scanner. This was how he heard a brief snippet of the street fire in Drake listing damages and injuries. They didn't mention him and Lucy by name, but they may as well have—Nana and Papa were calling daily, wanting updates on his condition.

"You need to call them back," urged Lucy. "They're worried." She had been fielding the calls, and she was tired of making excuses.

He shook his head painfully. "It takes me right back to when Eva was sick. I hear Papa's apprehension, and it's as if it all happened yesterday." Lucy knelt at his side and held his hand. She knew how time could shift and bend. One moment she would be there beside Eli. In a blink, she would be in an alley with a knife in her back.

"They're worried," she repeated. She handed Eli his phone and turned down the volume on the television as he dialed. "I'll give you some privacy." She tried to release his hand, but he clutched it.

"Don't go."

Eli reassured his former father-in-law that he was out of the hospital and recovering at home. They spoke for less than a minute before Owen took over the phone. Eli put it on speakerphone, so Lucy could hear.

"I made you a card, and Nana helped me mail it to you."

"That's awesome, Little Bird. I'll watch for it." His voice was choked and hoarse.

"Are you getting better in the hospital? Why did those men hurt you? Is Lucy there?" The rapid-fire questioning told them both how confused he was.

"I'm at home. Lucy's taking care of me now. I'm the luckiest duck in all of Drake." He wiped his tears with the back of his hand. "I love you, kiddo."

"I love you too, Dad. Can I come home now?" Eli handed the phone to Lucy. He was too distraught to speak. He'd been avoiding Skype while the bruises faded, but he would have loved more than anything to see his son's face. Lucy took the phone and walked out to the kitchen. She told Owen he wasn't missing much. She told him those men were confused. She told him to hold tight, and they would see him in a few more weeks. She told him his father was just fine. She lied, and lied, and lied again. But when she said she missed him, it was from her heart.

She handed the phone to Kali, who was happy to take over. "How's my favorite nephew?"

Lucy understood Nana and Papa's worry. She was dealing with similar concerns from her own parents. The news coverage of the event had waned, but their fears remained strong. It was the first time she could remember her parents asking her to come home. But Lucy knew she couldn't bring herself to leave Eli's side. Not now. Not yet.

CHAPTER THIRTY-NINE

BOB MARSHALL STOPPED BY THE HOUSE A WEEK AFTER ELI HAD BEEN RELEASED from the hospital. It was the first time Lucy had heard the doorbell, a lingering chime of tinkling bells.

"How is he?" asked Bob, standing in the formal entry.

"He hasn't left the couch since he got home," Lucy murmured. She didn't want Eli to hear. "His bruises have faded, but the other injuries are far from healed." She led Bob into the great room to see for himself. It was early. The sun had only just risen over the tops of the apple trees in the orchard and was now streaming in through the windows on either side of the French doors.

Bob sat down in the chair opposite the sectional where Eli could see him without turning too much. Eli's hair was a mess, and he hadn't had a shave since the nurses took care of him in the hospital.

"Big day tomorrow," said Bob. The AVID march was scheduled for the following day. "How you doin'?"

"I wish I could be there," said Eli, struggling to prop himself up on the mountain of pillows behind him.

Bob scowled at Eli. "Nonsense. Look at you. If I see you anywhere near Drake Park tomorrow, I'll beat you to a pulp myself."

Lucy left the room to give the two some privacy and put on a pot of coffee. From the kitchen she could hear their voices speaking seriously with small injections of muted laughter. It was music to Lucy's ears. As much as Eli loved to laugh, he hadn't had much of a sense of humor lately.

Ten minutes later, Lucy emerged from the kitchen with the full pot of coffee and three empty cups.

"None for me, thanks," said Bob. He gripped both arms of the chair and pushed himself up. "I've got to be off. Too much still to do before tomorrow." Lucy didn't envy Bob's position. He was still undercover with AVID as they planned their big march, and helping out with the Push Back rally at the park. Two such dynamically opposed causes.

Lucy walked Bob to the door. "Thanks for stopping by. I know it means a lot to him."

"Don't mention it. As for tomorrow, Lucy. Stay put. Take care of our invalid over there," he tipped his chin in Eli's direction. Lucy smiled and opened the door. As she closed it again, she heard the television switch on.

Eli had been parkedon the couch for days, and everyone was getting tired of the never-ending drone of talking heads. Lucy took the remote and shut the TV off.

"Hey, I was watching that!" He reached, but she held the remote just far enough away. He couldn't take it without getting up.

"You can get yourself to the bathroom, so you can get yourself upstairs," said Lucy.

"Maybe we could stuff him in the dumbwaiter," Kali teased as she descended the stairs. Eli cursed her for making him laugh. It hurt too much.

He reached for his crutches and began hobbling to the foot of the stairs, with an 'I'll show you' pout on his face. It was all Lucy could do to not lose herself in laughter as she and Kali walked up with him. Step--*thump*, step--*thump*. He had one hand on the banister and an arm around his sister while Lucy held the crutches. Step—*thump*, step—*thump*. It took ages to reach the landing.

Once Eli managed to get to their room, Lucy made a nest of sorts around him. She had him propped up with pillows against the headboard, and his leg supported with pillows further down.

He looked so comfortable, she climbed in beside him and closed her eyes for a few.

AN HOUR LATER, Eli gave her a nudge. "Lucy, Lucy, I need my pills. Lucy." His nest had toppled, and he laid cockeyed and compromised. After setting things straight, she slipped back downstairs to get his pharmacy of prescriptions from the kitchen, where Summer and Kali sat at the table, discussing their plans for the Push Back the following day.

Lucy walked past Thomas, who had made himself comfortable in the great room watching M*A*S*H in a Netflix stupor, periodically roaring, "I love this show!"

The guns were arranged across the granite island, and Mia was going through the checklist. Who would carry what? Would they need more ammunition?

At Mia's suggestion, Summer and Thomas had signed up for shooting classes at the range after Eli's beating. Summer could now boast of her eighty percent accuracy, and Thomas could joke about the other twenty percent. Lucy's only lesson had been the afternoon spent in the orchard with Eli.

"I didn't think the permits went through," said Lucy.

"Alex is still working on that," said Mia. "He's applied through the county to avoid the city hall scrutiny. They haven't given the green light yet, but we're preparing anyway. Just in case."

"Everything all right up there?" Kali giggled. Lucy couldn't understand her fascination with Eli's injuries, past and present.

"He's fine. Just popped down to get his meds." Lucy was envious of the comradery. She was the one who had set this operation in motion and felt left out of the grand finale. "Kali, I should go with you," she blurted out. "I should be there."

"Eli needs you here." Kali stood and helped Lucy collect the pill bottles she was assembling into a small box. "We'll keep you in the loop. I promise." Lucy's rational mind struggled with her emotions, but she nodded. Kali was right.

THAT NIGHT, LUCY took her time examining each of Eli's bruises, stitches, and bandages. His spleen incision was healing slowly, and the dressing needed to be changed often. The pins in his leg and the head trauma were the most painful, but the broken ribs were a close second. His bedside table was full of painkillers, antibiotics, steroids, creams, and some unfamiliar medications.

To relax, Lucy and Eli shared stories in the dark—of childhood, family, dreams, and fears. Lucy had already heard his account of being locked up in the garden shed by his sister, but she didn't stop him as he retold it now. She sensed he needed to be heard out before he could get to his most pressing thought.

"Every time I close my eyes, I see the flames from that night and that monster kicking you." He turned his face to hers. "Lucy, I didn't know what else to do." His words were slurred. "He was going to … you know." Eli's voice was drifting off. Lucy thought about the ogre's grip around her ankle as he readied to kick. If Eli hadn't come when he did, Lucy didn't know what she would have done. But he did, and it nearly killed him. "Are you—all right?" he managed to ask groggily.

Lucy fought back the sting of tears accompanying the lump in her throat and reached for the tall glass of water on her bedside table. She had a few medications of her own, though they were less potent than Eli's—something for her anxiety, and something for the pain of her broken wrist and cracked rib.

The wrist troubled her the most. It ached night and day. A constant reminder of that night, the sting of smoke from the blaze, the horror of Eli's beating, and the utter shock of seeing Ben Wyatt for the first time in years.

The stiff wrist brace she had to wear was a nuisance. It was tight and itchy and kept her from doing more than wiggling her fingers—and even that was painful.

She picked up the Xanax and rolled two tiny disks out onto the table. *As needed* was stamped on the bottle. One by one, she put them in her mouth and chased them down with the water, followed by one of the painkillers.

Lucy had told Bob about seeing Wyatt at the park fire. He had thanked her. "I'll get him, Lucy," he had said. "That's a promise."

Now, Lucy heard sirens off in the distance. She looked to Eli, but he was fast asleep. She wondered which of the pills was responsible for that.

She wasn't the least bit tired, so she got out of bed and padded down the main stairs, doing her best to avoid the places where the steps creaked. Kali was still in the kitchen, heating water for some herbal tea. The others had gone.

"I've locked up," said Kali.

"Windows too?" asked Lucy. Kali nodded.

They waited for the tea to steep, both lost in their own thoughts. Lucy knew Kali wanted her to share her feelings, and she would have if she could just put them into words.

For Lucy to express herself truthfully would mean trying to explain her dread of something dark and ugly. She could never reveal it without sounding like a raving lunatic. Images flashed through her mind: fire, violence, Ben Wyatt. Eli's battered body, and how she'd failed him. She was right there. She should have stopped it somehow.

"How are you, Lucy?" asked Kali.

"I'm fine," Lucy lied, quietly sipping the piping hot tea.

"No, you're not. But I get it. I did the same thing when ... you know. Just remember that when you're ready to talk, I'm here to listen. And if you don't want to talk to me, I'll find someone else, okay?"

Lucy nodded. It was all she could manage.

CHAPTER FORTY

LUCY WOKE AT SUNRISE TO THE *WOO-WOO-HOO* OF A MOURNING DOVE. *TODAY'S THE day*, she thought as she rubbed the sleep from her bleary eyes. *And I won't be there.*

She was resolved to staying behind to look after Eli. Besides—physically, she wasn't in any shape to participate in the rally, and psychologically, she wasn't in any shape to confront Ben Wyatt. But she did want to see his face when he discovered he was trapped. She wanted to see him handcuffed in the back of a police cruiser as it took him off to prison.

She thought back to the courtroom in California, where he had pleaded *not guilty* to sexual assault, attempted rape, and assault with a deadly weapon. He claimed that it was *Lucy* who had assaulted *him*—that she backed him against the wall, and the knife inadvertently punctured her kidney. It was bullshit, but the jury had seen through him enough to lock him up, and she had done what she could to rise above the trauma. Now here she was, still trying to rise above. In part, that meant tending to Eli, who she loved more and more each day.

Lucy listened again to the dove, sounding like a lost soul, and then regarded her bedmate and his harmonic snore.

A loose Velcro strap on her wrist brace snagged the bedsheet, and she was tempted to remove the whole apparatus. It itched, and her forearm was getting rubbed raw by the cuff.

What time was it? Nearly eight. She rolled out of bed and retrieved her clothes from the floor, then slipped down the hall for a pee. The house was still and peaceful. Kali and Mia were meeting Summer and Thomas at the Chrysanthemum House to wait for Bob's signal.

With the air conditioner already cranking despite the early hour, Lucy headed down to the kitchen to get the coffee going and pull something together for Eli to eat before his next dose of painkillers.

She was sitting at the kitchen table, waiting for the coffee and scrolling through the news feed on her phone, when Summer called.

"Hey, Lucy."

"Hey, how's everything at central command?" Lucy teased.

"We're loaded for bear, but you'll be happy to know the permit did not go through for our open carry."

"I would be happier if AVID hadn't gotten one. Why the double standard?"

"No idea," Summer said.

"Think the mayor had anything to do with it?"

"As far as I know, he is still clueless. The plan is to take the bastards by surprise, and I don't think Alex would have compromised that. As soon as Bob gives the signal, we're going to walk up to the square. There's probably eighty people in this house, Lucy. I had no idea how elastic it was! Nikko has another fifty at his place."

"WHAT'S THE STORY, Morning Glory?" mumbled Eli sleepily as Lucy set the small tray down beside him. He put his glasses on.

"Hope you're hungry." Lucy looked down at the tray. She had been a bit overzealous, filling plates with toast, fruit, eggs, and yogurt.

Eli struggled to sit up enough to handle the cup of coffee. She helped him get situated, then made herself comfortable beside him.

"I hope you plan to help me with this," he laughed, looking at the tray.

After filling their bellies, they curled up together and fell back asleep. Two hours later, Summer called from the rally. Lucy looked over at Eli, still snoozing.

"The press is all over the place," she shouted over the noise behind her. "We're going to be on national television!"

"Does AVID suspect what you guys are up to?" Lucy worried that any news coverage could blow the whole plan.

"Bob says they're clueless. Their whole ugly lot is down at the high school in a disorganized mess. Their march isn't supposed to start for an hour. You should see the turnout here, Lucy. It's phenomenal!"

Lucy thanked her friend for calling, then checked her news feed, which was full of updates and videos of the AVID march, currently beginning at the football field.

AVID members milled about, united under the flags of nation, state, and city. Ben Wyatt held a fourth flag—the AVID flag, with red and black stripes, and in the center, a hawk clawing out the eyes of a dove. He was wearing an oversized black T-shirt with the AVID flag on the back and A.V.I.D. stamped across the front. It looked like he hadn't washed his jeans in weeks.

Where was he living? thought Lucy. *Who was hosting him?*

Streamed video showed the small-town stadium humming with the chatter and chants of over two hundred men and women, openly packing. They looked like a rag-tag militia. Some wore the black T-shirts issued for the march.

Lucy cringed to see Ben Wyatt being treated like a hero. Fans waited to get selfies, and handlers doted on him.

Mayor Church stood in the announcer's box with words of encouragement, even as he reminded them to respect city property and remember their manners. The laughter was thunderous.

An interview with Lamar Hill revealed a map of the planned route. It was shaped like a coil that led directly to the square. Hill suggested it was a python coming in for the stranglehold. "We'll be making a few stops along the way," Lamar said, wheezing with the effort of having to string so many words together. He pointed to the map with black stars marking Planned Parenthood, the city hall, the free clinic, and the charred remains of the social service office. "When we reach the park," he wheezed, "Mayor Church and Ben Wyatt will make their speeches."

AVID had journalists of their own, Lucy noticed, looking at the footage on her phone. He pointed to a press van with the logo of a local conservative radio station and a popular cable news channel.

It was evident that the march was propaganda, intended to frighten some and recruit others.

Eli mumbled something and Lucy put down her phone. "Hey." She smiled down at him. "Welcome back."

"What time is it?" he asked.

"Almost noon," Lucy said, propping him up. "The march is just about to start. I've been watching the news feed."

Lucy picked up her phone and found a live podcast that sounded promising. "... Ben Wyatt planned the event himself" the host said. "But local AVID supporters, such as Harlan and Lamar Hill, had a great deal of input—securing the permits, notifying their followers, mapping the route, writing the speeches, and assembling friendly press. The primary draw today is Ben Wyatt." Lucy turned up the volume so Eli could hear it better.

"Yes, agreed," a co-host interjected. "He's a powerful draw. Wyatt's vision for a perfect nation, developed while he had been incarcerated. Am I right?"

"Oh, his passion goes back much farther. The seeds of Ben Wyatt's vision were sown early in life," said the host. "Born into a poor family outside San Diego, Wyatt was still a boy when his father died. His mother ran off soon after, with a man identified as Raul Domingo. Ben and his brother were left to fend for themselves." Lucy imagined the AVID sleuths were already looking up Raul's name and whereabouts.

"So, at the tender age of seven, Wyatt and his brother were left to grow up in foster care. Three foster homes in the first year rejected the boys. They were bounced around from family to family until, at ten, Ben split from his brother, and landed in a foster home in Los Gatos, California. There, Stan and Evie Carter showed him right from wrong. They explained that the trouble with the world was only going to be fixed by strong, white, Christian men, and the women who supported them."

"Old fashion family values," mumbled Eli.

Lucy recalled what Bob Marshall had said about Stan and Evie Carter at one of the Push Back meetings. They were racists in a country that was rapidly becoming more diverse. Wyatt learned that brown skin was ugly, dirty, and evil—and that if he got too close, they would bring him down to hell, too. That went for gays, Jews, Muslims, and just about any other US minority.

The host continued. "Ben Wyatt left the Carters when he was seventeen, for a job he was promised in the college town of Santa Cruz—a pizza place on the main drag. It meant throwing dough and shredding cheese for the better part of the day. He lived in a studio apartment above an old machine shop, but he was glad to be living life on his own terms."

Frustrated, Lucy turned off the program. "I remember that pizza place. The owner was a racist asshole."

Summer beeped in with a video chat. Lucy lifted the phone to include Eli. "Lucy," Summer shouted over the crowd. "Bob just texted that they're getting close! The Push Back has filled the park. If AVID wants any turf here, they will have a fight on their hands—and we're ready for one." Summer turned her phone so Lucy and Eli could see the crowd.

Signs, large and small, were everywhere. The atmosphere was festive. The faces in the crowd glowed, alert with anticipation.

"Eli," Thomas said, snatching Summer's phone. "This is for you, man, and all the other victims of those assholes!"

"Sorry, 'bout that," said Summer, yanking her phone back. "He's pretty pumped up. Everyone is. Oh! Here comes the mayor." Summer held her phone up and over the heads of the crowd, so Lucy and Eli could see what was going on. The mayor rounded the corner at the coffee shop to a sudden burst of hollering and shouting.

"Do you see this?" shouted Summer. Summer's video was bouncing around so Eli and Lucy couldn't see anything clearly.

"No. Tell us what you see," Eli said excitedly.

"They came up Washington Street and the mayor had this shit-eating grin on his face. He didn't seem surprised. Now he's blabbing on about something. I can't hear him over the crowd. Listen to them!" Summer held her phone out and Lucy and Eli heard, *Stand down! Stand down!* "That's our team," said Summer looking down to her phone. "Here come's Roy's group! It's a full press!" She held up her phone to the crowd, but Lucy and Eli couldn't make sense of it. "We have them outnumbered!" Summer squealed.

Roy had assembled a collection of out-of-towners—including dozens of newly deputized officers from the county sheriff's office, and a small contingent from the local National Guard.

Summer had to sign off. It was too difficult—not to mention dangerous—to manage the phone and the jostling crowd.

Satisfied that the Push Back seemed to be working, Lucy set her phone to silent and plugged it into the charger on her nightstand. She rolled over to face Eli, who winced with pain, trying to inch closer to her. She got the message and scooted over.

They dozed off, and when Lucy woke, she reached for her phone to check for messages. *No!* Her chest tightened and she gasped for air, as the color drained from her face.

CHAPTER FORTY-ONE

LUCY WOKE ELI WITH A SHOVE. "WE'RE IN TROUBLE." SHE READ THE TEXTS aloud. "We lost Wyatt," "We're searching for Wyatt. The weasel gave us the slip. Pick up your damn phone." She jumped out of bed and threw on a sundress from the foot of the bed.

Summer's voicemail message was hardly recognizable—almost a shriek. "Jesus—Lucy, Wyatt never showed up at the park!"

Bob's voicemail said, "Eli, Wyatt's headed your way. I'm sure of it." Bob coughed. His voice was rough. "Get the hell out of there! Fast!"

Another voice message from Summer said, "Bob says he's headed your way. Lucy, get out!" Lucy heard the panic in Summer's voice. Her friends were on their way, but the roundup at the park had scattered AVID, and the roads were all blocked.

Lucy's mind reeled as she looked out the window. She could just see the edge of the driveway, but she heard nothing.

"Do you see him?" asked Eli, swallowing something helpful from his bedside pharmacy.

She helped him out of bed. He was shirtless, and his long cast protruded from the over-sized basketball shorts.

"No, but that means nothing. We need to get to the garage. Can you drive?" She took one look at him. "Of course you can't. That was a stupid question. Eli, I can't drive stick. What about the Prius?" Eli shook his head. It had sat so long, it wasn't drivable. "Can you get down the stairs?" Lucy remembered the difficulty with which he'd climbed them. She had tears in her eyes, but they disappeared with a quick swipe of her index finger, and she pulled herself together. *Focus.*

"We can do this. They're on their way."

"Eli, Wyatt has a head start," Lucy panted.

"We'll hide." He opened the door and cocked his head to the back stairs. They started walking when a downstairs floorboard creaked. Lucy's heart skipped. She thought about the pocket pistol, the Colt Mustang Eli had given her. It was in the gun safe where it did her no good at all.

A few more steps to the back stairs seemed like a mile, but they managed with Eli balancing one hand on the wall and the other around Lucy for support. They entered the stairwell and fumbled for the light switch. Eli reached for the door and closed it behind them as quietly as possible, then locked it to slow the bastard down. She looked up to the servants' rooms.

"No," whispered Eli, "Down."

Eli relied heavily on the banister, descending the steps one at a time, struggling to be as silent as possible. Step—*thunk*. Step—*thunk*. The only way Wyatt wouldn't hear them was if he was deaf. They had cleared a half dozen steps when they heard doors being opened and then slammed closed. Wyatt was searching the house, and he wasn't even trying to be quiet.

Moving quicker, by necessity, they arrived on the main floor and listened in the narrow and dimly lit stairwell for any clues as to where in the house Wyatt had traveled.

While they were stopped, Lucy checked her messages. "They're nearly here," she whispered to Eli.

"We can wait here, on the stairs—doors are locked," Eli said, puffing through labored breaths.

"Locked doors didn't stop him from getting in the house." Lucy was breathless too. They could only guess where Wyatt would be.

Lucy gazed down the last flight of steps. She didn't think she could hold Eli's weight much longer, but she wouldn't rest until she had him secured.

They were hit with a blast of cold, damp air as soon as the basement door opened. Lucy's eyes and nose stung from the dust and mold. The basement was dimly lit by windows along the top of the wall, but they were too small to climb through, and too high to reach. Before her eyes could adjust, she spied someone standing nearby, and yelped. But it was only a collection of items poking out of an old oil drum—canoe paddles, fishing poles, Eli's lacrosse stick. The basement was every bit as scary as Owen had suggested.

Looking about, Lucy noted some storage racks and a workbench beside a ramp.

"Is that a door?" she asked.

Eli grunted—the pain was getting the better of him, and he spoke with difficulty. "Yes. This used to be the cellar. It leads out to what used to be the vegetable garden—by the shed."

With effort, they crossed to the battered workbench, where Eli supported himself while Lucy, as quietly as she could manage, began to clear space beside it. She discovered an old five-gallon paint drum.

He gritted his teeth. She could see where some of his stitches had pulled free on his back. He was holding the shoulder that had been dislocated, and had recently supported his weight on the banister.

She sat him down on the paint drum with his leg sticking straight out, and imagined the two of them holed up in this little corner of the basement as Wyatt burst through the door. They were defenseless. She needed to get to her pistol.

Lucy crept up the ramp to the cellar door and lifted the two by four from the brackets on either side.

"Lucy, don't be crazy!" Eli rasped.

"I'll be right back," she whispered. "I'm just going to get the Colt."

"We'll be safe here. Bob's on his way." The anguish on his face was part physical pain, and part frustration. Lucy ignored him, lifted the latch, and pushed up on the cellar door.

She stopped, allowing her eyes to adjust to the bright sun. Wyatt was waiting for her on the other side. He reached for her, but she dodged his grasp and ran, panicked, across the crushed rock of the driveway and into the orchard. Heart pounding, ears ringing. She struggled to work out a plan. *Get him away from Eli.*

She couldn't see Wyatt, but she could hear his heavy footsteps and picked up her pace. There was the old pump house she could probably hold out in until Bob showed up. How much farther? There it was. She was focused on the door when her dress caught on a branch. A tug, a rip, and she was free, but Wyatt was gaining on her. She would never make it to the pump house.

"This was not the plan, Wyatt," she hissed, as her right foot landed on something sharp. A shock of pain pierced the ball of her foot, but she didn't stop. She couldn't. Lucy turned west toward the road, then north to the driveway. A steady trickle of sweat ran down her back. Her loose hair was a tangle about her damp neck.

The house came into view, and she cursed her lame foot and the heat for slowing her down. Just as she reached the edge of the gravel drive, Wyatt rushed up behind her. He caught her by the hem of her dress, breathless and enraged.

She spun around to face him, digging deep for the strength to stand tall. With a quick swipe of his leg, he knocked her legs out from under her. She was suddenly overwhelmed by the same confusion, fear, and nausea she'd felt that night years ago, in the alley. She could have been hiding quietly in the basement with Eli—but now she was flat on her back, sharp bits of gravel pressing into her skin, as her tormentor straddled her. *Please, Bob—where are you?*

"Now you know who I am," he said, in that sickening voice. He pinned Lucy's hands above her head as his shifting weight pressed her more firmly into the gravel. Sweat collected under the wrist brace, and she found some wiggle room. With a little work, she could slip out of it.

"I should have finished you off in that alley," he hissed, as he unbuttoned his grubby jeans.

"Stop it!" she screamed. "You disgusting pig!" She fought, squirming and twisting, legs flailing, until she slipped her sweaty hand from the brace and slapped him. The pain ripped from her wrist through to her shoulder. The slap was a reflex, really—excruciating, but effective. She had his attention.

"Just what are you trying to prove?" Lucy screamed. The pain in her chest mounted.

His eyes glazed over as he looked down at her. His red, blotchy face seethed with anger. He was going to hurt her. She worked hard to use her own rage in defense—as she had that night in the alley. He reinforced his grip while working on getting his zipper down.

"No!" she screamed. It was her rage against his.

He had her good arm tightly pinned above her head—his one free hand had pushed her dress to reveal her panties. He pulled at his jeans, exposing himself. She was horrified by his arousal.

"Get off of me!" Lucy screamed, her free hand pushed at his chest and lashed his face.

"I want to hear you say my name," he panted. "Say it like it means something. Or I'll fuck your brains out, you Mexican whore!" His hand was on her crotch, a grip so strong it made her gasp. From the depths of her anger, she released a bloodcurdling shriek. With her injured hand, she lashed her fingernails across his taut, reddened neck. "You bitch!" he squealed.

"Stop!" The gravel dug into her flesh as she twisted beneath him.

He tightened his grip on her one arm and released his grip from below to slap her face. But as he lowered his body to force himself on her, he was struck in the head. Another blow hit him in the small of his back.

"Get off her." Eli held the lacrosse stick high over his head, his voice like steel. "Now." Sweat ran down the sides of his face and dripped from his bare chest—but Lucy saw no sign of pain.

Wyatt stood slowly, bits of dirt and gravel dropped from his knees as he tried to pull up his pants. Lucy lurched to one side, trembling, while Eli held the stick high and grimaced. He swung again—at Wyatt's face this time. Wyatt ducked and caught sight of Lucy running back toward the orchard. He ran recklessly after her, stumbling.

Lucy headed for the pump house, still hampered by her foot. Wyatt was hurting, too, but five feet from the door of the pump-house, she was hit from behind. She fell to her knees, and a hand on her back pushed her into the earth.

"Quiet." The voice was deep and vaguely familiar. Lucy turned her head to see Agent Thompson. "Shh," he said.

"Where..."

"*Hush*," he scolded.

They heard a gunshot, and the ensuing reverberation through

the trees. Then Agent Thompson's radio crackled. "Bring her back. We have him."

Lucy staggered from the orchard behind Agent Thompson. She limped across the gravel drive to Eli, bent and barely standing. Her dress was torn and filthy, her face smeared with the grime from her hands and blood from her fall. Eli crumbled at her feet.

"Are you two all right?" asked Bob, jogging toward them. Lucy looked up into his flushed face, then down the driveway as Officer Bradley appeared in his patrol car with Summer's Subaru following close behind.

Lucy nodded at Bob, but she wasn't all right, neither was Eli. It was a ridiculous question. Bob laid a kind hand on Lucy's shoulder. "An ambulance is on the way. Everything is going to be okay." He stepped away to join Agent Fitzgerald loading Wyatt's black Denali into the back of a van. Lucy overheard Bob talking to Fitzgerald. "I can't tell you how sweet that was,"

Bob had shot Wyatt in the knee and taken him down himself. Yes, thought Lucy, that probably felt sweet to Bob. A win. But to Lucy, cradling Eli's head in her lap while they both shivered in the throes of shock, it was a horror still. Perhaps that sweetness would come later. Perhaps.

CHAPTER FORTY-TWO

TWO AMBULANCES ARRIVED. ONE FOR WYATT, WRITHING IN PAIN. BOB climbed in beside him vowing not to let the bastard out of his sight. The FBI had their man, and he was going to spend the night in the county jail, while preparations were made at the nearest federal prison.

The other ambulance was for Eli, who was nearly unconscious as they lifted him to the gurney. One paramedic pulled the dressing from his spleen incision and did his best to stanch the bleeding. Lucy rode along in the ambulance while they patched up her foot and wrapped her injured wrist. Kali and Summer would meet them at the hospital.

The fuss in the emergency room reminded Lucy of the night of the fire, when Eli was carted off to surgery to repair his spleen, while Lucy received attention to her foot.

A rusty bit had punctured the ball of her foot, and it was now wedged deep. Removing it was a minor procedure, which left her foot tightly bandaged.

They'd asked when she had her last tetanus shot. She had no idea, so they plunged a needle into her arm.

"Where's Eli," asked Lucy as the nurse left the room. Someone further off was crying. Another person shouted. The emergency room was noisy and lacked privacy.

"He's back in surgery," said Kali, drawing the curtain around the bed.

Summer bent over Lucy and gripped her hand. "Lucy," she whispered. "Wyatt is finally gone." The excitement in her voice could barely be contained. "You're free."

"I'm free," repeated Lucy. She didn't feel free. She felt as trapped and burdened by his spirit as ever. The sound of his voice still rang in her ears. She still felt the weight of his body on her thighs. The image of his face still burned in her mind.

Lucy looked away. The resident psychiatrist was expected any moment—but that was against Lucy's wishes, and she was annoyed with Kali for setting it up. She wasn't interested in speaking with a stranger.

"Hello, Lucy. I'm Doctor Chan." Kali and Summer left the room as Lucy looked up into the disarming black eyes of the psychiatrist.

"Hello." She thought of Doctor Stewart greeting her after her attack in California. The immediate connection she'd had, and the candid conversation. Lucy didn't feel so forthcoming this time, regardless of Doctor Chan's eye contact and passive demeanor. She was withdrawn in a way that felt entirely different from the first time. It sickened her to know that she had this point of reference to use as comparison, to know that one assault was not like the other.

"You can call me Maggie if you like—if it would make you more comfortable." Lucy shook her head. "All right, that's fine." Doctor Chan's voice was steady, cautious, and kind. "I would like to tell you a little something about myself, if that's all right with you." If it meant Lucy didn't have to talk, she was all for listening to the doctor's story.

The story was personal. Doctor Chan too had been assaulted as a young woman. She was only nineteen at the time. Rape, in China, was blamed on the victim, so it was years until she was able to address the damage that had been done. She had been beaten, raped, and abandoned by her attacker. And she had been beaten again when she returned home—this time by her mother, who kicked her out of the house. She had been labeled an embarrassment to the family.

When she finally got the help she needed, she had to confront a pain far worse than the physical bruises. She had to come to terms with the violation of her innocence, the rejection from her family, and her abandonment to the streets. Therapy allowed her to forgive her family. It was the violation she had never been able to free herself from, but instead accepted as part of who she was.

"Lucy, I understand how you are feeling. I've been there. It's hell, but it's not your fault."

"I am not a victim." Lucy repeated the words Summer had asked her to say months earlier.

"Who says?" Doctor Chan took Lucy's hand. "It's okay to acknowledge the victim, as long as you understand that that is not your only identity. Do you understand what I'm saying?"

Lucy nodded, and the doctor continued.

"Who are you, Lucy? What do you want out of life? What brings you joy? The answers will evolve throughout your life—but as long as you *have* answers, you will be fine." The cadence of the doctor's voice had nearly convinced Lucy of this. Nearly.

Dr. Chan laid a compassionate hand on Lucy's arm, then turned to go, pulling the curtain closed behind her. Lucy heard Kali ask a question and the doctor answer.

The hushed voices mingled with the other sounds of the noisy emergency room, as Lucy strained to hear what was being said about her. But they were speaking about Eli. He had just come out of surgery. While the procedure had gone well, Kali suggested that Doctor Chan would need to swing by his room as well when his sedation wore off.

Lucy tried to get out of bed, but the curtain opened and Summer stepped in.

"Where do you think you're going, Missy?"

"Eli." It was the answer to Summer's question, but also Doctor Chan's. He was what she wanted out of life. He brought her joy.

"Can you stand on that foot?" Lucy slid out of bed and tried to put weight on the injured foot. "How about a wheelchair?"

"No, I can do this." She put the weight on her heel. "See?" Summer fetched her clothes, and Lucy tossed off the hospital gown. She disregarded the bruises on her arms and legs as she dressed. The mark on her face still showed the imprint of Wyatt's hand—the spread of his fingers as they'd lashed across her face. She looked away from the mirror to where Kali and the doctor still stood. Doctor Chan looked back with an understanding nod.

Lucy hobbled to the elevator with Summer beside her as they went to find Eli.

"There you are," said Eli. Lucy's heart leaped at hearing his groggy voice. "Are you all right?" he asked.

"Much better now," she answered.

"Me too."

CHAPTER FORTY-THREE

LUCY COULD NOT HAVE BEEN HAPPIER TO SAY FAREWELL TO SUMMER BREAK. September brought with it many new developments with the reopening of the Chrysanthemum House. School had begun a week late due to the legalities, but they were now a month into the new and improved arrangement, with an additional teacher and six more students, including Owen Alexander Moon.

"Out with the old and in with the new," cheered Summer the day they closed on the purchase of the house. She was referring to the ousting of AVID, most of whom had crawled back under their rocks, but many who now sat in jail, including Ben Wyatt.

Mayor Church was pushed out of office after confessing his role with the organization in looking the other way while they ran amok doing whatever they wanted. The police department too, had gone through a clean sweep.

The city was rich with bumper stickers, T-shirts, and yard signs touting "Together We Shall Soar Above, Roy Bird for Mayor."

The Hill brothers were behind bars, collected at the AVID march with so many other members, and still awaiting trial. Bob Marshall had managed to collect enough lower level members, that the evidence and witnesses would likely see the two in prison for years.

Roy Bird and Alex Bridges stepped in, along with three deputy council members, to take a vote on who would stand in as interim mayor. They nominated Roy.

His campaign which had been in its early phase before the Push Back, was running strong. He had one opponent, a young man named Charles Franklin, who had as much as admitted that he didn't have a chance of beating Roy. "In fact," he was quoted by Tina Reynolds, "I would vote for the man myself."

"**WE COULD USE** a fresh start," Eli said, sitting across from Lucy at Bistro 88. "Don't you think?"

The restaurant had changed little since they'd been here last, but it was nearly October now, and the outdoor patio was closed.

"A fresh start?" Lucy set down her menu and took a sip of wine.

"Well, let's see what Jasper has to say. I'm probably jumping the gun, but if he can figure out a way to release the accounts of the estate and get the business back, I'm thinking—just thinking at this point—that I would reopen the doors to Moon Harvest." Eli was much recovered in the month since Wyatt was arrested, but hadn't gone back to work yet. While Beth allowed an extended leave of absence, he was bored and at loose ends.

"Oh, Eli. Is that what you really want? I mean, the social service office is on the cusp of being fully refunded. Could you really let that all go?"

"Good question." The rubble had finally been cleared from the fire. The whole block was now under construction. "I think I could. Yes, I definitely could." He took the last bite of his Greek salad and emptied the bottle of Cabernet into their glasses. She could see the gears turning in his head. "My father had a vision of adding fresh and frozen produce, and I think I could make it happen. Think of all the jobs, and how much they could help this community. I can do it. But it all hinges on Jasper."

"You couldn't do it on your own? I mean—you have equity in the house, collateral. You could get a loan to get your own business going, couldn't you?"

"I probably could, but let's hear what Jasper has to say," Eli said, smiling. "Sounds like you're on board."

Lucy couldn't begrudge him this wish. It wasn't like it had come out of nowhere. During his recovery the last month, Eli had sent Jasper all the documentation he could get his hands on regarding the cannery and the estate. Steven Hanson, the longtime family lawyer did not seem to be in any hurry to resolve the case, and Eli wanted a second opinion.

As promised, Roy Bird had been helpful. He and Eli had sorted through a dozen or so boxes of records from the cannery. One held the bulk of legal documents, another held the tax records going back three years before the company closed its doors, and the rest dealt with accounts and personnel records. Kali cajoled Steven Hanson into sharing his discoveries with Jasper, and he did so—reluctantly.

"Happy birthday, Lucy," Eli said, lifting his last sip of wine. She grinned and tapped her glass to his. They were celebrating her twenty-fifth birthday.

"Thank you." She was grateful for many things. Eli was at the top of the list; Owen, a close second. Then there were her friendships, her parents, and her sister. She was also thankful for the success of the school. But it was her relationships—the people in her life, and the love she felt for them—that she was the most grateful for. *What brings you joy?* Doctor Chan had asked. When she toasted, it was for all of that. Joy was surprisingly easy to come by these days.

Lucy still felt the burden of responsibility for their turbulent summer. She knew that none of those things would have happened had she not been the lure for Ben Wyatt. But Eli never once blamed her. His office had been bugged long before AVID was involved. The mayor and his cronies had the potential to cause those issues and more with the police force in their pocket, and corruption running through their veins. Even without Wyatt, Mayor Church and others would have kept their stranglehold on the community, stripping what they could from the neediest.

Those days were a memory. Now it was autumn. The leaves were in transition into the brilliant reds, oranges, and golds that were the hallmarks of the season. The ducks were fleeing the sanctuary of Drake Park, seeking warmer weather.

We could use a fresh start, Eli had said. And like the Magic 8-Ball, all signs pointed to yes.

CHAPTER FORTY-FOUR

ELI APPEARED ON THE PATIO TO WATCH LUCY AND OWEN AS THEY CLEANED UP THE garden. Lucy was telling Owen a story, as she often did when they worked together. It was an effective strategy for keeping him close. Tales of young things vexed by witches, or drowsy princesses who slept soundly until awakened with a kiss. Lucy had discovered that Owen was a romantic at heart—much like his father.

"Stop staring at us. You're making me self-conscious." Lucy shook her clipper at Eli. She had been concentrating on the final prune of the season, using the mental checklist her sister had left. The perennials would but cut to the ground, except for … she was thinking. The roses, the hydrangeas, and what else?

"Looking good! Can you take a break? I need to tell you something."

"That's it for today, Owen. Why don't you go wash up?"

"But the story," he whined. "What happened to the boy? Did he get the dragon?"

Lucy set her pruner in a basket beside the gate as she held it open for Owen. He stood firm, waiting for an answer, so she crouched down beside him and said, "It doesn't end well for the dragon. Now go on." She gave him a quick paddle on his bottom, and he ran inside.

Eli met her at the gate as she plucked off her gloves and dropped them into the basket. His cast was now half what it was, only covering the lower part of his leg, and it made getting around much easier. Eli slipped an arm around her waist and bent his forehead to hers.

"I just got off the phone with Jasper." He kissed her.

"I'm guessing it's good news." Lucy laughed, and he kissed her again.

"Better than good."

They walked up to the house, where Kali waited for them at the patio table. Lucy sat down beside her, and Eli took a seat across from them.

"To make a long story short," he began, "the business default was to keep the assets in trust until future plans could be sorted out—whether or not to sell the business, or decide who would actually take it over if there was any interest in doing so."

"Who's the trustee?" asked Kali.

"Grandpa."

Kali's mouth dropped open. "Well, that's inconvenient. I thought you said this was good news."

"Right, so that's where we have to go with what our lawyer did way back when." Eli explained that six years ago, the family lawyer didn't just set up their grandfather as trustee for the business, but for the private estate as well. Upon the grandfather's death, Kali and Eli were to take over as trustees—but that message had gotten buried.

"It was a smart move, actually. For all these years, the assets have been frozen, but also the corporate status. No one needed to manage a thing."

"And now?"

"Now, we need to make a few decisions and sign some papers."

"And then?" asked Kali.

"And then, dear sister, we will be very wealthy." Eli giggled. Lucy and Kali were dumfounded. "Say hello to the two co-owners of Moon Harvest."

"What?" cried Kali.

"It's a long story, but to make it easy, you and I will go to Madison this week to sign a few documents and issue a release of the estate funds as well as the business holdings." He stood up and gave his sister a hug. "We, sister, are rich."

"Eli," said Kali, looking annoyed and shaking her head. "I don't want the business."

"Um, what? Are you kidding?"

"No, not kidding. I'm just fine doing what I'm doing. Mia and I are looking for a place." Eli rolled his eyes. She and Mia often talked about moving in together, but it had never come to anything. "And I think I've found an office that will work." She tipped her head and smiled a little. "But now that there's a little more money to work with, we could find something a bit nicer."

"Okay, wait—you don't have to work at the business. You can just be an owner, you know—I'll do the day to day stuff." Eli was not going to let his enthusiasm take a hit.

"Brother, you know squat about running that business, much less any business. What are you thinking? I say we sell it."

AS THE SIBLINGS hashed things out, Lucy and Owen decided to go for a walk. Most of the apples had been picked already by the local gleaners.

It was Beth, of course, who organized the whole operation. She performed magic with her new Community Cooperative, a project she'd started outside of her position with the social service office to add an additional layer of security to the neediest of Drakes population.

Even so, there were a few wrinkled apples to be found on the trees as they stepped carefully over and around the spoiling fruit on the ground, inhaling the heavy scent of sweet fermentation. It was attracting bugs of all sorts; flies, grub worms, gnats, fruit flies, and bees.

The aggressive bees seemed threatened by their presence. Lucy was about ready to go back to the house and let them have the whole mess, when Owen picked what looked like a good apple off the ground and was stung on the palm of his hand. His yelp was heard back to the patio, and Eli hobbled into the orchard. Owen rebuffed Lucy's attempt to carry him back to the house; instead, they ran, meeting Eli along the way. He reached for his son and slipped. Lucy and Owen continued to the house. When Eli caught up to them, Lucy had Owen sitting on the kitchen counter and was examining the sting. He was crying freely, and Lucy was talking to him calmly about what a fast runner he was, and agreeing that bee stings do hurt very much.

She cleaned up his hand and pulled the stinger, then made a paste of baking soda and water and applied it liberally to the sting and began to sing a little song about bees and honey that came to her from the furthest reaches of her brain. Had her mother sung this?

A glance at Eli standing in the doorway made her laugh—and that made Owen laugh, too, through his small hiccups of sobs.

"He's just fine, Eli. Aren't you, Owen?" Owen rubbed his eyes, and she looked back at Eli. "Go take a shower." Kali watched the tender moment from the kitchen table.

"Oh my gosh, you're heavy," said Lucy, lifting Owen to the floor.

"What's for dinner?" he asked.

"Panini sandwiches. Not much time for anything more, I'm afraid. It's getting late. Kali? Chicken sandwich for you?"

"I'm going out, but thanks." Kali stood beside Lucy as Owen marched out of the kitchen. "You remind me of my mom. I've wanted to tell you that for ages." Lucy smiled up at her, and Kali went on. "You have since day one, but especially now."

"Thank you, Kali. That means a lot to me."

"You're so much like her. Something in your voice, the way you move, the way—I don't know, exactly. Maybe it's because you spend so much time with kids, like she did as a volunteer at the school."

"I wish I'd known her."

"Me too. She would have loved you. Dad too."

"What was he like?"

"Did you see that picture in the hall of Grandma Moon?" Lucy nodded. "That could be him, sometimes. He was strict, practical—but also tender. Homelife was important to him, but the cannery took so much of his time and attention. That's another reason I don't want Eli to get involved. He's got such a good thing going right now."

"That's what I told him, but I think he's pretty serious about it."

"It will be an adventure, I'm sure." Kali gave Lucy a warm hug. "Goodnight, Lucy."

Bit by bit, Lucy was getting to know their parents, and realizing that despite their untimely exit, they were still a part of this family and home.

Lucy pulled down the panini maker from the top shelf of the walk-in pantry and started building toasted sandwiches with some of the leftover chicken from the other night.

Owen returned to the kitchen, still red around the eyes, and still moaning about how much it hurt. Lucy served him right there at the table, and he was half-finished when Eli stepped in.

"Mm—you smell sweet," said Lucy as she sat him down beside Owen and laid a hot panini on his plate.

"Lucy's Diner. Get it while it's hot," he joked. "How's your hand, Little Bird?"

"It still hurts," said Owen, with another tear spilling from his eye.

"I lost count how many bee-stings I've had from that orchard," Eli said.

"Did it hurt you too?"

"It hurt like the dickens."

"Lucy, were you ever stung by a bee?" Owen asked.

Lucy sat down with her plate and smiled at him. "Not by a bee, but I was stung by a jellyfish." Owen's eyes opened wide.

"Finish up there, Little Bird. It's time for bed."

Owen finished nearly his whole meal, so Lucy gave him a little cracker with honey dripping from it for his "sweet treat"—to remind him that bees do good things too—then ordered Owen upstairs. Eli picked up his son and tossed him over his shoulder while Owen squealed with both irritation and delight.

"Lucy—the dragon, remember?" Owen called down the staircase.

"I remember, Owen. I'll be up after your bath."

"Shower!" he corrected her. That's right, she remembered, baths were for babies. It's what he'd declared when he returned from Wisconsin covered in mosquito bites, scabby knees, and a scar on his behind from climbing under a barb wire fence. Like father, like son.

A great calm came over Lucy as she settled into the sectional and woke up the television. The cable news pundits were replaying the highlights from the Senate hearing for Supreme Court Justice. It appeared that Brett Kavanaugh would forever be remembered for his assault of Christine Blasey Ford as a teenager and the fact that he was very fond of beer. Lucy was fond of beer, too—but was not at all fond of Kavanaugh or the way the whole assault had been swept under the rug in favor of a political agenda. It was the ultimate Me Too moment.

Lucy clicked off the TV and made the rounds, locking doors and turning off lights. She heard Eli call to her from the top of the stairs and jumped out of her skin. One more aftershock left behind by Ben Wyatt. Eli recognized the significance of her flinch and met her halfway down the stairs. He put his arm around her and led her up to Owen's room.

He was snuggled with the Winnie the Pooh—resurrected from the window seat—under one arm, and a stuffed R2D2 pillow under the other. Lucy knelt beside the bed with an abbreviated end to the dragon story and kissed him goodnight.

"I love you, Lucy," Owen said.

Lucy's heart leaped. "I love you too, Little ..." It wasn't her place to use his family's pet name. "Little Owen. Sweet dreams."

Eli watched her through the open door of the bathroom as she went through her bedtime routine. She thought about how comfortable they had become with each other, and how comfortable she had become with Owen and life in their house.

When she finally climbed into bed, the sheets were cold, and she quickly found herself seeking the heat from his warm body.

"Little Owen?" Eli grinned.

"I'm sorry."

"Lucy, you can call him Little Bird. He would love it. So would I."

CHAPTER FORTY-FIVE

"CAST-OFF DAY" STARTED WITH THE MUFFLED GRUMBLINGS LUCY HAD grown accustomed to. It itched, it stank, and Eli felt like he was lugging around a small child. Even though it had been reduced to half its previous size, it was still an annoyance.

Now he would be able to run and play with Owen, drive his beloved car, and give Lucy a proper tumble in the sheets.

Dr. Franzki was waiting for them at the reception desk when they arrived for the final cut.

"Are you ready for this?" He smiled broadly, displaying his perfect teeth.

"More than ready."

The procedure was over so quickly, it was hardly worth the anxiety Lucy had felt on the way over. Dr. Franzki held the offensive cast out to Eli, who shook his head vehemently. It was only a reminder of that awful day.

"Right, well—I want you to take it easy. No pole vaulting or rock climbing," he joked. Lucy pulled out a pair of his old jeans. The basketball shorts had been abandoned long ago, replaced with a couple of pairs of pants that had to be cut to squeeze his leg through. Eli was thrilled to see his beloved jeans, but as he tried putting them on he discovered with a "harrumph" that the button was a little harder to fasten. Lucy hid her smile.

OWEN WANTED TO celebrate Cast-Off Day at the Haunted House, which recently popped up in Gardner's Grocery parking lot. That idea was promptly nixed. Lucy had had enough frights in her lifetime.

"Let's walk up to Drake Park."

"We can stop at the new SamSams for a Red October and some soda. How about that?" The Red October was the monthly sub special. Lucy and Owen agreed, and they set off for the town square, bundled for the autumn chill.

Kali and Mia emerged from the toy shop and joined them on their blanket under the Old Oak. Kali handed Eli a gift wrapped in plain white tissue paper with a red ribbon tied around it. After hemming and hawing about not wanting any gifts, he pulled the ribbon and revealed a framed photo of him when he'd returned from the hospital. His leg, newly wrapped in the full-length cast, and protruding from the baggy shorts, was propped up on the arm of the sectional. He was bare-chested, but for the tight bandage wrapping his torso. Any visible skin was splashed with the vivid purples and blues of major bruising. One eye was swollen shut, and his broken nose was taped on either side.

"Looks like you were hit by a truck," said Mia.

"You were hit by a truck?" Owen took the picture from his hand.

"No, no. I was badly hurt, though. You remember? When you were at Nana and Papa's?"

Owen nodded but couldn't take his eyes from the picture. "Thanks a lot, Kal," Eli mumbled sarcastically.

"You've come a long way, brother. Kudos."

Lucy gently removed the photo from Owen's grip and handed Eli a gift of her own. Everyone laughed when he revealed the Nike running shoes—a not-so-subtle hint at the weight he'd gained while out of commission. Eli groaned as his sister patted his belly, and he reared his liberated leg back as if he was going to kick her.

Lucy leaned in close and whispered, "I got some too. We'll run together—when you're ready." She had put on some weight, too, since living out at Eli's she was no longer walking and biking everywhere.

"I made you a card." From Lucy's tote, Owen produced a twice-folded sheet of orange construction paper covered in red heart stickers. Eli read the card and held his arms open wide to Owen, who practically threw himself into them.

THAT NIGHT, LUCY and Eli stretched out on the patio under the radiance of a moonlit sky. The air was cold enough that they could see their breath, but they were comfortable under their blankets. Eli was happily liberated from his cast, and they were overfull from the chicken piccata Lucy had prepared for their Cast-Off Day dinner.

They sat quietly, digesting their thoughts and their meal until Lucy broke the silence with reminders of her folks coming out to help put the orchard to bed. She was hoping to get something on the calendar—and that led them down the path of what may lay in store with Moon Harvest.

"I'm excited about the future," said Lucy, her voice calm and soft. She was thinking about his new venture and the progress of her school.

"Me too. I've been thinking about it a lot." Eli paused longer than necessary. It reminded Lucy of the night they passed a joint with Summer, and he zoned out to the word "fidelity."

"Yes?" she urged him on to finish his thought.

"I would never presume …" He swung his legs to the side of the lounge chair to face her. "I hope." He cleared his throat. "Since we've known each other, we've been through enough to write a novel. The good, the great, the terrifying, the brushes with death, and the start of something epic." He took a deep breath. "Remember that night with Summer when I got hung up on the word *fidelity*?"

"I was just thinking about that," she said tentatively, turning to face him.

"It's because it reminded me of something." Eli reached into his pocket and pulled out a ring with a beautiful, single, pear-cut diamond set in white gold. He held it up, pinched between finger and thumb, and watched her face with each word he spoke. "This belonged to my grandmother. It was her wedding ring, and … I want you to have it." He placed a hand on his chest. "I mean ... I want you to wear it ... hope you would." He pushed his thick hair away from his eyes. "Lucy, I come with baggage—the loss of my parents, the responsibilities of this house, my son, and now quite possibly a business. I know it's probably not what you imagined for a couple just starting out, but—well, you would make me the happiest man in the world if you could look past all that and ... I want you to ... will you ... marry me?"

Lucy's heart hammered so hard she could hear it. "Oh, Eli." She smiled at him and looked at the ring he still held between his fingers. His grandmother's ring. Another piece of the family legacy.

"Will you?"

Lucy shifted from her chair to sit beside him, hip to hip. She held the ring-bearing hand in hers and said, "Eli, I have baggage of my own. Baggage you've felt obligated, in your way, to carry for me—so you know the burden of it all." She paused. "If, after knowing that—after everything that's happened because of it—you still want to keep me around, then yes. Because I can't imagine a life without you or Owen." They laughed as he tried to slip the ring on her trembling finger with his trembling hand.

Lucy noticed an inscription along the inner band. A chain of symbols she couldn't read.

"What does it say?"

"*Fidelity.* It's Hebrew."

CHAPTER FORTY-SIX

*P*LEASE DON'T WRECK, PLEASE DON'T WRECK, CHANTED LUCY'S INNER VOICE AS she pushed the button to start the car and put it into gear. It was Kali who had insisted they get the old Prius drivable while Eli's BMW was in the shop. The former had been in the garage so long that it needed everything from a tune-up to a fresh set of tires.

Lucy had driven it for the first time the previous day and did her best to shake the feeling that she was receiving far more than she could give.

Driving that car gave her a strange connection to Eli's mother. The hairbrush in the glove box with her brown and gray hairs woven through the bristles, the half-used scented lotion, and Chapstick in the small console under her elbow were physical artifacts that Lucy didn't feel empowered to remove. But she also felt a spiritual connection as she sat in the driver's seat, looking in the rear-view mirror at Owen.

A rap on the window shook Lucy out of her reverie. Trying to roll the window down, she locked the doors instead. Eli stood outside the door, laughing.

"You sure you know how to drive?"

"Very funny. You saw my driver's license, remember?" Just the night before, they'd discussed it concerning her upcoming name change. A legal name change.

Eli leaned into the window. "It's just one night." One night with Owen as her sole companion while Eli and Kali went to Madison to meet with Jasper. She was looking forward to it.

They had decided to keep their engagement to themselves. Preferring to make a big announcement when Eli returned. Lucy wasn't sure how she contained her excitement. She was still reeling with the idea of being a permanent member of this family, and of this house.

"Go, go on, git," said Lucy. "You'll be late for Jasper, and we have to get to school."

"Bye, Dad. See you later." Owen had missed nothing from his booster in the back seat. Lucy managed to roll down his window, and Eli reached in for a classic Owen strangle-hold.

"Easy, Little Bird," he laughed. "I'll be back tomorrow. You take care of Lucy for me. Can you do that?" Owen nodded emphatically.

ELI SKYPED LATER to say goodnight to Owen. "How are things going there? Have you had your bath yet? How about your story?" Lucy heard the longing in Eli's voice. She wondered how he coul tolerate Owen's trips to his grandparents twice a year.

"We're reading *Nate the Great*. He's a detective who really likes pancakes. Dad?" Owen got very close to the screen.

"Yes, Owen?"

Owen whispered directly into the small microphone on Lucy's laptop. "I love you."

"I love you too, Little Bird," said Eli.

"Dad?"

"Yes, Owen?"

"I love Lucy too." He giggled.

"You and me both, kiddo." On the screen, Eli's smile was priceless. "I'll be home tomorrow. How's that?" Owen nodded and yawned.

"Night, dad."

Lucy was standing by to end the call but gave Eli a wink before she closed the laptop.

Once Owen was tucked in, and Lucy had made the rounds—turning off lights, locking doors, and so on—she went back up to find him fast asleep. Then went into her own room to call Eli.

"How's Madison?"

"It's beautiful. We had lunch on the Union Terrace while we

waited for our meeting with Jasper." He sighed. "Sure wish you were here. You should be part of this. It's your future, too, right?" Lucy had considered going along, but with school, and Owen, it was more practical to stay behind.

"Of course. You know I'm behind you, whatever happens." Lucy had been contemplating Kali's subtle critique of her father's time spent at the cannery. Would Eli let Moon Harvest take over his life?

"That's pretty much up to Kali right now. Jasper invited a guy named Bryce McNeil to the meeting. He works for a sister company called NextGen Management that settles Business Estates like Moon Harvest. Bryce said that Moon Harvest is not the first business that has been left in the hands of unwitting relatives. They'll either help us sell the business or help with the takeover if we decide to keep it. That's my vote, but Kali is standing her ground." That made Lucy laugh. She could just imagine Kali sitting with legs and arms crossed, not giving an inch. "As it stands, the business is a fifty-fifty split. We have equal shares. So, whatever we decide to do, we will profit equally."

"What happens if you keep the business?" asked Lucy.

"NextGen would take over temporarily—hiring, training, and devising a business plan. Then, when they feel like we're up to speed and ready to control things, they will make a gradual exit. And if we sell the business, they're able to facilitate that as well."

"And Jasper thinks you should use this guy? Bryce?"

"Jasper assured us that NextGen is above-board, licensed, and qualified to handle any type of business—including our concept of fresh and frozen produce processing and distribution."

"Well." Lucy laughed. "Listen to you with the business jargon."

"Right? I'm so into this, Lucy. I can taste it."

"Is there a third option? Could Kali just be, like, a silent partner?"

"Now who's talking jargon?" They laughed, both giddy with the prospect of a new future. "It was hinted at as a possibility. I would run the business, and Kali would still be part owner and have as much a say in what goes on as she wanted. We're going to sleep on it and meet up again tomorrow." Lucy heard the irrepressible excitement in his voice.

While they spoke, she toyed with her ring, flipping it this way and that, slipping it on and off, rubbing her finger over the inscription, and finally just admiring it on her ring finger.

After saying goodnight to Eli, Lucy looked in on Owen one last time before climbing into bed. Tomorrow, they would tell him their news, and then it would be public. She had been thinking of this all day—telling Julia, her parents, and Summer, predicting their reactions. Is there a word for this kind of happiness? Joy, bliss, contentment. Lucy searched her internal thesaurus as she drifted into a joyful, blissful, contented sleep.

CHAPTER FORTY-SEVEN

LUCY AND OWEN SAT ON THE PORCH SWING AS THE LAST FEW KIDS WERE COL-lected by their mothers. The leaves from the star magnolia were nearly all yellow—some had already released their grip on the season.

Lucy was thrilled with Owen's progress in school. He was now reading *The Wind in the Willows* with only a little help on some of the more difficult words. He loved that book as much as she had when she was his age. He had been disgruntled at first that she could not be his teacher—Summer taught the younger kids.

Lucy and Summer put a lot of thought into the division of responsibilities. The addition of a high school curriculum and a new teacher meant Lucy was teaching less overall—her role was more administrative. More students required tighter curriculum planning—and, given that they now had a mortgage on the Chrysanthemum House, tighter budgeting as well.

Owen swung his feet rapidly, trying to keep the swing in motion. Lucy touched her foot to the porch rail and pushed off. She thought of all the evenings she had spent on this bench with Eli, remembering the first day he had surprised her with a visit, and how her heart had soared to see him.

"Are you happy, Lucy?" asked Owen as the last student drove off.

"Yes, Owen, I am very happy."

"Me too." Owen watched her face and said that he had made a wish at bedtime last night. She remembered the "star light, star bright" routine they had begun earlier that summer.

"And?" she asked.

"I can't say, or it won't come true." He urged another push of the swing.

"It was a good day, wasn't it?"

"Mm-hmm."

"You miss your dad?"

"Mm-hmm—but all of the other kids have moms too."

Lucy thought for a moment as she stopped the swing with the toe of her shoe. "Yes, Owen, but you have so many people who love you." She put her arm around his shoulders and looked into his sweet face.

"I made a wish, though," he said with a sly smile. Lucy squeezed his shoulder.

She wanted so badly to tell him but knew how much Eli wanted them to tell him together. She wasn't going to steal his thunder.

AS PROMISED, ELI was waiting for them when they returned from school. He had so much news for Lucy before they could even think about telling Owen anything, so he invited her to walk while Kali watched Owen.

"Life is about to change dramatically," said Eli.

"Yes, I'm aware." She grinned.

"Well, yes, there's that." He took her hand, swinging it along as they walked toward the tree garden in front of the house. "But more than that."

Kali had relinquished any thought of selling the business. She would hold her shares and receive compensation along with benefits. Eli would receive equal compensation with the addition of a salary.

As for the personal finances, Jasper reminded them that the savings, retirement, and anything remaining in investments would be shared equally. This included assets also held in their grandfather's name.

The house had already been released to them, but the single caveat to the estate would be Kali relinquishing any ownership of the house once Eli remarried—or they could sell the home and split the windfall before he remarried.

"What was that last part?" asked Lucy.

"The house is mine—well, yours and mine, when we get married."

"And Kali is all right with that?"

"She is."

"What about the whole story about your grandpa's brother? I thought that was holding things up. Whatever happened to that?"

"Uncle Ernie died two years ago. Jasper opened that can of worms to the survivors and found a grandson who was moderately interested in the business, but not as an owner. They waived all rights. It's all ours, whatever we want to do with it."

Eli explained the agreement they signed with NextGen Management. They would begin setting up the office in two weeks while they threw out a wide net to find talent in the area. The prediction was that it would be six months until Eli could fly solo. He wasn't quite that confident.

Then he began the litany of personal accounts he had access to. The assets were split down the middle, and he and Kali were each worth sixteen million—not including the value of the business, which hadn't yet been evaluated.

They stopped walking and stood in the dwindling shadow of a chestnut tree, which was in full fall color and had dropped enough leaves that Lucy and Eli were standing on a carpet of yellow.

Lucy batted her eyes. "Sixteen *what?* Million?" A perfect V of geese called to one another overhead as they headed for their winter home.

"All managed by Jasper's firm until we get a local adviser, who this guy Bryce will help locate." He gave her a tight squeeze. "Unimaginable." He shook his head. "My folks were only a fraction of that. The bulk of the inheritance was from Grandpa. All his assets had been frozen until the business was decided—he had written that in his will. Apparently, he wanted us to struggle a little. To feel the pinch—the plight of most Americans."

"To build empathy? He thought you and Kali needed more *empathy*? Did he know you at all?"

"Oh, yes, he knew us. He knew we were too young to understand the struggles of life. His will mentioned 'walking a mile in another man's shoes.'

"I'll say. Eli, this is a lot of information." She stood still and folded her arms, not looking at him. "I'm blown away."

"So am I," said Eli. "It's daunting. I don't think we could do this without the NextGen company. I feel like Grandpa's watching over me." Lucy nodded. A soft breeze rustled the remaining leaves in the canopy overhead and released a shower of colorful leaves.

"Your mom and dad too, I'd say. Let's go talk to Owen."

CHAPTER FORTY-EIGHT

"**L**UCY'S GOING TO BE MY MOM? FOR REAL?"

"For real," said Eli. This kitchen table moment had begun awkwardly, with Eli nervously stumbling over the announcement, trying to find the right words.

Lucy's heart pounded excitedly. Had they moved too fast? It had been nearly six months since she was drawn in by Eli's gravitational pull. The concern for her in his eyes that day was now replaced with the sparkle of joy and love. Their initial attraction now included mutual respect, affection, devotion, and shared trauma.

"We should have a party!" squealed Owen.

"Yes, absolutely," replied Lucy.

"A big party!" he added. Eli and Lucy exchanged amused glances. "With balloons—and cake!"

"All right, party planner, take a break—time for bed," Eli said, taking his hand.

"And dancing!" Owen bounced up the stairs, jabbering along the way.

It took the better part of an hour to get him to unwind, but the warm shower, five chapters of *Nate the Great*, and copious hugs wore him down until he could no longer ignore his exhaustion.

"Goodnight, Little Bird," said Lucy, gently sweeping his bangs from his eyes.

"Goodnight … Mom." Lucy was just about to speak when Eli rested his hand on her arm. She looked into his soft gray eyes and nodded. When they closed Owen's door, Kali was waiting for them in the hall.

"There's someone here to see you."

"Me?" asked Eli.

"Both of you."

Their visitor was a tall man in a black suit. He stood in the front hall with his back against the door, as if he dared not come further without permission. They barely recognized Bob Marshall—clean-shaven with his hair cut short and neatly combed. But the moment he saw them, he took two long strides to shake Eli's hand, then set his other hand on Lucy's shoulder. They were wary of his grim expression.

"I have some troubling news," he started, with a bow of his head, and Lucy's heart sank. There had been no preamble—no "What's new?" or "How are you doing?" Nothing to indicate this was anything like a social call.

Eli invited Bob into the dining room. Bob took the head of the table with Eli and Lucy to his left and right. Kali sat beside her brother, as Bob began to explain the chain of events leading to this visit.

While Ben Wyatt sat in jail, AVID had not lost its momentum. Locking him up had only fanned the flames of his organization. He was a martyr now.

Drake was quiet for the time being because of their successful rally—but that wasn't going to last. Sitting at the controls of AVID's internal operation was Stan Carter, Wyatt's foster father. There was also an infusion of funds from an anonymous source.

"This benefactor came up with bail," said Bob. Lucy gasped. "As of tomorrow morning, Wyatt can walk while he awaits trial— despite firm resistance from the federal prosecutors."

Lucy turned her attention to the clean-shaven GI Joe. "What was the ultimate charge? What are we fighting?" The words were sickeningly familiar. This conversation had taken place years ago with Nathan Weil, her court-appointed attorney in California. Here she was again.

"Two counts of third-degree burglary, and a charge of third-degree sexual assault. In this state, that's a misdemeanor."

Eli pounded his fist on the table. The dense wood absorbed most of the impact, but everyone at the table understood his rage. "He's a terrorist!"

"Easy, Eli. Currently there is no law against domestic terrorism.

We must use the tools we're given. But it's not all a loss. The burglary is still considered a felony. We have the potential to lock him up for ten years."

"What's that worth in real time?" Lucy thought about the earlier reduced sentence, even after Wyatt had nearly killed her.

"Five, maybe seven years." Lucy couldn't believe her ears. "They're working on a plea deal."

"What does that mean?" asked Eli.

"He cops to a lesser charge and gets a lighter sentence. In return, Lucy won't have to testify. It'll settle out of court. It's pretty straightforward." Bob rummaged through his satchel and plopped a thick folder on the table.

"That's why I'm here. I've been at the courthouse all day. The district attorney's office asked if I would be the acting liaison based on our relationship." He opened the folder to a set of documents Lucy needed to read over and sign. "He's pleading guilty to sexual assault. It has the lesser of the two sentences—just one year, and he can work it off in work-release. If the plea deal falls through, this all goes to trial, and we're back to the possible ten years."

"Where is he now?" asked Eli.

"He's been in the federal corrections in Illinois, forty miles from here. Tomorrow, though, he's on the streets. It's not ideal. The bail seemed unattainable, but we underestimated these guys. The feds filed charges, and we're waiting to hear back from the court. It just takes time."

"I'm so confused. You're saying he's just free to roam, meet members of the organization, plan another attack on harmless citizens." Lucy was dumbfounded. "I don't want to have anything to do with this."

"It's out of my hands."

"If I sign the papers, he's on work-release. Is that like probation?"

"Not exactly, but something like that. He has to show up every day, on time. If he doesn't, he gets locked back up."

"Then he's accountable if I sign. If I don't sign, he's free as a bird until trial. Is that right?"

"No. He'll still need to meet with the police regularly, obey the law, and stay away from AVID. But you'll have to testify."

Eli pushed his hair back and gritted his teeth. "What kind of assurances do we have that he won't come after Lucy again?"

"The FBI is still monitoring the whole situation. And I have two agents right outside who will watch for him."

"What should I do?"

"I can't make this decision for you. There is a strong possibility that Lucy is no longer his priority. He has been discouraged from coming anywhere near her, and from meeting with the organization. There is a tail on him to make certain of it and two agents out front as a precaution."

"Is Lucy safe?" Eli was on the edge of his seat, his hands fastened in his lap. Bob shrugged one shoulder, then nodded. It wasn't the most convincing answer.

"When is the trial?" asked Lucy.

"Trial is set for December 30, I think."

"You *think?*"

"Unless something happens before then."

"What would happen? What are you thinking?"

"Well, if he breaks the terms of his bail release by doing something illegal—leaving the state, meeting with AVID—or if he's ..."

"Dead?" Lucy's mind was on the gun safe.

"Dead? Well, yes, that would certainly keep him from the trial." Bob smiled weakly. "I was going to say if he comes anywhere near Lucy." He looked from Eli to Lucy, who toyed with her ring.

It was quiet at the other side of the table, where Kali sat all eyes and ears. *An occupational habit.*

Bob cleared his throat. "Lucy, about the papers—what do you want to do?"

"Ten years if I don't sign?"

"You'll be called as a witness. Both of you." Bob tapped his fingers lightly on the file. Lucy picked it up and opened it to the first document. A mug shot was fastened to it. *That face,* she thought with revulsion. She closed the folder and handed it back to Bob.

"I'll take my chances." She'd have to testify, but it meant longer jail time.

"All right—I'll leave you to it, then. Eli, you have my number. He pushed his chair back and stood, stretching his arms. Lucy and Eli walked with Bob to the front step and stood under the bright lights of the front entry. Lucy pulled her sweater tight around her against the chill. Two men emerged from a black sedan in the driveway, dressed casually in jeans and sweatshirts. Lucy remembered them both from the incident with ICE.

"You've met Agents Fitzgerald and Thompson?" Agent Thompson stepped right up them, his tall and lanky body towering over Lucy. Eli reached out and shook his hand, then offered his hand to Agent Fitzgerald. Lucy spotted the cuff of his tattoo sleeve around the exposed wrist and his shaggy red hair stuck out in all directions. He looked as if someone had just pulled him out of bed at three in the morning. Perhaps they had.

"Call me Fitz," said Fitzgerald, "everyone else does. I have a thing for nicknames. This guy here is Slim." He patted Thompson on the shoulder.

"I'm outta here," Bob said. "Thanks for your time, Lucy." Bob shook Eli's hand and walked the other agents back to their jet-black Chrysler 300, where they would spend the night.

By the time Lucy and Eli joined Kali in the kitchen, she'd opened a bottle of champagne, which she'd smuggled in that afternoon to surprise the newly engaged couple.

"A toast," she declared. "To our expanding family! Welcome, Lucy."

"Thank you, Kali." Lucy raised her glass to her future sister-in-law.

CHAPTER FORTY-NINE

"**S**TRESS," SAID ELI, STANDING ON THE FRONT PORCH OF THE CHRYSAN-themum House. "The doctor said my headaches are from stress. Take that away, and ..."

"Piece of cake," said Lucy, with a knowing grin. It was all either of them could do to put their troubles aside. The spirit of Ben Wyatt followed them everywhere—given that he was on bail with the trial pending—and Moon Harvest was far more work than Eli had anticipated. Lucy and Owen were left to their own devices most nights, just as Kali had feared.

"Is that all he said?" Lucy didn't feel comfortable challenging Dr. Franzki's diagnosis, but there must have been more.

"Pretty much. I got the full exam—blood pressure, ears, eyes, heart."

"And how is your heart?"

"You should know." He put his arms around her and kissed her full on the lips while curious students watched from the window.

It had been two weeks since his last migraine, and he had planned to cancel his appointment, but Lucy insisted. She believed that migraines were always a symptom of something else, and her imagination had conjured ailments even WebMD had not suggested. The beating he had taken could very well cause subtle, longer-term problems.

The cannery was transforming before their eyes, but the price for such rapid development was that Eli had less time with the people he loved. Eli agonized over ever-changing design plans he did not understand, and interviewing candidates for jobs he was not familiar with. The weight of it all made him anxious.

"Shay says it will be six more weeks of construction, but I'll be behind my father's desk in three," said Eli. The news lifted Lucy's spirits. "If it weren't for you, Lucy, I'd be sunk."

Shay was the transitional CEO of Moon Harvest. He was an energetic thirty-something hipster with a man bun and pale blue eyes. Lucy had met him just once and marveled at his enthusiasm for the project. When Shay was satisfied that Eli was up to speed, the reins would be handed over, and Shay would stay on temporarily as a consultant.

It wasn't just Shay who pushed Eli. An interim personnel director named Kelly Fields also loaded Eli with resumes and human resource documents to review.

The construction site was a whirlwind of activity. Dust and noise contributed to the headaches as much as the workload. The portable office was continually buzzing with activity regarding construction, hiring, budget, and planning. Eli had a lot to learn, and it seemed the timeline for acquiring that knowledge kept speeding up because of Shay's ceaseless drive.

Each night Eli returned home exhausted, and Lucy would draw him in, feed him, and put him to bed. Owen was already in bed when Eli got back most nights. He would look in on him and worry that he was screwing up, but Lucy assured him that this situation was temporary, and they would get through it.

Gone were the days of lingering lovemaking and sweet nothings. No more nibbles and giggles under the sheets. It was lights out when Eli's head hit the pillow. That too, Lucy said, was temporary.

Eli looked across the street to the duplex where he'd first seen GI Joe, the man he'd later come to know as Bob Marshall. "I need a break."

"I know you do." Lucy brushed her fingertips over his open palm, and he giggled. He was ticklish in the strangest places.

They said their goodbyes, and he left for the cannery. It would be another late night, thought Lucy, as she reentered the school to the prattle of children's voices. The teachers were clearing the tables from lunch and trying to regain some control.

"Everything all right?" asked Summer.

"He said it's stress."

"Yoga. Meditation maybe?" Lucy was hip to both, but convincing Eli to make time for either was going to be a challenge.

She had her own ideas about stress relief. The next day, while Owen was occupied at school, working out the building blocks of multiplication, Lucy slipped out to put her small plan into action. With a packed lunch, and the best of intentions, she set off to the construction site.

To say Eli was taken by surprise was an understatement. Lucy had walked in on him, elbows fastened to the desk, head nestled into the heels of his hands, his hair draped in front of his eyes, and utterly alone in the portable office.

"I've come to steal you away," she said, with mischief in her eyes. Eli's head snapped up, and it took just a blink of his eyes to focus on her.

"Not a moment too soon," he replied, winding his way across the office to embrace her. They stood like that for a long moment, warming in each other's arms—but just as she tipped her head up for a kiss, the door opened, and a sudden gust of wind invited a few autumn leaves inside.

"Hope you're not planning on going anywhere," said Kelly, looking from Lucy to Eli. "We have an interview in half an hour."

"You can handle it," said Eli, still looking at Lucy. "I need a break." And with that, the two left Kelly to her own company and drove into town for a picnic under the Old Oak.

It was the middle of October. The park had recovered from its own trauma, and the rabble-rousers were long gone. The trampled grass had regrown and was entering winter dormancy with the night temperatures now sinking into the thirties.

The framework for the whole block of burned-down buildings was nearly complete. It was a wonder how quickly the reconstruction was going. The social service office was going to occupy a larger space than before.

As they lay beneath the Old Oak, its leaves now a deep bronze, the pair made themselves comfortable on the quilted blanket, borrowed from Lucy's old bed at the Chrysanthemum House.

"Thank you," said Eli, staring up into the branches.

"Are you hungry? I've packed a lunch." Lucy opened her tote bag and pulled out some egg salad, and a tub filled with plump green grapes.

"Starving." Eli reached for the grapes and pointed to the bench where he had sat with her the day they met. Despite the circumstances, Lucy loved thinking back to that day.

"My hero," she teased, and he grinned.

"You know, as much hell as Wyatt has put us through, we can thank him for introducing us."

"I thank Mia."

"What?"

"In the toy shop when you and Owen were outside, she pointed you out and said, 'He's single.' If not for that, I would have just gone home, no matter how cute you were."

"You thought I was cute?" His smile grew.

"Beyond cute. Almost as cute as Owen." They laughed.

"I knew there was a reason I fell for you."

Lucy remembered the first time he'd told her how much he loved her, and she reminded him of their run down the hill to the Chrysanthemum House just afterward.

Neither mentioned the fire or the beating Eli survived in the park, but they looked up into the oak's branches and acknowledged the ultimate witness to all of it—the relationship between their growing dependence on one another and the presence of the insidious Ben Wyatt.

Lucy looked at her watch and began packing up, just as he'd taken the last bite of his sandwich.

"What? Is our reminiscing over so soon?"

"Nope," she answered. "Not quite." It was 3:30, and time for phase two of her plan. Summer would have the house empty of another breathing soul, taking responsibility to deliver Owen to Aunt Kali.

They packed their things into the rear of the Prius and drove down the hill. All the while Eli joked about being literally hijacked until they pulled up in front of the Chrysanthemum House.

"I want to take you back to last spring," she said as they climbed the few stairs to the front porch. "Before Wyatt, before lawyers, and before the rebirth of Moon Harvest." She took his hand and pushed the front door open, leading him up the stairs and into her old room, where the bed was made up, and the blinds were pulled down.

"Oh, you clever, clever girl." They were back, for the time being, in their bubble, naked and utterly consumed with one another for the better part of an hour.

Eli reached high over his head in a satisfied stretch, his hands pushing against the headboard. Was this your prescription for treating my headaches, because if it is, it worked." He grinned at Lucy laying contentedly beside him.

"Happy to help." She placed her hand on his chest and felt the thumping of his heart.

"Kelly's going to be pissed, though."

"May I remind you—she is not your boss." She ran her fingers from his chest up the length of his throat and rested them on his mouth which stretched into a wide smile. He took her by the wrist and removed her hand so he could speak.

"It doesn't feel that way. Between her and Shay, I'm being pushed and pulled from morning till night. I miss you so much, you have no idea." He pushed a strand of hair from her face. "Should we set a date?"

"I don't know. Maybe we should wait for the dust to settle with the new business—and the trial." Her voice drifted off.

"You're thinking about the trial." Eli slapped his forehead. "Of course you are. I'm so sorry. My mind has been on the renovation and all that mess." He waved his hand in the general direction of the cannery. "I'll be there with you—don't worry about that. In fact, you'll have your own cheering section. It'll be bigger than Owen's fan base at a T-ball game."

"Oh, that reminds me. His first soccer practice is next week. We need to get him some cleats." Lucy swung her legs over the bed to get up.

"Just where do you think you're going? Get back here," said Eli reaching for her arm. Lucy sidled back against his warm body and gave in to his soft kisses. At some point, they'd drifted off, and Lucy woke to Eli, staring at her.

"What if it was possible to go back in time and change things?" he asked.

"How far back?"

"Exactly—how far back would you go?"

Lucy had played similar mind games since the attack in California. "I would go to a different college. No, I loved that school. I would ..." She thought hard. "I would not have worked in that coffee shop."

"But then you wouldn't have come to Drake. We wouldn't have met." Lucy wondered if she would sacrifice the love of Eli and the Chrysanthemum House to not have had Ben Wyatt haunt her dreams, or AVID terrorize this town?

"What would *you* have changed?" she asked him.

"I wouldn't have dated Eva."

"But then you wouldn't have Owen, and you wouldn't have moved back to Drake. Again, we wouldn't have met."

"I disagree. I think that our paths would have crossed anyway. Somehow. I think we were fated to be together."

"I like how your mind works." Lucy giggled. "The best of both worlds."

It was evening by the time Lucy returned Eli to the cannery. He was relieved to see so few cars in the parking lot but discouraged at the sight of Kelly's dusty white compact.

Kelly was sensitive enough to leave the two alone to say their goodbyes. Eli said he would still need an hour or two there at the cannery.

"Eli," Lucy pointed out. "This is no longer a cannery. You'll need to find another term."

He looked around at the renovated buildings. "I'll think about it." He kissed her quickly before she drove off.

OWEN WAS ALREADY tucked into bed when Eli came home that night, with an armload of files, his laptop, and a bottle of wine.

"She sent me home for a long weekend. Guess your little scheme to liberate me had a bonus effect." Eli set the wine down on the kitchen counter as Lucy fished around for the opener.

"What's with the files?" she asked, nodding at the stack he'd plunked on the kitchen table.

"Homework," he smiled. "To do at my leisure. It's the resumes, and the few positions we still need to fill." He filled their glasses with the Pinot Noir, and they moved into the great room where Lucy wedged herself beside him on the sectional.

"Cheers." It had been a wonderful day. Her plan had worked out better than she had imagined.

"Cheers."

CHAPTER FIFTY

Lucy was curled up on the sectional with a mug of strong coffee, watching the usual pundits speak about the gruesome Jamal Khashoggi killing in Turkey. It had been nearly a month since the story first hit, but the president's refusal to admit he'd known anything about it kept it in the news with bizarre Tweets and fresh rumors.

Breaking news announced the identity of the shooter from the Tree of Life Synagogue in Pennsylvania, and Lucy wondered if that incident had anything to do with AVID. What were they up to these days?

When she heard Owen tramping down the stairway, she scrambled for the remote to avoid any inevitable questions.

"Hi, Mom." He plopped himself beside her, wiggling his bare toes, and she set down her mug to put her arms around the cuddly little boy. His hair was growing out, and the soft curls had returned.

"What do you want to do today, Little Bird?" Lucy asked.

Eli called from the kitchen, "It's a beautiful day. How about we drive out to the cannery? I'll show you two around." Owen got to his knees and faced the doorway behind them as Lucy retrieved her coffee. She turned to Eli, approaching them. He'd been stir-crazy without the daily excitement of the business revamp, so Lucy knew it was a good idea to get him out of the house. Also, she wanted Owen to see why his father was working so much.

"I'll drive," she said, sending Owen off in search of his shoes.

Eli was right. It was a beautiful Indian Summer day, and she didn't want it wasted in front of the television.

Owen listened contentedly to the playlist while they drove along the country roads toward Moon Harvest. He tried singing along to the bluegrass lyrics of Brown Bird, but it came out sounding like nonsense.

Lucy turned to Eli, "We have a party to plan."

"A Halloween party?" Owen chimed in. "I'm going to be Chewbacca."

"No, not a Halloween party—sorry, Owen," Eli called to the backseat and turned to Lucy. "An engagement party."

"We could use the great hall," suggested Lucy.

"I love it," said Eli. "It needs a little elbow grease, but everything is there. Do you think Thomas would bring the band together for us?"

"I'll text Summer when we stop."

"We'll need some time," said Eli. "How about Saturday, the week after next? That gives us a full week before the grand opening." *And two months to the trial.*

By the time they'd arrived at the cannery most of the details for the party had been decided, including using Nikko to cater, and asking Thomas if the Genial Disposition would be available.

Lucy texted Thomas as they crossed the lot to the new front doors with a massive sign, reading Moon Harvest Wholesale Produce posted overhead. Just as Eli unlocked the door, his phone rang.

"Hey, what's up?" Eli said. *"Excuse me?"* He followed Lucy and Owen inside and closed the door behind them. "Got it. I'm not happy about it, but I got it."

"Got what?" asked Lucy, eyes wide at what she saw around her. Chrome and glass, high-set ceiling fans and glossy tile floors converted the dark and dingy space she and Eli had visited last summer into a stylish show of industrial chic.

"Two of our new hires were red-flagged for being AVID members. Bob said to keep them. They could be useful. And he's sending Fitz in to interview for some grunt job to keep an eye on them.

"Spies spying on spies," said Lucy, keeping an eye on Owen as he explored.

Eli shook his head. "Will this never end?" Lucy looked around the waiting area with black leather chairs and large prints on the walls of farm scenes like orchards at sunset, and vineyards that went on for miles. She took Eli's hand and pulled him close.

"Eli, it's beautiful." She was breathless with excitement. Whatever Bob and Fitz were up to seemed unimportant at the moment. "Look at what you've created."

CHAPTER FIFTY-ONE

THE TREES WERE AT PEAK COLOR WHEN LUCY, SUMMER, AND THE NEWLY ADDED teacher, Lizzy, set off for the arboretum at St. Charles College. Every year at this time, they sent a school bus to collect the students from the Chrysanthemum House and individual home schools to tour the grounds with a knowledgeable docent from the botany department—usually a teacher's aide who needed a little extra cash.

Lizzy had been an asset on their tour. She was a horticulture buff who seemed to know more than their docent and would interject small fun details about the trees that amused the children, such as Ginkgo trees had been around since the age of the dinosaurs, and the spread of a trees roots underground were as wide and the tree canopy aboveground.

They'd seen quaking aspens, silver maples, red oaks, and river birch. The whole tour was sprinkled with footnotes compliments of Lizzy.

The tour finished with a trip to the large fountain in front of the college library where Lucy stood, waiting for Summer and Owen to catch up. They were in an animated conversation with Owen's friend, Anika.

When Lucy turned her attention back to her own small group, she looked straight ahead into the eyes of Lamar Hill. She didn't recognize him at first. The beard was gone, and he wore a knit cap with the school logo embroidered on the front.

"Looking for someone?" he asked. A numb feeling washed over Lucy, and her head filled with static. In a flash, she was thrown back to the previous summer. The listening devices, the ICE raid, the office burning down, the riots, and Eli's bravery, which landed him in the hospital.

Flustered and confused, Lucy collected the kids and stomped toward the waiting bus. She finally caught up to Summer, who was surrounded by the younger students.

"Owen has some exciting news for you."

"Summer, I just saw Dum Beard," murmured Lucy. "*Summer.*" She gripped her friend by the hand. "I just saw Lamar Hill."

Summer looked over her shoulder. "Where?"

"He was by the fountain. He lost the beard, so I wasn't sure at first, but his name was on his work jacket." That was all she could say. Her mind was cluttered with flashing images and the instinct to flee.

She hurried onto the bus with her heart racing at a sprinter's pace. She sat beside Owen, who was saving a seat for her. *Not again,* she thought.

"Mom, look. Look." He poked her shoulder. "*Look!*" Lucy looked at the boy beside her, but the image was blurred, so she wiped her teary eyes with the cuff of her sweater and saw Owen pushing a lower front tooth a little this way and that. "Have you ever seen the tooth fairy?" he asked, innocently.

"No, Owen. No, I haven't." She smiled at his sweet face. "Not yet, anyway."

Her nightmares had dulled in the past couple of weeks—replaced with ideas for the party, and concern for Eli's transition into the business. But sometimes she could still be triggered into a flash of fear.

With this physical reminder, she was reintroduced to the havoc AVID had brought to Drake. She may as well have just seen Ben Wyatt himself for the fear that pierced her chest and clouded her head.

Lucy pulled her phone from the inside pocket of her jean jacket. She intended to text Eli with the news, but her hands were shaking like the quaking aspen they had just seen in the arboretum. Instead, she put her arm around Owen and pulled him closer, unconsciously fitting her armor around them both.

THE HOUSE WAS empty when Lucy and Owen returned. Eli was working late, and Kali was seldom home unless she had scheduled an appointment.

Lucy sent Owen to wash up in the hall bath as she fixed a small snack to keep him busy while dinner was in the works. She was making harvest soup, which Owen promptly renamed Moon Harvest Soup. It would be easy for him to navigate with his loose tooth.

The ground turkey sizzled in the pot while the celery, potatoes, carrots, and onions filled the countertop, waiting for their turn at the chopping block. She closed her eyes for a breath or two in a weak attempt to push Lamar Hill from her head.

It occurred to her that Owen had been taking a very long time in the hall bathroom, so she turned down the heat and left her post to look in on him.

She found him standing precariously on the yellow plastic footstool, leaning into the mirror to get a good look at his wiggly tooth. He grimaced, growled, and giggled. Lucy seized the opportunity to take a quick video for Eli.

After their guided tour of the revamped facility the previous day, Lucy had a new appreciation for the work it took just to get the place up and going. She was thankful Eli's headaches had not been an issue lately. *Knock on wood.*

Perhaps the headaches had abated because he saw his vision taking shape, or that he was surrounded by capable people like Kelly and Shay.

It was evenings like this that she appreciated the kitchen as it was. Sitting at the antique table nestled at one end, the room transported Lucy to the little kitchen of her childhood home. She could pretend, for the time being, that she wasn't in a house that went on for days. From wall to wall, floor to ceiling, the Moon house demanded a large family as Kali had suggested.

She imagined children of her own, though she couldn't fathom loving them any more than she loved Owen.

Still rattled by Lamar Hill, Lucy was also comforted by Owen and the regularity of their routine. She looked forward to doing the dishes—she would wash, and Owen would dry—followed by the bedtime ritual, which would include the latest edition of the new *Star Wars Chronicles*.

By the time Lucy climbed into bed that night, she discovered Eli had already beaten her to it.

"What? When did you? How?" She stumbled with her line of questioning as he pulled her close and began kissing her neck, effectively silencing her.

He was the sweet yet passionate man she had fallen in love with. A man both attentive and responsive in the privacy of their room and the comfort of their bed. The moon that night was just a sliver in the sky, shedding little light on their intimacy. In that darkness, with the hoot of a lonely owl outside their window, the two got reacquainted.

Eventually, Lucy told him about Tweedle Dum. He assured her they were going to be all right. She was safe, and there was nothing to worry about. The words were inadequate for how she felt. AVID was on the rise right under their noses. Nothing to worry about did not cut it. She was worried that any peace they had experienced wasn't going to last.

They had installed a security system in the house a while back, when Eli and Kali were dreaming of all the things they could do with their windfall. Bob recommended a system tough enough to keep intruders out, but easy enough that even Owen could operate it. Despite that, Eli couldn't wrap Lucy up tight enough to make her feel truly safe, and she longed for the day when he would no longer have to work such long days at the cannery.

"The business is nearly there." She listened halfheartedly as he ran his fingers up her arm and down the length of her naked back. His voice resonated through the fibers of the bed. "It's nearly functional now ... rudimentary way that allows us all to get a feel for things before ... operation gets up to speed." And she drifted off to sleep.

CHAPTER FIFTY-TWO

THOMAS AND HIS BAND WARMED UP IN THE GREAT HALL WHILE THE OTHERS swept, mopped, and polished the floors, or cleaned the expansive windows with ladder and squeegee. His bass player had moved to Florida, but fortunately Eli learned that Shay played bass and he agreed to fill in. Shay fit right in with the band, and Thomas couldn't have been happier, since it was mostly original material, and Shay needed to learn the whole set.

The music lightened the mood in the ballroom, and Thomas joked about speeding up the tempo to encourage the slackers.

"Hey," said Summer, brandishing her squeegee and bucket of window cleaner. "I'm no slacker!"

Thomas blew her a kiss. "Love you, babe. Forgive me?"

Owen wiped his brow with a dramatic flair and a toothy smile—less one tooth—as he took one of his frequent breaks from brandishing his dust mop along the wood-paneled walls. It was clear someone would need to come in behind him, as it looked a little spotty in areas—but Lucy was proud that he even elected to take on the chore in the first place.

Mia said she would be by later with tequila and mixer—one of the incentives that kept Summer busy atop her stepladder.

The engagement party was in three days, and there was still so much to do, but Lucy's suggestion to have Nikko cater the party had been a masterstroke. Nikko assured them that if their guests never remembered the party, they would surely remember the food.

Eli was waiting for enough of the floor to clear so that he could run the rented floor polisher—a machine much more daunting than he had expected. In the end, they all took a shot at it, relieving one another as their arms gave out. Owen was a little disappointed that he didn't get a turn, but he got over that quickly when Mia arrived with her promised contribution plus a small carton of chocolate ice cream.

"Nothing like an old-fashioned work party," said Bob, walking into the enormous room. Owen had already escaped to the kitchen to dish up the ice cream, and the band followed Mia down the hall to the great room.

Lucy wiped her hands on her jeans, and then approached Bob. "Can I offer you a hasty margarita?"

"Maybe later." Bob walked deeper into the room, his eyes wide as saucers. "Sheesh, look at this place. I thought I'd seen it all when I sat down in your dining room."

"Credit to my grandfather. He was a bit of a show-off," Eli said.

"No joke. Never seen anything like it."

"What brings you by?" asked Eli, reaching for Lucy's hand.

"Just making the rounds. Got Thompson out there now." He pointed out the window.

"Everything all right?" Eli gave Lucy's hand a squeeze.

"It should be. Don't worry, but the guys at your warehouse are acting squirrely. I just want to be sure it doesn't have your name on it. It's Fitz' job to blend in there. How's that going?"

"He's on the loading dock with them. Fits right in," said Eli. "No pun intended."

"We have him wearing a mic, you know. He's getting some wind on a rumor that Wyatt is up to something. I don't know if it's true, but ..." He trailed off. "You might want to think about getting out of town until the trial."

"That serious?" asked Lucy.

"No. Not yet. Well—maybe. I'll let you know." Bob leaned into Eli as if to share a secret. "On second thought, maybe I'll have that margarita after all."

THE GREAT ROOM was buzzing with energy. A bag of chips and store-bought guacamole sat open on the coffee table, as Owen ate his fill. *So much for dinner.*

"We should listen to Bob." Eli was standing so close behind Lucy, she could feel his warmth on her back. "The party can be canceled." He was right on both counts, but they'd worked so hard, the food was ordered, people invited, and only three days to unravel it all. Besides, she really wanted to have a party in that room.

"Is that what you want to do?" She turned around to face him. "Cancel all of this?"

"We'll go to your parents. I'll get to see where you grew up. Owen would love the aquarium." He was making the best argument in favor. She heard him loud and clear. They should go. But …

"Time for me to split." Bob reached for Eli's hand but gave him more than a handshake. The embrace was genuine. "What about getting out of Dodge, Eli?"

"Can we think about it?" Canceling was canceling, whether it was today or tomorrow. Lucy's heart fluttered nervously. Was Eli giving her space to think—or was he also having second thoughts?

CHAPTER FIFTY-THREE

I F LUCY HAD KNOWN THE CONSEQUENCES OF THEIR DELAY, THEY WOULD HAVE packed their bags and left that night. But she and Eli decided to follow through with the party.

Eli added one more surprise. As long as so many people were coming together to celebrate their engagement, he suggested they take it to the next step and exchange vows. After the fireworks, they would drive to the airport and catch a redeye to San Jose. Lucy's excitement couldn't be measured.

The tickets were bought, their bags were stacked just inside their bedroom door, and they told no one. Julia and her parents had flown in the night before, and she hadn't even told them. The secrecy lent an element of excitement to the party. Anticipation.

The great hall glimmered under the light of polished crystals that hung from the ceiling. Nikko had prepared enough food to feed the whole town—Beth assured him that any leftovers would do just that.

Lucy stood at the top of the stairs, where she could see the early arrivals assembled in the great room. Her parents were doting on Owen, who was behaving uncharacteristically shy. They were trying too hard.

"Are you seeing this?" Lucy asked the house. She had taken Kali's words to heart, seeing the home as sentient as any other member of the family. The sights and sounds of a grand party had been absent for years, and she felt gratified to bring it back—just as she and Eli hoped to expand their family, a topic they visited the night before.

Roy Bird looked up at her from the foot of the stairs, and she joined him. Together, they walked down to the sewing room and closed the door behind them. Eli leaped from his chair on the other side of the room.

"You two ready for this?" asked Roy. Lucy thought her heart was going to burst with excitement.

"We're ready." Eli gripped Lucy's hand. Monterey was going to be a honeymoon. It was one of the reasons Lucy had hoped Owen would click with her parents.

"It's remarkable how many of your friends and family have come together tonight. I can't express how much this means to me to be part of this."

"We're glad you agreed," said Eli.

"So, I just wanted to make sure we had everything in place. Vows?"

"Check," Lucy laughed nervously.

"License?"

Eli handed over the marriage license. They had decided to take the name Mondschein. The paperwork to change Owen's name, as well sat on the sewing table and would be mailed in with the marriage certificate.

"All right," said Roy, "When the band takes their break, I take the stage. I'll say a few words, then you two will join me with Owen." Lucy and Eli nodded, grinning. "Afterward," Roy smiled, "Thomas will set off his fireworks on my signal."

Butterflies did not begin to explain how Lucy was feeling. Part of her wished Roy would just marry them right then and there in the sewing room, where it was quiet and private. The public spectacle was Eli's inspiration. She did not love it, but she loved Eli and would do anything to make him happy.

They reemerged from the sewing room and entered the front hall hand in hand to greet guests. Lucy cringed at the stack of gifts piling up on the hall table. The invitations had explicitly requested no gifts.

Two six-year-old hands picked up and set down nearly every box with curiosity and a little confusion.

"Are you getting married today?" he asked unwittingly.

"Many people like to bring gifts for engagement parties too," explained Lucy with a broad smile at Eli.

Beth arrived with Rachel and Rayanne. "I know, I know—you said no gifts. It's just a little something." The box took all three of them to carry into the house.

Beth complimented Eli on his style. Lucy agreed. The new slacks and button-up shirt were a perfect fit. Owen was outfitted similarly. That morning she and Eli watched one another prepare for the day as he set out his new clothes, and she styled her hair.

Lucy dressed in a thin white sweater and a blue and white maxi-skirt with a pair of low heels. It was dressy enough for the occasion, yet comfortable enough to dance. It was her wedding— she was sure there would be lots of dancing.

Summer was in the great hall playing emcee for Thomas's band, the Genial Disposition. The great hall filled as more guests arrived. Some danced, but most were milling around the tables of delicacies prepared by Nikko and a few of his employees, who were working their tails off. His catering business was going well, thanks to a little seed money from Eli and a special discount from Moon Harvest.

It was nearly dusk, and the lighting in the room grew bright by the six chandeliers, which hung two by two down the length of the room. Whatever anyone may say, the Moon family was not one to leave a job undone—even when that job was challenging. Cleaning the chandeliers was a case in point. Eli and Kali had put their heads together to remember how it was done, and managed to work it out with the help of a certain curious boy, who discovered a switch behind the stage curtain, which lowered the giant fixtures to the floor, where they could be washed, dried, and polished. With another flip of that switch, they returned to their original position.

Owen was thrilled to revisit his discovery this night, in full view of all the guests. Eli was horrified as one descending chandelier nearly toppled Nikko's centerpiece. Lucy scrambled onto the stage to flip the switch back and return the chandelier to its proper place high above their heads. All the while Thomas and company provided a silly circus tune. The guests stood in awe of the scene and applauded Lucy's valiant save.

Eli and Kali resisted the urge to send Owen to his room, and instead ordered him not to leave either Eli's or Lucy's side. That's when Bob quietly appeared beside Lucy. Arriving late, he made a point of behaving like a guest—but Lucy had the strong suspicion he was on the job.

"Everything all right?"

"For now," answered Bob. "Thompson's watching the door. Fitz is walking the perimeter."

"Thank you." Lucy looked for Eli, who was keeping a close eye on Owen. When their eyes met, he touched the corner of his mouth. She smiled. *I love you too.*

The band stopped playing when Roy appeared on stage. The crowd looked up as he cleared his throat. Eli appeared beside Lucy as they prepared to join Roy. *Here we go*, thought Lucy, taking Owen's hand.

Bob stood on the other side of Owen, quietly observing the crowd. The bank of windows along one wall was broken up by a pair of French doors, and some thoughtful soul had just opened them wide. She looked down at Owen. "How are you doing, Little Bird?" She thought he was looking at the open door, but soon realized it was two windows down. Owen tightened his grip on her hand. "Owen?" She looked up at Bob, who also stared—so she looked too. It was dark out. The sun had set an hour earlier, but one thing was clear. Standing outside, with his face clearly lit by a flaming cigarette lighter, was Ben Wyatt. Lucy pulled on Eli's hand and pointed.

Bob tapped his ear, "Wyatt outside the great hall. Let's get this son of a bitch." He ran, pushing past Tina and another guest, and stopped briefly at the open door, where Fitz thundered past him at top speed. He followed. Just as they rounded the corner of the house, one of Thomas's fireworks soared into the sky with a piercing whistle, shedding light on a rainbow piñata that burst into flame and set off a spectacular show as the entire collection of fireworks blew up in a fountain of sensational pops, screams, and whistles.

Lucy stared at the flames, temporarily mesmerized.

As none of the guests outside of their little circle knew a thing about what was going on, they all went out to watch the display. Lucy looked frantically at Thomas, who shook his head. He hadn't lit the fireworks. It was Wyatt, she thought, the piñata was his idea. He'd used it to torch the whole collection of Thomas' fireworks. She grabbed Owen, who was still frozen in place, and gave a nod to Eli while pointing her finger to the door.

Lucy smelled smoke—and it wasn't the familiar gunpowder smell from the fireworks, nor the smoldering paper mâché piñata. She thought back to the arson that summer when Eli's office was burned down to the ground along with the entire block. The same smell was in the air, and the same eerie light was cast on the scene by the fireworks as the spectacular show spewed from behind what remained of the piñata.

Most of the guests stood outside the great room with their backs to the windows, spellbound by the fireworks, and warmed by the flames. It had occurred to a number of them, though, that something had gone terribly wrong and they were frantic to get away from the flames. Lucy lost Eli in the madness and took Owen into the hallway. "Eli?" She looked toward the great room. "Eli?" she yelled. She thought she heard an answer and ran in that direction.

As they passed the main staircase, an arm reached out to stop her. It was the monster who'd kicked her at the park. She turned with Owen and ran with him back down to the great hall.

"Eli!" she screamed—but before they could get there, the monster caught her arm. He gripped her wrist with the strength of a gorilla. She held firm to Owen, but when she realized that she couldn't free herself, she sent him in search of his father.

Lucy watched, powerless, as a terrified Owen stormed down the hall toward the great hall where Ben Wyatt emerged from the open door of the dumbwaiter. Wyatt swept up the boy, a wry smile on his face. As Lucy fought to free herself, he hoisted Owen over his shoulder and disappeared.

Kicking and scratching, she managed to frustrate her captor enough to loosen his grip. There was no time to think as she ran furiously in pursuit. She followed Owen's screams through the dark passage behind the dumbwaiter to the open door at the other end.

Everyone was in the back of the house, distracted by the spectacle Wyatt had orchestrated. Lucy caught sight of branches moving and focused on Wyatt's back as he disappeared across the front of the house into the dark orchard. Owen screamed with terror, but it was barely audible over the screams of the fireworks.

Where was Bob? Where was Eli? In her desperation, she looked around, hoping to catch sight of Agent Fitzgerald, but he was nowhere near. She was on her own, and there was no time to run for help.

Lucy brushed off the cold and plunged headlong into the orchard. She didn't have to go far before she heard the cries of the boy she loved so dearly.

"There she is," said Wyatt, in his eerie high-pitched voice. "I knew she would come. See how she loves you? See how she would do anything to get you back?" He held a knife to Owen's throat. Lucy witnessed the paralyzing fear on Owen's sweet face and the glint of moonlight on his tear-streaked cheeks.

"Owen, I'm here. Everything is going to be all right," she said, unconvincingly, through her trembling voice. She stepped closer, not knowing how she intended to free him, and looked at Wyatt. "Let him go. I promise I'll do anything you ask. Just please, let him go."

"Anything?"

"Yes, just let him go. Now please ..." She was two steps from them when Wyatt pulled the knife away from Owen's neck.

He grinned. "Too late." Wyatt slipped his knife into Owen's back, drew both arms up to reveal the bloody knife, and ran.

A dome of silence crashed around Lucy so forcefully, she couldn't hear her own anguished screams. The earth rolled under her feet like a California earthquake, rocking her from heel to toe. She went numb, then dropped to her knees and crawled to where Owen's small, limp body lay. As she pulled him to her chest, her tears spilled in an endless stream, and she struggled to breathe.

A mass cry from the front of the house sounded like a dull thrum. The world around her was suspended as she muttered, "Owen, Owen."

Bob Marshall pulled at her arms to release her grip. She couldn't let go. "Lucy. It's over. He's gone. Lucy."

"No!" she screamed like a wild animal.

Eventually, he succeeded, and Agent Fitzgerald led her, blind and stumbling, to the edge of the orchard, where she collapsed.

She didn't bother wiping the streams of tears and snot from her face. What was the point? There was no shutting it down. In fact, just when she thought it couldn't get any worse, Eli appeared at the garden gate. She heard the squeal of its rusted hinges and the crunch of footfall as he approached her, wearing the concern on his face she recalled from the first day they met.

She tracked his gaze from her to Agent Thompson, who kneeled on the back of a beaten man. Wyatt was caught. Then he turned to see Bob Marshall emerge from the orchard with his son's lifeless body draped between his arms, just as the first snow began to fall. The heartache Lucy felt seemed insurmountable. She couldn't begin to imagine a path out of the darkness, but she knew she would never find it alone.

CHAPTER FIFTY-FOUR

LUCY HELD HER SHOPPING TOTE FIRMLY OVER ONE SHOULDER AS SHE WAITED IN line for a sticky bun at the farmers market spring kickoff. The tender young leaves of the Old Oak fluttered in the chilly spring breeze, and Lucy pulled her jacket tight around her expanding belly. The baby bump had just become obvious in recent days, but any pride or joy she may have felt in a typical first pregnancy was tainted with the loss she and Eli had suffered the night of their engagement party.

Owen—his smile, his curls, the bounce in his step, his eagerness to learn, the longing in his big brown eyes, his heartfelt embraces—weighed on them both as they came to grips with his death. They certainly hadn't moved on, and how they had managed to move forward was anyone's guess. A day at a time? No. It was a moment-to-moment ordeal. It hurt with every breath, every step, and every tiny memory of him.

She tried not to think of the scene in the orchard, but the memory could not be stripped from her mind. It haunted her dreams and drifted into focus when she least expected it. Wyatt's self-satisfied face. Owen dropping to the ground. The blood. Her screams.

What could they have done differently? There were too many answers to that question and none were satisfying. The mountain of blame, guilt, remorse, and regret could never be summited. But therapy taught them their grief was not fatal. That moving forward was not the same as moving on.

Forward meant following through with the marriage, as a small gathering of friends and family, who stood by them through their suffering, stood witness to their commitment to one another.

Forward meant taking a step back from Moon Harvest and allowing Shay and Kelly to hold the reins a while longer.

Forward meant moving across the hall to the master bedroom and watching the sunrise over the orchard.

Forward meant filling the house as Mia moved in, and they prepared for the arrival of a little Mondschein—the first of many, they hoped.

Here, with the farmers market in full swing around them, Eli put his arm around Lucy as she sat down beside him on their bench and handed him half of the sweet treat. He kissed the frosting from her lips and patted her belly. The child—girl or boy—would be named Kestrel. Another Little Bird, as the spirit of the first one lived on.

"I see congratulations are in order."

Lucy looked up with alarm, then smiled when she saw Bob Marshall approaching their bench. "Thank you, yes," she smiled and rubbed her belly.

Bob reached out to shake Eli's hand, and Lucy scooted over. "I have some news." Eli and Lucy exchanged worried glances. "It's Wyatt again. Mysterious, really."

"Just tell us, Bob." Lucy braced herself. "Escape? Release?"

"Did the Feds drop the charges?"

"No—he was found suffocated in his cell early this morning."

Eli's sigh of relief was as expressive as Lucy's. The emotions, hormonal or not, rose to the surface, and Lucy cried tears of relief. She was free of him at last.

"I thought that was you." Beth joined them from across the street and reached for a hug from Bob.

"Good to see you again, Beth. I hope you're well," he said.

"I will be as soon as Lorena gets up to speed." Lorena, Beth's trainee, was from Tuscon. Lucy empathized with the young Mexican American. It would be years, if ever, before she'd adapt to the summer humidity and the bone-chilling winters.

"She's no Eli, I can tell you that—but we're getting there. Mayor Bird has been a Godsend to the office. We're certainly not hurting for support from the city."

Eli shared the news about Ben Wyatt, and Beth whooped with joy. "Hope he rots in hell."

"Here, here," said Bob.

Lucy felt a wave of nausea and handed what remained of her sticky bun to Eli, who took one look at her and suggested they move on.

"I hope you can stick around, Bob," said Eli. "We're having some friends over tonight and would love it if you could join us."

"I'm traveling with Jenny, my wife. Mind if she tags along?"

"Thrilled!" said Lucy. "We'd love to meet GI Jenny. Hope she likes enchiladas. Summer and I are making enough for a small army."

"Well," he said, laughing, "she can eat like one." He winked at Lucy. "She's expecting as well. Seven months along. How is Summer?"

"She's still at the school but helping to get a satellite Home School Project up and running in her hometown." Lucy didn't know what she'd do without Summer, who had taken on so much more than trapping spiders in the corner to protect her.

"And Thomas?"

"Thomas? The band is on tour in the Southwest. It seems the Genial Disposition has caught on coast to coast. They just released a new album last month. He and Summer just got engaged too, but they're waiting until the tour is over. Mid-September, they're saying—but you can ask Summer yourself tonight."

"Looking forward to it. You don't look so well, Lucy. I'm sorry for keeping you. We'll catch up later tonight then?"

"Yes—and bring your bags, there's plenty of room," added Eli, standing and helping Lucy to her feet.

Lucy's world was forever changed, for better and for worse. She'd surrounded herself with the positive energy of people who loved and supported her. And she regularly checked in with Dr. Chan, who reminded her to ask herself who she was, what she wanted out of life, and what brought her joy. Without disowning the victim within her, she acknowledged her strengths and was grateful for Eli's steadfast love and compassion, and the close friendships she'd formed.

For now, the spirit of Ben Wyatt had been removed, the spirit of Owen endured, and the spirit of Lucia Perez Mondschein persevered.

END